SKY HIGH

THE GLITTERING SNOW PALACE OF PLEASURE ON TOP OF THE WORLD. FOR EVERY MAN AND EVERY WOMAN WHO EVER DREAMED OF LIVING OUT THEIR FANTASIES . . .

JAKE CHAFFEE: Big, lean, suntanned. He staked his entire fortune on a dream, and now that dream was threatening to blow . . . sky high.

CASSIE LAMONT: Her beauty, and the strength of her love, offered Jake a fabulous new beginning.

ZEKE GIBBS: The old man had the pride of ownership and a vengeance that could topple Jake and his mountain.

DUD DRUMMOND: A wildly imaginative PR man who could make anything click—except his own marriage.

DOROTHY DUTTON: Notorious, wacky, preserved-in-aspic *grande dame.*

COUNT MOMO: Her dapper, dauntless, dangerous seventh husband.

CORNELIA DE VOS: Beautiful, successful lover of lovers —and oil fields.

PEPI PRAGER: Who carved perfect tracks on ski trails and young girls.

TOD RUBIN: The only thing he tracked . . . long-lost Nazis.

SKY HIGH

The high adventure of *Aspen.*
The high drama of *Grand Hotel.*

SKY HIGH
Tom Murphy, Jr.

BANTAM BOOKS
TORONTO
NEW YORK
LONDON

*This low-priced Bantam Book
has been completely reset in a type face
designed for easy reading, and was printed
from new plates. It contains the complete
text of the original hard-cover edition.*
NOT ONE WORD HAS BEEN OMITTED.

SKY HIGH
*A Bantam Book / published by arrangement with
G. P. Putnam's Sons*

*PRINTING HISTORY
Putnam's edition published January 1977
Bantam edition / January 1978*

ISBN 0-553-11115-9

Published simultaneously in the United States and Canada

Bantam Books are published by Bantam Books, Inc. Its trademark, consisting of the words "Bantam Books" and the portrayal of a bantam, is registered in the United States Patent Office and in other countries. Marca Registrada. Bantam Books, Inc., 666 Fifth Avenue, New York, New York 10019.

PRINTED IN THE UNITED STATES OF AMERICA

To the memory of Whizzer,
a true and gallant friend.

October, 1968

The white Learjet was like its owner: lean, thoroughbred, confident. The control stick felt good in Jake Chaffee's big suntanned hands as he retraced the trails of his pioneer ancestors, heading back from San Francisco toward Denver at five hundred miles an hour.

It was a business meeting. Four Denver bankers liked Chaffee Development's latest project, a huge shopping mall in San Diego, and they wanted Jake to do something similar for them. Probably he would. For these days Jake was only happy building, creating, turning nothing into something. A jealous competitor had accused him of playing God. And while Jake merely shrugged and grinned his easy grin, there was an irritating grain of truth in it.

Jake was half an hour early. The sky over Colorado was cloudless, perfect, blue to eternity. He asked and got permission to alter his flight plan. Then Jake Chaffee went exploring from a vantage point Columbus never knew: twelve thousand feet straight up. Jake loved to weave his way among these great brute mountains, seeing what the eagles saw, peering down into valleys where no man had ever set foot, leastways not to live and tell of it.

Over jagged gray granite pinnacles older than time but still sharp enough to kill, up foaming creeks pure with melted snow, along meadows fringed with stands of immemorial Colorado spruce, the silent shadow of Jake's jet plane flickered and was gone, unnoticed. He threaded the Learjet idly up a valley. The steady muted whine of the twin jet engines only made the eerie quiet of two and a half miles up more palpable.

And then he saw it.

There below and a little to the right the lonely perfect shape of Sky Mountain rose to greet him. And in that instant, typically, before he even knew its name, Jake Chaffee began thinking of the mountain as his, the prize of discovery. Jake turned both his head and the jet with one fluid motion. He circled back for one more look at this mountain that thrust up above its valley like the holy place of some long-forgotten race of sky worshipers.

It was an early October afternoon carved by the sun from blue crystal. The valleys were still green, and groves of pencil-slim aspens dappled the foothills with gold. But the top of Jake's mountain was white with a hundred thousand years of never-melting show. "You don't know it yet, Mister Mountain," Jake said out loud, "but you just made a friend." At the wide end of the valley Jake could make out a gray thread of road snaking in and out of the mountains and heading more or less due north towards Steamboat Springs. This would turn out to be the controversial Highway 317. Just where the road cut through the widest end of the valley, there was a little town clustered around it. Jake circled the valley two more times and marked it on his flight map. Then he climbed three thousand feet and headed southeast for Denver.

Down in the valley a tall white-haired old man sat on the front porch of his ranch house; it was shaded by a grove of Colorado blue spruce his great granddaddy had planted there in 1849, just after he'd built the original ranch house, what was now with the kitchen wing. Zeke Gibbs looked up into the brazen October sky with eyes that were more than seventy-five years old but missed nothing. He saw, even before hearing its unfamiliar droning, the small white shape of Jake Chaffee's jet circling in the unclouded blue. Three times the elegant little jet swooped and circled and circled once again. *He's either lost,* thought the owner of all Sky Valley, *or just plumb crazy.* Intruders meant only one thing to Zeke Gibbs: trouble. He looked at the white jet as it gained altitude and disappeared over the edge of Sky Mountain. Good riddance! Then, with the accuracy of long practice, he spat over the neatly painted white porch railing into the shimmering dust of the front drive. Strangers!

December 1973: The curtain was about to go up on the ultimate ski resort.

Two hundred carefully chosen guests were being flown in for the opening festivities that would launch Sky High. Here, to this remote Rocky Mountain valley, would come the rich and the beautiful and the glamorous athletes and hangers-on of the jet set, with just enough press people to record the glitter and fun of it. Two weeks of skiing and fine food and amusement would be capped by the Sky High Challenge Cup, a pro skiing race that was scheduled for coverage on national television and by teams from three major sports magazines. And Sky High was ready: polished, glittering, expectant.

1

Jake Chaffee's eyes had been described in print as "steel-blue" and "sapphire-blue" but in fact they were neither. The color of Jake's eyes changed more often than water under a windy sky. It depended on his mood and the source of light and the imagination of the reporter.

Jake stood with a reporter, Dawkins of the *Denver Post,* in the long curving driveway that led to Sky High. Dawkins was taking notes and wondering why Jake had never gone into the movies. He had the looks, surely, and the charm: a tall man with a swimmer's flat-muscled build and a craggy, even-featured face. And those eyes. It was very easy to imagine Jake Chaffee riding off into Technicolor sunsets. But Jake Chaffee grew up land-rich in northern California and the movies had nothing to offer him. If the Chaffees thought about Hollywood at all, it was with the faintly amused detachment of founding fathers watching the lurid progress of some sequined Gypsy fair. The reporter snapped out of his reverie. Jake was saying something and Jake's time was limited. It was about the beams.

"There have to be five cheap ways to fake 'em. But that isn't the way we do things at Sky High." Jake's voice was easy, Californian, friendly.

"I see that."

Jake Chaffee played the young reporter like a fish, feeding the interview from one corner of his frightened mind. The two men stood smiling in the bright December noon, and the cold Colorado mountain wind touched them on its way up Sky Mountain. Jake kept on about the beams. The beams of Sky High were not ordinary beams. They had been hand-picked with the special permission of the governor of California from certain giant redwoods marked for cutting in Muir Woods. They had been trucked across the Sierra at great expense to frame Sky Lodge in glory.

Jake smiled and told his story well, touching the reporter on the shoulder as he pointed up the curving driveway to Sky High. Jake was always a physically compelling man, a toucher, a taster of wines—a top-down-Jaguar, shift-through-the-turn kind of man who flew jets and fought a chestful of medals' worth of air fights with MIG planes over Korea and accepted with ease and grace the quickly offered friendship of men and the love of women. From childhood Jake had accepted all the best as rightfully due him. The reporter laughed, flattered by the sense of intimacy, an easy victim of the magic.

In the hard crystal sunlight Jake felt one cold drop running down his spine, the sweat of fear. He laughed and began another story, running ahead of the fear with all the skills learned in forty years of gilded living, of being The Senator's son, winning at sports, riding long boyhood afternoons on purebred horses over Chaffee land that never seemed to end, living a life of kept promises and dreams that came true.

The two men stood looking up at the glittering thing Jake had built. Sky High took in Sky Mountain soaring four thousand feet above the valley floor, which was already eight thousand feet up in the Colorado Rockies. At the mountain's base the many buildings of Sky Lodge clustered like some Italian mountain village transformed by money and the genius of the architect Paolo Storione into a dream of luxury and comfort and good taste.

"I guess you could say," said the reporter, "that it has your name on it."

"You could say that." *Damn right it has my name on it,* Jake thought. *And my name is going to stay on it.* The first drop of sweat had vanished. Two more appeared to take its place. Under the English sheepskin coat, under the hundred-dollar cashmere turtleneck,

Jake shuddered like a small boy in his first cold shower.

The tangible reason for Jake's fear was that Knickerbocker Trust, the huge New York bank underwriting Sky High, was showing ever more serious inclinations to take the management of the resort out of his hands. But underlying that, and much more urgent, was that fact that in the five years it had taken to build the resort, Jake's life had changed dramatically. Jake felt that his whole future lay in Sky Valley now, with Sky High and the woman with whom he had fallen unalterably in love.

The problem was simple but the solution might not be. Sky High, like almost all big real estate developments, had been built with borrowed money. Fifty million dollars of it. Five years ago, in 1968, the funds had come easily out of the conservative Knickerbocker Trust. Raising money for a Chaffee project then was about as hard as giving diamonds away in front of Tiffany's.

Then two things happened that nobody, not builders or bankers, really anticipated. Inflation soared and the cost of labor and materials with it. A brick that cost 7¢ in 1968 cost 13¢ in 1937. And Jake Chaffee was determined to make Sky High the world showplace of all ski resorts. No corners would be cut. The story of the redwood beams was one of many: only the best and most beautiful materials were good enough for Sky High, and if the right materials didn't exist then Jake Chaffee saw to it that they were specially made. This produced a magnificent resort and a hideous balance sheet. And all during the construction of Sky High, the interest rate climbed higher and higher. Currently it was 10½%, with no end in sight. This meant that Sky High had to repay its loan (which had climbed to 52 million dollars) at the rate of 14½% quarterly. And Sky High had yet to pull in its first nickel.

When the last quarterly payment came due, in September, Jake had liquidated some holdings and made up the difference himself. He couldn't afford to do it again, and he knew he couldn't expect any help from his father or from Betsy either, since he was just about to ask for a divorce. He wasn't going to risk giving Betsy a hold on Sky High to use as leverage in a divorce battle. Jake's only hope was that Chaffee Development's financial wizard, Pete Woodbury, could negotiate an extension of payment from Knickerbocker Trust. But Pete had made his first stabs at doing this and met with a cold reception. Times were bad and getting worse. The financial world was infested with barracuda conglomerates that could sniff out a good project in temporary trouble and had the cash to do something about it. Several had come sniffing at Sky High already. But Jake swore he'd do anything to prevent control of Sky High from being sold out from under him, which was just what might happen if they couldn't satisfy the bank by the time the next payment was due, in just thirty days now, at the end of December.

Jake knew Pete Woodbury's latest phone call by heart, and not because he was so fond of the news it brought: "It isn't personal, Jake. You know they trust you . . ."

"But they maybe trust somebody else a little more?"

"Jake, everybody's running scared. Very scared, you wouldn't believe what it's like down here."

"I believe. And trusty old Knickerbocker is panicking right along with the rest of the sheep."

"They just might call us, Jake. We've got to face that."

"Do they realize Sky High's really all set to open this week? I know we've had delays, overruns: what big project doesn't? But, Peter, you just ought to see the place. The snow's perfect. We've got a base of eighty-nine inches already and it's only December first. Fabulous!"

"Sounds great."

"Pete, what about the land? The Knick's gotta take that into consideration, surely?" Jake knew that the real profit potential of Sky High—and every other chic resort—came not from rooms or recreation but from the appreciation of the value of land. Land at Vail, for instance, had soared from under five hundred dollars an acre to more than sixty thousand in less than ten years. There was no reason why Sky High shouldn't do at least as well.

"They aren't dummies, Jake. They see the potential.

But right now it's only potential. Sky High has to make a hit first. I'm sure it will. But right now the Knick sees it as a dream. And dreams don't have too much leverage on Wall Street these days."

"And everybody told Columbus the world was flat. Fuck them. You coming out?"

"I'll be there."

"Great. Bring Franny."

"Not this trip." Pete's voice went funny. Jake sensed another kind of tension in it. "She's all tied up with some kind of Junior League bullshit, you know how it is."

"Don't I just! Anyway, I got your note about Peng, Peter, and I'll try to keep him in line. But hell, he's part of the attraction. A big part for some people." Raoul Peng was the world-famous French chef Jake had imported to preside over the kitchens of Sky High. And Peter Woodbury, who checked every bill that went into the building and operation of the resort, had been fighting some of Peng's more extravagant requests. Truffles at thirty-two dollars the ounce, for instance. "Anyway," Jake went on, "after the press coverage we're bound to get from the opening party, hell, in a few months we ought to be raking it in." Brave words. When you're skiing fast and suddenly there's a patch of ice right in front of you and it's too late to turn, you can do one of two things. You can fall, or you can tuck in and shoot right across the ice hoping there's negotiable snow on the other side. For Jake Chaffee this was never a debate. He always ran right over the tough parts. And he hadn't fallen yet. Not yet.

"Fine." Pete's voice didn't sound fine. "Look, Jake, I'm doing everything I can. I'll talk to them again before I come out. Try not to worry. We'll think of something."

"OK, Peter. See ya on the slopes."

"So long, Jake. Love to Cassie." Somehow the click of Pete's phone, amplified over the two thousand odd miles between lower Manhattan and Sky Junction, Colorado, had to Jake's ears the hollow echo of a closing tomb. And Jake Chaffee was scared.

Jake's was a wonderful facade. It had served him

well for forty years before the cracks began to show. He wasn't much given to self-analysis. It was his ability to concentrate and focus his energies that made Jake Chaffee very nearly irresistible in whatever he took up. Jake soared through his life on a trajectory that could have landed him any place, including in the opinion of experts, the White House. And all of a sudden he was forty. Suddenly the unbroken chain of successes was suffering a little from stress fatigue. Lately, and for the first time ever, Jake had been forced to take a long close look at what he'd become and where he was going.

There was a reason for this. Her name was Cassie Lamont.

It was because of Cassie that Sky High mattered so much. It was for her that Jake finally faced the fact that his twenty-year marriage to Betsy Bellington was in ruins. Jake's need of Cassie magnified his fear of failing. He had a deep, irrational hunch that one failure might lead to another just the way one success had always led to another.

If Sky High failed, it would be in the future. But the failure of Jake's marriage was an accomplished fact.

Jake Chaffee and Betsy Bellington had met and matched with a kind of mythic inevitability, so perfectly did they fulfill the fantasies of everyone around them—the bright golden young man and the shy, perfect princess who met and felt something like love that was really only the reflected glow of the happiness their union created in family and friends and especially in the love-drunk press, whose clicking cameras became an extended counterpoint to all love songs of the Marriage of the Year 1953.

It took some time for Jake to realize that the soft pleasant surface of the girl he married was all she had to offer. There was a sweet, childlike quality to Betsy that was charming until it became boring and then maddening as the boredom filled up whole years until, at last, suffocating under its own weight, it turned to a kind of numbness and then to nothing at all.

The world of Betsy Bellington was a paper-doll world that did nobody harm. Betsy caused innocent pleasure for hundreds of people with her endless luncheons and cocktail parties. The emptiness that resulted in Jake's life was quickly filled up, as if by some kind law of gravity, by business projects and travel and by other women. Jake believed his life was settled, as well as it ever would be.

Until August 1964, when young Jon Chaffee, just turned ten, went laughing off to summer camp and never came home. By the time they got the phone call it was too late. Little Jonathan Chaffee woke up one morning with spinal meningitis and died in twelve screaming hours, beyond all medical help. It was the kind of shock that might have jolted some faltering marriages onto firmer ground. With Jake and Betsy, Jon's death just served to lock the doors that had already been closed between them. Jake continued to love his one remaining child, Eliza—a little rebel who constantly fought against her mother's attempts to turn her into a little Dresden doll—but he could no longer bear to spend much time in the white limestone palace at Hillsborough, California. Jake went through the motions of being a husband in order to make a real try at being a father to Eliza. He was never really sure it worked. He could remember too well from his own childhood how easy it was to see through grownup deceptions. But Jake continued to play his polite role in this charade that was, for Betsy, completely real. Betsy Bellington Chaffee, at forty, her one son dead and her daughter away at college, still held forth among gardens that never ceased blooming and servants who always seemed to smile and dressmakers who never dropped a stitch as they upholstered her ever-plumper form in silks and tweeds. It had been ten full years since Jake had made love to her. Sometimes he wondered if she felt the lack.

For Jake Chaffee, Sky High was the future. And as he stood in the driveway with the reporter looking up at the lodge and the mountain behind it, it was clear how beautiful that future could be. If he held onto it.

Everything depended on the success of the opening, and everything possible had been done to assure it would be a success.

The press conference that would begin in half an hour was the official start of the celebration. Talking to this reporter was really a kind of warm-up for the conference. The reporter, charmed, was asking all the right questions and Jake fed him answers out of one small corner of his brain, keeping it light, friendly, never showing that he was juggling dozens of more urgent questions or that he had been seriously frightened for days and weeks.

They started walking up the driveway toward Sky Lodge.

"Kind of a nice view from right here." Jake said it casually, spontaneously, knowing the reporter would be back with a photographer. Jake had actually spent a full day tramping the grounds with his architect, finding the best angles. From any angle, this was no ordinary resort. Storione, the most avant of the avant-garde Italian architects, had done his work well. Sky Lodge nestled into the base of Sky Mountain with unself-conscious ease. The sparkling white stucco-and-glass, redwood-and-stone buildings might have sprung organically from the flank of Sky Mountain.

"Tell me," said the reporter, "about Highway 317. We hear it's getting pretty controversial in these parts." Controversial was putting it mildly. The proposal to widen the one road leading up from Denver was causing passionate arguments all along its three-hundred-mile length, but especially in Sky Junction. Sky High itself had been debated, damned and praised from the first. A group of local landowners and conservationists had opposed the new resort bitterly and vocally. Their leader and the sworn enemy of Jake Chaffee was old Zeke Gibbs. Zeke's family had settled Sky Valley in 1849, fighting off Indians to do it. And they'd owned it totally and exclusively until Jake Chaffee came along. When Zeke Gibbs and his supporters found they couldn't stop the resort itself, they undertook a program of harassment. The fight for—and against—widening old Highway 317 was the latest skirmish in this struggle against Sky High.

The proposal to widen the road had been in the works long before Jake Chaffee set eyes on Sky Mountain. No one thought much about the project one way or the other until Zeke seized on it as a way to limit access to Sky High. Now a full-fledged legislative battle was in the works. The outcome was to be decided in the next session of the legislature, in January. And it was more crucial than Jake liked to admit: Pete Woodbury had figured out that having 317 as a four-lane instead of a two-lane road could mean as much as half a million dollars a year to Sky High. The difference between making it and not making it.

"Well, fella," Jake said to Dawkins with his best rueful smile, "the first thing you ought to know is, that road-widening project was on the books back in '67, before this place was so much as a gleam in my eye. And folks seemed to think it was a pretty good idea. Pre-Sky High, you understand." Jake looked straight into the young man's eyes to make sure he did understand, and for one thrilling moment the reporter felt, as Jake intended him to feel, just like one of the knowing insiders in a big-time real estate deal. "You know, don't you, that all this"—Jake made a sweeping gesture that took in all of Sky Valley—"used to belong to one man."

"Zeke Gibb's father?"

"Right. And can you blame Zeke for wanting it all to stay in the family? This valley belonged to the Gibbses for more than a hundred years. They got rich off it. And they—old Zeke anyway—are just hankering to get richer. So I'm the bad guy. I managed to buy part of his precious valley. I'm opening it up so other people—ordinary people—can enjoy the valley just like the Gibbses always have. Zeke seems to think it's his by feudal right. So naturally he calls me a crook and lots of other things you couldn't print even if I could remember 'em all. You've heard the song before: Jake Chaffee is raping the landscape, turning Sky Junction into a veritable Sodom and Gomorrah." Jake laughed his big easy laugh and the reporter had to laugh with him, seeing how foolish the old man's struggle must be. Only Jake knew it wasn't foolish, that Zeke Gibbs might win after all.

"Sounds like fun," Dawkins commented.

"It's a challenge, at any rate. Sure I'm for widening

317. That's a damned dangerous piece of road. Hell, look at the records. In the last five years alone eleven people have died in car accidents on 317. The irony of it all is, Zeke Gibbs's only son—and the son's wife—were both killed on that road, up near Steamboat Springs about ten years ago. It's too narrow, it's too curvy, it cuts too close to the mountains, there's falling rock and avalanche danger. Hell, it's a death trap and it always has been. But old Zeke will use it against me—against Sky High—no matter what the cost, or to whom."

"I'm beginning to get the picture." The reporter asked Jake more questions and got more answers, but Jake's mind was on automatic pilot. He was thinking back all the way to that blazing blue October afternoon five years ago when he first laid eyes on Sky Mountain. Five years? It seemed like five lifetimes. So much work done, and so much still to be done.

The reporter stopped writing in his little notebook after Jake finished a funny anecdote about luring the famous Raoul Peng from his three-star kitchen at Chez Midas in Paris to become head chief at Sky High. "The fact is," Jake said with an easygoing man-to-man chuckle, "that between Peng and Pepi Prager, Sky High Corporation had to sign away the mountain just about to where you see the eagle circling." But the bird Jake saw was not an eagle. It was a vulture, a turkey buzzard, lazily hitchhiking on the updrafts over a certain hidden cave halfway up Sky Mountain.

What Jake said about Raoul Peng and the ski pro Pepi Prager was true. They'd cost Sky High an arm and a leg. But Jake knew they'd be worth it. They'd better be. Peng's fame was such that even non-skiing gourmets had booked into Sky High months in advance. Could advance bookings be used as collateral to soothe the doubts of doubting bankers? Maybe. And Pepi had a following too. There were plenty of skiers who would follow the legendary Austrian anywhere. That was like money in the bank. Almost.

Jake Chaffee couldn't have said just when Sky High evolved from another interesting new project into an obsession that would change his life. Part of it was tied up in the troubles he had getting the resort off the ground: wresting half the valley from Zeke Gibbs, pleading for the necessary clearances, pitching for the money, rounding up the talent to actually build the place. Two long summers he'd sweated it out in Sky Junction just to be on the construction site every day. He'd walked every inch of the mountain with Pepi Prager, laying out ski trails, plotting lifts. He'd staked his name and his cash and maybe his whole future on Sky High, and now it was finished. The last nail had been hammered and the last coat of paint was barely dry.

Jake hoped the reporter felt the excitement building. Sky High had everything. Jake believed this absolutely. It had the most beautiful setting in the world's best snow country. Sky Mountain had the highest vertical rise of any ski mountain in America, and a huge, swift custom-built aerial tramway that could zip a hundred fifty affluent skiers a mile up the mountain in six minutes. It had the brilliant innovative architecture of Paolo Storione in his first American project. Sky High had Peng in the kitchen, Pepi Prager on the ski slopes and Dud Drummond's million-dollar publicity and advertising campaign to tell the world all about it. Sky High couldn't miss. Except that Sky High was on the verge of going broke before it even opened.

The reporter saw excitement flashing in Jake's eyes, felt the conviction in what he said. There was something thrilling about the man and his enthusiasm, and also something a little disturbing. The reporter decided he wouldn't want Jake Chaffee for an enemy.

Halfway up Sky Mountain the vulture kept circling.

Jake smiled at the reporter but what he was thinking was how his father would laugh to see him squirm, so anxious for a good press he'd spent nearly an hour with a ten-minute reporter.

One of Jake's earliest memories was having breakfast with The Senator as he ran down a list of possible press interviews and a male aide took notes: "He's a fifteen-minuter . . . scratch that one . . . nothing doing with that one either . . . invite that one to the barbecue . . ." You could learn a lot, hanging around Senator Jonathan Chaffee.

Once you survived the business—and it was a very demanding business—of being The Senator's son, almost everything else in life seemed easy. The Senator: tall as Jake and with the same movie-cowboy looks—the sandy hair pure white now—Jake's father had been a legend in conservative Republican politics for as long as most people could remember. Senator Jonathan Chaffee cloaked a shrewd and beautifully educated brain in a kind of folksy false simplicity that over the years had become second nature to him. "Never let the other guy think you're smarter than he is, kid," The Senator once scolded Jake when Jake used a long word instead of a short one; "they become defensive, and you don't get what you want."

Getting what he wanted had been The Senator's career. Twice he'd been offered—and twice refused—his party's nomination for the Presidency of the United States. His position grew stronger with every refusal, and the cumulative effect of his thirty-six years in the Senate was to have wielded more power in more ways than any President. Jake hated him.

"The flaming definition of a son of a bitch!" Jake lay next to Cassie Lamont in the big double bed of a motel near Steamboat Springs. He'd brought her down for a look at Sky High under construction, hoping to talk her into managing it for him. Innocently, she'd asked about his father. "He's a user, a schemer, a real old-time major-league hypocrite. He never had time for me, except to use me as a stage prop; never had time for my mother after she got sick, lived by himself in Washington all those years—which might have been a blessing when you think about it. Underneath that silver-haired, golden-tongued statesman is a mean, ornery little guy who wouldn't give you a bean unless he knew he'd get four beans back the next day."

"Sounds charming." Cassie would have given quite a lot to change the subject.

"That's just the trouble. He is charming, charming as hell. Charm the damned gold fillings right out of your teeth, that man."

"I know someone else"—Cassie said it smiling—"who could be said to do that sort of thing from time to time." Jake reached over and pulled her very close to him in the big bed.

Cassie Lamont . . . only when he met Cassie did Jake wake up to the fact that half his life had been wasted in compromise.

The first thing they did was fight. Jake found her running a small but very good lodge at Aspen. He was making a tour of just about every first-class ski resort, taking notes for Sky High. He'd asked for a double. She gave him a single.

"I asked for a double, Miss."

"Mrs. Lamont. I know. And I'm sorry; I called your San Francisco office and they didn't know where to reach you. So I reserved this. If you hate it, I'll try to locate you someplace else in town." She smiled over his rudeness, a small dark-haired girl with enormous brown eyes and with a slim body and the kind of neck that makes you think of ballerinas and fashion models. Jake was in a foul mood. It quickly began to get better. The single would be fine. No, she couldn't have supper with him. He'd planned on staying a day, he stayed a week. The third day she had supper with him. By the end of the week they were almost friends. By the next summer, lovers.

Jake had been looking for a manager to run Sky High. He found more than that in Cassie.

Cassie was thirty and three years a widow. Her husband had been the hot shot pro ski racer Burke Lamont, who got a little too hot one night and drove his Porsche into a tree at 110 miles per hour. This left Cassie nearly broke and with little Charlie Lamont to take care of, since her father was dead and her mother unhappily remarried and not able to help. It had taken Jake six months to sell her on running Sky High. And just a little longer to sell her on Jake Chaffee.

Cassie and young Charlie had moved into the main wing of Sky Lodge in August, practically camping out until the place was finished. But it was finished now, and the Lamonts had their own little suite of two bedrooms, a living room and a bathroom tucked into the first floor of the lodge behind Cassie's office.

Jake was building his relationship with Charlie Lamont slowly and carefully. He'd given the boy a dog, Whizzer, a perpetually smiling Golden Retriever who was now Charlie's constant companion and confidant. The child was painfully shy and uneasy among strangers. "It's a question of self-confidence," explained the child psychologist whom Cassie had visited the previous summer. "Charlie feels, unconsciously, that a world capable of taking his father away so suddenly might be able to do any amount of other damage. He needs more of what you obviously are already giving him: love and a steady environment. No shocks." Which meant, in short, no new father just yet.

Everything Cassie Lamont did, she did intelligently and in depth. And if the dice landed in a way that left Cassie playing father and mother, pal and psychiatrist, to her child, so be it. Jake loved Cassie for the way she dedicated herself to young Charlie, and Jake was genuinely devoted to the boy. But there were times when he resented playing second fiddle to a child, and with Cassie there was no doubt about it: Charlie came first.

So Jake's time with Cassie was squeezed into odd moments of the day and night as she gallantly and successfully juggled her demanding job with the demands of long therapeutic sessions with Charlie. Her treatment was working. Even Jake could see that. And what made Cassie happy made Jake happy. But Charlie was not the only reason why Jake, with uncharacteristic restraint, had held back from asking Cassie to marry him. He knew how she felt about marriage, burned badly the first time around. And there was his own daughter to think about. But the real reason he hesitated was that before he asked Cassie to share his future at Sky High, Jake wanted to be sure he had one.

"Have you been up the mountain?" Jake asked the reporter. He caught a glimpse of his watch as he raised his left arm to point. Nearly lunch time. Before his question got answered there was an explosion of rust-red fur as Whizzer sailed over the three-foot wall of snow left by the plow at the edge of the driveway. Whizzer bounded across to Jake and, rearing up on his hind legs, planted both man-sized front paws firmly on Jake's chest in greeting. "Down, Whizzer!" Jake laughed. "You wanna dance, feller? Where's your master?" Jake knew that wherever the big Golden was, Cassie Lamont's eight-year-old was soon to follow. And right on cue there came a small commotion on the other side of the snowdrift. "Wait up, please, bad Whizzer!" cried a small determined voice. Charlie Lamont clambered over the wall of snow, clutching a large half-eaten French cream puff in one hand and an old broken ski pole in the other. "Hi, Jake," Charlie said hesitantly, put off a little by the reporter; "Look what Mr. Peng gave me."

"Wish he'd give me one! Charlie Lamont, meet Mr. Dawkins. Mr. Dawkins is a reporter."

"What's a reporter?"

"He writes things for newspapers, Charlie."

"Words?"

"Word after word after word." Dawkins patted Charlie on the top of his bright red knitted stocking cap. "Looks like a pretty good cream puff."

"Wanna bite?"

"No thanks, Charlie," Dawkins said. "I think we'll probably be having lunch soon." If this was a hint Jake didn't need it. He'd learned at The Senator's knee that the press was always thirsty and nearly always hungry. He took Dawkins by the arm.

"How about I buy you a drink before lunch?"

"You're on." They turned to walk back to the lodge and Jake scooped up Charlie Lamont and carried the boy piggyback on his shoulders, which is how the prime mover of Sky High came to have chocolate sauce in his hair at the press conference.

"Charlie's mother," said Jake, "is one of Sky High's biggest assets. She's our manager, Cassie Lamont—maybe you've met."

"Any relative to Burke Lamont?" Dawkins knew his skiers.

"Burke Lamont," answered Charlie offhandedly, "is my daddy." The reporter said nothing.

The press conference was held informally in the Sky Bar before lunch. There were a dozen or so reporters, all guests of the management for the opening celebrations. Jake automatically counted the house, looking for potential trouble spots. There were none. Some of the reporters were from the sports magazines, interested only in the quality of the skiing: no trouble there. Some were society reporters sniffing out the newest Place To Be Seen for the jet set: they'd get what they came for. Jake walked into the big, comfortably furnished bar smiling easily like the good host he was. Aside from the press people there were some of his own staff: Cassie and the PR man Dud Drummond and Dud's wife Liz, who looked the way she usually looked at noon, as though she'd put in a long strenuous evening at the bar the night before. Jake looked at Liz Drummond and wondered how many free drinks he'd poured down that bottomless well.

Dud Drummond was in his late 30s and looked older. A little plump, slightly balding, with gray eyes that made sudden changes in direction like a frightened mouse and a smile that often came a few beats too soon—Dudley Lanier Drummond III was the head account executive for the firm Sky High Corporation had retained to spend one million dollars telling the world that the place to ski was no longer Zürs or Chamonix or Vail but Sky High, Sky Junction, Colorado. Dud Drummond sweated a lot and showed a few too many teeth for Jake's taste. But you had to hand it to him. He was very good at his job.

It was Dud Drummond who opened the press conference. He told a mildly funny joke about a fat lady on skis and then launched into his pitch: "Every great hotel in Colorado, or for that matter any great hotel or restaurant anywhere, is inevitably the creation of one presiding genius . . ." Dud went on in this stately vein for several minutes. For Jake's taste it was pretty heavy-handed. But the reporters listened respectfully. Finally, after passing out some handsomely designed and expensive press kits which contained glossy photographs for reproduction, Dud Drummond turned the press conference over to Jake.

"You have chocolate in your hair," Cassie whispered as Jake passed on his way to the big fireplace that was the focus of the room. Jake rode his fear like a wild horse, smiling over tightness in his gut, making a good show of it, deliberately lounging a little more than he usually might and smiling slowly with the instinctive actor's timing he'd absorbed through his skin during years of watching The Senator. If the press was with him, it could be worth a fortune in free publicity for Sky High. And it couldn't hurt in the coming battle for the widening of Route 317. Jake went into it easy-voiced and gentle.

"I don't know if we-all can live up to that fancy introduction, Dud, but we'll sure as hell try." His voice was surprisingly soft for such a big man, and it was the voice of a workingman's West, a voice that knew about roping and branding and sweat and survival. A stranger would have had to look in Who's Who to ever know that Jake Chaffee had a magna cum laude in European history from Harvard. And this, too, Jake learned from The Senator; it doesn't pay to sound better educated than the people you're talking to.

Jake went on: "And by 'we,' I mean every darn one of us here at Sky High. Because, no matter what the man said, this place represents the work and sweat and dreams and talents of a lot of people. I like to think Sky High's more than just another business proposition. Naturally, we aren't going to refuse anybody's money . . . [laughter]. When we decided to build a ski resort here, there were—there always are—a number of ways to do it. I think we did it right. We went far, far out of our way to make sure this land will stay just as beautiful as we found it. For instance: you'll never see an electric wire at Sky High. They're all buried. You'll never see a building more than four stories high, because we don't want to spoil anyone's view. All of the land we own—and there's thirty-five hundred acres of it—is a perpetual wildlife preserve.

"And, no matter how popular we get, the number of skiers allowed on the mountain at any given time is going to be strictly limited to what Pepi Prager feels is right for everyone's pleasure and safety. The Sky High Corporation has spent more than fifty million dollars to develop Sky High right. My numbers guys tell me we could have done it for half that if we didn't care too much what it looked like. Well, I guess you can see. We didn't exactly take the path of least resistance."

Jake paused, smiling, and took a drink from the mug of beer he'd set down on the huge slab of granite that made the mantelpiece of the fireplace. He glanced across the room at Cassie, who was looking at him intently with an expression that might have been interest and might have been worry and was in fact a mixture of both. She caught his eye and winked. He smiled. A drop of sweat slowly started down his backbone.

"Now," Jake continued, "if you can believe all that from a guy with—as Mrs. Lamont told me too late—chocolate in his hair, I'll buy you a drink and we'll get us some lunch. And if there are any questions, well, that's what I'm here for. And thank you for coming."

There were smiles in the audience and even a small ripple of applause. The press liked Jake Chaffee and he liked them in return. Jake knew their problems and he always tried to make their work a little easier. This was not a natural talent. Like many of his more visible charms, Jake's way with the press was the result of work and study, coached by The Senator.

The Senator once said something Jake never forgot, boy or man. "Let me tell you one thing, son," he advised in his best Abe Lincoln manner, "always be nice to reporters and servants. They rule the world." And from the time Jake was a teenager, the press was eating out of his strong brown hand.

2

Zembra Gibbs looked at her grandfather with growing apprehension. In less than five years she'd seen him change from a quiet but gentle man into someone who scared her, into someone obsessed. It was breakfast time in the big eat-in kitchen of Sky Ranch. And Zeke Gibbs was on the warpath again.

"Jake Chaffee's a yellow-bellied no-good slimy cheating sidewinder with the morals of a coyote in heat, and he'll turn this valley into Disneyland if I don't stop him first!" Zem had heard it all before, more times than she liked to think about. The rage seemed to fill some secret need in the old man. He cherished it beyond all reason. Zem Gibbs knew what the ranch meant to her grandfather. It meant a lot to her, too. But this was something else.

The big cheerful kitchen looked like a military war room near the front lines. There were maps marked in several colors, manila folders bursting with news clippings and a stack of lined yellow pads in case the aspiring architect of Jake Chaffee's downfall had any sudden inspirations. Only the good smells of an old-fashioned ranch breakfast brought a note of happiness into the room: Zem was fixing the meal for herself and her grandfather.

Zeke ranted on and Zem tuned him out and thought about her busy day. Since she'd dropped out of college, and since the onset of Zeke's war on Sky High, a lot of the day-to-day management of the ranch had fallen on her. She liked the work and did it well. She saw to the payroll, maintained the huge larder required to feed fourteen live-in ranch hands, and handled the paperwork, which was no light chore since Sky Ranch was a large and profitable beef and lamb operation.

What it boiled down to was that Zem didn't hate anyone. Not even Jake Chaffee. And after all, Sky High was an accomplished fact. Somewhere deep inside, Zem felt the new resort was actually a very attractive place: certainly, it could have been worse. And she loved to ski.

"How goes the battle today?" she asked from politeness more than concern. Route 317 had killed both her parents. The damn road needed to be widened.

"Chaffee's lying low, the sneak. Got a passel of little toadies doing his dirty work for him. And naturally there's plenty of greedy folks with land along 317 just drooling at the thought of all those Denver good-for-nothings trucking up here with their beer cans and their snotty kids . . ."

"And green money."

"And their money, naturally. It's progress, Zem. The litter by the roadsides and a big neon-lit sign selling cardboard hamburgers every five miles. Brought to you courtesy of the man who claims to love Sky Valley."

"Well, Gramps, I guess there are different kinds of love."

"Zembra"—she looked up as he said her full name; it was a portent, usually he just called her Zem like everybody else—"this valley is wet with blood Gibbses shed to get it and hold it. I never had to fight for the place. All that was done for me—and for you—more than a hundred years ago. But what that man did was wrong!" Zeke's huge hand came down on the tabletop. Cups rattled on their saucers. "And I intend to fight him with every ounce of strength I have, even if it's the last thing I do, and well it may be."

"Have I ever tried to stop you?" She looked at her grandfather and wondered why he felt he must justify his warfare to her.

"Of course not, child. It's just that sometimes I'm afraid you think I'm crazy."

"Gramps, if I don't get busy and fill last week's orders from Denver, you really will have something to go crazy about." She rose and walked out of the kitchen.

Zeke poured some more coffee. He didn't expect Zem or anyone else to share his feelings about Jake Chaffee and his damned resort. His rage against Sky High and the man who built it did not come from ignorance about progress. He just never figured anything like the invasion of the ranch could happen to him. He knew his temper upset the girl. And he got madder—at himself—for not being able to rein in that temper. There was no sense getting mad at Zem. She was too levelheaded. And she was all he had left.

Zeke got up from the table and walked across the polished, wide-planked kitchen floor to the window. The very planks he walked on had been cut from Gibbs trees and planed and pegged into place by Gibbses. Sky Mountain loomed two miles down the valley on the right, rising protectively over the thousands and thousands of acres of rich grazing land that lay asleep now under five feet of snow.

"Sleep well," said Zeke out loud, comforting his land; "you never know what you might wake up to."

Zeke Gibbs felt the rhythms of Sky Valley in every season. He knew its beauties and its darker moods. The life of the land was Zeke Gibbs's life. It was as simple as that. For three long-lived generations these proud acres had sustained the finest herds in the Rockies, all with the famous Gibbs Triangle-G brand on them, beef and lamb that were so well regarded no packer ever questioned the premium prices Gibbs stock always commanded. The vast Gibbs Ranch—more than seven thousand acres of it—stretched from end to end of Sky Valley and partway up the mountain. Sky Ranch had been run smartly and very independently by Gibbs men and Gibbs women, too, since 1849. When Zeke Gibbs was a bright-eyed nimble mountain goat of a boy back before the turn of the century, ten-year-olds carried Colt revolvers and knew how to use them, for the land still bred rustlers and prowling renegade Indians and men crazed with greed from the silver-mine towns like Aspen.

Sky Ranch and the valley it sat on had come to Zeke and his sister in the natural course of events. He'd never had to fight for a thing. For ranching or hunting on the mountain or trying to live up to his position as the leading citizen of Sky Valley, Zeke Gibbs had plenty of natural ability. He could cure a sick heifer, suck out a rattler bite and predict the first snowfall within an hour and an inch. But when it came to wheeling and dealing in the dark, twisted corridors of political influence, Zeke was an innocent. Partly because he was dead honest. And partly because, underneath his crusty exterior, Zeke Gibbs was a very shy and private man who believed to the tip of his toes that it is wrong for one man to have "influence" over another. All this made the battle harder. But Zeke was determined, and come what may Jake Chaffee was going to have a fight on his hands. A fight to the end. When you got right down to the grit, there were plenty of people with influence in Colorado who owed the Gibbs dynasty a favor or two. As far as Zeke knew, no Gibbs had ever wanted or needed to collect those debts. But if ever there was a time to do it, the time was now. The bill to widen 317 had been pigeonholed for years. Now it was being pushed by the Chaffee interests. It would come up for debate in the new year, when the legislature reconvened after the Christmas recess. And Zeke Gibbs would be ready.

It was very quiet in the big kitchen of Sky Ranch. Zeke stood at the window watching a vulture circling over some invisible dead thing and thinking that the ways of the Lord were strange and inscrutable. Jake Chaffee had descended on Sky Valley like a judgment. Even now, in the morning stillness, Zeke could hear Chaffee's knock on the ranch house door echoing down the five years since the day of his first visit.

"Mr. Ezekiel Gibbs?" Jake had driven up from Denver in a rented car. He stood at the front door of the ranch house tall and straight in an open shirt and blue jeans, bareheaded, smiling and looking like anything but the agent of Sky Valley's undoing.

"Yes."

"My name is Chaffee. Jake Chaffee." Jake put out his hand and Zeke shook it.

"Come in, young man."

"I guess you got my letter."

"I did."

"And?"

"And I could have saved you a trip, Mr. Chaffee. Sky Ranch is not for sale. Or any part of it." Zeke had led Jake Chaffee into the big old parlor of the ranch house, a room hardly used since Zeke's wife died some thirty years ago. Jake was carrying a large manila envelope. He put it down on a table.

"Will you at least hear me out?" Both men were still standing. Stiffly, Zeke Gibbs motioned Jake into one of the heavily carved, black horsehair-covered chairs that had been bought a hundred years ago in Denver.

"Mr. Chaffee, it's easy to understand your wanting land up here. Hell. It's some of the finest grazing land in the state. But you're too late."

"You mean, you've sold?" Jake's face was so crestfallen the old man laughed.

"Hell, no, son! I meant, you're a hundred and twenty-some years too late. That's about how long us Gibbses have held this valley. And we're figuring to hold onto it at least that long again. So you may have to wait some. And you don't strike me as a man who's used to waiting."

"That depends on what I'm waiting for. Would you consider a long-term lease on just part of the ranch?"

"No, son, I would not."

"Mr. Gibbs, I realize you're pretty well fixed financially . . ."

"And what color underdrawers am I wearing, eh? In this part of the world, Mister, we mind our own business. And I must be keeping you from yours. Whatever it is." Zeke stood up, hoping to end the interview.

"I could make do with as few as a hundred acres, if they were the right acres."

"Mr. Chaffee, I admire persistence as much as any man. Up to a point. You have reached that point. I don't expect you to understand how I feel about this place. Why should you? In 1849, my grandfather up and joined a wagon train out of Saint Louis. Twelve Conestogas they had, and fifty-nine people. Joshua Gibbs was one of twenty-two who made it to Denver. Then he came all the way up here. Cleared this valley with his own bare hands. Tended the land. Fought for it." Zeke's eyes bored into Jake Chaffee's with an intensity Jake never forgot, the look of righteous pride edging dangerously close to madness.

"Ever since, we Gibbses have taken care of Sky Ranch. And this land has taken care of us. Sky Valley is not a commodity, Mr. Chaffee. The money hasn't been printed that can buy what this land means to me and mine. Find yourself another valley, son. You don't want mine."

"I do, though," said Jake, standing. "And while you may not believe me, Mr. Gibbs, I also understand how you feel about the place. I grew up on a ranch too, out in Sacramento. Built by my own grandfather, just like this."

"What kind of man are you then, to run around after . . . what others have built up?" Zeke's voice was getting louder.

"What I do isn't destructive, Mr. Gibbs. If you could see some of my other developments . . ."

"Developments? Ha! Outrages, I call 'em. Yours or anyone else's. Crowds. Noise. Mess. And the Lord only knows what-all else."

"You'll have to face progress sometime. What I'm offering is the very best kind of development. The next guy might not care so much."

"There isn't going to be a next guy."

"Are you always this stubborn?"

"Son, I'm going to invite you politely to get off my land. And one invitation had better be enough."

"You make yourself clear." Jake smiled and extended his hand. It hung in the silent room: Zeke either didn't see it or didn't care to contaminate himself.

"Then you'll leave me alone?" Zeke demanded.

"That may not be possible."

"Get out of here!"

"Thanks for seeing me."

"Out!" Zeke was shouting. Jake picked up his envelope, which contained a complete aerial survey of Sky Valley, and walked toward the door. He opened it, then turned his head toward Zeke, who stood in the parlor, livid, fists clenched at his sides.

"I guess we're both stubborn men," said Jake. Then he walked out into the bright October afternoon.

Zeke Gibbs looked down the long valley at the thing Jake Chaffee had built on what had been half of Sky Ranch. He sighed. There were a dozen "if onlys" that might have kept Jake Chaffee out of Sky Valley. For example, if only Zeke's sister had stayed healthy, her half of the ranch wouldn't have come down to her daughter, Eugenia, who didn't care spit about Sky Valley or anyone in it. Or if only Eugenia hadn't gone East to college back in the 30s, maybe she wouldn't have sailed to France and married that slimy looking little count ("the No-A-Count" Zeke always called him, making it a bitter family joke). Eugenia, Countess de Bramafam, hadn't set foot in America, let alone Sky Valley, in more than thirty years. Even when her own mother died, Eugenia was yachting in the Aegean. She sent a big wreath of red red roses. Zeke fed them to the goats.

It was Pete Woodbury who dug up the fact that Sky Valley really had two owners, Old Zeke and the Countess Eugenia. Two days after he knew, Jake himself was on a Paris-bound jet armed with a map of the valley and a limit of two million dollars. Eugenia, who bore Zeke Gibbs no special malice but no particular affection either, found Jake's offer of a million two hundred thousand both unexpected and irresistible. The Chateau of Bramafam got a new roof. And Jake Chaffee got all he needed of Sky Valley.

The night Eugenia signed away her half of the ranch, Jake took her to the legendary Paris restaurant, Chez Midas, to celebrate. There Jake tasted Raoul Peng's cuisine for the first time. And, with the same quick rush of possessiveness he'd felt seeing Sky Mountain, Jake decided that Peng would somehow be persuaded to become the chef at Sky High. And that, too, happened in its time.

When Jake Chaffee next set foot on Sky Ranch, it was as its owner. Zeke contested the sale of the land and the proposed development. But here, too, Jake Chaffee had moved too fast and too cleverly for him.

Permission to develop Sky Mountain had been granted before Jake left for Paris.

Zeke Gibbs never knew what Jake had said or done to get the agreement from Eugenia, but as always he suspected the worst. And Eugenia, like Jake Chaffee, fast became a treacherous enemy.

But Eugenia was only part way down Zeke's long, sad list of "if onlys." If only Zembra's parents had lived, they might have had sons. They were young enough. If only Randy Gibbs had been going ten miles an hour slower when his big Ford wagon hit the ice on Route 317, Randy and Anna might be alive and with sons to help Zeke in his struggle. It had been a bitter night, ten years ago, when Zeke Gibbs picked up the phone to hear the sheriff of Steamboat Springs ask him to come identify the bodies of his only son and the son's young wife.

That night left Zeke Gibbs with ten-year-old Zembra and a heart permanently outraged. Zeke carried on alone with just the ranch hands and old Mrs. Sutter to do the housework and be some kind of mother to little Zem. Even then Zem had been the bright spot in Zeke's darkening world.

At ten she was already a beauty, a quiet fearless child who would roam the mountain alone with one of the sheep dogs. And when the snows came little Zem skied the three miles down to Sky Junction and the tiny four-room schoolhouse, moving over the frozen meadows with the quick grace of a mountain deer.

Zeke Gibbs was not an outgoing man, but he did what he could to see that Zem had good times, treats, sleigh rides with her friends and barn dances and regular trips to Steamboat Springs for the Saturday movies. From time to time he'd even take the girl all the way to Denver for a few days of shopping and restaurants and maybe even a play or a concert. Still, Zeke knew, there must have been lonely times for her.

In high school, Zem was popular enough but never really interested in boys. That changed by the time she went off to college at Boulder. At first, she hadn't wanted to go at all, but Zeke insisted she give it a try, and for the first year Zem seemed to like the college life. Then the summer after her first year at Boulder, something happened to Zembra Gibbs. His name was Bill Shepherd and he was a young doctor from back East.

A tall, quiet, dark-haired young man, all shoulders and dedication, Bill Shepherd had worked up to the top of his class at the Harvard Medical School and then decided he didn't want a fancy city practice after all. After his internship in New York City, Bill gave himself a little vacation: his first ever. He'd never seen America west of the Hudson River, so he postponed all career decisions, packed his battered Volkswagen and headed west. Bill was driving down Main Street of Sky Junction when he saw the sign. Strung right across the street, hand-lettered on a bedsheet, were the provocative words: SKY JUNCTION NEEDS A DOCTOR. Curious, Bill stopped the car right there, and at that moment Zembra Gibbs rode down Main Street on her chestnut gelding, Herbert. Bill had never guessed there was country like this, or girls like Zem Gibbs. Sky Junction was a town waiting for its doctor. Bill Shepherd was a young man looking for a life. The two quests converged in that instant, and neither Bill nor the town would ever regret it.

Zem was then wearing her usual work clothes, jeans faded to soft blue, scuffed old Frye boots, a tan army shirt and a dark blue bandanna to hold the molten-gold hair. She sat tall on the beautiful horse and regarded Bill Shepherd with friendly curiosity. She smiled, just a little, to be hospitable. After all, this was her town. Her valley. And, there was no denying it, Bill Shepherd was a fine looking young man in a place where young men of any description were few and far between.

They met, of course, soon after. For Bill Shepherd it was love: plain and simple and strong. For Zem, more of a loner, a girl who was thrifty with her emotions the way mountain people often are, this was as close to love as she'd ever come. Zem and Bill were quickly friends and soon they were lovers. A lot of things about them just naturally fitted together. Bill, like Zem, was a child of the mountains. He'd grown up poor on the outskirts of Rutland, Vermont. Scholarships and his struggling druggist father and a series of part-time jobs saw the quiet, very determined boy through Harvard College and the medical school. Bill interned at Columbia Presbyterian, mostly because he'd never been to New York. And there he learned a lot, including the fact that he'd never be happy in cities.

When fall came it found Bill Shepherd hanging out his shingle in a small rented house set back from the road behind the old sawmill in Sky Junction, Colorado. Bill Shepherd found a world in Zem Gibbs and that high mountain valley. The valley was their only problem. For Zem was restless. She hadn't seen much outside Sky Valley and was bound and determined she would before she took any vows or put down any roots.

"Tell me about New York," she'd say, lying next to Bill in his big old white-painted bed.

"It's big. But Sky Mountain's a lot bigger. And you can breathe the air out here and walk down the street without being mugged. Basically, New York is kind of a stone sewer."

"But isn't it full of fascinating people doing wonderful things, making history?"

"Making a great big mess is what they're doing. If people like that are around, I sure never met 'em."

"But didn't you want to?"

"Not specially."

"Bill Shepherd, you are provincial!"

"My province," he said, reaching for her, "is you."

Their two young bodies found each other in the wide iron bed, Zembra slim and fair, Bill tall and dark and quivering with love. Softly, softly his hands stroked her. For Bill, Zem was a continent of love, and the sense of wonder was always there no matter how often or how totally these two smooth young bodies explored each other. Quickly, instinctively, like some creature of the woods, Zem twined her slender legs around him and he thrust inside her, rising on his knees in the same motion, gasping and pulling her to him, flesh locked in flesh, love meeting love as their passion made a new world without time or boundaries or any rules at all but sharing pleasure.

And after the explosion as she lay pensive in the protective curl of his arm, Bill said quietly: "The only times I feel complete are when I'm inside you. Marry me, Zem. It just doesn't get any better than this."

"You are just wonderful." She looked up at his strong dark profile silhouetted against a patch of moonlight on the pillow. "But, honey, I am only nineteen years old. How do I know what love is?"

"You know because it's right here in this room, Zem. In this bed. In the air. Love isn't something you know. It's something you feel." His hand moved on her shoulder, stroking, comforting.

"Bill, we could stay here and fuck for the rest of our natural lives and I'd probably be happy."

"Only probably?" His hand was on her breast now, exploring, caressing.

"Very probably." She could sense his sex quickening. She reached out to help it, laughing in spite of herself. "You horny son of a bitch," she said, "taking advantage of an innocent mountain girl like me." And the magic began again.

Zembra Gibbs went back to college at Boulder that fall. Reluctantly. By the time spring drifted up to the mountains. Zem asked for and got a year's leave of absence. At least that was what the piece of paper said. In fact Zem Gibbs had no intention of going back to college. She privately resolved either to settle down with Bill, who was boiling over with eagerness to marry her, or to get herself out into the great world beyond these hills and gain a little perspective on her life. Sometimes she even contemplated a surprise visit to Aunt Eugenia and her No-A-Count, in their leaky Chateau de Bramafam.

Zem forced herself to get down to work in the little ranch office, conscious of her grandfather's presence in the kitchen. Gramps was getting gloomier and gloomier, and try as she might, Zem really didn't know how to handle it. Bill was a help. Zeke liked the quiet young doctor, and Bill liked him back. Zem loved the old man. This was a man who had spent his whole life taking care of Sky Ranch, nurturing the land, patiently making it better and better, helping people whenever he could. In Sky Junction the little public library had Zem's grandmother's name on it, thanks to Zeke. Zeke Gibbs was shy, as mountain people often are. He had the mountain man's well developed sense of self-sufficiency, great pride and a reluctance to intrude. Zem thought maybe it wasn't the mountains that made people this way but rather simply that people who were inclined to be loners made their way to the mountains. There was a streak of this mountain shyness in Bill Shepherd and in Zem herself, a kind of unspoken self-reliance that had the effect of shutting out the world. They felt no obligation to fill the mountain air with small talk, for silence had its own thousand voices in Sky Valley and there was always something interesting to hear if you had ears to hear it.

One thing, Zem knew, that would cheer up her grandfather would be if she married Bill Shepherd. Zeke liked the young doctor. Zem smiled as she worked, thinking of Bill. A girl could do a lot worse.

Zeke Gibbs meanwhile stood at a window looking down across the snow-covered meadows to the mountain. He could see the dazzling reflections the morning sun struck off the oddly angled windows of Sky Lodge. Still, the vultures circled, but now there were three of them. Zeke put down his coffee cup and walked across the kitchen to the big, crowded gun rack.

Zeke stood for a moment looking at these thirty-some weapons that made a kind of history of the Gibbs family in polished wood and oiled steel. Here rested the flintlocks that crossed the great plains. There were Colt six-shooters with barrels so long they were all but rifles, guns that helped win and hold this very land. Zeke reached up and took the newest of the lot, a slender, handmade English shotgun he'd ordered specially from Purdy's for Zem's father on the boy's twenty-first birthday. Zeke held the elegant, deadly thing in silence and then took it to the big kitchen table where, first spreading Sunday's *Denver Post,* he carefully began to clean and oil it.

3

"For a slick rip-off artist from Frisco, you were pretty good with those reporters, Mr. Chaffee." Cassie sat in her little office behind the reception desk at Sky Lodge, wondering what was wrong with Jake. Something. The press conference had gone well and the luncheon afterwards was a triumph for Raoul Peng. Now Cassie sat smiling up at him, feeling the electricity between them, wondering if she was just nervous, just imagining things.

"You're speaking to the great-grandchild of Lily Cigar. Of course it went well." He stood behind her and rubbed her neck.

"Who's Lily Cigar?"

"My most famous ancestor—ancestress. Lily Cigar was the biggest madam on the Embarcadero. So successful she ended up owning her own house, then a string of 'em, then real estate up in what is now Marin County. Lily met my great-grandfather, presumably in the line of business, hers, not his, and lo and behold they got married and that was the start of the Chaffee fortune, such as it is. My father, you may be sure, plays down the connnection. I think she sounds like fun, myself."

"So do I."

"So, when a Chaffee, heaven forfend, does anything whore-y, that's where it comes from."

"You are anything but whore-y."

"That right? I wasn't out there peddling it this afternoon? Hell, Cassie, I did everything but wiggle my ass at 'em. There are two reasons I never went into politics.

Most importantly, to piss off my father. Secondly, to avoid scenes like today."

"I'm not sure I understand you. What was wrong with today?"

"Let's just say that if I did convince 'em I'm a virgin again, maybe it wasn't so bad after all. It's only that I feel a little weird doing it. Putting the old scam on 'em."

"Is Sky High a scam, Jake?"

"I didn't mean it to be. But sometimes I think so. Sometimes I think Zeke Gibbs could be right."

"Know what I think?" She stood up and kissed him.

"What do you think?"

"I think you have chocolate in your hair." Someone knocked on the door.

Cassie stood up suddenly, wrapped her arms around Jake's broad back and buried her face in his chest. Cassie wanted this man, felt like part of him, knew he loved her, sensed that he wanted to marry her. But something kept pulling her back from the edge of commitment. Some small, insistent voice in her kept saying, "Hold it! You tried that once, remember? You fell hard for one beautiful, flashy guy: are you going to make that mistake twice? How do you know Jake's not just doing a number on you, like he does on the rest of the world? Do you really know this man? How many times will you have to get burned before you get smart?" The voice was very persuasive. Almost as persuasive as Jake Chaffee. And between the two of them, they were doing a fine job of tearing her apart.

Two things kept Cassie on an even keel. One was Charlie. The other was the fact that Cassie was a smart woman with a sense of humor who refused to waste her energies in self-pity. If her marriage to Burke Lamont had ended badly, it had begun in good faith. They'd been too young and too crazy about each other to see what was obvious to any stranger: that Burke Lamont for all his charm was the kind of boy who never grows up. If he had lived, the marriage would have died anyway. Cassie knew that and held no bitterness against Burke or against men in general. Cassie frankly liked men, liked sex, liked the simple warmth of having a man around, but that sharp little voice kept right on warning her not to give herself completely to any man or any thing. She squeezed Jake and let go. The knock on the door sounded a second time, more insistently.

Dud Drummond came in, precisely one minute early, as always. Raoul Peng slipped noiselessly in behind him. Cassie, all business, sat at her desk in the small, beautifully designed private office that Storione had tucked in behind the main reception area. Cassie had the strong, high-cheekboned look of American Indian women, and in fact one of her great-grandmothers was supposed to have been part Cherokee. Cassie was also a fine athlete with a quick, attentive mind and a real affection for people. Jake paid her a generous salary plus the free suite of rooms and a nursemaid for little Charlie. She was a bargain at that. Cassie somehow managed to juggle all the different claims on her time in a sweet, almost gentle and completely feminine style. Yet she was better organized than most men Jake had ever done business with. Under Cassie's hand Sky High ran like the very expensive, well-oiled machine it was. And Jake Chaffee realized, even as he admired her work, that he was being juggled, gracefully, along with a dozen other parts of Cassie's life. That grated on him, even though his main rival was Sky High itself. Jake intended to straighten that out. There were other managers. But there was only one Cassie and he wanted her all to himself, completely, and soon.

From Cassie's point of view the situation was more complicated. An affair with Jake was one thing. She could handle that, keep it in its own special corner of her life. And in fact she had handled it successfully for more than a year now, keeping it light, making no vows and asking none. That was the way to play it. Except that Jake wanted more and more of her, and Jake, Cassie knew too well, had an astonishing track record for getting what he wanted.

Ever since that night four years ago, the night Burke died, Cassie had been slowly picking up the fragments of her life, making a future out of hope and guts and her love for Charlie. Now along came Jake Chaffee, smiling and rich and handsome as any prince, and every bit as charming. Jake was ready to shake up her life all over again. If she let him.

"Where were we?" Cassie asked of no one in the room in particular. Dud Drummond, very correct and slightly incongruous in a business suit, sat in a little chair next to Cassie's desk taking notes. Jake and Raoul Peng stood against the wall. "We seem," Cassie went on, "all set for tonight. Raoul has big plans for the press dinner."

At this, Raoul Peng smiled his thin, humorless smile. Peng was a lean, dark and almost boyish looking man, the son of a French mother and a Chinese father. Peng spoke French with a curious Far-Eastern lilt and English with virtually no accent at all. "It is to surprise them," he said. "They will be expecting the food to be French and very fancy. So Peng gives them all-American, as you say, and very simple."

"That is," said Cassie with a laugh, "Raoul's idea of simple. We start with fresh brook trout . . . "

". . . stuffed with a mousse of Alaskan crab," Raoul broke in softly, as if talking to himself. "This with a light mustard sauce. Then, a perfectly simple noisette of lamb—Sky Valley lamb at that—with just a little clear brown sauce and your fine small pink potatoes. *Asperges*—ah, rather, asparagus—with the Chez Midas hazelnut puree. A salad. Then, for dessert, and to give the place a bit of a name, an invention: Sky Mountain. Which is a small cone-shaped mousse of maple syrup decorated with crème Chantilly and chopped-walnut praline—the mountain, you see, with snow upon it."

"It sounds perfect, Raoul." Jake, who hated any meeting that lasted more than five minutes, shifted his weight restlessly.

"But there is one problem." Raoul, as always, spoke softly.

"What's that, Raoul?"

"I cannot do it."

"Come on, Raoul. Of course you can do it." Jake thought Raoul was making some inscrutable Oriental joke.

"The budget you have suddenly imposed on me makes meals like this absolutely out of the question."

Raoul looked at Jake with the eyes of one betrayed. "We made no mention of such limitations, Jake, when I agreed to come here. I did not leave the most successful restaurant in Paris to run a hot dog stand."

"Raoul, listen. Nobody's putting any limitations on you. Take it from me. I know Pete Woodbury's been hassling everybody about costs. It's just that the price of everything is skyrocketing and Pete feels he has to keep on top of things, you know, keep a tight rein on the budget. But don't take it personally. He does it to all of us, Raoul. It's his job."

"And shall Raoul Peng cook up a tight rein for this Woodbury? Has Peng achieved three Michelin stars by cooking tight reins? Has Mr. Woodbury ever eaten a tight rein? I am not extravagant in my kitchen, Jake. But we do not build the Parthenon without marble." Raoul suddenly whipped out a sheaf of papers, forms ordering supplies from Denver and New York and even Paris. The forms had been heavily red-penciled, with many question marks and annotations. "This," Raoul went on, his voice rising from whisper level to nearly normal, "this outrage came to me this very morning, Jake, from your Mr. Woodbury. Look! He questions that I buy truffles. The little greenhouse for fresh herbs, soul of my cuisine. Can't we use powdered? he says. Jake, I am sure that if this person is associated with you he must be clever in many ways . . ."

"He is."

"But please keep him out of Raoul's kitchen!" Peng's voice got softer and softer as his outrage reached a climax. But no one in Cassie's little office doubted that the master chef was very upset.

"Raoul, truly, I apologize. I wasn't aware of this. Pete looks over all our requests—in detail. It's his job. But you're perfectly right. You can take my word for it. I'll keep Pete Woodbury the hell out of your kitchen. Now. How about the wines for tonight?"

"Also a surprise. In fact, quite thrifty!" Raoul permitted himself a smile. "Again they are totally American. With the fish, a Blanc Fumé from Mondavi—lovely wine. With the lamb, hand-picked Gamay Beaujolais of Sebastiani—perfect for the mountains. Truly, I never dreamed America had such wines. I had thought of a champagne with the dessert, but, considering . . ."

"Of course we'll have champagne! And the hell with Pete Woodbury! After all, it's the press, and it's money well spent."

"The Korbel Brut Nature, then," said Raoul. "I believe we have enough on ice."

Indeed they did. Raoul Peng had worked closely with Storione to design the kitchens and wine cellar at Sky High. The huge wine cellar was cut back into the living rock of Sky Mountain, which served as a natural insulator, keeping the wine at a temperature never higher than 55 and never lower than 48 degrees year-round. This made it possible to truck in huge supplies of wine in the summer, when the passes were sure to be open, and store them in ideal conditions for practically indefinite periods of time. Already, on opening, Sky High could boast the finest and most extensive cellar between Chicago and the West Coast: nearly ten thousand bottles of carefully selected vintages.

Jake Chaffee owned an interest in one of the better small California vineyards, and under his auspices a small cuvée of special soft red Zinfandel and an equally rare Sauvignon Blanc were bottled under the Sky High label with Raoul Peng's signature and a notation that he had selected them personally for the tables of Sky Lodge. Jake's intention was to make these bottles collector's items—they could not be bought in any retail store—and to send them as gifts of the house to the tables of certain favored patrons and to people who might become patrons. This had been Jake's idea and he was proud of it. It gave Sky High one more exclusive feature and was the kind of thing people talked about.

Raoul Peng looked at Jake and Cassie and Dud Drummond, and he smiled with something close to affection. They were really such fools. And they were playing so perfectly into his capable hands, it was almost as if he had written the script.

"If you will excuse me then," Raoul murmured, "I really must be getting back to the—how do you say it, the salty mines?" They laughed politely at his little joke, although no one in that room thought Peng was funny.

Let them laugh, thought Peng. This Sky High, this preposterous creation, was to be but one more stepping stone in the glorious career of Raoul Peng. Even now, in the offices of one of America's biggest food conglomerates, contracts were being drawn up that would make Raoul Peng an instant millionaire. Raoul well remembered his meeting with the legendary art collector and *conglomerateur,* Norbert Styron. Styron, so different from Jake Chaffee, was much more Raoul's kind of man. He spoke quietly to Peng in near-perfect French, while gently swirling a crystal thimble full of vintage Armagnac. Jake talked fast in English and drank bourbon. Styron's proposition was simple and very appealing. He felt that the American public was ready for a line of truly fine gourmet frozen foods. These would be sold at very high prices—at correspondingly high profits—to the millions of middle-class housewives all over America who were just discovering that there was more to life than dry steaks and wet vegetables. But what the line needed was the endorsement of a world-famous chef. (Styron didn't mention he had already tried Julia Child and been refused.) If only—and here was the one area of doubt—if only Raoul Peng were just a little better known within the United States. Peng then brought up the subject of Jake Chaffee's offer, which had just been made, and which brought with it a full-scale international publicity campaign.

This fitted in perfectly with Styron's plan. The Styron Food Corporation wouldn't be ready to introduce the new line for at least one year. By that time the Sky High publicity would have done its work. Peng's name would be known. All Raoul Peng had to do was make sure Sky High's cuisine lived up to its reputation all winter long. Then, in the springtime, Raoul Peng would be made a senior vice-president of Styron Foods at a contract of a hundred fifty thousand dollars per year, plus stock options that would make him rich while the marketing division made him famous.

Planning three meals a day for three hundred people is no easy thing even if the quality is low. When you have a world-famous reputation to keep up and the Styron Foods contract hanging in the balance, the pressures mount. But Peng was equal to the task. He had insisted on bringing his carefully trained sauce chef, René Latour, and also a pastry chef from Chez Midas. The rest of the help, sadly, was local. But Peng and his hand-picked team worked together like champion athletes, silently and with perfect mutual understanding. With keen and practiced eyes, Raoul Peng looked down the length of his gleaming domain. He'd be lucky to get the equal of this kitchen ever again. No effort or expense had been spared to make this the Versailles of all hotel kitchens.

At the far end of the big room behind glass was a big fish tank with separate compartments for fresh and salt water. At this moment Peng could see two hundred pedigreed Dover sole that had been flown in live from Britain and trucked up from Denver in special tanks. They would be offered at enormous prices as a curiosity for the very rich, just to demonstrate beyond all doubt that the kitchens at Sky High could satisfy almost any whim. Below the swimming Dover sole, banked in ocean sand, dwelt scores of clams and oysters fattening for the knife. Above these oyster beds, huge green lobsters crawled ponderously across the expensive sand, dragging their armor to a battle they had no way of knowing was already lost.

In the fresh-water tank, schools of fat sleek Rocky Mountain trout swam merrily. Once more, Peng smiled. Sixty beautifully pearlescent trout, just minutes from the tank, were being stuffed with a delicate mousse of crab. Farther down the brightly lit and perfectly ventilated room, one hundred twenty lean and tender noisettes of lamb were being trimmed and spiced and brushed with home-churned unsalted butter. At a side counter smoothly topped with butcher block, a sullen older woman was slowly peeling asparagus stalks. These would be washed and tied into sixty individual little packages of six stalks each and then boiled for no more and no less than seven minutes, immediately before serving.

Raoul walked quietly down the length of his kitchen, giving a gentle word of advice here, a compliment there, now sampling a sauce, now adding a touch of herb, a drop of lemon, or slightly adjusting the heat of a burner. There was a surprising lack of noise and temperament in Raoul Peng's kitchens. A journalist had once attributed this to Raoul's supposed oriental calm. In fact Peng was a lapsed Lutheran and the calm was simply the result of organization and efficiency.

Peng had trained in three very well-known kitchens, all in a continual state of comic-opera excitement complete with oaths, screams, insults and flying saucepans. In such kitchens, Peng thought, the supreme act of creativity was that any dish ever reached a customer. So when the time came—and it came quickly—for Peng to supervise his own kitchen, he tolerated no such goings-on. Temperament was noisy and inefficient—and it curdled the Hollandaise. Instinctively, Peng picked up a wooden spoon and tasted the hazelnut puree that was slowly simmering in a copper pot. It needed more thyme.

Back in Cassie's office Jake looked restlessly from face to face and wondered if any of them could read the fear behind his confident smile. They were working hard, working well, acting like real pros, and right in their midst stood Jake, the focus of it all, a secret Jonah who alone among them knew he might just be the agent of Sky High's shipwreck. It wasn't a good feeling and it stuck in Jake's consciousness like a pebble in a hiker's boot. Cassie was in the middle of her briefing and everything she said was important. Too important, he thought, suppressing a sigh.

"So it looks like they'll be pouring in all week." She was flipping through her card file on scheduled arrivals. "Tomorrow we get the Arabs and, Jake, you don't happen to know what we call him, do you? I mean, he isn't really the sheikh, is he?" Dud Drummond had the answer to that one. Dud made it his business to have a complete runndown on all the celebrities he'd booked into Sky High for the opening blast. Everyone in Cassie's little office had a stake in the success of the opening celebrations. And as Dud Drummond worked his way down the list of the rich, the prominent, the notorious guests who were about to arrive at Sky High, every one in that room had his own private set of doubts and hopes to deal with.

"Niris Reza Herat Bir-Saraband," said Dud, "is next in line to the throne of Bidijar, where all that nice oil comes from. Niris travels with a private jet, two wives, five servants and a brace of snow-white Royal Afghans. I trust we've got space for the whole circus."

"Done." Cassie, as always, cool and efficient.

"And on Sunday," Dud went on, "we get the infamous Dorothy Dutton."

"A challenge to Raoul," said Cassie, smiling at the thought. "She's on a diet that consists entirely of peanut butter and beer. The beer we've got. The peanut butter is ordered. But what he does with it . . ."

"Peng never yet refused a challenge. He won't refuse this one." Jake frowned as he thought of "La Dutton," as the press liked to call her. Dorothy Dutton was rumored to be either the richest or the second-richest woman in the world. She was well into her sixth decade and her seventh husband, a fiscally and sexually ambivalent Italian count called "Momo." Momo's full title was Count Massimilliano Ruvo di Putignano-Squillace. He and his unblushing bride were notorious scene makers, crockery hurlers, and pursuers of any sexual object that wasn't tied down. But La Dutton was as famous as she was rich and the world press followed her every move. And even while Jake wondered what havoc she might wreak on his beautiful resort, he knew very well that wherever La Dutton stayed was *the* place to stay.

Cassie looked down at La Dutton's file card. "So, just to be sure, I've asked the market in Steamboat Springs to save me an extra two cases of Skippy peanut butter. It's the only kind she'll touch."

"Crunchy or plain?" Jake snorted.

" 'Crunchy,' says Madame la Contessa Ruvo di Putignano-Squillace, 'is for the nouveaux riches!' Plain she wants it, so plain she'll have it. I'm not sure I believe any of this, either." Cassie put back the Dutton file card.

"Noel Northcliff is coming, isn't he?" Dud Drummond had pulled many a string to get the famous gossip columnist to spend two weeks at Sky High. Cassie flipped to the N's.

"Even as we speak. He's on the noon flight into Denver and so is, Cornelia de Vos. I authorized an Eagle Airlines charter to pick both of 'em up and fly them to Steamboat, and our limo will collect them from there, scheduled for two-thirty."

"Good work." Jake nodded. He hated to spend the money for luxuries like the charter, but at this stage of the game there was no point in not doing things right. "Do the same for Pete Woodbury, will you, Cassie? He'll be on that same flight, only tomorrow."

"Done. And, Jake, you know that Eagle plane has room for four. Why don't I have TWA make an in-flight announcement before they set down in Denver, just in case anyone else on that flight is headed for Sky High? Won't cost a penny, and it's great free publicity."

"I'll take care of it, Cassie." Dud Drummond smiled to cover his irritation at not having thought of this himself. "You must be up to your ears."

"It's great you got us Northcliff, Dud," Jake said, anxious to cut the meeting short. "Between him and La Dutton and the de Vos lady and the Arabs, we ought to get some pretty good coverage all over the world." But Dud Drummond looked pensive.

"I wish," said Dud, "I wish for a nice famous Jap."

"Dudley Lanier Drummond the Third, you are shameless, absolutely shameless." Cassie giggled.

"Where the gold is," said Jake, grinning, "the Japs will not be far behind. By this time next year every aspen tree on the mountain will conceal at least two small yellow transistor millionaires and their Nikons."

"God willing!" said Cassie, half to herself.

"Well," added Dud Drummond with his PR man's instinct for letting his clients know he was earning his fee, "don't forget we also have Buck Washington." The recently retired but still very famous black superstar pro quarterback of the Los Angeles Rams was at loose ends. Thirty-four years old and at least four times a millionaire, Buck Washington had retired three years ago and quickly made three bad movies, did some youth work, signed on as a TV sports reporter, quit that, and made headlines all the while. The most recent ones involved his split with Olivia Pelham, the blonde, eloquent and carefully publicized leader of the women's liberation movement. And now Buck Washington was coming to Sky High to learn skiing. Alone.

"Not to mention whoever shows up for the Sky High Challenge Cup." Cassie followed the ski racing circuit with the added interest of someone who had been part of it. "Your idea of getting Pepi to come out of retirement for the downhill was pure inspiration, Dud. That alone will get us bags of coverage."

"Plus," said Jake, "we'll have the whole regular pro contingent in the Cup event: Spider Sabitch, Annie Famouse, maybe even Killy himself."

Cassie looked at Jake. "It's all coming together at last. We're not full up yet, but we will be by this time next week."

"And the revels will commence." Dud pulled out a much revised schedule of the next two weeks' events. "Tuesday is the sleigh ride to our side of Lake of the Sky for mulled wine and ice skating. Old Zeke Gibbs can't do anything to stop that, much as he'd like to. Then, Wednesday at cocktail time is the wine tasting conducted by Raoul Peng himself, which is something they'll be talking about for years. Thursday we'll have either Judy Collins or somebody like her as a surprise entertainer after dinner. On Friday I've laid on three choppers to fly the serious skiers up to the snow bowls on the north face of Sky Mountain—with Pepi to guide them personally. We'll only be able to take about two dozen, Jake, but you can bet they'll be talking about it for the rest of their lives."

"They'll also see the potential of the hill." Jake knew that people who could ski well enough for the helicopter ride up to the three great snow bowls on the back side of the mountain would be just the kind of people to invest in Sky High land. "Hell, in five years this place will make Vail look like a molehill."

"Then," Dud Drummond went on, "on Saturday we're trucking in five dogsleds for anyone who wants to ride through the woods—that'll be especially good for the kids. And so it goes. Every day something different, all leading up to the big pro race. Some schedule."

"You're doing fine, Dud. Just fine." Jake stretched and yawned. "But now I've got to go track down Pepi about that race. Anyone for a little skiing?" This, Dud knew, was directed at Cassie. Dud hardly ever skied himself.

"I can't now, Jake," Cassie said a little wistfully. "I really have a mountain of stuff to do, including that damn broad's peanut butter."

"Maybe tomorrow." Jake grinned.

"Maybe tomorrow," she said, casually.

They are so cool about it, thought Dud Drummond, so businesslike. They do it so well. Dud knew, as everyone knew, that Cassie and Jake Chaffee had been lovers for more than a year now. It was by all appearances a pleasant and casual affair. There was, Dud knew, a Mrs. Jake Chaffee back in California, but Mrs. Jake Chaffee had never set foot on Sky High and as far as anybody could tell apparently had no plans ever to do so. Cassie's husband was dead. It's all so simple for them, Dud thought, not with malice but with regret because for Dudley Lanier Drummond III, things were not simple at all.

4

Well, thought Noel Northcliff, laughing so hard he almost spilled his champagne, you had to say this for Cornelia de Vos, bitch goddess of the jet set: she was a very funny lady. NN—as the world knew him from the famous initials that signed his widely syndicated column, *Living It Up*—leaned back in the wide first class jet seat and howled, "Darling, you don't mean it!" He sputtered. Across the aisle, a fat businessman looked up from a complicated feasibility study in wonderment that this lean, distinguished-looking man and his strikingly beautiful blonde companion should be giggling like schoolchildren.

"But darling, it happened." Cornelia de Vos giggled: "There he was, three in the morning, naked as the infant Jesus, peeing into the Grand Canal from the third-floor balcony of the Ca d'Oro. While from the ballroom, one could hear the distant strains of a Strauss quadrille. It is the *definition* of what's happened to poor Venice. And, Noel"—she fixed him with a meaningful glance from her wise gray eyes—"you simply would not believe the size of his . . ." Cornelia de Vos leaned very close to the famous society gossip columnist and whispered into his ear. And Noel Northcliff roared still again. Very little of what Cornelia had told him would ever appear in print. NN had long ago discovered that titillation sold more newspapers than muckraking. The reason for Northcliff's tremendous acceptance by the rich and the powerful was that they knew he was essentially a kind, if bitchy, man who never breathed a word of the real scandals.

For example, NN would tell at witty length about Dorothy Dutton's new passion for peanut butter, her various baroque ways of serving it, and her futile attempts to convert her fashionable friends to a steady beer-and-peanut-butter diet.

But NN would not tell about the less amusing side of Dorothy Dutton's personality. He knew, but wasn't telling, the story of the muscular, darkly handsome seventeen-year-old Moroccan longshoreman who had been picked up one day last year by La Dutton's famous white Bentley limousine, in which she cruised looking for additions to her sexual menu. The young Moroccan had been seen to get into her car on a Tuesday in June. And three weeks later he stepped out of the white Bentley in front of the American Express Company's Morocco office, where he opened an account with a certified check for fifty thousand dollars signed "Dorothy Dutton." NN knew all this because a friend of his was the manager of that branch of American Express and had naturally investigated the deposit of such an unusual amount of money by a hitherto penniless boy. At the time, NN had thought of La Dutton, who, well into her 60's, was more silicone than flesh, and of her Momo, who had probably enjoyed the boy as much as Dorothy—or more. *Not worth it, kid,* was NN's reflection, *not by a long shot*. But Northcliff was not casting himself as a moralist, but merely as a survivor. These people, whatever depths they might sink to in private, were, in their public character, Noel Northcliff's bread and butter. He treated them well, and they reciprocated. There were worse ways to make a living.

Noel smiled and looked across the console at Cornelia de Vos, who sat in the window seat eating an apple and taking an occasional sip of chilled white Burgundy. "I may have said it before, my dear, but you are looking especially ravishing." She was indeed. Cornelia had the kind of lean, high-cheek-boned beauty that always carries with it a breath of outdoors. She called to mind long sleek yachts and ski slopes and polished saddles. There was nothing of the candy-box, Gabor-type prettiness about Cornelia de Vos: hers was a more architectural kind of beauty which showed every sign of getting better looking with the years. If there were a Dutch Katharine Hepburn, thought NN, she might look like Cornelia de Vos. Cornelia sighed gently:

"Well, you are not invited to ravish me, darling. I'm coming out here for a bit of a rest. And the skiing, of course, which they assure me is heaven."

Noel looked at her with eyes that had seen everything and forgiven most of it. *She won't be there a day,* he thought, *before the best-looking young studs in the ski school will be braying at her door. And she'll open it.* Cornelia de Vos had a rather well-known sideline in young athletes. There was no harm done, NN knew. And, Noel was quite sure, de Vos gave as good as she got. He looked at her again. She might—just might-be turning forty. She looked thirty and her charm was timeless. Unlike many great beauties, Cornelia de Vos had a mind. She was an expert listener, which was a trait the kind of men who could afford her found irresistible. And this ability to listen served Cornelia de Vos admirably. She knew an astonishing amount about the ins and outs of world-class big business. She knew who was drilling for what in the murky seas off Indonesia. She knew who did what to whom in the boardrooms of legendary banks and corporations, and she also knew who did what to whom in significant bedrooms around the world. Men told her their secrets because they knew she could keep them. The only person who profited from what Cornelia de Vos knew was Cornelia de Vos, which was exactly what her men friends intended.

And in the ten or twelve years that Cornelia had been a certified member of the bigtime, she had done very, very well for herself. Considering the glittering impression she made, and where she went, and with whom, Cornelia's actual living expenses were very modest. Three famous designers of clothes gave her whatever she chose from their current collections and wrote the expense off as advertising, which it surely was, and of the best kind. Cornelia had none of the old-time courtesan's taste for jewelry. So she made do with one large cabochon emerald ring in a simple dull gold setting, which she wore everyplace. Cornelia had a small but beautiful chalet in Lausanne, the gift of a well-known Italian chemical tycoon, and this was her headquarters. Two international airlines gave her free first-class passage anywhere, because her comings and goings were so often pictured (the tail of the aircraft with its huge identifying logotype always prominent in the shots) and commented on in the press. Other than breakfasts, Cornelia de Vos couldn't remember when she'd last paid for a meal.

Cornelia had dabbled in films—and occasionally she did a little cabaret singing in her husky, beckoning voice which managed to be at the same time unmusical and unforgettable. Cornelia had written, in surprisingly controlled and witty English, a popular book on personal health and beauty maintenance. The fruits of these enterprises, plus frequent and generous gifts from admirers, had been invested through a discreet private bank in Liechtenstein. It wasn't bad, for a butcher's daughter from Delft.

Cornelia de Vos leaned back in the plush jet seat and closed her beautiful gray eyes. She wore the face of a woman without a care in the world. But she was almost dead broke.

"This simply can't be true." Cornelia had looked at her discreet little Liechtenstein banker in disbelief: "If you are joking, Carl, it is really not very funny."

"Madame de Vos, if only it were a joke." The plump, gray banker had always reminded Cornelia of a pigeon. He took off his gold-rimmed eyeglasses and polished them. "I can hardly believe it myself."

Cornelia stood silently, trying to sort out all the devastating new information in her mind. First, although her Italian coin-operated laundries were doing good volume, the Italian interest rate was spiraling out of sight, which meant that they would either have to inject large amounts of cash into the business or sell out a loss. That would not have ruined her, except that the same inflation was everywhere. No one had the money to buy fine works of art from the Tokyo antique import-export firm in which she was a partner. Even the Japanese were tightening their belts. Cornelia's flats in Bavaria were heavily mortgaged and suffering under the real-estate taxes that seemed to double every year. Her American bonds were depressed.

Cornelia looked the calm little banker in the eye. "What you're saying, essentially, is that I have no money. That in ten years I have gone from penniless to penniless. Congratulations, Herr von Messerstein."

"Madame, it is only temporary. You have your house in Switzerland . . ."

"And shall I sleep in the fields, then?"

"The Konigenstrasse flats, eventually . . ."

His matter-of-fact banker's words spoke the epitaph of everything Cornelia had hoped for. Inside her regal head, unseen by the smug little man, alarms went off and shock troops were rallied. Just when she'd begun to let herself imagine the struggling days were over, the trap was sprung and she was back almost to the beginning. Except that in the beginning she'd been fifteen years younger, reckless, ready for anything. Was she ready for this new challenge? She had better be. Carl looked up and was surprised to find his nearly bankrupt client smiling.

"Say it, Carl. What shall do? How do I save myself?"

"Get into oil."

"Oil? But hasn't the increase there already happened?"

"Madame, there is never enough oil. There never will be. The value of oil shares is unassailable, and the yields are going to be enormous."

"As you say, Carl. And what oil, exactly, shall I get into?" Cornelia remained cool, but she was in shock. This was enough to bring back all the demons that haunted her. These demons would appear whenever they were least expected and whisper in silken, threatening voices that no one else could hear: "One day, my dear, you will be old, and alone, and you had better not be poor when that happens." It was the demons who had made Cornelia invest every spare penny she could get her hands on. But the demons had neglected to warn her of the worldwide monetary crisis.

"Bidijar, Madame." The banker's voice was almost a whisper.

"Bidijar?"

"The Bidijar reserve, not quite so well known as the others, is thought to be the largest in all the world. And they are just beginnning to tap it. There are rumors of a public offering early next year. Perhaps we can find a way to participate in that offering, although the shares, I am told, will be strictly limited to the royal family. Still"—and at this juncture the banker looked shrewdly at his client—"still, there may be a way."

"We certainly must look into it." Cornelia smiled and shook his hand and walked out of the room like a queen. Inside, she was trembling. She took the next train to Lausanne and picked up a telephone. Very soon after that, Cornelia de Vos was on a jet, then another, bringing her closer and closer to Sky High. Because visiting Sky High for the gala opening parties would be a man one heartbeat away from full control of the Bidijar reserve, one of the richest men in the world and known for his fondness for blondes; Niris Reza Herat Bir-Saraband, younger brother of the Sheikh of Bidijar, whose throne sat, literally, on top of the Bidijar reserve.

The big jet had been gliding over the immense and, from thirty-two thousand feet, immensely boring red desert. Now there was a distinct lessening of altitude. Soon the NO SMOKING sign would flash on. Cornelia looked out the window.

"Look, darling, how flat it all is . . . and then, the mountains! Like a great stage flat, Noel."

"It's a a backdrop, lovey. Jake Chaffee had it done to impress us. He's said to be capable of anything."

"Do you know him?"

"Know his daddy, of course, The Senator. But I've only met Jake once. Good-looking boy. Very American, sort of an up-to-date Gary Cooper type. You'll probably like him."

"Who's to hate anyone that gives such nice invitations, just when there's not a drop of snow in the Alps?"

"Who indeed?" said Noel, as he fastened his seat belt for the landing.

The big turkey buzzard hung in the bright noon sky like the dark hand of an avenging god. High in the air, in the sun and the wind, this creature could sense carrion from an altitude of hundreds of feet that other animals might not detect at close quarters on the ground.

Far below Zeke paused, looked up, clicked the safety catch off the slender Purdy shotgun, and waited.

Zeke Gibbs generally took nature as he found it, but he'd always hated vultures. And the way he'd been feeling lately, his old dislike of the carrion birds built up in him and mixed in some strange way with his feeling about Jake Chaffee.

Zeke had grown to cherish his hatred. It had become the most important thing in his life, after Zem, and after what was left of Sky Ranch. Zeke watched the vulture and it got to looking more and more like Jake Chaffee. Jake, who had also flown uninvited into Sky Valley, Jake who sniffed out the moral carrion of Eugenia Gibbs's dead affection for the land and fed on it just like any vulture, any worm.

The bird circled lower, smiling death. Zeke raised the shotgun and tracked with the vulture for a few seconds and then, almost casually, pulled the trigger. The obscene head exploded, raining fragments of blood and flesh and beak onto its own motley feathers, which then fell twitching and fluttering onto the pure, expensive snow of Sky Mountain. Zeke turned and plodded back to the ranch.

Pepi Prager buckled on his skis and stood tall, stretching forward a little to check the tightness of his racing bindings. They were perfect. From where he stood, on the level space by the side of the big, terraced snack bar on top of Sky Mountain, Pepi could see the full sweep of the mountain ("the hill," he always liked to call it in his offhand way: "Let's take a run down the hill"). The bright December afternoon was doing its part to make all the promises of Dud Drummond's advertising campaign come true: SKI SKY HIGH said a series of full-color advertisements that, some of them, showed almost exactly the view that now lay in all its astonishing splendor at Pepi Prager's ski tips.

One of those advertisements showed Pepi himself; alone, dramatically sailing through an idyllic grove of snow-laden Colorado spruce, up to his knees in fresh, dry, talcum-weight powder snow, the stuff skiers' dreams are made of.

Pepi felt very good about Sky High. He'd been at the head of several prominent ski schools since he gave up racing twenty years before. The name Pepi Prager had appeared on a well-known brand of skis, on a special racing model that was still being sold, still making money. Pepi was not a rich man, but Sky High would undoubtedly make him rich. He had a small percentage of the profits, which showed every sign of being substantial. And he lived almost free. He had his own small but very handsome three-room chalet right in the Sky High complex, opening onto the ski slopes, so that all he had to do in the morning was buckle on his skis and glide a few hundred yards down to the base station of the Sky Lift tramway. He took his meals at the lodge, and he had unlimited credit at the bar, an important plus for public-relations purposes. Pepi drank very little himself, and then almost exclusively beer and wine, but the rich guests at Sky High would be flattered to have a drink with the legendary Pepi Prager anytime. Diplomacy was as important to Pepi's usefulness at Sky High as anything he actually taught on the slopes.

Pepi took a deep breath and smiled, surveying the dozen or more possible trails he could take down the mountain. He'd helped lay out those trails himself, walking up and down the mountain two summers before, poring over aerial photographs shot at various times of the day. Great care had been taken to lay out trails that would appeal to skiers of every degree of skill. The trails were well planned and carefully groomed. When trees were cut down, the stumps were pulled out completely and the holes filled in.

They'd had fun naming the trails, making a joke of it in the time-honored way of skiers. There was a trail named for just about everyone in the inner circle at Sky High, including little Charlie Lamont and his dog, Whizzer. Charlie's trail was called Charlie's Challenge, and it was the best beginner trail Pepi had ever seen, a wide, gentle trail that curved politely all the way down the mountain on the far western slope, more than two and a half miles of dead-easy, spectacularly beautiful skiing. Whizzer was just that: a very steep, nearly straight experts-only cut through the woods that existed purely as a test of nerve for the speed freaks. Whizzer was the kind of trail skiers would brag about around the fireplace after a few drinks.

The other trails had whimsical names meaningful only to a handful of people at Sky High: there was Pepi's Promise, a tricky, steep expert trail that was to be the course for the grand opening pro race in two weeks—thus the "promise," because Pepi had promised to make an exhibition run that day and try for a new record. Cassandra was named for Cassie Lamont. One trail was called Jake's Snakes because Jake had designed it himself with a curiously involved series of S-curve upon S-curve snaking down the mountain.

Cassie had named the huge, nearly perfect snow bowl China Bowl in the interest, she insisted, of international goodwill. It was hard to imagine the serious-minded denizens of the People's Republic springing for a holiday at Sky High, but that didn't stop Cassie.

All the trails were beautifully marked with large elegant signs designed by Paolo Storione. Behind each sign, and at other key locations all the way down the mountain, where weatherproof telephones to summon the ski patrol in case of emergency. It was, thought Pepi Prager, most satisfactory.

There were very few skiers on the mountain. The day was so perfect, Pepi decided on Jake's Snakes for no reason but to prolong his run. He pushed off and "skated" a little to work up some speed. Then he crouched in the racer's famous "egg" position, knees deeply bent and together, arms tucked in for maximum streamlining, and took the first four curves of the trail at racing speed.

Two girls having lunch on the terrace looked after Pepi in wonderment. He was quite a sight, skiing or standing still.

Just past fifty, Pepi looked about thirty. He was lean and very fit, with ice-blue eyes and hair the color of straw. There was something very regular and nearly expressionless about Pepi Prager's face in repose, a bland, youthful quality that gave him an air of boyish innocence. This plus his natural charm and Austrian good manners made a combination that many girls and women found irrestible.

Which was just fine with Pepi. In all the world, there were two things he cared about to the depths of his being: one was skiing and the other was sex. Sky High offered him large amounts of both. Few were the nights that Pepi spent alone in his little chalet. His girls never stayed long, but they left happy. The fact that most of his conquests came to a ski resort on vacation, stayed a week or two and neatly disappeared, suited Pepi right down the line. Because despite all the strength, skill and inventiveness he put into his lovemaking, the last thing Pepi Prager wanted was a serious relationship with anyone. He had reasons for this which were, to him, sufficient. No entanglements was his style, and he carried it forth with care and precision.

Pepi skied in a kind of rapture, abandoning himself to the hill, responding reflexively with all the nerves and muscles of his well-tuned body as he flew down the trail on skis that hissed and swooshed through the powder but hardly seemed to touch it. About halfway down the mountain, Pepi saw his youngest instructor, Jean-Pierre Belfort, giving a lesson to a middle-aged man Pepi hadn't noticed before. Swiftly assuming a cloak of diplomacy, Pepi skied down to the pair and asked how it was going.

"Pepi Prager, meet Mr. Tod Rubin," said young Belfort. Rubin awkwardly pulled off his ski mitten to shake hands.

"It is a pleasure, Mr. Prager. Your young man here is trying to make a skier of me, against very big odds. I have never skied before, you see." Rubin framed his words carefully, as if translating them first from some other language. Pepi smiled even more broadly, because the hairs on the back of his neck were tingling with a familiar, unwelcome sensation.

It was perfectly obvious. The man was a Jew. So Pepi smiled, all brothers together in the magic fellowship of the hill. "Well, you couldn't be in better hands." Pepi clapped Jean-Pierre on the shoulder. "This crazy kid is going to set the world on fire one day."

Jean-Pierre Belfort smiled modestly. He was a tall, broad-shouldered farm boy from Val d'Isère who'd made it young to the French Olympic downhill team but never to the coveted gold medal. Now he was teaching to support himself before having a crack at the newly formed (and lucrative) American pro-racing circuit. The big Sky High Challenge Cup race in two weeks would tell a lot about Jean-Pierre's chances for a racing career. He looked forward to it with hope—and, sometimes, with fear.

Pepi shook hands again, smiled and pushed off down the hill. There was no doubt about it. The man was a Jew.

Tod Rubin, meanwhile, stood absolutely still, watching the graceful blue figure darting down the mountainside. Then Tod spoke to Jean-Pierre: "He is quite a skier, isn't he, your Mr. Prager?"

"One of the best. He is, as we say, world class. Of course Pepi is not as young as he was, but he's still *extraordinaire.*"

"Yes," said Tod Rubin, slowly pulling on his mitten. "Yes. He is that."

Jean-Pierre waited politely. Tod Rubin was a bit of an odd customer, pleasant enough, surely, but not really the athletic type at all. Jean-Pierre would have vastly preferred a wildly beautiful eighteen-year-old girl or even her passionate, frustrated mother for pupils, both ripe for merry bedding later on. But, at twenty-five dollars an hour for a whole morning's booking, one could hardly complain. In time, Jean-Pierre thought, he might even make a serviceable skier out of Tod Rubin.

"If you'll just follow me, Mr. Rubin, and try to do what I do: like this!" Jean-Pierre pushed off, and Tod Rubin, clumsily but gamely, followed a few yards behind.

5

Jake Chaffee turned off the shower and reached for one of the big sky-blue towels. Like many things at Sky High, they were far from ordinary. The towels were huge, densely woven European-style bath sheets with SKY LODGE embroidered in heavy navy blue cord. The idea was to let them be stolen, to have the extravagant towels become permanent advertisements for the luxury at Sky High. The phone rang.

"Jake?" Pete Woodbury's voice was so clear it might have been coming from the next room.

"Speaking. What's up, Peter?"

"I've been thinking about the land."

"Cheerful thoughts, let's hope."

"Fairly cheerful, Jake. Look . At a very conservative ten thousand an acre we're sitting on more than thirty million bucks."

"What'd Vail go for when they opened shop?"

"I'll check. Right now land in the village is pegged at better than a hundred thousand an acre. And you can't get it."

"Knickerbocker can't be unaware of the fact that we've got clear title to just about thirty-five hundred acres."

"The thought processes at Knickerbocker Trust make a dinosaur look like a wizard, Jake. If during the next couple of weeks we can actually sign up a few customers at, say, fifteen or twenty thousand per acre, the cold platinum heart of the Knick might just soften up a little."

"Paolo Storione's already working up some sketches for houses. We'd have to retain design approval."

"Of course. So much the better. Makes it that much more exclusive."

"Well, Peter, it's nice to see you hopping on the bandwagon. For a minute there you had me worried."

"I'm still worried, Jake. There are just too many ifs in our little calculation. If the opening goes well, we could be home free. If not . . ."

"If not we change the name to Jake's Folly! Have a good flight. I'm sending a charter to fly you up to Steamboat. The lodge limo will meet you there. We'll talk when you get here."

"Thanks. And, Jake: fear not, OK?"

"See you tomorrow, Pete."

Suddenly Jake felt thirsty. He turned on the cold water tap and let it run colder and colder. At least one thing around Sky Lodge was free, he thought, filling a tall glass and relishing the taste of the clear, pure mountain spring water. Back East people were paying good money to get water like this in bottles.

Night came fast to Sky Valley. The shadow of the mountain poured across the valley floor in the late afternoon with the crisp finality of some great blackout curtain being drawn. Then for an hour the valley would be dark while the sky above held the fading remains of the day's sapphire blue. And this, to Jake, was the most beautiful of all the beautiful times of day. The mountain loomed dark violet-black against the lingering blue of the sky, and the empty ski trails were glowing phosphorescent lavender rivers banked by the black evergreens.

Jake looked at his big black-faced Omega wristwatch, which was so accurate it could divide one second into five equal parts. Time for a little diplomacy in the bar. Time to be charming. Time not to show the fear or the doubts or the apprehension. All right. So the ice was a little thin. That just meant you had to skate a little faster.

Sitting at the bar, Liz Drummond wasn't thinking at all. Which was the result of considerable effort. Not thinking about things had become Liz Drummond's main goal in life and she was getting good at it. Right now, for example, she was floating in a haze produced by a Valium chaser on top of three stiff glasses of bourbon. That took care of her mind. She had other ways of taking care of the body. For more than two hours Liz had been making several kinds of love with a tall, strong eighteen-year-old ski bum she'd picked up during a late lunch at the snack bar on top of Sky Mountain. The boy was good-looking but inarticulate which was just as well.

Liz in her mid-thirties was still a striking looking woman—as long as you didn't look too closely. Only people who had known her five years ago—before she married Dud Drummond—were shocked by the change in her. And Liz made a point of not seeing old friends these days. While they had been in bed, the boy reached for her and the sex began one more time. "Oh!" Liz had moaned softly, "oh, Bill." And without missing a beat, the boy whispered back, "My name is Ronnie."

Paolo Storione had designed the Sky Bar to be as unlike a typical resort hotel bar as possible. The focal point of the huge room was not the bar at all but a great cavelike fireplace built from native granite boulders excavated on the site. The fragrant spruce logs it held were so big that two of them would burn all night. Scattered around the room were low overstuffed sofas and chairs with even lower cocktail tables in front of them. The furniture was covered in subtle handwoven woolen fabrics in shades of beige and ivory and rust designed to complement the bold Navaho rugs that glowed in their primitive splendor from the polished wide-planked floor.

The bar itself was tucked into a corner and had only a dozen barstools. In his convivial Italian heart Storione found the spectacle of Americans drinking alone at their bars a sad thing, people strung out like so many crows on a telephone wire, washing away the pain of loneliness. Storione created the Sky Bar to discourage this, to invite cozy groups of people to cluster about the low tables in conversation, to simulate the atmosphere of a gracious home. The plan worked well.

Jake Chaffee paused for a moment at the entrance to the bar and he didn't have to make himself smile because he liked what he saw. This was what Sky High was all about. The big room soared twenty feet from the warm amber glow of the fire to disappear above in the impressive mystery of Storione's bold design. Yet the room was filled with warmth. The fire crackled reassuringly, while outside the vast picture window, purple Colorado twilight turned to black night.

Jake stood alone at the bar swirling the Sky Lodge house Zinfandel in a big balloon glass. Cassie, he knew, would be giving Charlie his meal. And although Charlie had started out by unknowingly being a major problem in Jake's affair with Cassie, the problem was getting smaller as the boy grew more confident of himself and more at ease with Jake. Jake knew the reason Charlie had made such remarkable progress this last year was simply because Cassie spent great loving chunks of her valuable time with the boy, explaining things to him and coaching him, giving him a sense of fun and discovery. Cassie, wisely, also encouraged Charlie to be an independent little boy. In this, the gentle fun-loving Whizzer was a big help. Whizzer became the playmate Charlie would otherwise have lacked, and they went everywhere together. The big red dog slept on the foot of Charlie's bed. When Charlie went skiing Whizzer went with him, romping down the steepest slopes in an irresistible doggy excess of enthusiasm. It was a happy arrangement, and Jake felt that in time Charlie would be able to accept him as a father. Which was exactly what Jake Chaffee wanted most.

Charlie brought on thoughts of Cassie. And thinking about Cassie led Jake to think about his own home life. Although these last few years you could hardly call the Hillsborough address Jake's home. And you could hardly call if a life.

Jake Chaffee and Betsy Bellington! How the newspapers had loved them when the engagement was announced. Pure storybook. He, the golden boy, rich and good-looking, The Senator's son. And she, Betsy, richer still and the only heiress to the huge Bellington sugar and pineapple fortune that had begun in Hawaii but filtered into San Francisco. Betsy, sweet, charming and just the slightest bit plump—baby fat she called it, shyly, when Jake took her in his strong brown arms.

All Betsy had wanted was Jake and Jake's children and flowers and sunshine and a life without any ripples in it at all.

For a few years it went that way. Jake and Betsy never fought, for raised voices and edgy tempers were not invited into Betsy Chaffee's magic kingdom. Their children flourished and seemed perfect, or at least like some picture-book dream of perfection: the girl Eliza and the boy Jonathan, named for The Senator.

If Jake had been less of a man it might have worked out. But Jake gradually developed a sense of being a spectator at some lavishly produced private theatrical performance, continuously playing in his own living room. Only Jon struck real sparks of love from Jake. Young Jon, even at ten, was a person, not about to be poured into any of his mother's large collection of fashionable molds. But with Jon's sudden death, the gilt-mounted fiction of Jake Chaffee's marriage died also.

The years since Jon Chaffee died had seen Jake become a demon worker, seething with plans and dreams and the energy to make them happen. He took part of his inheritance from his Chaffee grandmother and doubled it in building projects, then doubled that again. But it wasn't money that interested Jake Chaffee. It was the act of creation, of playing God in small ways, of making things happen.

Like all sophisticated developers, Jake worked largely with other people's money. And after his first successes people were more than happy to lend it to him. Jake Chaffee's name on a project was almost like FORT KNOX on a bar of gold. And as dream after dream became reality, Jake's dreams got bigger. Now he'd dreamed up an entire mountain. And for the first time ever a Chaffee project looked like it might not make it. *It's still going to work, dammit,* Jake told himself, *it's going to work because I'll make it work.*

Jake stood at the bar smiling, playing host. And counting the house. Maybe half the people in the room were press. "Investment spending" he'd told Pete Woodbury when Pete seemed apprehensive about the elaborate plans for the press introduction. Jake knew that the free drinks and fancy food and rooms and lift tickets ought to pay dividends in publicity for years to come. Reporters were the hardest-to-impress people in the world. They'd seen it all before. But nobody had ever seen anything like Sky High before. Jake looked around the room and felt good about the press party. They were enjoying themselves, these ladies and gentlemen of the press, basking in luxury that most of them, on their own, could scarcely afford.

Jake sipped his wine and wished for Cassie. It was a quarter to seven. Dinner was scheduled for eight. If she didn't show up in ten minutes he'd go looking for her.

Suddenly a hush fell on the Sky Bar. Heads turned as Cornelia de Vos walked into the room looking like a snow princess in slim white slacks and a white silk blouse and a long vest of white mink. Cornelia, tall and expensively suntanned and with her honey-colored hair simply pulled back under a satin ribbon—white—headed straight for Jake with a regal posture and a smile that could melt glaciers. "Mr. Jake Chaffee, I presume?" Jake introduced himself and accepted her thanks and bought her a drink—white wine.

"We're glad you could make it, Madame de Vos."

"Please! Cornelia."

"Jake."

"Jake!" she exclaimed: "I adore American names. Only in America could there be a Jake. It is like . . . something in a movie."

"Isn't it, though?" said a smooth voice at Jake's elbow. Noel Northcliff had joined them. The revels had begun.

—

6

Pete Woodbury flew coach. Sky High, after all, was footing the bill, and Sky High could use every dime. Still, it wasn't so bad. The 707 was only half full. Pete fastened his seat belt and leaned back, a compactly built six-footer with curly brown hair just a shade longer than the crew cut he secretly preferred. Pete looked younger than a man in his upper thirties. His complexion tended to be a little pink, and his large horn-rimmed glasses gave a collegiate air to the deep brown eyes.

Amazing, he thought, *how people are cutting back these days*. A year ago the plane would have been full. Pete, as always, took the window seat. He glanced across the aisle at a pretty redhead. She was intently working a complicated looking square of needlepoint. Pete had noticed her in the airport lounge. The lady was very noticeable, and it was a look he liked. She wasn't trying to be a kid, she wasn't too skinny, and the face, hair and body all looked very real. The dark mink looked real too, about ten thousand bucks' worth of real. Now there was a lady who obviously could afford first class, and she was riding coach too. A new mood was on the land. Pete hoped he could pull Sky High out of its tailspin before this tide of financial conservatism rose higher and engulfed the project. With a sigh he reached for his attaché case and pulled out the long, detailed projection of Sky High's future—if any. Somewhere in that labyrinth of figures, there might be a way out of the fiscal trap that seemed to be closing on them. Pete cast one last wistful glance at the redhead. *Restrain yourself, Woodbury, he thought. You're doing exactly what Franny's afraid you'll do.* Pete tried not to think about the unpleasant little scene at breakfast that morning. He tried and he failed.

"Well," Franny had said, her voice harsh from anger on top of two cigarettes before breakfast, "I still don't see why you have to go all the way out there yourself." She poured him more coffee. Franny was, Pete noticed, putting on weight.

"Honey, we've been through all this. I have to. Period. A fifty-million dollar deal that I helped put together is coming apart. I've got to look the situation over first hand."

"While I sit here with a candle in the window. I hate to miss the Clarks' party."

"Then go, for God's sake. There's no reason in the world why you can't."

"I'd feel funny. Anyway, they only asked us because of you."

"Then why do you care so goddamn much? He drinks too much and she's a little climber."

"But our Stacy and their Meredith. Pete, I've got to think of our position." Here it came. The litany.

"Fuck our position!"

"Pete! I only want what's best . . ."

"Tell me one thing that's best about the Clarks. Or even adequate. They use us and we use them, and for what? When was the last time we had someone over because we actually liked them?"

"Don't you like the Atkinsons?"

"That's just it. I love Tom and Ulla. And it's been damn near a year since we've seen 'em. And the last time they came here, that big dinner party, they practically had to stick pins in themselves to keep from falling asleep, they were that bored."

"So now I'm boring. Bravo!" Franny stood up from the table, flushing. "It's interesting, Pete," she said slowly, trying to get control of herself, "that you immediately assume it's *me* they were bored with. Do you think it's my idea of fun, sitting out here with nothing but kids and cleaning women to talk to? While you run off and play with the jet set? With all those pot-smoking ski bunnies with no minds and no morals? Have a good time, Peter. Have a very good time!"

Quickly, a little too quickly, Pete looked at his watch.

"I'm running late. Look, Fran: let's cool it, OK? Hell, it's just one more business trip. I'll be back in a week, ten days at the most. Then maybe we can park the kids and get away by ourselves for a few days." Franny stood rigid at the sink. He got up and kissed her on the cheek, and put on his coat.

"Sure, Pete. Have a good trip." The words hissed out like steam from a radiator. As he started up his Volvo in the attached two-car garage, Pete could hear the crash of his wife's coffee cup smashing where she'd hurled it into the sink. *That's my Franny,* he thought grimly, *tidy to the end. If she were going to stab me, she'd put on a hospital gown first.* Pete activated the electric garage door and backed out of the drive.

On the plane, across from Pete, Maggie della Robbia looked down at her needlepoint and smiled. Mom was going to love it. Probably the old lady's favorite possession was that old Belleek plate that hung in her sitting room. Maggie had found another plate just like it and had the pattern adapted onto needlepoint canvas for a pillow cover. The pattern was small bunches of bright green shamrocks scattered at random on a cream background and entwined, along the border, with a ribbon of sky blue. The pillow, just for the design work, had cost Maggie over two hundred dollars. *Every once in a while,* she thought, *Nick's money actually makes someone happy.*

Nick's money certainly hadn't made Maggie happy. Which was why she was on that jet. These days it hurt Maggie with an almost physical pain to think about her husband. But she thought about him a lot anyway. Day and night. It was only this last year that Maggie had been able to face the increasingly obvious fact that her marriage of over twenty years was a gold-plated ruin.

Maggie Flynn had married Nick della Robbia when she was seventeen and barely out of convent school, and he was only twenty.

"Let me not kid you, Father," Maggie had told her favorite priest, Father Kevin O'Donnelley, in a private consultation just last month, "I married Nick for sex. In those days we called it 'love.' But what I was in love with was his body. And now I suffer for it." Just like they said. The sins of the flesh.

Nick della Robbia at twenty had looked to Maggie's convent eyes like a pantheon of Roman gods all rolled into one. His body was lean and rippling with muscles and bulging with sex. Well, he should have been strong, working the way he did, hauling bricks to construction sites. Then, there were Nick's eyes. Maggie had never seen eyes like that outside a movie house. Huge, dark brown, liquid, most of the time half covered by those lazy eyelids. Lately Nick's eyes had taken on a reptilian aspect to Maggie. But at seventeen, they were pure Rudolph Valentino.

The Flynns, of course, were up in arms at their Maggie taking up with an "Eye-talian." But there was no stopping it. And at least he was a Catholic. They met and wed and bedded within two months. *And,* Maggie reminded herself with a wry little smile, *if I had to marry for sex, I sure picked the right boy.* For a year they made love so often and so enthusiastically it got to be almost comical. Then a parade of little della Robbias came along. First Kerry. Then Angela. And Nick, Junior. And finally, David.

"Before I knew it, Father, ten years went by. Just like that."

"You must have been very busy," he said, not hearing the irony.

"Extremely. I mean, four little kids and hardly any money. Not that I minded. You see, I was still in love. I had Nick. I had these beautiful kids. I was happy."

"You still have the children, Mrs. della Robbia." Ever since Nick put a new roof on the church, Maggie had been "Mrs. della Robbia."

"I'll have them no matter what. But they're gone, Father. They're teenagers and older. I'm not one to cling to them. You see how it is. The kids gone. Nick gone. And here I am with a big empty house and an empty life to go with it. I really think I want a . . ."

"Not a divorce?" From the tone of his voice, she might have been plotting a murder.

"I have to face it sometime, Father: our marriage is over. He just doesn't care anymore. And not just about me. He hires other people to run the business. He doesn't really see the kids. Not my bigshot. All he wants is the big Cadillac. The flashy silk suits. Vegas. Paradise Island. And all his oily pals with no visible means of support. Not to mention the floozies."

"That too?"

"He's been seen. Father, if I ask Nick for a divorce, he'll probably give me one and good riddance. I'm getting to be an embarrassment to him. Cramping his style, as it were. I guess what I came to you for is for you to tell me it's OK, that I won't go to hell and all that."

"Divorce is never OK, Mrs. della Robbia."

"I've been doing a lot of thinking, Father. And one thing I think is, hell isn't quite so scary when you're already there. I have paid my dues in hell, Father. Now I want out."

"Is there someone else? I mean, for you."

"Oh, no. Not at all. You flatter me."

"You are a very attractive woman."

"I'm a middle-aged housewife who's plenty tired of lying in a bed I never made. If that makes any sense."

"But you married for better or worse."

"And marriages are made in heaven—by the handicapped!"

"Bitterness won't make it any better."

"Well I know it. Father Kevin, listen. I am as good a woman as best I can be. Corny as it may seem, I really do try. To do good. I raised my kids to be as good as I knew how to make them. In spite of their father. I don't screw around like certain other so-called ladies I could mention. But here I am middle-aged and what's ahead for me? I mean, you can only spend so much time at the beauty parlor. I'm going to waste, Father, and frankly it scares me. A lot."

"There are so many ways you can be useful . . ."

"Good deeds? Father, that's bullshit. Forgive me. But I have rolled my last bandage and emptied my last bedpan. Martyrdom just isn't my idea of fun, Father. I feel the minutes of my life ticking away like some kind of time bomb in a bad movie. You asked me if there was anyone else. Sometimes I wish there was. Anyone. The other day I found myself looking kind of hungrily at the kid who mows our lawn. He's sixteen. I went upstairs and locked myself in my room and cried for an hour. Does that shock you? Am I going crazy? Sometimes I think so."

"Mrs. della Robbia, can I suggest one thing?"

"Sure, Father. I hoped you would."

"Take yourself away for awhile. Someplace you've never been. Go for a week, maybe two. Sometimes a change of scene can really help a person sort things out. When you get back, we'll talk again."

"It's a deal."

"Enjoy yourself. You deserve it." He smiled a smile full of unspecified promises.

"Thank you, Father Kevin. I'll try."

"Do you believe in miracles?"

"Once I did."

"They happen, Mrs. della Robbia. They can sometimes be made to happen."

"I hope so." She stood up and shook his pale hand and went home. And that afternoon a thick sky-blue envelope came in the mail containing an invitation to Mr. and Mrs. Nicholas della Robbia to attend the opening festivities at Sky High. Della Robbia Brothers was doing very well: they were always getting fancy invitations these days. It seemed like an omen, and Maggie was ready to believe in omens. She'd loved skiing ever since she'd learned with the kids. Nick, of course, could never be dragged to a ski resort. Maggie picked up the richly engraved invitation. Even the name seemed right, "Sky High," she said out loud in the expensive silence of the della Robbia entrance hall, "you are just what the doctor ordered!"

Maggie put down her needlepoint while the jet raced to take off. This was the moment she always dreaded. Somewhere she'd read that the first few minutes after takeoff were the most dangerous time in a jet. Usually when Maggie flew it was with Nick or the kids. Being alone didn't help the fear any. Her body tensed. Fists clenched, Maggie braced for the moment of takeoff like a kid waiting for the dentist to start drilling. As usual, she missed it. Only when she felt the jet climbing steeply into a turn did Maggie realize they were airborne. The jet veered left and Maggie looked across the aisle where Pete Woodbury sat alone, poring over his financial report and quite oblivious to the motion of the plane. *Just look at him,* she thought, *that is what a husband should be.* To Maggie, he looked like a husband. A well-cared-for husband. A kind of sexy well-cared-for husband. *Probably plays squash to keep in shape.* Maggie contrasted Pete's trim body with the two-hundred-twenty-pound lump that years of ever-richer living had made of Nick. Involuntarily Maggie shuddered, thinking of the last time Nick tried to have sex with her—whenever that was—and how she'd grimly put up with it, with the fat torso sweating over her, with Nick della Robbia grunting with effort, not passion, half drunk and unaware that Maggie accommodated him simply because she was too bone-weary to resist. As he grunted to a quick climax, Maggie simply lay there. *His women earn every nickel they get out of him,* she thought.

Across the aisle Pete Woodbury sensed her eyes on him. He looked up and smiled. Maggie started to smile back, blushed, and quickly turned away. Damn! She'd dropped a stitch. That meant she'd have to pull out a whole row. *God,* Maggie told herself, *is punishing me for impure thoughts.*

Now it was Pete's turn to stare. She looked like a woman who took pride in the way she got herself together. An individual. Pete thought of Franny who went through life masked in the safety of styles that had been fashionable somewhere else, six months before. Franny Woodbury looked and dressed exactly like most of the other women in their set. They were like an army, these Valkyries of the upper middle class in matching armor by Gucci and Vuitton, talking about their lost individuality. The best design a dress or a scarf or a shoe could have, Pete thought, was some French faggot's name big enough to read across a room. This told the world you were classy, just in case the world needed to be reminded.

"Our Stacy and their Meredith." Even the names of their kids floated uncertainly like plastic ducks on some pool of fashion. Right now it seemed to be Fake English-Distinguished for the girls (Kims, Hathaways, Stacys and Tracys) and Fake Biblical simplicity for the boys (Adams, Jasons, Jareds, Davids). Their position? Positions were for sex manuals. What, Pete wondered, would Franny do if she were suddenly penniless in a trailer in Kansas? What good would her damned position do her then? Pete realized he'd been staring at the redhead for five minutes without really seeing her. She was furiously tearing out a row of needlepoint. Well. It was going to be a long flight. He went back to his report. Sky High was in big trouble. Pete wondered if the redhead could be induced to buy a couple of acres at the world's most glamorous new ski resort.

Across the aisle, Maggie della Robbia retreated into needlepointing the row she'd messed up. In went the needle, drawing the oyster-colored wool thread precisely through the canvas. She loved to needlepoint. Something about the precision of it appealed to her. All you had to do was get to the end of the row. Then the next row. Everything was organized and if you did it right, it came out right. Unlike life. In a way the rows of her needlepoint were like the days of her life. But for years now, as she lived her careful days, the rage had grown within her. There had to be more to life than this. Maybe, just maybe, she'd find it at Sky High. Whatever it was.

Tod Rubin looked at himself in the mirror. He was in his mid-thirties but could have been any age. Medium height, compact build, dark hair worn slightly long, pilot-style eyeglasses, expensive sports clothes: *Still and all,* he thought, *it doesn't quite add up. You are really not cut out to be a sporting type.* Then he smiled at his reflection and took another sip of the excellent room-service coffee. Tod Rubin was not in any sense an extravagant man, but somehow the unreality of being able to order a croissant high in these remote Rocky Mountains delighted him. And such croissants! He broke a fresh one in half, buttered it, and spread it with orange marmalade from a small blue earthenware crock. Thank heavens for the skiing lessons, or he'd be getting fat as a house. Rubin looked at his watch. Fifteen minutes until his appointment with Jean-Pierre Belfort. As always, Tod Rubin would be on time.

Tod liked the young French ski instructor. Jean-Pierre seemed to Tod all instinct and action, not a thought in his handsome head. *And just as well, too,* reflected Rubin; *he will be infinitely more useful that way.* Tod buckled on his brand new ski boots, stood up and pulled on the inconspicuous black nylon parka. Then he turned and looked out the big window onto Sky Mountain. Lovely! And worlds away from the drab little offices above the cigar store in Neutor Gasse off the Schottenring in Vienna. Some aspects of Tod's work were not altogether unpleasant.

He picked up the handsome Sky High brochure that lay on his dresser and opened it to the page that featured the ski school. There was, of course, a big photo of Pepi Prager, tanned and smiling, his head framed against a sky of deep Rocky Mountain blue. Yesterday Tod Rubin had canceled his ski lesson and gone into Sky Junction, carrying a neatly wrapped little package. There, by airmail special delivery, he had posted the package to himself at the Neutor Gasse address. There were reasons for not leaving this simple chore to the hotel staff. For inside the little package were three copies of the Sky High brochure and a carefully cushioned beer glass that Tod Rubin had discreetly removed from the Weinstube. The beer glass had Prager's fingerprints on it. *We will soon see,* thought Tod Rubin as he smiled and paid the clerk at the post office, *whether Mr. So-called Pepi Prager is going to be Neutor-alized.* That was their little joke at the office, that they "Neutor-alized" people.

Neutor Gasse 23B, a dingy suite of offices, was the world headquarters of STYX. And STYX, named for the river of Greek mythology where the living cross over into the world of the dead, was the last remaining fully functional organization devoted to hunting down Nazi war criminals.

Tod Rubin had not sought out his present career.

STYX found him. Tod had been drifting his way through law school at the University of Vienna in the 1960s. He lived alone in what had been an aunt's apartment on the top floor of an old mansion in the Währingerstrasse. It could have been an attractive place, if Tod had cared to fix it up. Somehow, he never got around to it. Also living alone in the old house was a lively little bird of a man, Herr Professor Doktor Knabel. Herr Professor Doktor Knabel and Tod fell into the habit of occasionally taking a meal together in a café, and sometimes afterwards they would go back and play chess. On one such evening, the professor looked up from a move he was contemplating, and said: "Rubinsky, I feel we know each other well enough now, that you will forgive me if I say something of a personal nature."

"But, of course, Herr Professor."

"Tod, I am worried." It was the first time the professor had called Tod by his first name. "For it seems to me that there is no purpose in your life. Tell me: have you any plans, plans for after the University?"

"I'm afraid not, Herr Professor. I hadn't really given it much thought. Perhaps teaching . . ."

"If you were going to teach, you would know it by now—in your heart, almost like a religious calling."

"I could go into business, I suppose, but . . ."

"How do you feel about the Nazis?" The question came quickly, cutting into Tod's aimless ramblings.

"By every right, I should hate them, I should want to kill and destroy them even as they killed and destroyed us. But, Herr Professor, if we have learned anything from the Nazis I think it is this: that hate is expensive. Hate is greedy, Professor. It feeds upon all the emotions, consumes them, until all that is left is hate and more hate: there's no end to it."

"Bravo!" The professor stood up. "That calls for a glass of wine. You do not disappoint me, Tod. But tell me. How do you feel about justice? Just suppose you should be offered a job—no, not a job, a career—that would allow you to use your mind to its fullest, and your law education too, and would help bring certain proved Nazi war criminals to justice? Would you take it?"

Tod looked around the immaculate, old-fashioned parlor. Was the old man crazy? Sometimes people who had been through too much to bear went right out of their minds. But something told him the professor was quite sane, and more than sane: very clever. He, Tod, who had never dared to dream of the future, was suddenly being offered a future ready-made. A future with purpose in it. A way, perhaps, to atone for a shapeless guilt that had haunted him since the end of the war, the feeling of having gotten away with something—his life—for no good reason. In that instant Tod Rubin made his most important decision yet.

"Are you in this, Professor?"

"Tod, I *am* it. Do you know of STYX?"

"Of course. The river."

"I mean STYX, the organization. We are as the Americans like to say, very low-profile. STYX is a sort of international intelligence agency. We deal in one subject only. In depth."

"Nazis?"

"Exactly. Only very rarely is our work publicized. What we do, Rubinsky, is the groundwork, the digging, the archaeology of the suspect's past. And, of course, we work very quietly. When we have the irrefutable evidence, only then do we turn it over to the appropriate government."

"Professor Knabel, how is this STYX financed?"

"Inadequately!" The professor sipped his wine appreciatively. "Prosit!" They clinked glasses. "You might say we exist out of other people's petty cash. If we deliver a suspect to a nation with which we do not have a standing arrangement, then we simply work out a special price. Our investigations tend to be very costly, and to take a very long time. Take Eichmann, for example."

"You've got Eichmann?" Tod was astonished. The infamous Nazi had eluded all efforts to track him down for twenty-odd years.

"We will have him, probably within a year. And then you'll see some publicity, my boy."

"And you are responsible for tracking him down?"

"There are many and many of us, Tod." The little

professor's voice got softer, unconsciously, as if someone might be listening. "Eichmann has taken six years of the most arduous research on three continents. And we don't have the bag tied up yet."

"But, where is he?"

"Let's just say, he's not in this room. Or in Europe."

"Then you don't trust me?"

"I trust you entirely, Tod Rubinsky. But that is information I give to no one. No one." The professor moved his bishop. "Checkmate."

That had been twelve years ago. Tod Rubinsky started as a researcher in the dingy offices at Neutor Gasse 23B poking his way through box after dusty box of brittle old files, writing reports, learning his history. It wasn't a pretty history, but Tod learned it well. Soon he knew the SS and the Gestapo and the slave-labor camps and the death camps like old friends. He traced careers of certain people thought to be still alive, tracking them from horror to horror to oblivion in 1945, when all records abruptly ended.

The work suited Tod. He was methodical, quiet and very shrewd. Herr Professor Doktor Knabel promoted his protégé from straight research to intelligence analyst. He began evaluating the dozens of "raw" intelligence reports that came to Neutor Gasse every week. More than twenty years after the holocaust, people were still seeing Martin Bormann behind every tree. The file of Bormann sightings occupied one whole wall of a room. Knabel's opinion was that Bormann could hardly have survived that last day in the Hitler bunker, yet still, they kept the file open. You never knew. Tod graduated from analysis to field work, the actual tracking down of suspects. And here he really came into his own. Tod's scholarly approach, quiet ways and inconspicuous appearance rendered him virtually invisible. He scored conviction after conviction, feeling no special joy beyond the satisfaction of a job well done. It was this curious lack of passionate feeling for his grim assignments that made Tod Rubin (as he called himself in America) so effective. He never got carried away. The professor, who kept up a lively interest in many things—chess, the soccer matches, opera—often worried about the emptiness of Tod's existence. Tod had few men friends, and women only now and then. After a time, the professor stopped worrying about Tod and accepted him for what he was: quiet, steady, colorless, and very good at his job.

Tod exchanged his regular glasses for sunglasses and walked out of his room. He got his skis out of the rack next to the outside door, stepped into them, clicked the bindings shut, pulled on his ski-pole straps and skied down the gentle slope to the base of the tramway, where the ski instructors met with their pupils every morning. Jean-Pierre wasn't there yet. *I wonder whose bed he'll come hopping out of,* thought Tod good-naturedly. Then Prager appeared, all suntan and charm, carrying his own skis and the skis of a slightly plump middle-aged lady pupil. Pepi passed close to Tod Rubin and favored him with a smile. Pepi's wide-set blue eyes caught the morning sun. Yes! The little fleck of brown was unquestionably there, at the outside of the iris of Pepi's left eye. Just where the old lady in Brussels had said it would be. All of Rubin's well-honed instincts told him Pepi was his man. Yet, and yet . . . these were not accusations to be cast about lightly. Tod looked at his quarry with the interest of a naturalist about to pin down a new butterfly in his collection. *And are you really Carl-Heinz Waldemar, the Wolf of Westerlo?* He was surer and surer the answer would be "Yes!"

Tod looked at his watch. If Jean-Pierre wasn't here in five minutes, he'd ask for another instructor. After all, STYX's money was financing this adventure. Tod thought back to the old woman in Brussels, and how they'd debated whether it was worth the expense to send him there from Vienna.

"She bases it all on a photograph?" Professor Knabel was skeptical. There had been many false leads.

"Yes, but a good one, a four-color portrait in a magazine. She says his face is changed. Also the hair color: Waldemar had brown hair, this man is blond."

"That's easy enough."

"Even the teeth are different, more even. And the nose has been reshaped."

"Well, then, Tod, how in the world does she identify him. After twenty-eight years?"

"The one thing you can't alter. His left eye—blue—has a fleck of brown in it. That shows in the photograph."

"And you think there's something to it?"

"I can't say why, professor. It feels right in my bones." The professor had learned, over the years, to respect the feelings Tod Rubinsky got in his bones. "And it makes sense," Tod continued; "we know he is—was—very vain. We also know he was a promising skier in high school. Born and brought up in the Austrian Tyrol, after all."

"The Wolf of Westerlo, is it?" The professor put his fingertips together as if constructing an imaginary little church. And suddenly, the slender old hands became fists. "Go talk to her, Rubinsky, if you feel like it."

La Mère Olivier must have been eighty. She was a fat little creature, stooped, with finely wrinkled, almost translucent skin. Dressed all in black, with a black woolen shawl over her white hair, dark eyes twinkling with interest, she looked like a creation in porcelain as her gangling great-grandson helped her into the magistrate's office in the central police headquarters in Brussels. It was a large, dark-paneled room furnished in heavy oak and red plush chairs. There were just the four of them: Tod, the old lady, her great-grandson and the magistrate, a thin, nervous-looking individual who obviously considered it all a waste of time.

"Please, Madame, tell your story," said Tod in unaccented French. The old lady arranged herself in one of the chairs. Her short legs dangled, not reaching the floor.

"Never," began La Mère Olivier, "did I expect to see that face again in this life. In fact, many are the times I prayed I would not. He is a very, very bad man, Your Honor." Her voice was thin but steady. She was obviously in full possession of her mind. The old lady continued, addressing all her remarks to the magistrate. "Perhaps you know what we call him?"

"The Wolf of Westerlo?"

The magistrate's tone of voice indicated he'd rather

be almost anyplace else but in this room. Tod was used to that. So few cared anymore. But la Mère Olivier cared. She went on. "He earned it. Even before the horror of the schoolhouse. It may be given to all soldiers to do bad things, so be it, war is war. But this one enjoyed it. I know, you see, too well . . ."

"How do you know, Madame?" Tod interrupted her as gently as he could.

"I was the cook." Her round little head pivoted to inspect Tod. "In his house. May God forgive me, it was a way to exist. I often stole food, passed it on to others. Ah! Had he thought, this man, he would have killed me. Of course, the day they left, the day of the schoolhouse . . . no one thought. The Amis were routing the Huns, they were nearly within sight, their artillery was falling all around, and even as the fire rained down on us, we thanked God—silently, of course—for we knew, and the Huns knew, it was over. They'd lost. But what no one knew was that the worst was not over. This man, this wolf, Waldemar, had all the schoolchildren of the village locked in the schoolhouse. Hostages, you see? Well, on that day . . ."

"Yes?" The magistrate was getting restless.

"On that day, Your Honor," she continued with dignity, "there was great activity in the manor house. Trucks. Many Huns. Packing. And, of course, looting. They came and took everything out of my larder. The silver, what there was left of it. Paintings. Just before noon, I became very frightened, for I thought he would kill me. In the midst of the uproar, I made my way out to the hen house. Even the hens knew something was up—they weren't laying that day. Well, Your Honor, I simply kept on walking. Up the hill and into the woods. And there, in a secluded place I knew, I hid and watched. Soon, the trucks began to pull away. Then Waldemar, in his big olive-colored Mercedes, with the swastika flags on it. He drove down the hill and into the town and stopped the car at the schoolhouse. It was the old schoolhouse, you know, all made of wood. From the trunk of the car, the driver—not Waldemar—took a can, a metal can the same color as the car. He opened the door of the schoolhouse and poured something all over the place."

"And Waldemar?" Tod prompted her gently.

"He stood there smoking a cigarette. The driver reported back to him. Then . . . oh God!" She sobbed and covered her eyes with trembling hands. Then she composed herself. "Then Waldemar walked slowly to the open front door of the schoolhouse and very deliberately flicked his lighted cigarette through the door. There was a huge burst of flame. Flames everywhere. And the screaming! I hear that screaming in my dreams, Your Honor, to this day. You see, he had barred all the windows. So his hostages couldn't escape. He—Waldemar—stood for a few minutes, watching his handiwork. Then he signaled his driver to drive on. They all drove out of town, to the East. And I never saw him again until this picture in the American magazine." The magistrate held the magazine for Tod's inspection. It was a good photograph, accurately reproduced. So often, STYX had to work with blurred, black-and-white material. The caption read: PEPI PRAGER TO GO SKY HIGH.

"But Madame," asked the magistrate, "what, exactly, makes you so sure this is the man? You have said his face is different."

"I know that face too well, Your Honor. This one"—and she pointed to the magazine—"has made his hair much lighter. The nose had more of a curve to it in the old days. But one feature does not alter. His eyes. His cold, evil eyes. He had, you know, the mark of the Devil."

"Madame Olivier, really!" This was getting too much for the nervous Belgian magistrate. He shot his immaculate cuffs with the air of a man fighting the forces of ignorance. But Tod listened attentively.

"He did, as I sit here, Sir. In one eye, the left, is a pointed fleck of dark brown. On the left side, the outer side. That—my grandmother once said—is surely the mark of the Devil. And what, I ask you, could be better proof than for such a mark to appear on such a man?" With that the little old lady rested her case. Tod thanked her and the magistrate thanked her. Tod was sure the woman was right. When you hate and fear a man, and see him at such close quarters as a cook does, you don't forget his eyes.

Back at STYX, Tod did his homework. Pepi's background was cloudy, often a sign, Tod knew that someone had set about obscuring it. The first public record of Pepi was when he made the Austrian Olympic ski team. Coming, it seemed, out of nowhere, Prager took two gold medals, in the downhill and the giant slalom. Came to America, to teach skiing at Stowe. And ever since, with ever-increasing publicity, Pepi Prager had gone from success to success. From his pictures, Pepi looked to be about the right age, a well-conditioned early 50s. That fit, too. Waldemar would be that now, if he was alive. The beer glass should tell the tale. They had a set of Waldemar's prints back at STYX headquarters. Of course, even fingerprints can be altered. But the alteration shows.

"Bonjour, Mr. Rubin! I am late!" Jean-Pierre broke into Tod's reverie with a cheerful grin.

"Bonjour!" said Tod and headed for the bright new tramway, thinking at the same time of sunshine and death.

7

Cassie Lamont washed her face, splashed it with cold water and rubbed it down with the thick Sky High towel. That felt better. It had been a long day. She slipped on a bathrobe and went in to check on Charlie. Cassie's suite had two bedrooms, a small sitting room and a bathroom all tucked behind the reception area of Sky Lodge. Dimming the light in the hallway, Cassie opened the door. A shalf of moonlight cut the room nearly in half. The two sleepers were still and contented looking. Whizzer was curled up, a mound of furry red warmth on the foot of Charlie's bed, framed in the spotlight of the moon. Cassie gently, unnecessarily, adjusted the edge of Charlie's blanket. The boy slept on his side, curled up with one small hand reaching out like a swimmer in midstroke. Burke Lamont had looked just like that, sleeping: young as dawn and with everything ahead of him. Cassie turned suddenly and walked out, closing the door soundlessly.

She thought of Burke less these days, but every time she did it hurt.

The hotel maid had turned down Cassie's own bed and placed a blue paper cup containing three squares of milk chocolate on the night table. Each chocolate was stamped SKY HIGH in the bold typeface Paolo Storione had chosen for all graphics associated with the resort. As she did every night, Cassie collected the chocolate squares and put them in a tin at the top of her closet to be thriftily doled out to Charlie for treats. All the saving habits of her feast-or-famine marriage to Burke Lamont were still with her. Waste of any kind horrified Cassie.

She put the tin of chocolates back on the shelf and grinned at herself. With Raoul Peng feeding Charlie God-knew-what French delicacies at all hours there wasn't much point hoarding candies. Still and all, she wasn't going to throw them away. Cassie hung her robe in the closet and wondered if Jake would come by. He usually did and the private Jake was, in some way she didn't quite understand, different from the public Jake. Nicer. But the slickness was always there, never far from the surface, the charm Jake seemed able to switch on and off like a light to get whatever he wanted. What he wanted right now, Cassie knew, was Cassie. And every time he said so it tore her up inside. She wasn't sure she really knew Jake, the real Jake, the man behind the brilliant smiles, and the million-dollar trappings. Cassie turned toward her bed, frowned, looking for the book she'd been reading. Then she saw the box.

It was a square of dark blue leather, not wrapped. Stamped in gold were the words TIFFANY & CO. Cassie opened the box and gasped. Not entirely with pleasure. It was a ring. Dazzling. A wide band of Florentine gold was crisscrossed with bands of small diamonds that made a chain of X's all around the ring. Inside, in simple block letters, were her initials and his, and a message: I LOVE YOU. Holding the ring but not quite believing it, she sat down on the edge of the bed. So here it was. Jake forcing the issue. And so typically Jake Chaffee. The ring was perfect, just right for her, no fat vulgar solitaire screaming "engagement ring!" It could be worn on either hand, on any finger. But still it was more than a ring. It was a pledge. Cassie knew that if she accepted it, Jake would take that as an answer. And if she didn't accept it she might lose him altogether. She read the inscription aloud: "I love you."

"I do, too." His voice was soft. She hadn't heard him come in.

"It's lovely, Jake. You couldn't have chosen better. I can't accept it." Something trembled inside Cassie as she said it. There should have been a way to soften the blow. But she could only say what she felt.

"Hell, honey, it's got your name on it. I'm only the messenger." He laughed, trying to carry it off as a joke.

Jake looked at this puzzling woman and wanted her more than ever. With all the girls in the world who'd jump at the chance, trust him to pick one with scruples. The need for her cut into him, more than sex, sharper than pain. Jake knew she was hurting too, and he didn't have a cure for it. She met his eyes with an unwavering stare. There was a plea in it.

"I'd feel funny wearing it, Jake. It'd make me feel kept."

"I want to marry you."

"I'm a bad bargain, Jake. I don't come with any guarantees. For fairy tales to work, you've got to believe in them."

"I love you. That's not a fairy tale." She stood up, still holding the glittering ring. Why was life always painting her into a corner? She turned to the window, a black square in the paneled wall. There was no escaping. She could feel Jake's eyes, she could sense his longing.

"You're always so very sure of everything."

"One of us has to be."

"I just can't yet, Jake. I'm still so shaky. There's Charlie, and Burke. I've been trying to put the pieces back together, one by one."

He came to her and put his arms around her. "I used to be pretty good at putting things together."

"You're good at everything, damn you."

"What's that supposed to mean?"

"Only that you're so damn good-looking and successful, and so much a Chaffee that sometimes it scares me. I may not be able to handle all that perfection." She put the ring back into its box. Then she turned to him, pleading.

"Jake, please help me. You wouldn't want me to fake emotions I don't feel."

"No, I wouldn't want that." His voice was quieter now, across the room, his back to her, looking out into the blue-black night.

"I need more time, Jake."

"Cassie." He turned around and walked slowly to the bed, never taking his eyes off her. "I want you any way I can get you. I want you more than I ever wanted anything. And I'm sorry if you don't want to marry me." He picked up the box and closed it. This made a small snapping noise but it sounded to Cassie Lamont as though a huge prison door had shut on her forever. Jake stood in front of her and put his hands on her shoulders and managed a lopsided little grin. "You don't mind if I keep on trying?"

"Oh, Jake. Of course not." Suddenly he was gone. Cassie threw herself down on the bed and buried her face in the pillow, sobbing uncontrollably, muffling the sobs, hating herself for hurting Jake, for not being able to handle him better, for being so mixed up about so many things. Why, after all, wasn't she sure? Did she imagine, at age thirty and with an eight-year-old kid to support, that she was such a bargain? Who was going to come along better than Jake? Hell, there were plenty of women who'd marry him for the money alone, or the name. Or the sex. She looked up from the pillow and saw her left hand. Burke Lamont's simple gold wedding band was still on her third finger. They'd bought it for twenty-five dollars in Denver one crazy October afternoon, the day they decided on the spur of the moment to get married. Burke Lamont had been magical then. Nothing could stop him, not on a racing trail, not in bed, not anywhere. Then suddenly Charlie was there and that had magic too. Now her world revolved around the boy, and along came Jake Chaffee with every intention of shaking up her world all over again. Famous, powerful, handsome Jake, the mover of mountains—but Cassie still wasn't sure. She couldn't help wondering what would happen if one day the whole world stopped dancing to Jake's tune. How strong would he be if his luck ever ran out?

Cassie dragged herself up off the bed and turned out the lights. For a moment she stood in the darkened room looking out at the cold white world and the deep purple sky above it. All Cassie had to do was say one word and this could be hers. And Charlie's. And still she couldn't. She sighed and climbed into her lonely bed.

The door slammed behind Jake as he walked blindly out into the night, his sheepskin coat flapping around him, long strides taking him up behind the kitchen to the big garage where the Sky High vehicles were kept. He pressed a button and the huge door opened. His red Jaguar convertible was there, waiting, sleek and powerful and immaculate. He slid behind the wheel and turned the key. Twelve purring cylinders awoke and the garage filled with a low, throaty rumble. He sat in the Jaguar clenching the wheel for three full minutes before easing out of the garage and down the driveway.

Then he let it out. There were no other cars on the road. Jake sliced through the purple night at sixty, then seventy, then eighty, never using the brakes but downshifting like a race driver. The night air rushed over the windshield like a river of ice, so sharp and chilling it would have been painful if Jake's nerves had been in any shape to feel such things. Just before Sky Junction came the turn branching off the town road onto route 317. Jake took the curve at seventy-five and then he was on the highway, or what passed for a highway in these parts, headed north, towards Steamboat Springs. The wind roared in Jake's ears as the white needle of the speedometer crept up and up: past eighty, ninety, the hundred mark. The road dipped and curved and the Jaguar clung to it, the note of the engine lifting from a purr to a growl. One hundred and ten, said the needle. One fifteen. One twenty. A big trailer truck came lumbering at him out of the night. He dipped his headlights and flashed past. Then the road was empty again, as empty as Jake felt inside. What was he doing wrong? He knew with a hollow sureness in his gut that there was no answer, no trick, no technique. You can make many things but you can't make someone love you. Jake eased his foot off the accelerator. The white needle moved back down the dial. Finally, Jake shifted down and made a U-turn on 317, and headed back. The Tiffany box made a lump in his pants pocket. He hadn't noticed that before. It was cold, very cold. But Jake didn't want to think about the cold, or anything else right now except Cassie. And thinking about Cassie hurt too much. As the low red convertible nosed into the exit from 317, Jake Chaffee made himself a promise. The promise was that Cassie would be wearing that ring and his name with it, before another year was out. Tomorrow he'd talk to his San Francisco lawyers about the divorce. Maybe Cassie would feel differently when he actually had the divorce. Suddenly he smiled. There had to be a way. After all, there always had been.

Outside Cassie Lamont's window, Sky Mountain thrust its white-capped bulk into the night sky, keeping its silent watch over Sky Valley as it had done for a hundred thousand years. The moon lit up the mountain with a glow so bright it seemed phosphorescent. Nothing moved on Sky Mountain. Even the wind had gone to sleep. Only a few lights marked the town. The Gibbs ranch showed one light, on a corner of a barn. At the edge of Sky Junction an engine coughed to life and a pair of headlights blinked on. Zem Gibbs was taking herself from Bill Shepherd's warm bed to her own empty one.

Cassie stirred in her sleep, one thin arm flung out as if to ward off demons. The moonlight caught the band of gold on her finger and made it glitter. But there was no one to see.

Momo looked at his wife with a mixture of interest and disdain. She sprawled on the big bed, hair askew, one strap of the Dior gown in shreds, her face contorted into a mask of rage and frustration. The small-craft warnings were definitely out. *"Cochon!"* Dorothy Dutton's hoarse scream was punctuated by the crash of a big glass smashing against the steel wall of her double-stateroom aboard the oceanliner, the *Queen Elizabeth II*. The glass missed its smiling target.

"My flower!" exclaimed the target, Count Massimiliano Ruvo di Putignano-Squillace, lounging gracefully against the false mantelpiece of the suite sipping Dom Perignon champagne. "My little mimosa blossom. You are such a beguiling sight when aroused, Dorothy: so demure . . . so chaste . . . such an ornament to my house."

"Listen, you little cocksucker, I've had better titles than yours waiting on my table." Dorothy, already drunk, poured another glass of Jack Daniels. The *QE II* had run out of her Moroccan beer, Moro XX, but that was only one reason for her wrath. "If you think I didn't see you making eyes at that big West Indian steward . . ."

"Did you want him for yourself, my turtledove?" Momo spoke with a flawless Cambridge accent learned during five years spent as private secretary to a rich and homosexual British duke. "Really, my angel, you had only to ask."

"You disgust me!"

"That would be an achievement." He sipped the wine.

"What did I do to deserve this?" Dorothy cast her eyes towards heaven and knocked back half her bourbon.

"If the truth be known, I married you for the purity of your soul. As you, no doubt, married me for my boyish charm."

"You've got boyish charm, all right. Ha! Choirboys! Delivery boys! Boys from the docks . . ."

"That was your little fancy, as I recall." Momo twirled the champagne bottle in its silver ice bucket and poured himself another glass. From above, the ship's operatic foghorn sounded. It was three in the morning. The great liner was pulling into New York harbor. "But, my love, enough of this banter! Shall we go above, and greet the new dawn?"

"Fuck the new dawn." La Dutton drained her glass and teetered toward the bathroom.

"Such eloquence. Dorothy, I am touched. Is there anything I can do, my pet? Send for a stomach pump, perhaps? Or the ship's psychiatrist? I'm sure they have one." The bathroom door slammed. Momo could hear the burps and gurgles of his wife being sick. It was not an unfamiliar sound. He sighed, and put down his glass. He'd just go for one last spin around the deck. One never knew what might turn up.

Momo stepped out onto A deck and closed the door carefully. When she got this drunk, sleep came fast to Dorothy Dutton, and the longer she slept, the happier Momo would be. Especially if . . . but no, it was too much to hope for. He turned up the heavy satin collar of his dinner jacket against the predawn chill. Momo leaned against the rail near the bow. The sea was calm and the enormous ship had slowed nearly to a halt to take on the harbor pilot. A fine gray mist enveloped everything in a watercolor haze. Momo pulled out the slender platinum cigarette case that had been a wedding present from Dorothy. It had been made up by Bucellati, with his crest in diamonds and rubies and antique gold raised against the gleaming platinum.

"Got one to spare . . . Sir?" said a soft Caribbean voice at his elbow. Before turning, Momo looked out into the mist and smiled. There was something the English liked to say about the early bird . . . he must ask Dorothy. Then he turned, still smiling.

"I've quite a lot to spare, young man, now that you mention it." Momo held out the glittering cigarette case.

"Thank you, Sir." The tall black steward pulled out a box of wooden matches and lit Momo's smoke, then his own. "Just couldn't sleep this night, the sea being so quiet."

"No more could I," said Momo, looking at the wide shoulders under the white, fitting steward's jacket, and the muscular arms, the slender hips, and most of all at the strong, carved-mask ebony-smooth face. *Grade A,* thought Momo, drawing on the cigarette. *Decidedly Grade A.* "Getting a little chilly up here, don't you think?"

"You could say that." The steward's voice was flat, noncommittal.

"What's your name, Steward?"

"James, Sir."

"Well, James. I think we can dispense with the sir."

"Yes, Sir."

"Tell me, James," said Momo, placing his hand lightly on the steward's shoulder in what could perfectly well have been nothing more than a comradely gesture, "would it be out of line for me to buy you a drink? There seems to be some champagne going to waste in my stateroom."

"This is my own time," said the steward, "I can spend it any way at all." He looked into Momo's eyes, and Momo looked back unblinkingly. A deal had been made. The two men walked through the mist back to the suite. Gesturing for silence, Momo opened the door and peered in. La Dutton was snoring in her bed. Momo picked up the ice bucket and tiptoed through his wife's stateroom to his own, equally large, but, unlike Dorothy's, in perfect order. Momo poured two glasses of the world's most expensive champagne and held one out to James.

"To the future."

"To the present." Slowly, very slowly, James smiled. Momo, with the ease of long practice, hung up his own dinner jacket and took off his tie. Then he walked across the stateroom to where James stood, still smiling, and quickly but gently undid all the buttons on the black man's tunic. Underneath, James's black flesh gleamed like mahogany. Momo hung the steward's jacket next to his own, and went to work on other laces, buttons, buckles.

A little later, still standing, smiling, the black man laughed out loud: "I love it, man, I just love it!" But Momo's tongue was too busy elsewhere to reply. James reached down and touched Momo's immaculately arranged hair with a kind of affection: "I was born in a tin hut in Bridgetown, man, and here I am! The husband of the richest lady in the whole world has my big old prick in his mouth!"

Six hours and several amphetamines did their work before Momo and Dorothy were settled back in adjoining first class seats on a jet bound for Denver. She was trying to forget last night. Momo was reliving the end of it. They smiled at each other. He leaned confidentially across the console and kissed her newly lifted cheek: "It was really a lovely crossing, darling, don't you think?"

"I've had worse."

"And this place . . . this High Sky we're going to, it sounds exciting, doesn't it?" Momo was thinking of tanned blond godlike youths soaring down white mountains into his dreams. Which, typically, was exactly what Dorothy was thinking of at the same time.

"The name," Dorothy said flatly, "is Sky High. And American skiers tend to be heterosexual."

"Well, darling, don't always look on the dark side. Maybe they'll have some French ones." He noticed her glass was empty, and gestured for the stewardess. The stewardess returned with a bottle of Moro XX. When the *QE II* ran out of Moro XX, they also lost their richest customer.

Momo looked at his wife. You wouldn't believe she was nearly seventy. Everything that spas and exercise and surgery and cosmetics could do to create the illusion of youth had been done to La Dutton. Her nose was not the nose she had been born with. The cheekbones had been heightened, and the entire face itself lifted and tucked in several times. The eyes had been de-bagged, the breasts bouyed up and inflated with silicone. *Funny about the earlobes,* Momo thought, *nobody's figured out a way to take the wrinkes out of earlobes.*

Zeke Gibbs hadn't felt this good in years. The old man walked out of the exclusive Settlers Club in Denver in close conversation with his lawyer, Will Jefferson. Zeke, a little stiff in his beautifully tailored, seldom worn, dark blue suit, had just finished a gratifying luncheon with Jefferson and three Colorado legislators. The subject had been how to defeat the upcoming proposal to widen Highway 317. It was going to be a fight, no doubt about that. Well, Zeke was ready for a fight. The three legislators were against the widening for three very different reasons, which was exactly why Will Jefferson had chosen them.

Young Jed Regis was an all-fired-up conservationist, against anything and everything that disturbed the balances of nature. He considered Sky High an act of ecological rape. Zeke liked him. In tomorrow's mail, Jed was going to find a check for ten thousand dollars made out to his conservation organization, Friends of the Rocky Mountains.

The second legislator was another animal entirely: Dave Davis. Davis was a classic example of the smooth young politician on the way up. He had his sights on the governor's mansion and made no bones about it. Davis was good-looking, rich and charismatic. Probably, Zeke guessed, it was because Davis had money that he so vehemently took the conservationist side of the battle over 317. Davis was trying very hard to avoid any implication that he was hooked up with the state's big-business interests.

The third guest at the luncheon was old Henry Macintyre. Macintyre was the archconservative's conservative. He had made a long career of being against everything. If old Henry ever voted *for* something, the action had gone unrecorded. Predictable as he was, Macintyre had influence. He had evolved into a figurehead over the years—by sheer persistence as much as talent. Still, the name of Henry Macintyre behind a piece of legislation was guaranteed to win the approval of all the most conservative elements in the state. And, Colorado being Colorado, these archconservatives carried weight.

"I always knew you were a sly one, Will," said Zeke over an excellent cigar back at Jefferson's office. "But this time you've really outdone yourself."

"I'm always glad to help."

"And don't I need it! Let me tell you, Will: this is war. Jake Chaffee bushwacked me once. There is damn little I would not do to make sure he doesn't do it twice. I want to fight, Will, and fight hard. And if it costs money, I've got money." Zeke permitted himself a little smile, but his eyes were killer's eyes.

"Well," said Jefferson as he unlocked an old mahogany secretary and took out a decanter and glasses, "We're not home free yet. Jed Regis will make a lot of noise, be sure of that. Davis, well he likes to work on the inside. But he will work. Maybe slip it into a couple of speeches. As for old Henry, all we had to do there is point him in the right direction. But still and all, Zeke, don't count your chickens. Jake Chaffee has a lot more influence than he's letting on. Plenty of people in Washington owe his daddy big favors. And that can carry all the way out here."

"I'll take on the father and the son if it comes to that."

"And 317 isn't just your bridle path, Zeke, much as I wish it was. It goes damn near two hundred miles before it gets up to Sky Junction, and a good piece afterwards. That's more than three hundred miles lined with folks who stand to get rich—richer, anyway—if the road is widened. And some of those people are fairly influential in their own right."

"They call that 'progress,' Will."

"We're doing everything this side of murder." The lawyer poured two glasses of whiskey and handed one to Zeke. "Confusion to our enemies!"

"Amen!" said Zeke Gibbs with all his heart.

The old myth was acting up again. Buck Washington could feel it right down to his toes, which was some distance. Buck topped six-three in his bare feet. The black pro-quarterback threw his head back and laughed out loud. The girl looked at him again. They always did. Buck was alone in the first-class section of the LA-to-Denver jet. And the little blonde stewardess was exhibiting all the usual symptoms of a well-brought-up white girl fascinated but more than a little bit scared by the myth of the black superstud. Buck knew the myth for what it was, but he enjoyed it all the same. Why not get a little of your own back? Or a lot! Probably, he thought, she expects me to order watermelon juice and then rape her.

Buck's keen eyes followed the girl ("Annette, but they call me Netty") as she walked up the aisle. Nice ass. Nice face. Nice girl. He wondered how long her stopover in Denver would be. Hell, he could probably boff her right here on the jet. He'd done that once, traveling with the Rams cross-country. But that had been on a bet. Bumping and bouncing around a tiny jet toilet was not Buck Washington's idea of pleasure. Give him a long afternoon in a big double bed with Annette-call-me-Netty and she'd come out of there a true believer. Now she was walking back towards him, pretending to be casual. She handed him a hot towel. He smiled a slow, easy smile and asked for a glass of red wine. She'd be back with the bottle. After all, it was first class. And he was Buck Washington. And he was going to squeeze every last drop of pleasure out of the myth for just as long as he could. Life was short. Buck was bored. That's why he'd accepted Jake Chaffee's invitation to Sky High.

Annette/Netty came back with the wine. And left the bottle. Buck Washington lifted his glass and swirled it, savoring the rich aroma of the Burgundy. Maybe he would speak to that Netty about a date in Denver. And maybe not. Hell, there'd be action aplenty at Sky High, good no-strings-attached sack action. There always was.

The little private jet was white from nose to tail but on the tail was painted a large blue star crossed by a golden yellow scimitar: the crest from the state flag of Bidijar. The jet, a custom-built French Mystère, was white inside too: the walls were white, the deep cut-pile carpeting was white accented here and there with ancient silk Kashan hunting carpets in which white animals chased pink and blue animals over pastel hills and forests. The leather chairs and couches were spotless white and two snow-white Royal Afghan hounds lounged on the white carpet, their inquisitive black faces dulled with jet lag.

The owner of all this white-on-white sat alone in the main cabin reading the latest issue of *Skiing* magazine. Niris Reza Herat Bir-Saraband, in his thirties, was lean and fit, a compactly built olive-skinned man with enormous brown eyes and a thin but smiling mouth.

It was Niris's luck—call it good, call it bad—to be a younger brother. He was the younger brother by twenty-two years of the Sheikh of Bidijar, third in line to the throne after the sheikh's own two sons. The tumultuous politics of Bidijar made it prudent for Niris to become as nearly invisible and harmless looking in his native country as possible. Too many, and far too fanatical, were the little factions that simmered around the immensely rich little sheikhdom.

Niris, awash with money from childhood, found himself at school in Switzerland and in college at Oxford. He visited Bidijar once a year, and then as a private person, quiet, smiling, uncontroversial. And when his brother arranged marriages for Niris—two of them, politically useful ties to young girls from powerful families who had been raised in the strictest Moslem conventions—Niris smiled and agreed and fulfilled his husbandly functions so competently that both of his wives were pregnant more often than not. Out of kindness, Niris took his two wives with him everyplace, keeping them just as strictly sequestered as if they'd been left behind in the women's quarter of the palace of Bidijar, where, if the truth were known, they would vastly have preferred to be. The only times the royal wives were excused from Niris's travels was when they were having babies. The children were raised in the palace nursery with their cousins.

It would have been easy to go straight to hell with so much money and pleasure. But Niris was smarter than that. Early on, he discovered what a useful cloak this reputation as a playboy could be. The press did most of the work for him, turning a bright boy's love of pretty women and festive company into a worldwide myth while Niris was still in his teens. While often photographed in company with some of the world's better-known beauties, Niris hardly ever drank anything stronger than wine and never took drugs. He was fond of sex but far from obsessed by it. The playboy image came more from the splendor of the settings in which Niris lived than the way he behaved. The jet, the fabulous houses, the expensive presents he had been known to give certain ladies, all lent credence to a myth Niris did nothing to discourage. It was useful to be considered no more than a wastrel. The time might well come when Niris would prove the absurdity of this reputation. But that time was not yet.

And in the meantime there were new mountains to ski, new women to meet, new dreams to dream. If Niris had a true obsession it was skiing. He was fascinated by mountains and snow as only a desert-bred person can be. His schooling in the Swiss Alps had given him the chance to ski all year, all through his teens, and Niris had taken the opportunity to become a skier of nearly professional caliber, although he felt it unbecoming to race. So Niris looked forward to his time at Sky High. Sky High! Even the name had a kind of magic for him. There was an excitement to it, the promise of adventures. Niris smiled, and reached down to stroke one of the Afghans, which nuzzled his hand in return.

"Think of it, Snowball," said Niris in his startlingly

perfect Oxford English, "a whole new mountain to play with!" No one had ever dared suggest to Niris that he might be lonely. So he roamed the world in a search that had no name, pursuing he knew not what. Sky High would teach him.

Pete Woodbury closed the fat gray folder that held his financial projections for Sky High. The figures were every bit as depressing over Missouri as they had been over Pennsylvania. "Inflation roulette" was the joke around Knickerbocker Trust, only no one thought it was funny.

In one sense Jake Chaffee was lucky. Sky High was the only major project he had going at the moment. And it was completed. If they could just hold out for a few months more, Sky High might pull through. Barely.

Pete tucked the gray folder into his attaché case and looked across at the redhead, who sat reading a magazine, having hardly touched her lunch. Should he say something to her? He wanted to. But she'd just think he was trying a cheap pickup. And this was obviously no cheap lady. Let it be. Hell, he'd probably never see her again after the flight anyway.

Maggie turned the page. He was looking at her again. Would he say something? And if he did, would she answer? Suddenly she felt about seventeen again. Unsure of herself. She had to keep pretending not to notice, that was very important. Or was it? There had been too much pretending in Maggie della Robbia's life lately. She imagined a scene in which she, shy, Catholic, virtuous Maggie, got up from her seat, sat herself down next to the attractive stranger and said: "Hi, my name's Maggie and I think you're kinda cute." Just thinking it, Maggie blushed uncontrollably and giggled out loud. *Please, God: let him think I'm reading a funny story in this magazine*. Maggie della Robbia did not get up from her seat and talk to Peter Woodbury. Fighting to get back her composure, she merely turned another page in her magazine.

8

Mildred Rush looked at the pile of carrots she was supposed to be trimming and sighed. The pile looked to be growing bigger, darned if it didn't. And of course the headache was coming back again, a steady dull throbbing at the base of her skull. And she knew, she could feel it, the cold slanted eyes of Raoul Peng were on her from someplace in the big kitchen, disapproving, just waiting for her to make another mistake like the sneaky little Jap he was, Frenchified or not. Raoul Peng had shown her how to do the carrots. He even did the first one himself, his slender yellow fingers wielding the knife like an orchestra leader's baton, moving so fast a person could hardly see what he was up to with his sneaky foreign ways. Filthy little Jap. The carrots—hundreds and hundreds of them—had to be trimmed and peeled and then cut up into little matchsticks an inch and a half long and an eighth of an inch thick, no more, no less. Naturally that Peng couldn't have 'em sliced in nice little rounds like any decent person. Matchsticks! Mildred Rush sighed again. She guessed most of the guests at Sky High had never peeled a carrot in their lives, or done any other honest work either. Mildred rose up from her stool at the kitchen cutting table and went to a vacant sink for a glass of water. Somehow the headache made her thirsty.

From the other end of his immaculate kitchen Raoul Peng watched as the squat old woman made her slow progress from the vegetable counter to the sink and back again. "For this," he thought, "I am paying three dollars the hour." Peasants were the same everywhere.

Totally unreliable. Still, trapped as he was in the farthest reaches of the godforsaken Rocky Mountains, Peng had to make do. The Mildred Rushes of the world were a necessary evil. Well. It would only be a few months now. Mildred Rush, shuffling back to her stool, looked at Raoul, defiantly. To her surprise and consternation, she was greeted by his most charming smile. Sneaky Jap that he was!

Jake Chaffee looked hard at the sky-blue telephone ringing on his night table and let it ring again. Then he picked it up. These days he'd come to dread the phone. The news it brought was seldom good.

"Hello."

"Jake?" It must have been weeks, maybe months, since he'd heard his wife's gentle voice.

"How are you Betsy?" Even at the start, guilt weighed on the line like a row of fat cows.

"Well, I'm fine. But we have a problem."

"What's wrong?" Jake's concern grew with his knowledge that for Betsy even to admit something might be a problem meant it was both real and serious.

"It's Eliza. Eliza's gone."

"From school? When?"

One level of Jake's mind instantly clicked onto automatic pilot. He kept his voice level. He kept his comments logical. It wouldn't do to add his own fears to Betsy's. But he was afraid, and worse than afraid, guilty. Wherever Eliza was, she needed him. It wrenched his gut to face the fact that he hadn't really thought about his own daughter for weeks, maybe months. Betsy's gentle voice went on, a voice from the past.

"I called her yesterday, Jake. You see, when an eighteen-year-old hasn't written or called for a week or so, naturally . . ."

"You were worried."

"Jake, I went right over there. Nobody in the dorm's seen her for at least two days. Her car's gone. It isn't like Eliza to go away without telling me—or someone."

"Did you call the police?"

"I wanted to talk to you first."

"I haven't heard a word since . . . well more than a

month." It had actually been two months. Jake bought the girl a fancy dinner the last time he was in San Francisco and promised himself he'd see more of her, starting right then. But somehow that promise hadn't been kept.

"She took her skis, Jake, and some of her ski clothes. I thought she might be heading for you."

"Let's hope so. She didn't leave a note, or tell her friend . . . what's-her-name?"

"Florry Hudson. No. Not a thing. I'm worried, Jake."

"Of course you are. Me too. Betsy, I'm glad you went down there. The way things are here, it'd be tough for me to get away right now. We're just opening up shop. But I will, if anyone thinks it'll help."

"I'll talk to the police first. You do whatever you think best, Jake."

"I'll get going on the FBI."

"You really think they might help?"

"How could they hurt? I mean, if there's any question at all of kidnapping . . ."

"Well, Jake, I'm sorry to trouble you. I realize how busy you must be." If Betsy had been more of a woman there might have been more of an accusation in her voice. As it was her words were no more than a fading echo.

"Nonsense. Call me as soon as you hear anything."

"You too. Good-bye, Jake."

"So long, Betsy. Try not to worry." The click of Betsy's phone a thousand miles away triggered more memories than Jake cared to deal with. He picked up the blue phone and dialed his father's private number in Washington, D.C.

"The mole," read Cassie Lamont, "had long wanted to make the acquaintance of the badger."

"What's a badger?"

"It's a kind of animal, Charlie, sort of like a raccoon. We don't have them here."

"Is it a good animal?"

"In this book it is," she said, smiling. Charlie always wanted to know the motivation of anything new in his life. "But in real life, I'm not so sure. Shall we look it up?"

"Sure."

They looked in the big dictionary.

"How about that," said Cassie, "we do have badgers in America. And—see?—they look more like groundhogs than raccoons. Well, we may have 'em, but I've never seen one."

"I bet Whizzer's seen one."

Cassie touched the boy's arm. Charlie never knew it, but every move his mother made was first weighed on the scale of his future. What was she giving Charlie in considering Jake Chaffee as a stepfather for him? Some days she couldn't separate her own complicated feelings for Jake from her worries about the boy's development. Some days a nagging little voice asked her if she was really prepared to let her life be run by an eight-year-old. The answer, today as always, was "Yes!"

There was a knock at the door and Jake poked his head in.

"Hi, Charlie. Sorry to interrupt, but, Cassie, when you have a minute . . ." The look on Jake's face told Cassie it was important.

"We were just finishing. Charlie, maybe Whizzer could use a little fresh air, OK?"

"OK, Mom. Come on, Whizzer. We'll go find you a badger." The boy and the big Golden Retriever bounded from the room.

"What's up?" Cassie stood and kissed him.

"Just what I need right now! Eliza's disappeared from Berkeley."

"Oh, Jake! When?"

"Well, Betsy just called. But she's been gone two days. Without a word to anyone. Her car's gone. We're putting the cops on it, naturally. And my father's trying the FBI. I keep telling myself she wouldn't do anything stupid, that she knows she can tell me anything . . ."

"And you end up blaming yourself, right? Don't. In the first place, it might not be anything bad. Kids get restless. It happens."

"Betsy thought she might be heading up here."

"Let's hope she is."

"Hope. And pray."

"Look, if she took the car, it's not too likely she was kidnapped, right?"

"Cars crash. There are such things as hitchhikers."

"Jake, this isn't like you. To look on the bad side."

"It's just that, hell, what kind of a father have I been to my only kid?"

"It isn't my place to say it"—Cassie's temper came seldom but strong—"but what kind of a mother has she had either?"

"I know. It's just that there are such damned scary things going on. That Hearst kid, for instance. Eliza could easily be a kidnap target . . ."

"Jake, listen: if the cops and the FBI are on it, there isn't a thing you can do. There's no ransom note or anything like that?"

"Nothing. Just—nothing."

"But you have every reason to believe she just went off by herself. Keep believing it, Jake."

"I guess I'll have to."

"Once when I was sixteen, I ran away for a whole week."

"So did I. Except I was seventeen, and I worked in a logging camp in Oregon for a month just to see if I could do it. The old man damn near killed me when I got back."

"Eliza sounds like a kid who can take care of herself."

"Please God!" Jake spoke with a confidence he was far from feeling inside.

Cassie knew the man too well by now to be completely taken in, but she also knew there was nothing she could do to help, not at the moment anyway. So she thought of a way to change the subject. "Speaking of problems," she said, "I had another run-in with Raoul this morning. He keeps trying to fly cream in from Paris. Do you know what cream costs, flown in from Paris?"

"I can imagine! Cream, for God's sake. What's wrong with good old American cream?"

"*Alors,* eet ees not *crème fraîche!*"

"Tragic. What did you tell him?"

"Well, I wanted to tell him to go take a flying fuck back to France. But I guess that wouldn't have been quite diplomatic of me. So I told him how to make fake *crème fraîche.* It's easy. Just simmer down our heavy cream, and then blend in about ten per cent sour cream when it's cool. Works like a dream."

"Raoul agrees?"

"Mais oui! Except, the bastard is getting on my nerves, Jake. He looks like an angel. I'll be the last to deny it. But there's something sneaky about him."

"I think you've seen too many 1940s propaganda movies featuring the Yellow Menace."

"If you say so."

"Where'd you learn to make fake French cream?"

"From a real French lady. Burke's mother. She's about twice as French as Peng ever dreamed of being."

"It's an ill mother-in-law that blows no good." He put his arms around her neck and kissed her. Just being in the same room with Cassie made him feel better.

"Jake?"

"Mmmmm."

"Don't feel guilty, OK?"

"I'll try."

"We'll both try."

Jake kissed her again, but his mind was speculating on what Zeke might be up to. It was not a very romantic thought.

The unfamiliar aroma of peanut butter mingled with the more traditional scents of onions, baking bread, roasting meat and bubbling stock pots in Raoul Peng's kitchen. Peng sat alone at his desk. In front of him was an open giant-sized jar of Skippy peanut butter and a spoon. Peng knew that one of the great challenges of his career lay before him. And he was determined to live up to it. Two weeks of catering to Dorothy Dutton and her bizarre insistence on an all-peanut butter diet! It was enough to defeat a man of lesser resources. But not Raoul Peng. He would meet it and master it and make it look easy. Raoul Peng would not be defeated by the mad whim of a neurotic American millionairess. Indeed, there might be a way to turn the crazy situation to his advantage.

Meticulously, on a fresh sheet of his menu-planning notepaper, Peng was listing the possible culinary variations on peanut butter, inventing as he went along. There were many. He would make the infamous La Dutton peanut butter breads and brioche; peanut butter crust for peanut mousse pie. There would be peanut butter gnocci, both au naturel and deep fried, and sometimes the gnocci would appear floating in bisque of peanut soup. Peanut hollandaise might garnish an omelette. And peanut butter ice cream was a possibility worth considering. As were: peanut butter meringues, a gratin of peanut butter and onions, and peanut butter soufflé. The possibilities were, if not literally endless, certainly intriguing to a mind of Peng's creative resources. La Dutton would be pleased. And when Dorothy Dutton was pleased, the world at large generally knew all about it soon afterwards.

Thoughtfully, Peng dipped his spoon into the grainy brown puree and tasted. "Peanut butter puff pastry!" he said out loud, oblivious to the glances this performance was drawing from the kitchen help: "Even peanut éclairs!" If there was to be madness, he thought scornfully, it would be of the most elegant kind.

Liz Drummond had long since stopped trying to hide the bottles of bourbon. And Dud Drummond had stopped trying to hide them from her.

In the five years of their marriage, Dud had tried just about everything love or money could do to help reverse her downward slide. Nothing worked. Not the thousand-dollar-a-week sanatorium in Connecticut, not the hundred-dollar-an-hour Park Avenue psychiatrist, not threats or reasoning or trips to far-away places: wherever she was, Liz Drummond quickly found a bottle or a pill or a man. It could be any bottle, any pill, any man. There was one simple but overwhelming answer to the obvious but unasked question of why Dud stayed with her. He loved her. Like all doomed love, this was an accident of nature. There was no logic in it.

Dud looked at his wife and sighed. Sticking with Liz

was an act of hope in itself. Their life together had become a question of getting through the day, day by day. He could tell that this would not be one of the better days. Liz sat at her dressing table in the big sunny room, slowly and expertly making up her face, which was hangover-pale under the honey Sky High tan. It was still a good face: high cheekbones, widely-set eyes that were somewhere between blue and green. Too good a face to waste.

On the dressing table next to her pots and tubes and jars was a glass of bourbon only slightly diluted with tap water. It, too, had become a vital part of Liz Drummond's morning ritual, right up there with tooth brushing, powder and paint.

"How are you?" he asked.

"Liz Drummond is barely alive and living—if you call it living—in East Bejesus, Colorado."

"I thought you were getting to like it."

"It'll do." Liz picked up her glass, sipped from it and met Dud's eyes in the mirror. "It's as good a place as any to play out the last act of our little soap opera."

"What do you mean by that?" Threats were not Liz's style.

"I'm finished. Checking out. Leaving. *Ciao.*"

"Don't."

"This was a new game. But Liz was always playing new games, and always losing. Dud gathered all his resources of love and pity to make her lose this one.

"And do you know why?" she asked, quietly.

"Don't leave, Liz."

"It's kind of funny, actually." She laughed. It sounded like someone drowning.

"Liz, please. Don't."

"I've come to pity your pity." Her voice went tense.

"I don't want you to leave, Liz."

"I cannot abide those hopeless wet looks."

"Think it over, Liz."

"Or your meaningful silences."

"Where would you go?" He was almost out of control now.

"Or your gallant air of quiet desperation."

"Liz. You need someone to look after you." It always came back to this.

"Righty-ho. Now we're getting down to it. Old Liz needs a keeper. Just listen, you'll hear her, up there in the attic, rattling her chains!"

She was playing to the balcony now, pitching it high, adding gestures. Dud knew all the signs of a storm gathering. This was one of them.

"I can help, Liz."

"The first Mrs. Rochester."

"At least, let me try." He touched her shoulder. She cringed.

"It's your fucking trying that's killing me."

"I don't understand." He really didn't.

"Do you not? Well, old buddy, you aren't alone there. Dudley, look. Can all the for-better-or-worse stuff, OK? You can't help me. And I, well, I can hurt you a lot. I've already managed to mess up your sleep and your sex life. Next, it'll be your job. You think I don't notice the way people like Jake Chafee look at me? And pity you? You'll start hating yourself—if you don't already. I'm calling it off, Dud. The show is folding. I'm doing what you'll never have the guts to do."

"I love you." The words hung in a sudden silence and faded, a dream of a bridge, leading nowhere.

"I really think you do. Which makes it worse."

"Where would you go?"

"The logical place is San Francisco. 'San Francisco is where the dream stops.' Funny. I read that in a book once. It was the first sentence. And I can't remember one other word of it." Her voice became a small girl's voice, filled with wonder. She took a long pull on her bourbon.

"You don't know anyone in San Francisco."

"I have a knack for making friends. I'm such a warmhearted kid."

"You are." He had to think, to keep it in the present tense.

"I'm a drunk and probably a nymphomaniac and I've got a mean streak that makes Route 66 look like a bridlepath."

"I won't let you go." Dud said it as though he knew a way of keeping her.

"I'm gone, Dud. Long gone. Yesterday afternoon in this room—on that bed—I spent hours balling some teenaged ski bum whose name I don't even remember. If ever I knew it."

"You can't shock me, Liz." It came out so softly, it was almost a whisper. Dud turned from his wife and looked out the window. The mountain was still standing, the sky was still blue, the earth was in its usual orbit. He touched his face, hoping she wouldn't see the tears as he wiped them away.

"Don't I know it!"

"Will you promise me one thing?"

"Probably. I'm a very promising girl." She continued applying makeup.

"Don't leave right now. It's only for two more weeks. Then maybe we can both go take a look at San Francisco. If you still . . ."

"Jesus!" She slammed a jar hard on the dresser. "Do you ever miss the point! Sure, Dud. Quit a job you like. Ride off into the sunset with your blushing bride. No sale. Thank you very much."

"Will you at least wait till I'm done here?" He was fighting for a couple of weeks. Dud knew in his heart he'd be just as willing to fight for hours, minutes.

"Sure. Why not? It hardly matters, at this point."

"Take it easy, Liz, OK?" She turned to him and started to get up. Then she thought better of it and sat down again. For the first time that morning Liz Drummond looked her husband in the eye.

"It's time to cut your losses, pal. Buddy." She managed a grin.

"We'll talk about it later, Liz." Dud bent over and kissed her on the cheek, then walked out of the room. As he went down the hallway, Dud stood a little taller and even smiled. The years had gradually bred into Dud Drummond a major talent for self-deception. Now it worked on him like a drug, all that was left between his self-respect and screaming pain. There just might be a chance. At least she was willing to listen to him, to give him a little more time. There was hope. As long as they both lived, there would be hope.

Zem Gibbs smiled as she started her long ride up Sky Mountain. It was a glorious morning. Two inches of fresh powder had fallen unseen in the night, and the sky soared cloudless over the mountain. Only the tramway moved in the clear morning light. Far below her on the right, Zem could see the ranch, smoke curling up from the kitchen wing. *How tiny it is,* she mused, *when you think I've spent practically my whole life in that little valley.* Zem thought of her grandfather. He'd be down there still, stewing in his own poison, scheming and pulling strings and doing just about anything to get in Jake Chaffee's hair. Zem paused for a moment and looked down at the ranch again. Surrounded. Zeke Gibbs was making his last stand after the battle was lost.

A black speck appeared in the sky and grew bigger. Zem's quick eyes recognized it, and she shuddered. A big old turkey buzzard flew toward her and began circling over a patch of woods. About a third of the way up the mountain. *Coming back for dessert,* she thought. Yesterday there had been three of the disgusting creatures.

An hour and a half later, Zem stood tall on her skis at the rim of China Bowl. The huge, almost perfect concave snowfield was empty under the topless sky. High above the edge of the bowl on the right loomed the ice, rock and snow cornice that had been called Widow's Peak ever since Zem could remember. Even Zem, fearless, as a child had been forbidden Widow's Peak. In summer it bred rattlers, and in winter more serious dangers that attacked without warning: avalanches and hidden crevasses. Widow's Peak had earned its name many times over in the old days. Zeke himself kept away from it. Still, it was spectacular to look at, curling up more than five hundred feet like some enormous ocean wave just about to break. It was strictly off limits to skiers, marked and roped off with big orange warning signs. Zem smiled and watched the miniature white cloud of her frozen breath vanish into mountain morning. There were no sounds at all, no wind, no skier's shout, not a bird song.

The bowl had been well-packed for days, and now it wore the new powder like a wedding dress. It was the best time of the day for a skier. Zem pushed off, half hating to mark the new powder but thrilled to be the first to make tracks across the finest snow bowl in the Rockies. Zem skied China Bowl easy, not wanting the run to end. She swooped and glided down the inside rim of the bowl, throwing up long plumes of white crystals that seemed to hang in the air a supernaturally long time before settling down again. She moved fluidly, musically, and she laughed out loud from the raw joy of it. Zem threw her head back and yodeled, "Yeeeo-dee-oh-hooo!" At the bottom of the bowl two men stood watching her performance in silent admiration. She recognized Jean-Pierre Belfort and neatly stopped next to him.

"*Allo*, Zem. That was beeeutiful!" said Jean-Pierre, grinning. "Maybe you give me a lesson, OK?"

"Oh, sure. You really need help, Jean-Pierre. Like I need a third leg." Zem liked the young Frenchman and the playful puppylike way he approached any pretty girl.

"Zem, this is my pupil, Mr. Rubin. Zem Geebs."

"Good morning," said Tod. "You do ski beautifully."

"Thank you. I was skiing this bowl before it had a name. I grew up here."

"You are very lucky, Miss Gibbs."

"I guess I am." Zem smiled at the curiously formal Austrian. "I'm also playing hookey from the ranch's office work, so I'd better be trucking along. Nice meeting you, Mr. Rubin. So long, Jean-Pierre." Zem thrust her ski poles into the snow and pushed off. In seconds she had disappeared around a curve in the trail.

"That's a beautiful young lady, Jean-Pierre."

"You said it. But she is, what-you-say, spoken for."

"Married?"

"I am betting she will be. To the young doctor of the town, Beel Shepherd. Nice fellow."

"Bad luck for you, Jean-Pierre."

"Perhaps." The boy shrugged philosophically. And

grinned. "But there are other fishes, are there not, in the river? But now, we should be skiing, OK?"

"Let's go." Jean-Pierre pushed off down the Milky Way trail with Tod Rubin struggling gamely behind him.

Seething with annoyance, Raoul Peng gave three more strokes to the glittering French Sabatier knife he was whetting to a surgical edge. Old Mildred Rush had called in sick that morning. Headache and a fever, she said. Well, what could one expect? There was no discipline, no loyalty among such people. She probably had a hangover. Or just felt lazy. If she wasn't back on the job tomorrow, he'd have to find someone else.

With a small sigh of regret, Pete Woodbury abandoned his attempt to flirt with the redhead. The plane's intercom system crackled and a stewardess said, "Ladies and gentlemen, we are beginning our descent to Denver's Stapleton International Airport. Please observe the no-smoking sign when it appears. If any of our passengers are enroute to Sky High, we've been told there is a charter flight waiting at the airport with two available seats. Please contact one of the flight crew if you wish to use the charter. Thank you." Immediately after this announcement the redhead pushed the call button overhead. A stewardess appeared and Maggie asked her to arrange a seat on the charter.

"Excuse me." Pete leaned across the two empty seats and smiled at Maggie. "Are you going to Sky High?"

"Why yes. I am."

"Let me introduce myself. Pete Woodbury." He put out his hand and she shook it.

"Maggie della Robbia. I take it you're a skier, too."

"Well, I am, but this is a business trip. I've been helping with Sky High's financial arrangements." He smiled as though this was merely a question of raking in the money. Hell, she might be a prospect for a condominium. She sure looked like she could afford one.

"That must be very interesting, Mr. Woodbury."

"Please. Pete."

"Call me Maggie."

"Sometimes it gets a little *too* interesting. But I have a confession. All the way from Kennedy I've been trying to work up my courage to talk to you."

"Well!" Maggie laughed. "I'm glad you finally made it. I hate to travel alone, myself."

"Can I buy you a drink at the airport?"

"If we have time before the charter leaves."

"We will. Hell, it's my charter. He'll leave when we want him to leave."

"That's pretty fancy." She looked at him apprais-ingly. "I'd love a drink." The seat-belt sign flashed on and Pete moved back to his place and fastened his belt. And smiled. The trip to Sky High might have a silver lining after all.

Eliza stepped harder on the small accelerator pedal. All she saw was the road. All she heard was the wind. And all she could think of was Sky High, and what she might find there. The lacquer-red MG was topping 80 miles an hour on Route 317 when the state trooper pulled it to the side of the road. He got out of his car but left the blue rooftop light flashing. A thin blonde girl sat at the wheel of the MG, tense and alone, looking straight ahead. He knocked on the window and she rolled it down.

"License and registration, please."

"Shall I tell you where the fire is?" There was some-thing dead in her voice, a kind of burnt-out anger. The trooper ignored her cheap joke. "This is a dangerous road, Miss Chaffee. The speed limit is fifty-five. For a reason. Two weeks ago I had to scrape a boy not much older than you off a rock just down the road a bit. He didn't believe the limit, either. I clocked you at eighty."

"That fast? I guess I just wasn't thinking. I've been on the road for hours and——"

"And you're much too pretty to kill yourself. I'm not going to take you in. But do me—and yourself—a fa-vor, OK?"

"Sure."

"Cool it."

"I really will." She looked at him for the first time

and smiled a smile that made everything in her face warm up. "And . . . thank you."

"Anytime." He smiled and handed back her wallet. "Fifty-five, hear?"

"I hear you." Eliza Chaffee rolled the window up and pulled back on to Route 317. She'd never seen Sky High. In fact, she'd never been asked there.

Living away at Berkeley had taught Eliza Chaffee a lot, most of it the hard way. She learned, for the first time, that rational, independent thought and action were widely admired. She learned the several uses bright young people make of each other's minds and bodies. But the fundamental thing Eliza Chaffee learned at college was that, whatever her future might bring, it did not include any more episodes of Life With Mother.

Luckily for her, Eliza inherited her father's energy and love of life. She tried to see Jake whenever she could, which turned out to be not often enough. Jake had missed whole chunks of his daughter's life: her times with him were so rare and special that she hated to spoil the atmosphere by dragging out her private problems. As far as she ever let Jake know, everything was just fine.

It wasn't, of course—it never is—and eventually the pressure of making all her own decisions while simultaneously fending off Betsy's social advances on one hand and negotiating meetings with Jake on the other just got to be too much. She felt the campus closing in on her. So one day she threw some clothes into a bag and locked her skis onto the MG's ski rack and headed east for Colorado. That was two days ago. Two days of steady fast driving broken only by a parade of bad hamburgers and one night in a motel.

Keeping the MG's speed within hailing distance of the limit, Eliza noticed the beauty of the landscape for the first time. These mountains were special. And from what she'd heard Jake say about it, Sky High was special too. Maybe he'd give her a job as a waitress or something. Or maybe he'd boot her right back to Hillsborough.

The red sports car gobbled up the miles and Eliza didn't even try to stop the familiar fantasy from replaying itself in her mind. She was on trial and on the witness stand. The judge was not amused.

"Take pity on me, Your Honor. I'm an orphan."

"Is this woman not your mother?" The prosecuting attorney wagged a longer finger at her. Betsy smiled sweetly.

"My mother vanished years ago, I swear it, into a cloud of money."

"And is that man not your father?" Jake sat at the side of the courtroom, handsome as ever, posing for the eager photographers, smiling, apparently unaware of the life-or-death drama being being played out in front of him.

"I worshiped him as my father. But he was a false god, Your Honor. He turned from me in my hour of need."

"And what, my child, was your need?" The judge's voice had a hollow sound to it, a voice from a tomb.

"Why, love, Your Honor! What does everybody need?" The girl on the witness stand in the dream rose to her feet and blinked back tears. Real tears fell on Eliza's cheek. She blinked and blinked again. A highway sign read: SKY JUNCTION 25 MILES.

"Did you have a good day, Whizzer?" Charlie Lamont's thoughtful suntanned little face broke into a grin of welcome. Every day at two-thirty the town school bus dropped Charlie at the end of the long driveway that led up to Sky Lodge. And every day Whizzer was there waiting for his master, tail wagging, dancing and romping from pure anticipation. Now came the great adventure of the day.

Boy and dog raced up the driveway and into Sky Lodge, where Charlie quickly changed into his ski clothes, looked in on his mother and, after a fast cup of good hot chocolate, Charlie and Whizzer would bound out into the snow to catch the lift up the mountain for one last run, and sometimes two.

There had been quite a debate about letting Charlie ski alone. The eight-year-old had been skiing four years and there wasn't a trail he couldn't get down in style on his small fiberglass skis. And, with the ever-present

Whizzer, he wasn't really alone. Cassie, naturally, worried, but she couldn't deny Jake's argument that they should do everything they could to build the boy's self-confidence. And skiing alone did just that. It led Charlie to meet people on his own, but in protected circumstances. He was already the mascot of the whole ski school, and the instructors loved to ski with him if they had a free moment. Cassie and Jake went with him whenever they could.

Like most big Rocky Mountain resorts, Sky High closed the tramway at three-thirty, two hours before sunset. The idea was safety, to get everyone off Sky Mountain before night fell. It was cold and lonely on the mountain after dark, and the last hours of the skier's day are the most dangerous, with skiers tired and the slopes sometimes icy.

The tramway made its six-minute run up the mountain, and Charlie took off alone down the trail called Wardance, closely pursued by Whizzer, who bounded joyfully down like a dolphin through the ocean, perfectly in tune with his element. Wardance was an expert trail, steep and stacked with an endless series of the hard, rounded bumps skiers call moguls. Charlie loved moguls more than most full grown skiers because he was small enough to treat each like a separate little mountain. He headed fearlessly down the trail and skied around the moguls one after the other in a kind of roller-coaster rhythm using the big bumps for leverage in his turns, winning admiring glances from adults resting by the trail side. Charlie skied so well for his age that heads turned whenever he was making a run. He had a natural athlete's feel for economy of motion and showed every sign of growing up to be the world-class skier his father had been.

"Your dad would be proud of you, Charlie," Jake had said one afternoon when the boy finished an especially good run.

"My daddy is dead." Charlie looked Jake in the eye, not in sorrow and not in anger, but with a look that clearly indicated there were parts of Charlie's psyche where visitors would not be welcome. It would be a long time before Jake mentioned Burke Lamont in Charlie's hearing again.

Down and down Charlie went, around and around, bobbing out of sight behind the bigger moguls, followed by the flash of rust-colored fur that was Whizzer. Whizzer had a different way of negotiating the moguls. He leaped from top of bump to top of bump with all the spirit and agility of a mountain goat.

Wardance was a chute of a trail, steep and straight and a lot shorter than most of the others on Sky Mountain. At the bottom, it melded into the easier Skyway trail. Charlie paused at the place where the two trails joined and waited for his dog. And as soon as Whizzer came sailing over the top of the final mogul to land, puffing for breath, at his master's feet, "Your dad would be proud of you, Whizzer," Charlie said gravely, "he really would."

"*Aaaaaaauuuuuughaa!*" A loud Tarzan yell filled the quiet air as Jean-Pierre Belfort came flying down Wardance alone and with all stops out, his skis barely touching the tops of the moguls, skiing at the farthest edge of control, using every ounce of instinct and guts and muscle to squeeze one more tenth of a second out of the implacable clock that is every racer's archopponent. Jean-Pierre took the last mogul as a jump and came soaring twenty feet in the air to land close to Charlie and Whizzer in a cloud of powder and enthusiasm. "Wooof! Hi, Charlie. Hi, Whizzaire."

"That was good, Jean-Pierre."

"I thank you. When I am alone," he said, rolling his brown eyes dramatically, "I become Tarzan."

"You're funny." Charlie laughed. He liked the young Frenchman.

"Will you ski down with me, Charlie?"

"Sure. Come on, Whizzer."

Jean-Pierre led the way, skating a little at first to work up some speed. Then, conscious of the eight-year-old behind him, he took the wide inviting Skyway trail in easy loops. Charlie followed close behind and gave a remarkably good imitation of Jean-Pierre's perfect form.

"*Aaaaaaauuuuuugha!*" yelled Jean-Pierre, Tarzan once again.

"*Aaaaaaauuuuuughaa!*" answered Charlie, laughing. Whizzer, as usual, was silent, absorbed in the joy of the game. A few late skiers on the trail paused in admiration as this oddly matched but happy procession sped past them into the twilight.

9

Noel Northcliff stood at the bar and smiled. He'd been right to come. NN sensed stories forming in the air around him. The world, for Noel Northcliff, had long been divided into two simple categories: story material and nonstory material. And virtually everybody in the bar at Sky High was, or could quickly become, the focus of an NN acecdote.

Dorothy Dutton had entered the room wearing a sable jacket over wide silk trousers, her masklike face half hidden behind enormous lavender eyeglasses which, NN happened to know, were for decor only. Maybe she had one of her well-deserved hangovers. But La Dutton clung to Momo's limber arm like a schoolgirl, all innocence, love, flirtation. There was sure to be a scene.

In a corner near the fireplace Niris lounged on one of the low couches, sipping sherry and talking to Pepi Prager, negotiating ski lessons. Pepi glowed, a postcard picture of Nordic health, good cheer and self-confidence. No wonder he felt good. Niris had just offered him ten thousand dollars, cash, for a week of private lessons. Turning down the oil heir's proposition gave Pepi nearly as much pleasure as the offer itself. He was sure Niris would understand: that just wouldn't be fair to the others. An hour a day, surely—but at the regular rate. They shook hands and exchanged the understanding looks that flash between leading players in games of big-time power. It was agreed that, perhaps, when the Sky High season was over in June, Niris and Pepi might take a week or two in Portillo, Chile, or perhaps the new mountain in New Zealand everyone was talking about.

There were more than fifty people in the room, Noel guessed, but the scale of the place was so huge and the furniture so artfully positioned that there was no sense of crowding. Outside, the ski slopes turned from pale blue to violet as night came to Sky Mountain. A spruce fire crackled in the big stone fireplace, perfuming the air with evergreen smoke. The room glowed. And the people in it glowed. Not a one of them was less than very good-looking. A few were world-class beauties. A sense of ease and fun and bottomless money hung in the air. This was their game, a portable Olympiad of chic, and they played it like champions. It was for this that they trained like athletes: to be slim, to be sleek, amusing, to be in love or with the prospect of being in love very soon. But perhaps above everything else the thrust of their lives was simply to keep a reserved seat on the merry-go-round.

In an odd way, Noel thought, they all look as though they're related to each other. There were more perfect teeth in this room than Ecuador, for instance, might have seen in all its history. Noel Northcliff just loved it.

Buck Washington, impressive in a black turtleneck and embroidered blue jeans, walked into the bar with Jake, laughing. Dorothy Dutton's violet eyeglasses followed his progress towards the bar with the slow sinister regard of an enemy gun turret in an old war movie, silent but aware. Jake knew Buck from California. Jake was a rabid football fan, and it was at his suggestion that the flamboyant ex-quarterback had come to Sky High. Soon there was a small crowd around the two men. They moved to a vacant couch and began a discussion of the next year's pro season.

Cassie stood at her bedroom window thoughtfully tying a silk scarf at her throat. Five-thirty. It wasn't like Charlie to be so late. She looked out at the mountain. Sky Mountain loomed purple under a darkening sky. Usually the mountain seemed like a huge and friendly presence, as its protective bulk stood between Cassie and the world. But now there was something cold and threatening to all that rock and snow, something ominous. Without knowing why, Cassie shivered. Then she smiled, and looked at her watch. Sometimes she had to pull herself up short to stop from becoming an overprotective mother. Left to her own devices, she'd worry about Charlie so much, she'd want to keep him in bed all day. There were at least a dozen places Charlie and Whizzer might be lingering after their last run. They could be having a Coke with one of the instructors. Or Peng might be plying them with his latest pastry. Cassie checked her reflection in the mirror and decided to make a quick search before she let her intuition drive her into a panic. She turned and looked out the window again. The mountain was almost black now. Black and cold and deadly. She hurried out to look for her son.

Now Cornelia de Vos entered the Sky Bar with Jean-Pierre Belfort. Cornelia was all in white. This time it was a soft, silky white, the white of moonlight shimmering off snow. Her wide trousers were some dense, rich silk, and the simple turtleneck top was an intricately crocheted silk, Her tawny hair was pulled back by a white ribbon. Alone of all the women in the room, Cornelia wore no jewelry other than the inevitable large emerald ring. Jean-Pierre, smitten, cavorted by her side with the unself-conscious delight of a puppy. Jean-Pierre was a fine foil for de Vos. He was tall and brown-haired and tanned nearly mahogany by the mountain sun. Cornelia, who spoke six languages perfectly, joked with the boy in unaccented French. They came to the bar and she switched to English and introduced Jean-Pierre to NN. Noel smiled. It was just as he expected. If there was a good-looking young athlete anywhere in the woodwork, Cornelia de Vos would draw him out like magic. Noel looked at them like some wise old uncle. Let them have their fun.

It was in this cheerful setting that Sky High's first big crisis broke.

Cassie, pale with worry, hurried into the room and went straight to Jake. Apologizing to the group, she drew him aside: "Charlie's missing. Oh, Jake! I'm terrified he might be on the mountain."

"When did you last see him?"

"Right after school. He went skiing with Whizzer. Like they always do. But neither of them came back. Jake, I'm scared."

"The ski patrol cleared the mountain an hour ago." But Jake's voice was grim. No ski patrol was perfect. Sky Mountain was huge. It was the easiest thing in the world for someone to crash off a trail and lie there unseen. He took Cassie's hand and held it, hard. They both knew how deadly a mountain can turn in the night and the cold. Then Jake's mind came to life with its usual efficiency. "Call Frank Carson." Carson, who lived in town, was the head of the ski patrol. "I'll alert Pepi, and he'll get all the instructors. We'll get every guest who's an expert skier and comb that hill from top to bottom. Tell everyone we meet at the tramway in half an hour." Impulsively, he kissed her. Cassie went to make the calls.

Jake went first to Pepi. "We've got an emergency. Charlie Lamont didn't come back from the mountain. We'll have to get up a search party."

"Count on all of the instructors, Jake. An even dozen. Are there lanterns?"

"Yes. The patrol's got big ones. If you can round up the ski school, I'll work on the guests. Cassie's getting to the ones who live in town. We meet at the tramway in half an hour." Jake looked at his watch. Six-thirty. The light was gone now. It would be cold on Sky Mountain. And the boy might have been there for two hours. Long enough to be badly frostbitten. If not worse.

The big room emptied. Everyone who could wanted to help. Those who weren't expert skiers helped on the ground: alerting the hospital in Steamboat Springs, making phone calls. But mostly they just milled about, making half-thought-out suggestions that no one listened to. The air of chic festivity had evaporated with Cassie's first words.

Cassie telephoned Bill Shepherd. Zem was with him. They jumped out of bed and into their ski clothes.

Charlie Lamont lay on his back in a snowdrift halfway up Sky Mountain. The moon was coming out. It would be a clear night, but Charlie didn't see the moon. He drifted in and out of consciousness, aware only of the soft warm presence of Whizzer tucked in next to him and aware, too, that something was very wrong with his leg. Charlie didn't remember falling. The run with Jean-Pierre had been so much fun he decided to squeeze in one more. Charlie and his dog caught the very last ride on the Sky Lift.

The mountain was nearly empty then and not as friendly looking as it had been. When they got to the top Charlie could see shadows flowing down the valley like spilled ink. Something told the boy Wardance might not be a good idea for him, alone, at this time of day. Charlie shivered. "Come on, old Whizzer. We'll take the easy way." And he pushed off down the wide, gentle beginner's Milky Way trail. Milky Way circled gently around the right side of Sky Mountain. Even for a fairly tired Charlie, it would be a breeze.

The late afternoon chill had turned the morning's soft powder hard. Milky Way had been well-skied all day. There were ruts. But Charlie skimmed down the trail, making Jean-Pierre's Tarzan yells re-echo from the silent black spruce trees that walled the trail. Half in deep shadow and half in the yellow late afternoon sun, the boy flew down the gently curved trail. There were no sounds, but the hiss and slap of Charlie's skis on the hard-frozen snow, his occasional war cries and the panting of the Golden Retriever coming on behind.

The effortless sweep of turn into turn had an almost hypnotic effect on the little skier. Charlie was going faster than he realized, not because he was a daredevil, but because there was no one else on the hill for comparison. He skied faster and faster. When he caught an edge in a frozen rut it happened so fast it was like a dream. The ski edge caught and twisted, and Charlie instinctively shifted his weight to counter the pull of the trapped ski. Probably nothing could have saved him from a fall, but this sudden weight shift turned his trapped leg into a lever that catapulted him into a somersault and sent him flailing through the air ten feet before he came down hard on his left leg and broke it. The place where Charlie fell was only three feet beyond the edge of the trail. Just far enough to make him invisible when the ski patrol cleared the mountain some twenty minutes later.

Charlie blacked out immediately. He didn't see or hear the three ski patrolmen who came down the trail searching, deliberately yodeling and pausing to listen for cries for help. Whizzer by that time had found his master and lay silently guarding the unconscious boy as the ski patrol passed by.

When Charlie revived, it was with Whizzer's wet nose nuzzling his cheek just like he did every morning in Charlie's warm bed at the lodge. "Good morning, Whizzer," he said weakly. Then he realized where he was. It was dark on the mountain. The injured leg was twisted under him and throbbing. Charlie leaned back and tried to straighten out. He put his arm around the big red dog. Then he fainted from the pain.

Fifty anxious people gathered at the base of the tramway. There were a dozen instructors, fifteen Ski Patrollers, Jake and Cassie and Pepi Prager and Frank Carson. The rest were guests. The Ski Patrol had eight powerful electric torches, and Frank Carson divided his men into eight search groups. Each group would have two Ski Patrollers and one or two instructors. Eight groups to cover twenty-three trails. It would be sheer luck if they found Charlie on the first sweep. And while nobody said so, it would be lucky to find him at all in the immense darkness of Sky Mountain.

Jake gave the signal and the tramway began its smooth ghostly ascent of Sky Mountain. Jake and Cassie stood holding hands at the front of the car. It was a curiously beautiful ride, and they started it very quietly. Jake new, and Cassie knew, this was no routine search for just another kid. Charlie Lamont was just about all his mother had to hold her life together.

As the softly humming cables lifted them above the valley floor, they could see the almost full moon begin its nightly courtship of Sky Mountain. The moonlight glinted off the silent ski trails. Far down the valley they could see the clustered lights of Sky Junction and the one pale yellow dot that marked Zeke Gibbs's old ranch house. Jake drew Cassie closer.

"He's all right. I know it."

"Jake, if . . . I lose Charlie . . . God! Why did I let him go up there alone?"

"Because the kid can ski. Because he's got a good head on him. Because Whizzer's with him."

"He's dead. I can feel it."

"Stop that, Cassie. Cut it out."

"I'm sorry."

"It counts a lot that Whizzer's with him."

"Let's hope so," Her voice was getting more desperate with every word.

"You know where Goldens come from? They were sheep dogs in the Ural Mountains, which have to be about the coldest mountains in the world. In fact it gets so cold there the shepherds can't take it. So what they do is leave their sheep and a few Golden Retrievers and a stock of food in the mountain pastures all winter long. Those dogs take care of the flock for months on end. Now if a Golden can take care of a whole herd of sheep for a winter, it figures he can take care of one small boy for a couple of hours, right?"

"I think I'm going to pray."

"We're all praying, Cassie. One way or another."

"God could not be that much of a sadist."

"Cassie. He's all right. I feel it."

"Everything's always all right for you, isn't it, Jake?"

"Not always."

"Jake. He's out there dying."

"We've got the best skiers in the world. We'll find him."

"In what kind of shape?"

The tramcar glided to a halt at the top of Sky Mountain and the fifty searchers got out as quietly as they had got on. The eight groups of searchers prepared to ski the fourteen trails on the list of trails that might have appealed to Charlie. Everyone expected at least two sweeps of Sky Mountain, and maybe more. Pepi handed out chocolate bars. It was cold, and few of the searchers had eaten since lunch.

Quietly and with torches flashing the eight little groups split off to probe their several trails. In the still

December moonlight every one felt a humbling sense of the power of Sky Mountain.

Over the top of the mountain torches flickered off the snow and swept from side to side of the empty trails. The searchers sideslipped along the very edges of the trails, peering intently into the black woods. The theory was simple: if the Ski Patrol missed the boy the chances were he was off the trail. Which trail, and how far off, might mean the difference between Charlie alive and Charlie dead. Some shouted. Some listened. The boy's name echoed down Sky Mountain and hung in the frosted air: "Charlie! Charlie! Charlie!"

The answer was a silence so enormous and forbidding that it took on a physical presence. The silence became their enemy more than the cold or the night. "Charlie! Charlie! Charlie!"

Cassie and Jake were in the party that took Wardance. It was the toughest of the trails Charlie might have chosen, and they knew he had taken it on his first run of the day.

To Jake, the fact that Charlie skied Wardance once that day made him sure the boy would pick some other trail for his only other run. But Cassie didn't agree, and Jake wasn't going to budge an inch from Cassie. They skied side by side, at the edge of the trail, sideslipping their skis slowly, calling out and pausing to listen at frequent intervals. "Charlie!" Cassie's voice was never large. Now it was at the point of cracking. "Charlie!" Jake waited until she slipped down to him. For a moment they paused, silent, listening. He put his arm around her. Cassie's slim body was shuddering with quiet sobs. Jake said nothing. He just held her. And that is how they stood when Jean-Pierre's red signal flare lit up the sky like a smile from God.

Jean-Pierre and Frank Carson led the search down Milky Way. Though Milky Way was the easiest trail to ski, it was also the widest. There was always the possibility the boy might have fallen in the middle of a very wide trail and been overlooked by the Ski Patrol sweep. "Charlie!" Jean-Pierre called. "Charlie!" Silence. They made their cautious way down the trail all but oblivious to the eerie beauty of it.

The skied without talking for fear of missing a call for help.

"Charlie! Charlie!" The shouts got more urgent as the party made progress down the trail and the chances of finding the boy dwindled.

About halfway down the trail, Jean-Pierre tried something new: "Whizzaire!" he shouted into the wall of trees, "Whizzaire!" Silence. Then, just as the young Frenchman was about to move down the trail a little, there came, unmistakably, the throaty bark of the big red dog. Again, Jean-Pierre called. And again Whizzer barked, twice. They were close now. The dog was not far off, and on their left. Finally Jean-Pierre flashed the torch and its glow reflected from Whizzer's eyes. The big dog lay calmly where he was, guarding the unconscious boy and keeping him warm.

Charlie Lamont lay sleeping next to the dog. One cheek had the telltale white spot of frostbite. But he was alive. Frank Carson quickly splinted Charlie's leg, injected a stimulant and got him on the toboggan. Whizzer rode the aluminum ski patrol toboggan too, crouching next to his master all the way down Sky Mountain.

Jake and Cassie stood close together at the edge of the trail, his arm around her, Cassie's upturned face pale in the red glow and paler as the flare sank and died. They had no words to say.

With one instinctive motion they turned on their skis and pushed off down the steep trail as fast as the moonlight and their emotions would let them. Jake led the way with Cassie close behind. They flew down the mountain, a pair of silent shadows darting and gliding among the even darker trees, pausing only once for breath during the run down Sky Mountain. Their concern turned them into skiing machines with one fixed goal: to be at the bottom of the mountain before Charlie got there. At the lodge they stopped and took off their skiis. And waited.

They didn't wait long. The red flare had started all the searchers down the mountain as fast as they dared ski. Soon Jake and Cassie were the center of a milling group. None of them knew who had found Charlie, or what shape he might be in.

"He has a good parka on." Cassie spoke softly to no one in particular. "It's a down parka. Very warm." What she was thinking was, *What if it isn't the cold at all? What if he smashed into something? Broke his neck. He could be paralyzed. He could be dead.* Cassie was not fearful by nature, but nature had made her a mother and she felt the gut fear of all mothers, the instinctive certainty that only she stood between her child and the pitfalls of the world. Jake stood by her, holding her hand and saying nothing. He'd said it all. Now the most he could do was be there. Their eyes were drawn to Sky Mountain. Here and there a lingering torch flickered on the trails. Now and then a shout cut through the night.

"They'll be here soon." Jake shifted his weight inside his big yellow ski boots.

"Do you believe in God?" Cassie's voice was just this side of a whisper.

"I think I'm starting to." He squeezed her hand.

"Me too."

A torch came into view near the runoff from Milky Way. It was moving much slower than a normal skier's pace. They knew it must be the toboggan. Slowly, slowly the torch moved towards them. As it drew nearer they could make out the dark funereal shape of the toboggan, black against the snow, pulled by one tall skier and restrained from behind by another. Four other skiers, anonymous in the darkness, flanked the procession on both sides. They looked like pallbearers. The pressure of Cassie's hand on Jake's arm spoke her fear more eloquently than words. The procession drew nearer, but slowly, like some dream sequence in a movie. Jean-Pierre, seeing Cassie, left the procession and skied up to her. "He is OK, Cassie," said the Frenchman with a grin; "the leg is broken—but not badly. Your Charlie is going to be fine." But before Jean-Pierre had quite delivered this news Cassie broke away and ran stumbling up the hill toward the toboggan. Halfway there, she slipped in the soft snow and fell, picked herself up, and ran on. They stopped the parade. Cassie knelt next to the toboggan. Partially revived by the injection, Charlie was awake now and almost enjoying his free ride. "Charlie. Oh, my Charlie!"

"Hi, Mom. Whizzer and I had a ride. Didn't we, Whizzer?" The dog barked happily. Charlie looked up at his mother and frowned. "Why are you crying, Mom? What's wrong?"

"Nothing, Charlie. Nothing's the matter. Everything's just fine." Cassie turned her head aside to hide the rush of tears. Then the ski patrolmen picked up the toboggan and used it as a stretcher to bring the boy inside.

Bill Shepherd leaned over Charlie. "Do you mind needles, Charlie?"

"Yes, I already had one." The boy's voice was drowsy in the sudden warmth of his own safe bedroom. The flush had returned to his cheeks. Bill Shepherd had neatly cut Charlie's ski pants all the way up to the seam to get them off without disturbing the fracture. It felt like a clean break just above the ankle. Bill made a firm temporary splint and bandaged it and set about giving Charlie an anesthetic. Tomorrow would be soon enough to X-ray and apply a cast. Meanwhile the boy needed warmth and rest. One toe was frostbitten, but that would come back as Charlie's circulation improved. Jake and Cassie stood at the foot of Charlie's bed. Whizzer sat on his haunches next to them, watching Bill Shepherd alertly as the young doctor worked over Charlie's leg.

"Well, it's just a little sting, Charlie. And it'll help the pain. You've been pretty brave already. Now I'm going to ask you to be brave again, OK?"

"OK." Charlie winced as the hypodermic needle went into his arm.

"Good boy. That wasn't so bad, now, was it?"

"Not really." Already Charlie's small voice was fading into sleep. He looked at Whizzer and smiled. "Good night, Whizzer." His eyes shut before he was quite through saying it.

"You're lucky, Mrs. Lamont. That dog probably saved Charlie's life."

"I know. I know."

"He'll be fine. No more skiing this season, though."

"I think we've all had enough skiing for the moment." Cassie managed a laugh. "How about a drink, Doctor?"

"Sounds fine. Thanks."

They were just leaving Charlie's room when Jean-Pierre poked his head in. "Charlie is OK?"

"Jean-Pierre! I didn't even thank you." Cassie stood on tiptoe and kissed the young man on the cheek, which made him blush furiously.

"Ah, Cassie, I did nothing." He pointed dramatically at Whizzer. "*There* is the hero." They all laughed and went to have a drink.

There was excitement in the bar. Although the adventure had lasted only two hours, everyone had a theory about it. The room was filled with reporters who knew a good human-interest story when it dropped into their laps. Cassie and Jake were surrounded and quickly begged off: yes, there would be details and pictures tomorrow. Yes, the boy was going to be fine. Yes, the dog was a hero. Yes, Sky High had an absolutely crack Ski Patrol. Finally they disentangled themselves and joined Bill Shepherd in a corner. Bill had a beer. Cassie and Jake sipped red wine. "I think, Doctor, I may be your next patient." Cassie smiled over her big wine glass. "I am in shock."

"Please call me Bill. You have every right to be in shock. We all are, kind of."

"How is he?" Zem Gibbs had waited in the bar while Bill attended Charlie. Now she separated herself from a knot of admiring ski instructors and perched on the arm of Bill's chair.

"He's going to be fine, Zem, thanks." Cassie liked the girl. Any quarrel between Zem's grandfather and Jake Chaffee was not allowed to intrude. Jake liked the girl too, what he knew of her. "Well," said Cassie, raising her glass, "here's to the scariest night of my life. May I never have another like it."

"Here's to happy endings." Bill Shepherd lifted his glass to Cassie but looked at Zem.

"Amen!" said Jake, meaning it. "You know what? I am famished." None of them had thought about eating. They descended on Peng's dining room like Biblical locusts, hungry and thirsty and revved-up by their adventures. Jake insisted that Bill and Zem join them. Sky Junction's only doctor was a good man to know. Especially if he was going to marry the girl who would own Sky Ranch. They found a round table at the window.

"What in the world," asked Zem, looking at the handsome sky-blue menu, "are quenelles de brochet?"

"Fish meatballs!" said Jake with a grin. "And very good they are, too." Jake looked up as a busboy handed him a note. But he didn't have to read it. There in the doorway stood a tall, thin, nervous-looking girl dressed in old blue jeans and a tired sweater. She hesitated and looked at the floor. "Eliza!" Jake ran to the girl and kissed her.

"Daddy, I'm sorry I didn't call first."

"Cut it out, honey. I'm thrilled to see you safe. You must be starving." Jake felt a twinge of guilt. He'd been so worried about Charlie, he hadn't thought about Eliza for hours.

"I am starving, kind of. Been driving since yesterday morning."

"Well, you'll join us. Naturally. We're just starting. But first, you've got to call your mother. She's going out of her mind. You know, we do worry."

"I know." There was a dead tone in Eliza's voice. Jake looked at her quickly: for a moment she sounded drugged. But her eyes were clear.

"OK. Go wash up and call your mother and then join us here. Use my room for now. We'll settle you someplace else later on." He hugged her and handed her a key.

"OK, Daddy. You're sure you're not mad?"

"I am delighted. I haven't seen nearly enough of you lately, Eliza. Now, scram!" The girl walked out of the dining room and Jake went back to his table. "Never a dull moment."

"Eliza?" Cassie had seen the family resemblance.

"Eliza. Thank God."

"Well," said Cassie, "that's two missing persons accounted for. This must be our lucky day." But something in her eyes spoke of things other than luck. A day of reckoning was coming to Cassie and Jake, and in her innocence Eliza just might have brought it with her.

"I think," said Zem, "that fish meatballs sound absolutely fascinating."

"I'll settle for a quiche," said Cassie, "my tummy is still up on that mountain." They all placed their orders and Jake got busy with the wine list. He ordered a Sauvignon Blanc from a small California vineyard, one of his favorite white wines. Then he leaned back and stretched a little and sipped the wine he had in his glass, the house red. And he smiled. It had been quite a day. But Sky High had proved up to it. He looked around the big, handsome dining room. Most of his guests were finishing their late supper. The room was beautiful and so were the people in it. The food had better damn well be beautiful. All around him Jake Chaffee could feel his dream coming true. He thought of the long day and the search and the rescue and how it all conspired to bring him closer to Cassie. Jake smiled. Life was good.

10

The Eagle Airlines twin-engined Beechcraft climbed in a wide circle west of Denver and headed straight into the Rocky Mountains. Maggie and Pete Woodbury sat side by side behind the pilot. The pilot, in typical ski-country fashion, wore blue jeans, cowboy boots and a plaid lumberman's shirt. He had shaggy dark hair and a full beard, and if Maggie had known he used to be a captain for a Pan Am 747 before moving to the ski country, she would have felt a lot better about the flight. As the little plane entered the first range of mountains it hit an updraft, and bucked a little.

"Sorry about that," said the pilot cheerfully, "just one of our friendly local thermals." Maggie's hand shot out automatically and sought Pete's hand. She clutched him as if her grip alone could keep the Beechcraft in the air. She looked at him and forced a grin: "I forgot to tell you—I'm the world's worst coward."

"Shall I give you my famous number about how we're a lot safer up here than walking across Fifth Avenue on a quiet Sunday in August?"

"Thanks. But Fifth Avenue has a way of not heaving up and down underneath me."

"I'm like a kid about flying. Can't get enough of it. If I lived anywhere else, I'd get my license."

"Really?"

"Partly, it's the beauty. But more than that, it's a miracle, a kind of continuing astonishment, that we really did it. To fly! Amazing."

"Sometimes it's a little too amazing for this lady." But Maggie laughed. For the first time in her life she almost didn't mind flying. "My favorite miracle is the telephone. This year my youngest went away to school for the first time. And guess who was homesick? Me! I held out for nearly a week. Then I called. And just the sound of his voice changed everything. He hadn't fallen off the edge of the world after all."

"How many do you have?"

"Kids? I have four: Kerry, Angela, Nick Jr., and David. It was David who went away this fall. Now they're all away. I feel like a candidate for Sun City."

"In that case I'll reserve my plot today. I've got two girls myself, Stacy and Muffy. Nine and twelve. So we're just facing up to the boarding-school thing. And I sympathize. It can't be easy."

"It isn't. For all the times I've yelled my head off, for all the broken windows and broken bones and the record player melting my eardrums, every year when it's time to send 'em back I shudder. I'm one of nature's natural-born doormats."

"One of nature's better ideas, if you ask me. Your kids have one gorgeous mommy."

"Pete Woodbury! I love it."

The plane was following a valley. The peaks on their right were gold in the slanting light of late afternoon. Maggie sat back, happy and as close to being relaxed as she'd ever be in an airplane. "I brought it on myself, of course," she continued; "I'm sort of an education freak. My own education—if you could call it that—was really pretty pathetic. So I did a big 'My Kids Will Have It Better' number, and away they went."

"Comes a time when we all have to ask ourselves what, exactly, is left for us." For no reason he could put his finger on, Pete felt at ease with this stranger. He was saying things he'd never think of saying to his own wife.

"I wonder about that," she said, "a lot."

"It's why so many guys work so hard."

"And why so many wives spend so much time having floors you could eat off. Did you ever know anyone who ever ate off a floor?"

"I did. But he was a dog."

"As along as the treadmill is in motion, all's right with the world. It's kind of scary."

"Very scary. The enormous effort not to think."

"Or feel." Maggie could hardly believe some of the things she was saying. In all her marriage she'd never had a conversation with Nick even remotely resembling this one. His idea of communication was to ask her to pass the sauce. "The reason I came on this trip," she said, looking at him intently, "is to forget a lot of things." There was a slight bump as the Beechcraft feathered its wings for the descent into Steamboat Springs.

Mildred Rush lay sweating with fever in her dark cabin on the outskirts of Sky Junction. Weakly, she pulled the worn pink blanket up over her shuddering breasts because she knew that before long the chills would come. And always there was the headache, steadily pounding at the base of her skull like an army of construction workers armed with jackhammers drilling into rock—and she was the rock. She lay there, a lumpy shape in the lumpy bed. Softly, for there was no one to hear, Mildred Rush moaned. He had fired her. That sneaky little Jap had told her not to bother coming back to Sky High, they'd send whatever was due to her. As she lay there in dark and in pain, Mildred Rush could see his tight little yellow face smiling in triumph. The gloating Jap face seemed to float near the ceiling even though her eyes were shut tight against the pain. Why didn't the aspirin work? It always worked before. The face seemed to float down closer, gloating and grinning in its fiendish Japanese way. He was a Jap no matter what they called him, no matter how Frenchified he was with his sneaky Jap ways and his fancy French airs. Mildred Rush clenched her few remaining teeth and drifted off into a feverish sleep.

For the third time Tod Rubin asked at the desk for messages. And for the third time there were none. He knew it was futile: what mail didn't get to Sky Junction by noon simply didn't get there until the next day. These Americans could get to the moon quite casually but apparently getting a letter or a wire from here to there was beyond them. An odd and endearing people, the Americans. Of course, there might be a long-distance phone call . . . if the fingerprints on Pepi Prager's beer glass matched the fingerprints of Carl-Heinz Waldemar, late of the SS Corps.

Tod went back to his room and picked up a parka. He'd go for a walk. Three-thirty in the afternoon was a quiet time inside Sky Lodge. The last dawdlers had left the dining room an hour ago. It would be an hour yet before the most enthusiastic skiers quit the mountain. The bar was empty except for the dapper figure of Count Momo Ruvo di Putignano-Squillace perched on a bar stool explaining to the young bartender just how to pour Dorothy Dutton's beer. "From quite high up, you see, never less than six inches above the center of the glass for maximum oxygenation. Which produces the maximum head." Momo smiled boyishly and demonstrated. The boy behind the bar nodded. You had to be nice to the guests no matter how wigged-out they seemed. It was worth it, for the free skiing all morning long.

Tod Rubin passed through the lobby and out onto the terrace. The evening's chill was sending cold messages across Sky Valley. Already the far side of the valley was in shadow. Tod looked up and got a brief glance at the Eagle Airlines' Beechcraft that was carrying Pete Woodbury and Maggie della Robbia into Steamboat Springs. He crossed the terrace and took a path that wound up the slope past the north wing of Sky Lodge. Each unit was complete unto itself although in fact they were all connected by interior corridors. Tod climbed the path until he came to a small circular turn-around ringed by low evergreens. It made a miniature terrace overlooking the runoff from the Sky Mountain ski trails.

One small chalet stood in untypical isolation at the end of this terrace. Next to the massive redwood door was a discreet brass nameplate: PEPI PRAGER. The brass lock looked solid too, not easy to pick. Tod walked to the far side of the little terrace as if to get a better view of the skiers. He was close to Pepi's door now. He looked around the side of the chalet, hoping there might be a side door that would be easier to work on unobserved. But the snow, of course, would give him away. Unless he chose a time when snow was falling to cover his tracks. There had to be a way to get in. Tod leaned casually against the split-rail fence that edged the terrace and looked at Pepi's chalet in frank speculation. What secrets might be found inside this honest-looking little house? Was there any element of sentimentality—or, more likely, of pride—that might have compelled Waldemar (if he *was* Waldemar) to keep some reminder of the past? Tod resolved that if he hadn't heard back from STYX the next day, he'd have a look.

He knew Pepi's daily routine pretty well by now. As the ski school's star attraction, Pepi's teaching day was a long one. He was booked for every hour, two weeks in advance. He gave private lessons all morning long and then lunched, very publicly, at the Skytop restaurant on the very peak of Sky Mountain. And even when the day's skiing was over, Pepi's work went on. He usually went straight from the slopes to the Sky Bar, mingling, laughing, and adding glamor to the après-ski atmosphere. This was part of this job too, to be charming and highly visible around Sky Lodge: the celebrity-in-residence. Pepi Prager was unquestionably a very busy man. *He'd be busier,* thought Tod, chewing on a pine needle, *if he knew who's breathing down his arrogant Austrian neck.*

Tod shivered, half in pleasure, half in fear. It was a new sensation, taking the initiative. The professor would be astonished. In fact, Tod was astonished himself.

Eliza Chaffee looked at her father over a brimming cup of hot chocolate. "I'm not your little girl anymore, Daddy."

"More's the pity." He reached across the table and took her slender white hand in his wide brown one. They had been sitting in a quiet corner of the Skytop restaurant for nearly an hour, talking in low voices. Jake had learned a lot. So had Eliza. "I was upset that you didn't let your mother know, that's all. But now you're here, I love it. How long has it been, since we skied together?"

"Four years and three months."

"You ought to be the one who's mad at me."

"Daddy, I know why you haven't been home much. You don't have to apologize."

"I guess we never really talked about grownup things, have we?"

"I used to be kind of bitter about that." Eliza sipped her chocolate. "But now I understand. At least I think I do. There just isn't much point in talking to her, is there? Mummy, I mean. The message does not get through." Jake looked at his daughter and thought of all the time and love he'd meant to give her, and how he'd failed. It was amazing, he thought, that she turned out this well. And he resolved as he sat there not to let this unexpected second chance pass him by.

"Your mother is a good person, Eliza. She means well."

"So did Marie-Antoinette."

"She hasn't a mean bone in her body."

"Daddy, I'm not sure she has *any* bones in her body." She was looking right at him and he couldn't hide the flash of agreement that came into his eyes. "It's not just that she's out of touch. Plenty of parents are that. It's that she doesn't *want* to be in touch—ever. With anything."

"It's that bad?" He smiled ruefully.

"Last spring she gave a tea dance. A *tea* dance, for God's sake. And not as satire. She got all upset when I couldn't come, and shall I tell you why I couldn't go to Mummy's tea dance? I was in New York that weekend, having an abortion."

"Oh, Eliza. My God. I'm sorry. You should have told me."

"I'm sorry too. I can't recommend it as entertainment, Daddy. But it wasn't your fault. It got myself into it, and I got myself out."

"Honey, if you'd called I could have hired you a specialist, or helped, with something."

"And buy us out of a sticky situation. Oh Daddy, enough. I didn't come here to ask for pity, and I'm sick of thinking about the whole mess. We'll make a deal, OK? We won't talk about my love life and we won't talk about yours." Eliza looked straight in Jake's eyes. "We'll keep our little secrets to ourselves."

"Eliza, I don't know what you may have heard . . ."

"I hear a lot. You aren't exactly Mr. Nobody, Dad. People have eyes—and tongues."

"And they talk about Cassie and me?"

"Some people do."

"Well, Eliza, they'll probably be talking more. I'm sorry you had to hear it through rumors, instead of straight from me, and I hope before you make any judgments you'll get to know Cassie for yourself. She's very special, Eliza. I've asked her to marry me." Jake saw the surprise in Eliza's face.

"What did she say?"

"She's not sure."

"Well, that's a new ending to an old story."

"If you knew Cassie," Jake said, "you'd understand. She's quite a woman."

"I'm sure she must be," Eliza said, dropping back in her chair. "She seems very nice. But I never thought . . . marriage?"

"Look, Eliza, I want you to stay at Sky High for a while. I'll wire the college that you're sick. Get to know Cassie. Give her—give us—a chance. Will you do that?"

"Sure, Daddy."

"I'm too young to just throw in the towel, right?"

"Right." She kissed him and laughed quickly. "You know, I think I'm a little jealous."

Jake hugged her. "Eliza, you know you're still my best girl."

"I guess so, Daddy—but you'd better not let Cassie hear you say that."

They walked hand in hand out of the restaurant and buckled on their skis. For a moment Jake and his daughter stood side by side looking at the panorama that stretched for miles in every direction below them. "This," said Eliza in a reverent whisper, "is some beautiful mountain." Then they pushed off and skied down Sky Mountain and the only conversation between them was the hiss and crackle of their skis on the fine dry snow.

Cornelia de Vos made one last sweeping turn and then flashed to a stop in a spray of powder not five feet from the door to her wing of Sky Lodge. In one easy motion she knelt to unbuckle her ski bindings. Cornelia dressed for skiing in a lightly quilted nylon jump suit that fit like paint. This was white with a red circle in the middle of her chest. "My Japanese flag," she called it. The effect was dramatic. She looked like an elegant target bobbing down the slopes. Cornelia picked up her skis and poles and slid them into the wooden rack by the door. Niris's two white Afghans were frolicking loose in the new snow but their master was not to be seen. She watched the dogs with amusement. Soon. Soon the time would be ripe. She had felt his eyes on her in the bar last night before the rescue, as she stood with young Jean-Pierre. Soon an introduction would be made in the easy style of ski resorts. Perhaps by dear Noel. By Jake. Or even by Jean-Pierre himself, so amusing in his puppylike jealousy. As yet, he had nothing to be jealous about. Cornelia thought of the young Frenchman and laughed. The slender white hounds chased each other over a big snowdrift and disappeared. She thought of the Bidijar reserve and its rich black oil oozing from the hot desert halfway around the world. Yet perhaps, very near.

Dorothy Dutton sat at her dressing table making up for the cocktail hour. Her hands moved among pots and tubes and brushes with the swift assurance of a professional. It had been more than thirty years since water had been allowed to touch La Dutton's face. The look she achieved was built up layer upon layer in subtle washes of color much in the manner of an old-master painter working his canvas. There was, to begin with, an under-coating of moisturizing cream. Then came a toner. Then a very light film of makeup base. A glaze of liquid powder overall. Then individual highlights and shadows and blushes, all expertly blended to create a color scheme of dewy health and freshness on her fine-grained near seventy-year-old skin. The eyes, of course, were a project unto themselves. Hair by hair, eyelashes were painstakingly cemented into place once a month in

Paris. There was a special lightener to eliminate any suggestion of bagging underneath the eyes. Subtle shadows made her eyes seem more widely spaced, deeper, more compelling. A touch of mascara was brushed on with the finest Austrian sable-hair artist's brush. Then, her special scent, "DD," unobtainable commercially but sometimes given at Christmas or birthdays to special friends. Her hair, tinted to the original chestnut of her youth, was simply pulled back in a twist, waiting for one of her four impeccably crafted wigs. Momo lounged in a chair by the window, observing this process with the respect it deserved as a triumph of art over nature.

"Tell me, Momo," she said absently, "when did you first have sex?"

"In the womb, my dear. Most assuredly in the womb."

"No. Really."

"With a man, at age ten. With a girl, at thirteen. With various barnyard animals . . . but you don't care about the barnyard animals?"

"How immeasurably corrupt you are."

"Nothing, Dorothy, is bottomless. Not even that trench in the ocean. And you?"

"You'll laugh. It was the stable boy. Things like that really happened in those days. I mean, one couldn't possibly, not with someone of one's own class."

"Hardly. So. It has come the full circle then. From stable boys to stable boys. Or the equivalent."

"So it would seem. Is there any Moro XX?"

"Of course." He got up and went to the small refrigerator that masqueraded as a night table in every bedroom at Sky High. It was packed with two dozen tall brown bottles of the Moroccan beer. Momo popped off the cap and poured a tall glass of the pale amber brew and handed it to his wife. "Cheers!" he said, smiling sweetly.

"Cheers!" She sipped the beer with appreciation and wished for some of the peanut-butter shortbread Peng had made for her breakfast. She looked at Momo with a rare surge of approval. He was too beautifully dressed, as always. Brown suede trousers cut in a mockery of a cowboy's blue jeans clung to his narrow hips. Tan cashmere turtleneck. Brown suede boots which matched the trousers exactly. "That color becomes you, Momo."

"Thank you, my dear. You're looking heavenly tonight yourself. Do you like it here?"

"It's got something. The people are nice. Pity we don't ski."

"His name is Jean-Pierre Belfort."

"Whose name?"

"The beautiful young Frenchman you were admiring last night."

"Ah, my so-observant Momo. Well, he is beautiful. But that hussy de Vos seemed to be rather in control, from what I could make out."

"Don't be too harsh, my pet. I hear she's quite amusing."

"As hookers go."

"Not quite a hooker, Dorothy. Simply a brave young girl trying to make her way in the world."

"From bed to bed to bed."

"Now Dorothy, that was hardly charitable. People in glass palaces . . ."

"I never asked for a cent."

"I should hope not. But let us be frank. Is doing it with money a more attractive moral proposition than doing it for money?"

"Momo, I couldn't give a flying fuck if de Vos hooks her way to the moon before Sunday. Let's not fight, shall we? Especially not over the likes of her."

"You are at your most charming when you are most diplomatic, my dove." Momo glided across the room and kissed her lightly on the forehead as he had learned to do, where it was least likely to disturb her makeup.

Cassie closed her account book and stood up. It was time to look in on Charlie. She walked past the registration desk on her way to the kitchen for hot chocolate. And nearly bumped into Tod Rubin. "Excuse me," she said, "is there anything I can help you with, Mr. Rubin?"

"Oh, thank you, but no. I was hoping for a message, but it doesn't seem to have come."

"Sometimes the mails get a little slow when the snows

come. But it'll get here. Sooner or later."

"That is just what I feared."

"If there's anything we can do . . . maybe send a wire?"

"Oh, no. Thank you very much." He smiled and walked into the bar even though he didn't particularly want a drink. Anything to cut the conversation short. Cassie shrugged and went on her way. Tod Rubin looked troubled. She hoped it wasn't anything about the hotel.

Charlie Lamont sat up in bed working a large jigsaw puzzle. His new cast made a big mountain halfway down the bed. Whizzer sat on the foot of the bed, his face between his paws, looking expectantly up at Charlie, wondering when they were going skiing. Bill Shepherd had taken Charlie to his office that morning for X-rays and a cast. The break was clean, a few inches above the ankle, and promised no trouble. But it would be better to stay off it for a few days all the same.

"How goes it, Charlie?"

"OK, I guess. Except I can't find the top of the castle." Cassie pulled up a chair and sat next to the boy while he drank the hot chocolate. "Take an old lady's advice and look in that pile on the right. And do me a favor, will you?"

"Sure. What?"

"Don't let Whizzer sit on your cast, OK? We have to keep it really straight for a few days."

"Whizzer wouldn't hurt me, Mom."

"Of course not, but sometimes he gets frisky and that is just what you don't need."

"Whizzer is a hero. Aren't you, Whizzer?" All afternoon the reporters had been streaming in for pictures and Charlie's version of the story. Within a few days the rescue would be international news, much to the delight of Dud Drummond, who organized the publicity as though the whole episode had been his invention.

"Sure he's a hero. Charlie, did I tell you Jake's daughter drove up for a visit?"

"Nope."

"Her name's Eliza. Later on I'll bring her in to meet you. She's very nice."

"How long is she staying?" he asked, not caring.

"I'm not sure. Probably not long. Charlie?"

"What?"

"Know how many times your father broke his legs?"

"I bet never."

"He broke his right leg three times and his left ankle once. And that was just in the six years I knew him. He always used to tell me, 'If you don't fall, you're not trying hard enough.' So, don't feel bad, all right?"

"I don't feel bad, Mom. Just dumb."

"Well, you aren't dumb. You're brave and a good skier and I love you to pieces." She bent over and kissed him. Charlie squirmed, embarrassed but pleased. Then Cassie stood up again. There was a pile of work to be done.

11

No one believed his real name was Noel Northcliff although in fact it was. "Noel Northcliff" had a made-up sound to it, a bit too slick, stagy, as-written-by-Evelyn Waugh. Noel stood in his room thinking about shirts. When you have been a kid in the slums of Liverpool with one shirt to your name and that one none too clean, shirts take on a special importance. Noel opened the redwood dresser and smiled. Two dozen of the finest shirts in the world seemed to smile back. They lay in rows, an aristocracy of silk and Egyptian cotton and cashmere, self-confident shirts, shirts that could do no wrong. An old man in Jermyn Street in London did nothing but make such shirts. He made them for two members of the British royal family, for three kings (one reigning, two in exile), for the Aga Khan and for Noel Northcliff. Money alone could not buy them. To be accepted as a customer by the little old man in Jermyn Street was to gain admission to one of the world's most exclusive clubs. Northcliff counted having done this as one of his proudest achievements.

He looked in the mirror and was pleased to find the suntan he'd picked up on the beach in Sardinia last week was sustaining itself nicely in the sunlight of nine thousand feet in the Rockies. "Snow tans," thought NN, making a mental note for later use in his column, "are actually quicker and deeper than beach tans." It must have something to do with the reflective qualities of snow. This could be material for a feature article in, say, *Vogue*. A quick few thousand dollars and the article would practically write itself. One checkout with a dermatologist would do it. And what dermatologist wouldn't be thrilled at being mentioned in a Noel Northcliff article?

Tomorrow he'd call his agent in New York. He'd been out of touch nearly a week now. But wherever NN was in the world's most sybaritic playgrounds, he was working and working hard. The smile and the well-honed irony masked a mind that could retain information like a computer. In his chic little town house on West Twelfth Street off Fifth Avenue in New York, NN had his own small research center complete with a microfilm read-out machine like the ones at the *New York Times* library. Here, cross-referenced by country, by city, by sex and source of income, were all the people who might be of interest to the readers of *Living It Up*. Thus, on hearing of some debutante's bad behavior in Palm Beach, NN could instantly produce the names of her dowager grandmother's first five husbands, her dog, her hairdresser and her yacht. This gave NN's writing a depth and color that other society columnists lacked. It had taken him years to create the filing system and he was justly proud of it. Every two years NN produced a book, and for every book, the microfilm files did half the work.

Noel tied an emerald silk scarf around his neck and put on a navy-blue Cardin blazer. Dorothy Dutton's card lay on the dresser. The card was a single slab of hand-laid parchment the color of old ivory. She had written in her unformed scrawl, "Dearest Noel, Momo and I would adore for you to dine with us tonight. Don't bother to answer, just meet us in the bar around seven. Love, Dorothy." She was up to something. NN wondered what.

Noel's microfilm file had a whole cassette devoted to the bizarre career of Dorothy Dutton-Langfeld-Harper-la Princesse Parmentier-Schwartz-Lady Westfield-Morgan-Countess Ruvo di Putignano-Squillace. Looking at the splendid card and shrewdly guessing its cost, NN laughed out loud imagining her stationery bills. *Someday*, he thought, *I'll write her biography, uncensored. And what a best-seller that will make.*

Like many things in life, her story was more bizarre

than fiction would dare invent. Dorothy Dutton was the prototype of the Poor Little Rich Girl, a public figure from the cradle in a time when the lurid press devoted forests of newsprint to America's robber-baron rich. Dorothy: heiress to a four-hundred-million-dollar tobacco fortune, at age three the hotly contested prize in a scandalous custody battle, reared finally by a hysterical Baptist maiden aunt on the forty-thousand-acre Dutton estate near Asheville. Dorothy's father, Deke Dutton, won the custody battle but lost his daughter in a no-contest race between Dorothy and his first and abiding passion, sour-mash bourbon whiskey. By the time Deke Dutton achieved the ultimate bourbon blackout and died institutionalized at forty, Dorothy was sixteen and spending long musky afternoons in Asheville screwing the stable boy who was the first young man to smile at her motivated not by greed but honest lust. She would never be quite so happy again.

The Baptist aunt found them one gold September afternoon and fainted into a steaming pile of fresh horse manure, which, though impeccably Thoroughbred, did nothing to cool that lady's indignation. Auntie packed her bags and her trust fund that very night, and Dorothy found herself the ward of two very large banks and a holding company, none of which had any idea in the world what to do with her. She solved their problem by marrying one of the bankers, Preston Langfeld. He was forty, just the age her father had been, good-looking, rich and completely stupid. Yale, with its clubs and tailors and polished accents, had done everything it could for Preston Langfeld. But everything was not enough.

Two years of life as Mrs. Preston Langfeld failed to drive Dorothy mad with boredom, which says more for Dorothy's tough-mindedness than it does for life with Langfeld. She was nineteen and rather pretty and not stupid at all. They moved between their house on Fifth Avenue to their house at Oyster Bay and to other people's houses at similar addresses filled with similar people wearing similar clothes and not thinking as hard as they could. But Dorothy thought. And what she thought was, *There has to be more to life than this.*

Dorothy Dutton Langfeld went out to find that life,

armed with only her youth, her courage, her four hundred million dollars and her determination never to be bored again.

The first thing she found was J. J. Harper. JJ was tall, bony and a flaming communist. He believed passionately in free everything, including, of course, free love. Dorothy, delighted, dug out her oldest tweeds and sweaters and moved into Harper's cellar flat in Greenwich Village, where they ate undercooked pasta, drank raw guinea red wine and planned the revolution.

JJ would defend to the death any theory he cared about. When it came to facts, he was less brave. So Dorothy discovered the day she announced she was pregnant. She had imagined he'd be pleased: a child of the revolution and all that. JJ turned pale. Then he turned angry, accusing Dorothy of harboring the decadent values of the outmoded bourgeoisie. What he meant was, *Get rid of it.* Dorothy turned and walked out of the basement room and all the way up Fifth Avenue to the Plaza, where she checked into a suite and took an hour-long bath in the biggest tub in New York and ordered pheasant and champagne for one. So much for communism. The next day Dorothy's lawyers knocked on J. J. Harper's door. She saw him once more, at City Hall, the day they signed the marriage license.

Dorothy sailed on the Ile de France and was driven to a clinic in Zurich to wait for the baby. It was a boy, born prematurely and dead. She was twenty.

Paris offers many consolations to the young and the rich and the sad and Dorothy Dutton tried them all. She had never thought much about clothes. Paris taught her about dressing. There was something sensuous, dreamlike, in the long afternoons of showings and fittings at Chanel and Vionnet and Worth. The feel of priceless fabrics sliding on her thin body as seemingly disembodied hands draped and pinned and fitted and held up mirrors sent Dorothy into a kind of trance. From age twenty-one Dorothy Dutton would be a living testimony to the finest couture Paris could invent.

Dorothy had never cared much about food. Paris taught her how to eat. In Deke Dutton's château in Asheville a black mammy had made grits and gravy. In

Paris Dorothy learned the language of sauces and the significance of undercooked green vegetables and discovered that a meal could be a sensual experience.

Dorothy Dutton had never been in love. There had been three men in her life: the stable boy, Preston Langfeld, and J. J. Harper. The first two were expedients. JJ was an experiment that failed. But the word "love" wouldn't describe her feelings for any of them. Paris taught Dorothy about love.

There were five other baptismal names between "Jacques" and "Parmentier," and of course he was a prince. Jacques was thirty and tall for a Frenchman. He cared about two things: racing cars and sex. The Parmentiers were rich but conservative. Jacques had to earn his way in the racing world and he had done spectacularly well at it. At twenty-four he was the youngest member of the Bugatti factory team, with victories at Montlhery and in the Mille Miglia. He made headlines with his cars and his girls in the bubbly postwar years.

They met almost by accident, although they were fated to meet since the world they moved in was a small world fenced in by platinum. She was leaving a party early and he was arriving late, and a friend introduced them. "Enchantée," said Dorothy. "How do you do?" asked Jacques Parmentier, shaking her hand instead of kissing it because it was fashionable to be American that year, the year of Scott Fitzgerald and Hemingway and all the sad rich Americans in Paris. Then, still holding Dorothy's hand, he turned, murmuring something to his friends, and led her down into the courtyard and into his car, a flame-red Bugatti which only had room for two.

The engine growled to life and roared and settled into a throaty rumble as they sped along the Quai de la Tournelle towards the Seine. Soon they were on the outskirts, following the Seine to its birthplace in a blur of speed and anticipation. They were in farmland now and Dorothy could smell what she couldn't see: wet earth and barnyards and the mist from the Seine. Jacques slowed the car, but only a little, as they crossed an ancient stone bridge in the town of Corbeil-Essones. Then he cut off to a dirt road that soon led them to a pair of enormous wrought-iron gates standing open in the moonlight. The red Bugatti escorted its trail of dust along a drive flanked by three-hundred-year-old beech trees. The drive widened into a large oval courtyard with an oval reflecting pool in the middle. This pool reflected the white bulk of Parmentier-la-Fôret, the most beautiful château Dorothy had ever seen.

Jacques silenced the car and led her through a secret door built into the enormous front door. The main hall of the château was paved in stone and sparsely furnished. Jacques found a light switch and led her into a small drawing room with walls of faded green satin moiré, furnished in the style of Louis XVI. He pulled a hidden cord, and a butler in livery appeared. Supper was ordered. "My mother," said Jacques over a simple meal of cold pâté, cheese, salad and wine, "never comes here. She finds it drafty."

Later, in bed, it was anything but drafty. They made love in a huge feather bed with four posts and a canopy of worn red velvet. Jacques Parmentier proved his reputation as the best lover in Europe.

Dorothy Dutton Langfeld Harper became la Princesse Parmentier in a small family ceremony in the private chapel of the Parmentier town house in Paris. Jacques' family had serious reservations about his bride's suitability to bear the Parmentier heirs. But in France money conquers all, and no one on earth could dispute the suitability of the Dutton legacy.

They lived at Parmentier-la-Fôret for a year and half of fairy-tale happiness, while their youth and their well-matched desires and their inexhaustible money conspired to perfect the dream.

In the road named Moyenne Corniche there is a curve. The curve itself has no name although it is something of a beauty spot, high above Monaco. It was on this curve that Jacques Parmentier came flying out of control in his Bugatti blue Team 7 racing car in the Monaco Grand Prix of 1927. Something had gone wrong with the left front wheel bearing and the wheel buckled under. The car spun, swerved and then bounced over the stone wall, landing in a ball of deadly fire in a field of pink carnations.

Although there was no doubt who had been driving the car, Jacques Parmentier could only be identified by the ancient signet ring he always wore on his right hand.

Grief is not the right word for what Dorothy Dutton felt at Jacques' death. She went into an uncontrollable depression that lasted six weeks. During this time she stayed in seclusion at Parmentier-la-Fôret surrounded by nurses and flowers, drugged with a tonic she later discovered to contain heroin.

The Parmentier family closed ranks around the grief-stricken young Princesse and proceeded to make her life unbearable as only a determined French family can. Drugged, persecuted and alone, Dorothy remained virtually a prisoner in Parmentier-la-Fôret. She realized that with Jacques gone, she had no friends at all.

There came a day when the tonic ran out and Dorothy woke up with a clear head. She got dressed, ate breakfast, packed her jewels and a few keepsakes to remind her of Jacques, and walked down a back staircase to the stable where Jacques had kept his cars. Dorothy struggled to open the heavy stable door. Two low-slung open racing cars and a big town car waited. With a sigh, she flung her bag into the red Bugatti. Driving down the beech allée in the morning sunlight, Dorothy passed through the château gates for the last time. God, she decided, did not want her to be happy. Well, if she couldn't be happy, she could at least have fun. Smiling a tight little smile, Dorothy roared through the gates and never looked back.

For three years Dorothy Dutton dragged the name of Parmentier through the scandal sheets of the world, laughing all the way. La Princesse Parmentier gave a masked ball in Venice at which more than one guest showed up nude. La Princesse Parmentier chartered the biggest available yacht and with the help of forty-three friends proceeded to lay the Greek islands to waste all one summer. La Princesse Parmentier, for reasons unspecified, was *non grata* at the Dolder in Zurich. "The Swiss," she was quoted as saying, "have no imagination." Finally one night la Princesse Parmentier found herself in a marble terrace high above Beverly Hills in the humid and depressed July of 1931 saying "Why not?" to a slick but amusing gangster-turned-movie-producer named Aldo Schwartz.

Thus began Dorothy's brief but lurid Hollywood period. To Dorothy, who had devoted years and millions to creating her own fantasy world, the ready-made fantasy of Hollywood in the early 1930s seemed like an enormous toy created for her amusement. Bitter men with newspapers in their shoes fought for stale bread on the Bowery while millionaire ex-hatcheck girls wearing lamé and emeralds and fuck-me smiles came gliding up Dorothy's long driveway in improbable motorcars with unpronounceable names and fifty coats of hand-rubbed lacquer. The nights were filled with warm flesh and persistent laughter and the false poignancy of blues played by black musicians who lunched at the Brown Derby.

But like most people who play with toys, Dorothy's attention span was growning shorter and shorter. The enormous palm-fringed plaything tucked in between the Pacific and the Sierra was just beginning to wind down for Dorothy when Bunny Westfield sailed into her life, on a large white yacht.

Dorothy and Marion Davies were assembling a giant jigsaw puzzle on the terrace of Marion's house at Malibu. Slowly, imperceptibly, a very large white yacht slid up the coast and dropped anchor offshore. A white motor launch was lowered and a white-clad man climbed into it. He was carrying a package. Marion looked up through her big sunglasses: "Now who could that be?" The launch nudged its way into the beach and the man in white vaulted over the side, landing like a dancer on dry sand.

"I am here," said Bunny Westfield, "with your clotted cream."

"Bunny!" Marion jumped up and kissed him. Introductions were made. Bunny proved to be Charles, Lord Westfield. He was rich, well-educated, tall, eccentric, unmarried and with an international reputation as a practical joker. Dorothy had never met anyone like him. "I have sailed in that tub," Bunny said, "six thousand lonely miles to deliver Marion's highly illicit clotted cream." It seemed that Marion and Mr. Hearst had stayed with Bunny the year before while Hearst tried unsuccessfully to persuade Bunny to sell him a small thirteenth-century abbey. In Westfield Manor, Marion had fallen in love with clotted cream, and, for reasons best known to the United States customs authorities, clotted cream could not be legally imported. Thus, the characteristically wild gallantry of Bunny's gesture.

"This," proclaimed Marion Davies, "calls for a party!"

When the white yacht sailed for England, Dorothy Dutton Langfield Harper Parmentier Schwartz was on it. "The important thing," said Bunny as they lay nude in the moonlight, "is never to be bored."

For six years, from 1933 until 1939, Dorothy reigned at Westfield Manor as Lady Westfield, leading the racy set in England on a merry and well-publicized chase after several kinds of pleasure. This was the time of Dorothy's only real education. She read for the first time in her life, she saw the best theater. She and Bunny filled Westfield Manor with the wittiest and most interesting writers, actors, musicians and artists they could find. The ancient halls of Westfield Manor now rocked to jazz at dawn, after which beds that were part of the history of England creaked with the strain of many kinds of lovemaking. Through it all Bunny remained Bunny: kind and funny and unshockable. Their baby, the present Lord Charles, was born in 1937 to world-wide headlines. Dorothy was almost certain the child was Bunny's. Then the war came.

Bunny had been flying his own Sopwith Camel since boyhood. He was among the first to enlist in the RAF. And he was among the first RAF fighter pilots to be shot down in the Battle of Britain. Dorothy, Lady Westfield, was left with a two-year-old son and an estate to run. She tried very hard. Dorothy organized the farmers and sent meat and dairy products and grain to the local hospitals and orphanages. As the bombings got worse in the cities, she turned the seldom-used twenty-three room Queen Anne wing of Westfield into a dormitory for evacuated children. Her own baby had two nannies and three nurserymaids. While Dorothy spent as much time with him as she could, it seemed that some well-starched nursery bureaucrat was always taking Charles off to be washed or combed or potty-trained.

The war was therapy for Dorothy. For nearly two years she was too caught up in it to look at a man with any speculation other than whether he could be persuaded to till, sow, mow or polish the ancestral silver. Then the Americans appeared.

Dorothy's own private Americans were a highly secretive crew of Air Force intelligence operatives who requisitioned an old manor house ten miles down the road. Within two weeks they had the run-down place wire-fenced and fitted with mysterious electrical devices. It was June of 1943. Dorothy invited all the officers to dinner at Westfield.

The American general was an unreconstructed Tennessee redneck so marinated in whiskey he could scarcely talk. But his aide-de-camp was Johnny Morgan. Even Dorothy had read Johnny Morgan's book *Slumchild*. It had been the last big best-seller in America before the war, a frank, funny, sexy and scorching novel about a kid fighting his way to manhood in New York's Hell's Kitchen. The book had inspired great praise, great shock and record-breaking sales. Morgan was being talked about as a new Hemingway.

Now Johnny Morgan sat in the great dining room at Westfield Manor eating partridge whose distant ancestors had been hunted by Henry VIII. Johnny Morgan made Dorothy laugh.

"To the hardships of battle!" he said, smiling, raising his glass to her.

"Cheers, Major."

"Johnny!"

"Johnny. I liked your book."

"I like your canteen."

"Are you working on a new one?"

"I'm taking notes." He was a dark compact man with the build of a middleweight boxer: all chest and not much neck. You could imagine Johnny Morgan as a longshoreman or a truck driver or a prizefighter: it was surprising that he worked with words.

It soon became obvious that the general would have to be escorted back to the base before he became totally comatose. Grinning philosophically, Johnny Morgan steered the aged party out to their Jeep. The next week she asked him back alone.

"I can't figure it," He said, lying on her enormous feather bed, Dorothy's head nestled under his arm, his hard prizefighter's body relaxed after love.

"Can't figure what, Johnny?"

"Me. Here. This. It's not my kind of act at all."

"And what is your kind of act?"

"Less fancy."

"A slum, Johnny," she said, stroking his chest with one finger, "is a nice place to leave." He turned to her, rigid with desire.

Johnny Morgan became a fixture at Westfield Manor that year. But then 1944 turned into 1945. Johnny's unit moved to France shortly after D-Day. Only when he was gone and in danger did Dorothy know what the funny, blunt, sad-eyed writer meant to her. If she ever saw him again, she promised herself, she'd tell him.

The war had been over nearly a year and it had been six months since her last letter from Johnny. She tried to pull strings but no one would tell her a thing: it had been a very secret operation indeed. Lord Charles Westfield was now old enough to be packed away to boarding school to prep for Eton. Dorothy deferred to generations of Westfield tradition. The child left one wet September day, and Dorothy went into a funk that lasted two weeks.

She sat in the library one afternoon idly flipping the pages of *Country Life* and letting her solitary tea grow cold, wondering whether she could get through this day without jumping out of her skin. The library door creaked open and the voice of Webster the butler drifted in on clouds of arrogance: "Major Morgan, My Lady." He was thinner and the big eyes looked hungrier than ever.

"Marry me."

"Oh, Johnny. Of course."

They settled into Westfield Manor for Johnny to finish his war book. He went at his writing with the same energy and almost desperate honesty that marked everything he did. A year later six hundred pages went to

Johnny's publisher, and after six months, *Rage of Battle* appeared. All the other war books looked pale and artificial. Young Lord Charles had settled into the pattern of his aristocratic life. Johnny wanted to move back to the States. Over this they had their first quarrel: she was afraid of neglecting the boy. But Pan Am was flying the Atlantic in fourteen hours and before long the jets would cut that in half. Lord Charles was in school most of the time at any rate. They moved back to New York in 1948. Johnny found himself famous. That was the year he began drinking.

New York loved Johnny Morgan. They loved the way he wrote, his tough-guy directness, feisty manners and four-letter-word conversation. *Rage of Battle* won him a Pulitzer Prize in 1949 and all the literary world waited for his next book. It would be ten years coming.

Dorothy had designed his study on the third floor of the Sutton Place house, a small room lined with antique walnut bookshelves reminiscent of the library at Westfield Manor. She found him there one day in 1950 standing in a sea of crumpled paper and crying. It was two in the afternoon. He was very drunk.

"What is it, Johnny?"

"Phony. Everything. Everything. Every fucking thing I put down looks phony." She had no way of helping him because she had no more idea what was wrong than he did.

"Maybe you should try something different."

"May-fucking-be I should." He passed out on the tan leather Chesterfield sofa that had once belonged to Conan Doyle.

Johnny sobered up enough to try a play that folded to a dirge of critical scorn. He started two novels and left them undone. Dorothy began spending more time in England. Johnny began spending more time at "21."

They stayed together for some time, more from habit than anything else. The relationship had gone as sour as it had once been sweet. Dorothy began a series of casual affairs with increasingly younger men. She was past forty now and trying not to look it. She traveled, sometimes with Johnny and sometimes with her son. And she built houses.

Dorothy bought a small château on a tributary of the Loire because it reminded her of Parmentier-la-Fôret. She built a spectacularly modern beach house in Barbados for Lord Charles to visit on holidays. She sailed around the world alone and met a guru in Bali and stayed six months and bought a hilltop where she created teakwood palace. Dorothy discovered Acapulco and carved a marble mansion into the cliffside a thousand feet above the bay. She found Tangier and acquired a cluster of buildings in the old part of town which she had totally gutted on the inside while carefully retaining their shabby outside walls. Here she created a secret hideaway, an Arabian Nights fantasy of stone lacework, trickling fountains and a subtle all-pervasive sensuality.

Johnny Morgan hated travel. The war had been travel enough for him. Usually he stayed in the Sutton Place house locked up with his creative impotence and his booze. People had to be reminded who Johnny was. "Oh yes," they'd say, "Johnny Morgan. I remember him."

Johnny had met a young girl and decided he wanted her. She thought *Rage of Battle* was the finest book written by a living American. Dorothy made no protest and they were divorced quietly.

The adolescent Lord Charles was bemused by his mother's rich-Gypsy lifestyle. She was so unlike the mothers of his Eton friends. Lord Charles found his mother colorful in her way but ultimately vulgar. She tried, but never in the right ways. When Charles asked for a horse, she bought three famous Arabian stallions. That wasn't what he meant. When Charles took up competitive swimming, she built an indoor Olympic-size pool at Westfield. He found that rather showy. Before long their relationship would be reduced to an attempt at Christmas and a few weeks in the summer at one or another of Dorothy's hideaways.

At fifty Dorothy liked sex as much as ever. But she was finding it in stranger and stranger places.

Now she found that men her own age were too old. And the younger men who came her way expected more from the relationship than shared affection. The idea of buying sex was unattractive to Dorothy Dutton. But if she was going to buy it she was going to buy the best.

For several years in the late 1950s Dorothy had employed a series of private secretaries. These were always athletic young men in their late twenties who made reservations, mixed drinks, told jokes and performed the services a husband might, including stud service. It worked quite well until one of them decided to write his memoirs. Dorothy managed to stop publication, but it cost her a quarter of a million dollars, which was exactly what the young man had in mind to begin with.

It was then that she decided to marry Momo.

Dorothy was sixty and looked forty-five, Momo was forty-five and looked thirty. She knew all about him and he knew a lot about her. Their lack of illusions was a common ground. She knew Momo was poor, bisexual and without scruples. On the other hand he was genuinely charming, very good-looking if you didn't mind them slim and dark, the title was authentic and he could be kept in control.

Teams of lawyers set about drawing up a marriage contract.

Dorothy Dutton-Langfeld-Harper-Parmentier-Schwartz-Westfield-Morgan became the Countess Ruvo di Putignano-Squillace in a small private ceremony in Naples. Lord Charles Westfield sent flowers and regrets.

By the time of this, her seventh marriage, Dorothy had been a legend so long she scarcely noticed the publicity. Momo, however, flourished under the attention of the world press like a freshly watered begonia. This amused Dorothy, who required ever more baroque forms of amusement. In Momo Dorothy had found what she had long dreamed of: a permanent escort, pimp, stud and dinner partner. In Dorothy Momo had found what he had always lacked: a steady, well-paying profession.

Noel Northcliff, adjusting a handkerchief in the breast pocket of his blazer, smiled and reflected how perfectly matched they were, how like a well-made zipper their needs meshed together. NN wondered what in the world they were up to now.

Sky High was the only ski resort in America where you could find masses of fresh flowers in December. Cassie had a program of growing bulbs all season long. The paper-white narcissus were the first, already a success. Cassie stood watering a large copper bowl bursting with the fragrant blossoms, smiling as she thought of the two dozen other bowls that sat waiting their turn in a shed behind the kitchen. She also had hyacinths and crocus and five other kinds of daffodils. She looked at the narcissus with affection. They stood tall on slender stems, heads of creamy white flowers whose delicate but pervasive scent made a refreshing change from the aroma of wood and leather that hung in the air.

"As if," said Jake's voice behind her, "you didn't have enough to do. Next thing you'll be shoveling snow."

"I love them, Jake. They're so proud to be flowers."

"Well I'm proud you thought to grow 'em. They've been photographed three times already. That gal from *Town & Country* just about freaked out when she saw 'em. They'll be worth their weight in publicity."

"And we value everything by its weight in publicity?"

"You know I don't, honey. Are you still sore about Charlie?" Charlie's rescue had made headlines in the Denver papers and had been picked up by *Time* and *Newsweek*. Cassie hated personal publicity and feared kidnappers. DRAMATIC RESCUE ON MILLIONAIRE'S MOUNTAIN said the Denver papers. It made very good press for Sky High, and Cassie thought she could detect the Machiavellian hand of Dud Drummond behind the national coverage. Jake claimed ignorance, and he refused to take her concern seriously.

"Not really. I'm sorry if I'm grumpy. It's just that every part of our lives is so damned public here. I feel like I'm living in a department store window."

"Shall we sell tickets?" He took her hand and leered comically.

"You are impossible." But she giggled.

"How about trading that watering can for a glass of rotgut, lady?"

"It's a deal." She put the can back in her office and they headed for the bar.

The opening party was in its fourth day now. Everyone agreed it was an unqualified success. If this was the dress rehearsal, the show was sure to be a hit.

The physical design of Sky High proved Paolo Storione right on every count. People loved their handsome rooms with the textures of wood and stone and the warmth of the fireplaces and the sweep of the view out onto Sky Mountain. Peng's food exceeded all expectations as triumph followed triumph in a procession of culinary delights. He was clever enough to vary the menu in astonishing ways. Along with the classics of French cuisine, Peng offered brilliant alternatives at ever meal. One night he created authentic Peking duck with a memorably crisp amber skin and tender greaseless flesh inside. Another time, he produced a New England clambake with fresh clams steamed in real seaweed and broiled lobsters and cornbread. After lingering over their supper, the livelier guests found their way down to the Weinstube with its almost collegiate informality of rough stone walls, intimate banquettes and beamed ceiling, good wine and live music. Usually the music in the Weinstube was casual, with one or another of the young ski instructors or ski-bum waiters or waitresses picking out folksongs on a guitar. But tonight in the Sky Bar there was a special undercurrent of anticipation. Dud Drummond had announced a surprise entertainer would appear in the Weinstube at ten.

The Sky Bar was humming. Pepi Prager held court in one corner, Dorothy and Momo in another, and Buck Washington, surrounded by young people, in still another. Jake and Cassie circulated from group to group with the ease of practiced hosts.

Pete Woodbury came into the bar looking for Maggie. He'd been deep in meetings with Jake and Dud Drummond for two days and he'd hardly seen her. But Maggie wasn't there. Pete stood at the bar and ordered a bourbon on the rocks. He was sipping it when Jake joined him.

"Time-sharing," said Pete as though announcing a cure of cancer.

"Time *what*?" Jake had been immersed in the grim economics of Sky High for two depressing days now.

Pete, for all his ingenuity, had no miracle solution to their problems. The real money would come from the sale of land as building lots and as condominiums. Zeke Gibbs was going to have apoplexy. And Jake wasn't happy at having Sky Valley turn into the kind of pack-'em-in jumble that Aspen had become in fifteen years of badly controlled expansion. But it was a way out, and they needed a way out. Desperately.

"On the condominiums, we build four two-bedroom units for, say, a total of twelve thousand dollars per unit. We could keep it down to that, if we build enough of 'em. Well, that unit would sell for maybe thirty thousand—if we sold it outright. But with time-sharing we can damn near triple that, cash on the barrelhead, and it's probably an easier sale. It's the buy-one-week-a-year guaranteed number. Snowbird's peddling 'em at six thousand for a two-bedroomer for one week. It's one of your better legitimate rip-offs."

Jake frowned. "Rip-off" was very far from the kind of operation he wanted at his resort. Sure, it would all be perfectly legal as was the sale of TV dinners, in which the portion of meat averaged out to more than ten dollars a pound, and various other common ways of fleecing the public. Still, it *was* legitimate, and the Knickerbocker was breathing harder down their necks every day. Jake wondered just how far he'd go, when it came right down to it, to keep Sky High.

"And people go for it?" he asked.

"It's very new. But I'd say yes. Look at it from the buyer's point of view: he gets the use of a nifty condominium with a small cash investment. No hassle with reservations. It can be attractive."

"I can see every dentist in Duluth talking about 'my condominium at Sky High.' I think, Peter, that you may have struck paydirt."

"Strike some for me," said Maggie from behind them; "I've been hitting the dirt all day long, or rather the snow. That's a very fast mountain you've got out there, Jake."

"Here's our first customer. Mrs. della Robbia, how would you like to own a magnificent condominium at Sky High?"

"I won't even consider it until you call me Maggie. But, you know, I have thought about it. All my kids are ski-freaks and I'd like to get 'em someplace that doesn't have too much in the way of . . ."

"Temptations?" Pete laughed.

"Exactly. Aspen's getting pretty boozy and druggy for this lady. But Sun Valley's too stodgy, and I hate Vail."

"Sky High is the answer to your prayers, then. I'll get on the horn to Paolo tomorrow and start him on sketches. Cost the thing out, the basics at least, and Dud can work up a brochure."

"You guys never stop, do you?"

"It's my life," Jake said simply, smiling at her with eyes that didn't smile. "Sky High means a lot to me."

"You've done a wonderful job, Jake."

"Thanks. If you'll excuse me, I've gotta play at being Ye Host."

"There," said Maggie looking wryly at Pete, "goes a force of nature. I wouldn't want Jake Chaffee for an enemy."

"He plays to win."

"That's the American way, I guess. At least he does it with class."

"Pretty much. You seem a little down on Jake."

"I'm not really, Pete. In fact, I admire him. If the charm doesn't get you, the energy will. But there's a feeling of 'don't tread on me' about the man. Or am I wrong?"

"You're probably very right. Jake's a remarkable guy. He exudes success through his pores."

"While the rest of us just sweat?" She laughed.

"I think," said Pete, "that I could use another drink. How about you?"

"Speaking of temptations, why not? The same, please."

"Can you join me for supper, Maggie?"

"I would love to."

Cornelia de Vos was angry. Underneath the beauty, the confidence, the wit and the smile something was grating. Her own mother wouldn't have guessed it because Cornelia knew what the jagged lines of anger can do to a face. But here it was the fourth day at Sky High, and Niris hadn't made the slightest move in her direction.

Instinctively, she knew a time would come. She had played this game before and never lost. Something should develop to bring them together, and the next thing Niris would know, he'd be in love. Cornelia had that power and she recognized it as a gift, like perfect pitch or a flair for colors. She used this gift sparingly, with the same precision a great actress might, saving the blaze of talent for the big scene in the third act. In the meantime, idly, Cornelia amused herself with Jean-Pierre Belfort. She saw him now, glowing with the expectation of love, walking through the room with eyes only for her. Cornelia de Vos smiled and gave him her hand.

Momo Count Massimilliano Ruvo di Putignano-Squillace poured another glass of beer into Dorothy's glass. Graceful in all his movements, Momo had the beer-pouring down pat. His narrow hand seemed boneless as he raised the frosted bottle a good eight inches above the glass and poured the light amber beer directly into the center of the glass. The beer foamed and hissed as the glass filled, magically, right to the top. It was a neat performance and Momo took pride in it. He smiled at Dorothy. Dorothy smiled at Noel Northcliff, who smiled at both of them.

"I would never have come," said Dorothy, looking philosophically into her beer glass, "if it weren't for Raoul Peng. He is a genius with peanut butter. You must try this, my dear." Smiling girlishly, she scooped up a spoonful of steaming-hot peanut-butter soufflé. It was light and delicate and the color of faded mahogany. With it came a rich but fluffy peanut sauce. Dorothy was enraptured, and rightly so. "Not once," she went on, "has he repeated himself since we got here. Except when I asked him to. I wonder, Momo, what that man would ask to cook for me alone?"

"Shall I approach him, m'love?" The Edwardianisms of English flowed from Momo's Italian tongue in unconscious self-satire. He was a living dubbed-in movie.

"Do."

"That would be something, Dorothy," said NN, smelling a scandal, "to snare Peng from the clutches of Jake Chaffee."

"The slick son of a bitch'd probably make an avalanche fall on me!" Dorothy giggled at the idea of some new mischief. "I'll offer Raoul Peng a million dollars and an unbreakable contract."

"Once he knew us," said Momo sincerely, "he'd come to love us." NN sipped his wine and tried to keep a straight face. The Weinstube was packed. The banquettes that lined the walls were all taken and the little tables for two somehow held three or four. The buzz of voices was a little louder than usual. You could feel the anticipation in the air, a physical thing like perfume or smoke. An upright piano stood against one wall just to the side of the miniature dance floor. The room fell quiet.

A slender middle-aged man in black tie walked up to the piano, sat down and arranged sheets of music. Then the lights dimmed and a spotlight picked out a circle on the empty dance floor. Dud Drummond appeared, grinning like the Cheshire cat. "I promised you a surprise tonight, folks, and I'm happy to introduce a lady who's been knocking them dead all year in New York, America's newest recording star, the fascinating ROSETTA!"

Fascinating was the right word. Rosetta was a big Southern girl with a traffic-stopping figure and enormous brown eyes the *Times* had called "the sauciest dark eyes in town." The voice that came with those eyes was big and rich and expressive, and she was a born comic to boot. Her opening routine was a hilarious pastiche of songs using the name Rose. By the time she got to "Second-hand Rose," the audience was hers. She sang love songs in French, a Gospel hymn in full revival-meeting frenzy, songs that made the audience roar with laughter and blink back tears.

Pete and Maggie sat together, listening intently but looking at each other. Jake and Cassie were with a group in a banquette, loving it. Cornelia and Jean-Pierre held hands under the table. Pepi Prager looked at Rosetta with the wary expression of one whose emotions are always in perfect control, unable to understand why she could give herself so completely to a room filled with strangers. But they weren't strangers anymore. Before Rosetta's performance was over everyone there felt they'd known her all their lives. She stopped, at last, after four encoures. They could have kept her singing all night, but she had a jet to catch. Cornelia made the definitive comment: "If there was an American Piaf, it would be she."

For Pete Woodbury and Maggie, already acting like adolescents on the brink of falling for one another, the atmosphere of warmth and of love given freely acted like a catalyst. Before Rosetta's routine was through they were holding hands like schoolkids. They couldn't take their eyes off each other. Maggie had always been a warm person physically, a cuddler, a toucher, a hand holder. Pete was quite the opposite. His sexual relationship with Franny had become routine. What sex they had was quickly finished and almost furtive. It was as though they both had more important things to do. Maggie, of course, considered her marriage to be over. There was nothing to keep them apart but their own inhibitions. Thanks in part to the spell cast by the singer, those inhibitions were melting into a volatile brew of unstated yearnings that had been held back too long. They left the Weinstube together and, still holding hands, walked slowly upstairs to the quiet of Pete's suite.

Inhibitions were not on the list of things that worried Cornelia de Vos or Jean-Pierre. They left the Weinstube in Rosetta's wake. Minutes later they were in Cornelia's room in front of the fire, standing a foot apart, sizing each other up like contenders in a prizefight. The spruce fire crackled and perfumed the big room with a pungent forest aroma.

"So," he said at last, smiling, "we make love."

Cornelia's response was instinctive: she drew the heavy tweed curtains across the huge expanse of glass. Then with a dancer's graceful economy of movement, she unzipped the one-piece white silk jump suit and flung it on a chair and stood before him tanned and naked and smiling the sweet smile of all the virgin milkmaids in all the fairy tales of the world. Jean-Pierre too, was no stranger to speedy undressing. Very soon the room was filled with love just as Cornelia had always known it would be. They were both athletes of sex, and they did it very well, two superb bodies on the soft wool rug in the firelight, lost in their total allegiance to this elusive fragment of time whose only function was to flash gloriously across their sex lives for a moment like shooting stars on a summer midnight that die and are gone before we can gasp with pleasure at the pretty streak they make in the bottomless night. They both had the natural good taste not to mention the elusiveness. There had been many, many Jean-Pierres in Cornelia's life and many indulgent older women for Jean-Pierre. And there would be again. But they shared a secret, these two, and the secret was what made them so good at all the physical parts of love. The secret was, "Don't care too much. It will pass. As everything passes."

12

Pete Woodbury wasn't a drinker, but he had long since learned to travel with a bottle of good Scotch. His job took him to all parts of the country on short notice, and there always seemed to be a client who wanted—or needed—"just one more." Now Pete stood in the bathroom of his room at Sky High mixing Scotch and water for himself and for Maggie.

"Cheers!" He handed her the drink and indicated she might want to sit down. Maggie sat down primly with her knees so close together she might have been hiding something between them. "Cheers," she replied, not feeling cheerful because it had dawned on her that Mrs. Nicholas della Robbia, pillar of the church and mother of four fine children, was sitting in a married man's hotel room holding a glass of whiskey and thinking impure thoughts.

On his part, Pete was not particularly religious or even moral. His problem with things like extramarital affairs was that they tended to be messy. Pete had worked for years to make his life tidy. Anyone could check his books at any time. In fact the IRS had done that more than once and gone away satisfied. But Maggie della Robbia suddenly focused all Pete's doubts about whether his carefully built life was really worth having after all. When you really looked at it, his life consisted of one wife, married for wrong reasons, two attractive kids he never saw because he was too busy earning the money it took to maintain their "position." Pete sipped his drink while his mind spun its wheels trying to think of the right thing to say. It came out all wrong.

"I think I'm falling in love with you, Maggie."

"Do you ever watch soap operas, Pete? I bet you don't. Well, people in them say things like that all the time."

"People say things like that in real life all the time. Only not people named Pete Woodbury. I'm not sure I even said that to my wife. But I mean it."

"I guess I always try to crack jokes and hope problems will go away. I'm flattered, and touched, and let's face it, it takes two."

"That," said Pete, "is music to my ears."

"Funeral music." She gingerly tasted her drink.

"You really think I'm after a little quicky-cheapie, don't you, Maggie? Let me tell you. For fifteen years I've been a model husband. I've been so square you could build walls with me. And all this time, without me even noticing it, my life has been turning into something I didn't ask for and don't want. None of that has anything to do with you, except that you're the first thing I have wanted in a long time. I've known you three days and you've made me re-evaluate my whole life. Well, I'm a pretty good re-evaluater, Maggie. I get paid quite a lot for evaluating. And let me be the first to inform you, Pete Woodbury's situation stinks. I wouldn't invest a nickel in it."

"You ought to try mine."

"Problems?"

"The man I married turned into . . . something very unpleasant. We haven't had a real marriage for years. Not that he hasn't found plenty of consolations elsewhere. Every elsewhere. I should talk about soap operas! I'm living the old soap-opera cliché of, 'Let's keep things together for the sake of the children.' Well I've done that. God, have I done it. But they've gone now. And there I sit in that big house with a man I can hardly stand the sight of, so tangled up in everything I've heard about sins and sinners all my life I feel guilty even to think about you. Or anyone."

"We seem to be," Pete said with a tight little grin, "kind of like flip sides of the same record."

"With the needle caught in the groove."

"Do you realize how beautiful you are, Maggie?"

"Come off it. In five or so years I'll be a grandmother."

"Marlene Dietrich is a grandmother."

"I'm patterning myself more after Ma Kettle."

"I think it's time to stop kidding." He crossed to her chair and leaned down and kissed her on the cheek. Maggie instinctively put her hand up to touch his hand, a quick, cautionary gesture.

"Don't you see how easy we're making it for each other, Pete? If you think something's wrong with your marriage, you ought to fix it or get out of it. But not because of me. And the same is true for me. I really will leave Nick, sooner or later. But if and when I do, it has to be for my own reasons. If I left Nick for you, I'd be just as bad as I think he is. How could I live with myself then?"

"Let's fuck."

"Pete!"

"When was the last time either of us simply gave in to a nice uncomplicated desire? Let's just take our clothes off and make love. Right here and now and damn all the long, torturous thinking it out first." He started untying his scarf.

"Pete, look: I'm sorry, but I just can't operate that way." She couldn't look at him because Maggie knew that if she did all the walls would come tumbling down. So she got up and started for the door.

Pete caught her arm and held it firmly. He turned her to face him. He felt like a man who had just stepped off a cliff, and maybe only by hanging on to this woman he hardly knew could he save himself. "There isn't," he said gently, "anything in this world I'd like better right now than being in bed with you."

"And tomorrow morning?" All the girlhood fears came marching at her in their uptight ranks, uninvited guardians of conventional morality.

"You ought to know me better than that."

"I wish I knew myself better, Pete." Maggie was desperate as only someone can be who has lived all her life by the rules and suddenly wakes up to the fact that the rules don't work. "I always had an answer for every question . . ."

"Someone else's answer?" He touched her cheek. "You're forcing me into a role I don't like, Maggie. You're turning me into a seducer."

"There's a word out of my childhood. And it was always us girls who were in danger. They really did a job on us. Sex was dirty. All men ever wanted was to get into our drawers. Love was something you negotiated like a minefield. All that is in me, Pete. I can't just switch it off."

"You could try trusting me."

"It's myself I don't trust." For the first time she smiled. "Do me a favor, though. Don't stop trying."

He grinned. "That's one thing you don't have to worry about."

"Good night, Pete. It was a lovely evening." She kissed him and was out the door before he knew it. Pete finished his drink and poured another. Then he sat in the chair Maggie had just left and looked out into the night. Maggie's doubts and vacillation made him love her all the more. Here was a woman with no pretenses, no tricks. He set the glass down, wanting her so much it was a physical pain.

Zem Gibbs thought her grandfather was looking better tonight. Zeke sat across the kitchen table playing checkers with Bill Shepherd. Winning, more often that not. Zem was working on her quilt, an old-fashioned "friendship" quilt made from scraps of fabric given her by friends. There were colorful donations from women in town, pieces she'd found in hundred-year-old trunks in the attic, a square of Bill's old blue jeans that he'd cut off at the knees. Zem had got so she could tell the signs of madness rising in her grandfather the way you sense a storm coming on. This looked like one of his better nights. He'd been in Denver, conspiring, and that always made him feel better. Zeke's war with Chaffee had been in full force for five years now. To Zem, that seemed like forever. The time came when she took his outrage for granted. But lately, ever since the controversy over 317, he'd been getting worse, less and less in control, leaving the running of Sky Ranch more and more to Zem. The old man liked Bill. The meal had been fine. The checker game might be another good sign. Zeke made a triple jump, click-click-click. "Gotcha!" There was a boyish glee in his voice. Checkers was about all Zeke Gibbs had been winning lately.

As if reading his granddaughter's mind, Zeke turned to her. "There's a curse on that place, Zembra."

"Oh, Gramps! A curse?"

"I saw the vultures circling. Three of 'em. Right above that place." Zeke could never bring himself to say the words "Sky High." It was as though this denial of the resort's existence might make it disappear. "So I went up to check on 'em. Thought it might be a sheep straying off. Well, Miss Zembra, there was nothing." He looked at her triumphantly. She had no idea what the old man was getting at, but the whole performance scared her. If this wasn't madness, it was close enough. "Well, there was nothing there. And you know what that means."

"No, Gramps, I don't."

"It's a curse, honey, plain and simple. One of the oldest. I learned it from my pappy and he had it from an Injun medicine man older than the mountain, or so they said anyhow. Those Indians believed that when you saw the black buzzards circling over empty ground, there was death coming sure as sunrise."

"Whose death?" Bill had been listening in silence.

"The one nearest where they circled."

"But Gramps, there are hundreds of people down there."

"Then they all better watch out, that's all I can say." He laughed a dry, bitter little laugh. Zem shivered.

"Bill, maybe it's time I took you home," she said. "Gramps, the meal was delicious. I won't be late." She kissed the old man good night and slipped into a warm sheepskin coat.

"Good night, Zem, Bill. Have fun."

Zeke Gibbs stood and poured himself some more coffee. He knew he probably sounded crazy to these youngsters. But he also knew by instinct that something bad was going to happen to Sky High, and not just because Zeke Gibbs wished it. They'd learn, all of them. The mountain would teach them.

In the Jeep, Zem was nervous. "Bill, have you had any psychiatric training? I think he's going bananas."

"You're just too close to it. He is one fine old gentleman, Zem; don't knock him. He may be a little obsessed by the whole Jake Chaffee thing, but that's understandable when you think of the emotional stake he's got in Sky Ranch."

"I still think he's crazy. I mean, Indian curses, for heaven's sake. Really!"

"Look. I'm a medicine man myself, right?"

"Anything you say, Doctor."

"Well, believe me, there are plenty of things we just don't understand. People laugh at Lourdes, for instance. Maybe the cures are all in the victim's heads. But that doesn't make them less real to the cripple who can walk again."

"You mean an Indian might see a buzzard and die just to make the curse come true?"

"It's possible. Medical books are filled with similar things. People who really do die of broken hearts, for instance, which is just what I'll have if you don't get off your pretty white ass and marry me damn soon."

"Selfish! You have my pretty white ass in any case." Zem laughed and then turned serious. "But let's hope Jake Chaffee's guests don't know about that curse. The buzzards at least are real. I saw them myself."

"I think we can safely say," Bill chuckled, "that it's out of our hands."

Mildred Rush had spent nearly seventy years cultivating the mean temper that made her one of the least popular residents of Sky Junction. She was hard and spiteful and the sworn enemy of animals and small children. Every Halloween a shower of rotten eggs fell on old Millie's cabin from the concealment of the nearby spruce grove. No one in Sky Junction had more to do with Millie than they could help. No one came dropping in for a chat or a cup of coffee, because a chat with Millie inevitably turned into a vituperative monologue built on her favorite subject of how the world was rotten and how she was going to get some of her own back, the Devil take her if she didn't. Part of Millie's often repeated threat came true. She never got her own back, but the Devil did come and take her.

Millie's cabin was heated by an old iron wood-burning stove fueled by logs she cut herself and stacked outside the kitchen door. Now after several days in fever, she was too weak and crazy with delirium to put more wood in the stove. Late the same night that Rosetta sang at Sky High and Zeke Gibbs told Zem and Bill about the Indian curse, old Millie Rush woke suddenly and found herself shivering uncontrollably in the dark.

Frightened, she peered over the raggedy heap of old blankets and quilts. Millie saw the stove silhouetted cold and black against the window. Somehow the stove had gone out. In her fever-disoriented brain, Millie didn't realize what time had gone by since she took to her bed. Slowly, painfully, like some prehistoric creature emerging from the mud, Millie Rush dragged herself from the bed. Lordy, but it was cold. Cold and thirsty. What Millie needed was a drink, and not of water. Feeling her way in the dark, she opened the cupboard where the gin was hidden. Out came the bottle. She held it up in the cold beam of moonlight that mercifully hid the squalor of the little cabin, and took a long pull right from the bottle. Then another. There. That felt better. Wiping her lips with the arm of the old flannel nightgown, Millie set the gin bottle down on the table, forgetting to put back the top. She stumbled for the kitchen door. The door, which opened outward, was stuck shut with the below-zero cold of the winter night. Fuddled by gin and fever, Millie put her full weight against the flimsy door. It flew open and she flew with it, out the door and down the three wooden steps, landing headfirst against the jagged pile of firewood.

Three days later some schoolkids found her there.

The story was perfectly clear to the local sheriff: the gin, the cold stove, the fall, the freezing night. Mildred Rush was dead of misadventure, no foul play, and good riddance. Her death, mean as her life, was just what Sky Junction might have expected, if they'd given it any thought. Mildred Rush had no known relatives and no estate. She would be given a pauper's burial, after spending the winter at state expense in a vault in a funeral home in Steamboat Springs, until the ground got soft enough to dig graves. No one thought to do an autopsy on Mildred Rush.

Eliza Chaffee watched Cassie with the curious, analytical eyes of age nineteen. Cassie, for her part, wasn't about to be intimidated by any teenager, no matter whose kid she was. Jake had arranged for the girl to be a waitress in the Weinstube, which gave her a dorm room with the help, a free lift pass, and all day to ski if she wanted to. Eliza thought this was just fine. For one thing, it meant an indefinite holiday from college. It also gave her a chance to be near Jake for the first time in years, which was what she wanted more than anything else. Eliza's relationship to Cassie was a cordial armed truce. She didn't intrude on Cassie's time with Jake but rather sought out her father on his own time. Jake, asking Cassie about Eliza, got affirmative, but noncommittal replies: "She's charming, Jake." Eliza, asked about Cassie, said the same thing in almost exactly the same words, which made Jake roar, "She says the same about you, pumpkin, and the two of you are acting like a delegation of Manchurian diplomats."

"What do you expect, Daddy?"

"Well, honey, I guess I want you two to get on well together."

"I don't think she'd be the Wicked Stepmother, if that's what you mean. But Daddy, I hardly know the lady."

"How do you feel about what you see?"

"Daddy, you don't have to ask my permission."

"Don't play games, Eliza!"

"OK. Fair enough. I like her. I like the way she treats Charlie. I even think she's probably very good for you. It's just that I can't fake feelings I don't feel, you know."

"Of course I know. And no one wants you to."

Jake covered her hand with his hand. As much as he wanted Cassie, he wanted his daughter back. He wanted to make up to Eliza for all the times he'd been too busy, too selfish or simply too far away. He'd find a way to get them liking each other. Cassie and Eliza were the only women who mattered to him.

"Can I tell you a secret?" Eliza asked.

"Anything, darling, anytime."

"You're not exactly the worst father a girl could have."

"That's the best news I've heard in months."

Tod Rubin was normally a patient man, a watcher and waiter rather than a mover and doer. His STYX training confirmed the wisdom of a quiet, subtle approach. But something about the Pepi Prager case made Tod impatient, restless. Maybe it was this place, Sky High. Maybe it was being cooped up on this mountain with all these merrymakers, a fish out of water with no talent or inclination for acting the playboy. Tod Rubin had watched Pepi for a week now with skill and persistence. And everything he saw in the dashing ski pro fitted his conception of the man Carl-Heinz Waldemar might have become, given brains and luck and a great talent for skiing. A ski resort was a brilliant hideout. The transient, fun-seeking ambience precluded close relationships. And people who might have known him in his earlier incarnation were unlikely to be visiting a jet-set ski resort in 1973. Except for Tod Rubin.

Pepi's little chalet fascinated Tod. He must find a way inside it. Something must be delaying the identification of the fingerprints on the beer glass he had posted to Vienna. Tod was sure in his heart that Pepi would have kept some souvenir from the old days. Hidden, no doubt, perhaps meaningless to anyone who wasn't looking. But it would confirm the man's identity once and for all.

Charlie Lamont was up and walking now, still in his first heavy cast and crutches. The cast was decorated by kids in school and people at Sky High. Charlie's favorite was a Magic Marker portrait of Whizzer, done by Eliza Chaffee. They were becoming pals, just as fast and thick as Jake wished Eliza would make friends with

Cassie. Eliza knitted him a funny little half sock with a pom-pom on the toe to go over the cast. She taught him "go fish," the simple card game she had played with her own small brother Jon in the happy, dreamlike days of childhood before Jon died. But most of all, she kept the boy from being bored, and thus did the one thing most likely to earn the friendship of Cassie Lamont.

Jake sprawled in a chair in Pete Woodbury's room, eavesdropping on a telephone conversation Pete was having with someone crucial at the Knickerbocker Trust.

"Of course we know that, Bill. If I remember right, Snowbird lost a million-five the first year and a million the next. But remember, we aren't that big an operation. Sure. You have that figure."

"Buzz-buzz." Jake paced the room, fighting the frustration building inside him. Imagining the responses of Pete's contact at the Knickerbocker Trust was worse than hearing them. Pete went on, calmly, all the facts ready in his head, doing what he did better than anybody Jake had ever known. If being buttoned up counted, they'd win.

"Right," said Pete, "and there'll be a lot more. Sure Bill, you can count on it. Bye now. Best to Helen." Pete hung up. He looked tense. "Stay of execution. Bill Harkness has seen some of the early publicity, the thing in *Sports Illustrated* where they say we're better than Aspen. He thinks he can buy us a little more time."

"Time's what we're short of."

"He's uptight about 317, though."

"Did you welcome him to the club?" Jake's laugh had no humor in it.

"He doesn't know much about Zeke Gibbs, and you can bet your bottom ski resort I didn't fill him in."

"My biggest fear about Gibbs is that some day he'll really go round the bend and take a shotgun to me."

"Don't ever underestimate him. You know what the Utah environmentalists have done to stop the development of Snowbird. Well, Gibbs has the environmentalists here on his side. And he carries plenty of weight with the old-line conservatives, the guys who are automatically against anything new. And plenty of people just owe him favors. He's calling in all his debts, Jake, and he's concentrating everything on this next session of the legislature."

"With the help of Will Jefferson, no doubt."

"Exactly. And he's another one not to underestimate."

"I know the type, but not the man." Jake was restless, bored by all the background material. He only liked to be where the action was, and let someone else do the homework.

"Jefferson," said Pete, "is the power behind a lot of thrones in these parts. A lot like your father."

"Then he's someone to beware of." Jake said it flatly. Through all his problems at Sky High, he had refused to call on his father's influence, except about Eliza, even though it was his for the asking. The Senator asked too much in return. Jake promised himself that come what may he wouldn't—couldn't—go on his knees to his father. It would be exactly what the old man expected.

"We haven't exactly been idle, you know, Peter."

"Well, I know it. But we're far from a shoo-in, Jake, and probably we ought to be thinking how to handle it if we lose."

"I'd hate to have to call The Senator."

"I'd hate for us to lose."

"The old man would fix us up in no time. And I'd be hearing about it for the rest of my life. To him a political advantage is a political advantage, and God help anyone who owes The Senator a favor and doesn't make good when the time comes he asks for his own back."

"Family or not?"

"Family or not." Jake stood up and began pacing the room, which was a sign Pete knew well: he'd leave, and leave handling the problem to Pete Woodbury.

"What I'd like," Jake went on, "is for you to get us some quickie attitude sampling among the people who matter in that legislature. I don't care how you do it or what it costs. If it looks like we need heavier artillery, so be it."

"Done. I'll have it within a week."

"I appreciate it, Peter. You know what this joint means to me."

"I'm beginning to get an idea. It isn't just another Chaffee Development, is it?"

"Sky High," said Jake in a voice so low it was nearly a whisper, "is where I'm building my future."

To Dorothy Dutton the proposition she was about to set before Noel was irresistible. She had only to ask. Dorothy sat back in the armchair sipping her beer as though it were the rarest of white Burgundies. Momo, in a sulk because his attentions to Jean-Pierre Belfort had gone unnoticed, sat quietly pouring beers, lighting cigarettes and automatically making small talk as they waited for the arrival of Noel Northcliff. They didn't have to wait long. NN appeared two minutes after seven, glowing with health, wit and anticipation. It had been made clear to him that La Dutton was going to offer him a proposition. He hardly imagined it would be sexual. But propositions from Dorothy came trailing wagons of gold, and gold was a commodity that NN would never shun.

"Ravishing as always, my dear." NN bent nimbly from the waist and kissed Dorothy's hand.

"Noel, Noel, Noel, I'm a ruin and all the world knows it."

"Nonsense! You're just hitting your stride."

"What I like about you, dear Noel, is the shameless way you lie. What are you drinking?" With this, Momo imperiously signaled for a waiter.

"Chablis, thanks. But now, you must clear up this mystery."

"Done and done. It won't come as a surprise, dear Noel, that my life had been, shall we say, far from ordinary."

"But Dorothy, what an understatement. Wars have been fought over you, as well they might."

"Ha! They were very small wars, Noel. Police actions, they'd call 'em today. At any rate, I want to write my memoirs."

"Brilliant idea! Darling, they'll sell like hotcakes."

"No doubt." Dorothy drained off her beer and

Momo magically produced another. "But there is one little hitch. I can't write three coherent words. So, darling, I'd like you to be my official biographer. You know me so well, Noel. You would get the tiny innuendos a stranger might miss. Naturally, you'd be fully credited as the author with none of this 'as-told-to' crap. I want this to be *the* biography, not a puff piece. God knows, I'm way beyond needing flattery. Warts and all, Noel, dear. I'll even put that in writing. You shall never be censored in any way. The financial arrangements, naturally, we will leave to your agent. But I'm sure something satisfactory can be worked out. Now, please say yes."

"Yes." Noel's mind worked faster than his automated microfilm retrieval system. He knew practically to the penny and to the last line of publicity what it would be worth to him to be the author of such a book. America's most famous rich girl, uncensored! It was more than he'd hoped for. One of the things that made Noel such an effective society columnist was the simple fact that he shared the point of view of his readers: he was always on the outside looking in, no matter who made his shirts or how much caviar he consumed. The Dorothy Dutton book could certify his status as the world authority on the very rich. He smiled fondly at his benefactress, and gave the slightest nod.

"Darling! I knew you would. Oh, Noel, it'll be such fun. You won't lose by it, I promise." He leaned across the table and kissed her cheek.

"Neither of us will lose by it, my dear. But the only question, Dorothy, is simply of time. I really am very busy. There's the column, there are two books already contracted for, plus magazine features and talk shows and all that. Not to mention doing my homework at places like this. I suggest that you get busy with a tape recorder as soon as you can. When we get enough basic material, you and I can sit down and edit it. It's easy enough to hire researchers to dig up things like press clippings."

"But Noel, what exactly do I say to this bloody tape recorder?"

"You say it all, my dear. Begin at the beginning. Parents, birth, childhood, romances, marriages, your views of times and places, all interwoven with as much good gossip as you can remember. It'll be a ball."

"And I'll have dear Momo to help."

"Of course, my love." Momo said this in a monotone so glazed with boredom it could hardly be mistaken.

"Momo just adores literature, don't you, my love?"

"Passionately."

"Then it's all settled," said Noel. "I'll call my agent in the morning. What fun it'll be. I love you for thinking of me, Dorothy. Together, we can create a work of art."

"Unquestionably." Momo signaled the waiter to bring more beer.

Niris Reza Herat Bir-Saraband was one of the finest amateur skiers in the world. He had devoted his life to the sport. Yet everywhere Niris went, migrating like some exotic animal following the snow, he liked to take skiing lessons from the reigning pro. It is possible that no other man had skied in so many different places. Yet Niris was modest in his great ability and experience. He was in no way a show-off, as sometimes happens to very good skiers, and he always professed himself willing to learn.

Today he was learning from Pepi Prager, one of possibly five men in the world who were accomplished enough to teach Niris anything.

Though Niris, as always, had tried to sign up Pepi's services for the entire two weeks of his visit, he had found Pepi too involved with the opening publicity campaign to tie himself up. Pepi had also been shrewd enough to realize that playing a hard-to-get would enhance his value in Niris's eyes in the future.

The first regular lesson started after a leisurely luncheon served in Pepi's chalet. Niris was enchanted by the informality: it was exactly the right tone, as Pepi had guessed it would be. Then they skied down to the tram and in minutes were ski-borne down Sky Mountain. This first run was to get acquainted. Niris went first, instinctively heading down Wardance, one of the most challenging trails. Niris skied rhythmically, his legs close together, so close that Pepi could hardly see air between them. As the trail sloped steeper and steeper down a narrow cut in a spruce grove, Niris kept his speed in check with little flicking motions of his skis, defying snow and speed and gravity with such casual grace a stranger might think skiing was easy. Pepi, who had designed the trail and skied it often, knew better. At the bottom of Wardance, where the MOST DIFFICULT trail ran into a larger, easier bowl, Niris stopped and smiled at Pepi.

"Delightful. One of the best," commented Niris. Niris knew that his slightest compliment was worth tons of praise from less sophisticated skiers. Pepi instantly wondered if he could use this comment in publicity. He'd check with Dud Drummond that very night.

"You leave me in some distress," said Pepi with his most endearing boyish smile; "I am cheating to let you imagine you have anything left to learn." A touch of flattery never hurt when tipping time came around. Pepi was equally adept with fat peroxide widows who would never graduate from the baby slope but liked to imagine themselves as sporty.

"I know the form is there," said Niris with modestly downcast eyes, "but sometimes I wish I could be a little . . . more free, if that is how to put it. Sometimes, I see for instance a fat mogul and although I can execute perhaps three correct ways to ski around it, an impulse comes over me to simply leap over it. Which I don't do, because it might look, oh, a trifle showy?"

"But, your instinct is absolutely right. If you feel like jumping, well, dammit, jump! And we have just the place. China Bowl this afternoon will have every kind of mogul there is. And we'll jump them all."

"Just for fun?" This was a new idea for Niris, to do something in skiing just for the fun of it.

"Just for the very hell of it, as my wise old Austrian grandmother used to say." Pepi laughed his hearty man-among-men laugh, and Niris smiled eagerly in return. They would be boys together. They would have an adventure. Laughing and even from time to time yodeling, Pepi led the way to the nearest chair lift that would bring them to the China Bowl.

In less than ten minutes, Pepi and Niris stood at the

rim of China Bowl. The enormous sweep of this great natural snow bowl reached out in a nearly perfect circle for half a mile on either side of them. The bowl itself had been skied all morning, but the Sky High powder was so light and dry that this merely groomed the slopes and made them easier to ski. There might have been fifty people skiing China Bowl as Pepi and Niris contemplated their first run, but the bowl swallowed them up and seemed to be empty.

"You know this, of course," said Pepi, slipping into his role as instructor, "but the key thing in jumping the moguls is to be low on your skis in the first place, and to unweight just before takeoff. Anticipate a little. And be ready for the jolt when you land. It's the rhythm of the jolts, hop, hop, hop, that makes it work. Now, shall we?"

"By all means."

Pepi led the way, cutting straight down the side of the bowl to pick up speed. Then he turned nimbly to the right and sailed over the first mogul, not a large bump, but enough to give him an elevation of eighteen inches which carried him in free flight to the top of the next, larger mogul. And so he went, flying, his skis just grazing the tops of the moguls, changing direction at whim, cutting this way and that down the side of the snow bowl with Niris following in perfect imitation of his every move. They looked like a pair of mountain goats in flight from some unseen enemy. It was an astonishing spectacle and every one on the bowl who happened to glimpse the two airborne skiers was transfixed by the sight. One of these watchers, more fascinated than most, was Cornelia de Vos. Finally, gasping with laughter as much as for breath, the two skiers stopped at the bottom of the bowl. Niris looked at Pepi. Of all the ski instructors Niris had known, and he had known the best of the best, none compared to Pepi Prager. Fate and his own fundamental shyness had kept Niris from close friendships with men or women. Yet on this bright afternoon, after such a dazzling run, it seemed for a moment it might be possible. Niris came out of his shell a little. "Pepi, it was beautiful!"

Pepi grinned the grin of rakish adolescence. That it

was false did nothing to diminish its effectiveness. Niris grinned back, and for a moment the two men stood in the shared exhilaration that can make brothers out of strangers. Pepi laughed out loud. It was going to be a very good thing, having this one for a pupil.

It was then that Cornelia de Vos came flying down the opposite side of the bowl in exactly the same manner, soaring from mogul to mogul like some bird of the snowfields, blond hair flying loose behind her, slim dancer's body outlined by a blue jump suit, her face behind the pilot's sunglasses wearing a smile of practically saintly exaltation. More heads turned.

Cornelia sailed up to Pepi and Niris and flicked her bright red skis to a halt.

"Pepi, you are very naughty. You inspire me to do dangerous things." She laughed a laugh that held secrets and promises, and nodded at Niris, to whom she had of course been introduced.

"But you mustn't blame Pepi," said Niris with a shy smile, "for it is I who am at fault. Pepi is giving me a lesson, and I asked him to show me how to jump the moguls."

"You learn fast."

"I have the best teacher. But, seeing how you do it, Madame de Vos, it strikes me that all of us could learn from you."

"I was just showing off. Pepi brings out the devil in me. Usually, I am more sedate."

"Possibly"—Niris' voice dropped as if he were telling a secret—"we could persuade you to ski with us." Cornelia looked at him, then dropped her glance and smiled modestly. This was it, the long-awaited invitation, the moment she must nurture and build the way you build a fire from a spark. She decided to gamble. Niris was undoubtedly accustomed to having his smallest hint taken as official decree. Which was why Cornelia decided to refuse him.

"You do flatter me," she said with a grin. "But the fact is, I'm late for a lesson of my own. Perhaps tomorrow?"

"It would be an honor."

"Ski with us tomorrow after lunch, Cornelia." Pepi

chimed into the spirit of the invitation with his voice but not with his heart. He wanted Niris to himself, for whatever benefits that might bring. And the de Vos woman was definitely not Pepi Prager's type. She was several degrees too self-sufficient for that. Pepi liked them softer and more submissive.

"If I can, I'd love to. And thanks for a good show." She gave them her thousand-watt smile and turned magically on her skis where she stood and was off down the trail in a fine shower of pluming snow and a graceful semaphore of her long legs.

"She," said Niris, "is the show."

And all the way down the trail Cornelia hummed a little old Dutch nursery tune under her breath, something she did very rarely, and only when a delightful surprise had come to her. Just when she had almost despaired of the Bidijar reserve, it came flying down a ski trail at her! She kept humming the tune because in her heart she was five years old again and it was the eve of Saint Nikolas, her wooden shoes were out upon the well-scrubbed doorstep, and the old saint was going to come by in the night and fill them with unimaginable goodies.

It was by chance that Tod Rubin found the way into Pepi's chalet. Tod's solitary late afternoon walks had become routine now. Every day after skiing he'd go for a stroll before cocktail time. On this afternoon Tod went exploring around the back of the kitchens, a quiet figure so familiar by now that he practically disappeared into the landscape. Which was exactly what he wanted to do.

Behind the kitchen wing was a service road that led up the mountainside to the pumping station. This road was used once a week when a maintenance crew went up to check the pumps and the levels of water in the tank. The road was well plowed and Tod noted that there were many footprints on it, coming and going. The road followed Sky Lodge up the slope until it ended at Pepi Prager's chalet. Tod could hardly keep from running. Finally, casually, he did get there. And beyond, never pausing or seeming to notice where he was, the picture of an absent-minded idler.

Tod walked all the way up to the pumping station, took a good look around, yawned, and resumed his stroll back to Sky Lodge. But now the Viennese was smiling quietly to himself. A problem had been worked out, or very nearly. For this God-sent little service road ran right past the back wall of Pepi's chalet. There was no back door. But there was a convenient bedroom window, and the heavy brass hardware was exactly like the hardware on Tod's window in the lodge. He thanked some lucky star for the efficiency of American standardization. Tonight he would study that hardware. Tomorrow, with any luck at all, Pepi Prager would have an uninvited houseguest.

Jake really didn't have to make this trip to Steamboat Springs himself, but he hadn't driven the Jag for three days and the arrival of Paolo Storione's sketches for the Sky High Condominiums did add a certain urgency.

Route 317 was empty this morning. Jake grinned and added pressure on the accelerator. The white needle on the clock-faced speedometer passed fifty, then sixty, and was easing towards seventy when Jake spotted the lone hearse lumbering up a grade just ahead. The hearse bore Colorado plates and a small, faded white sign in the rear window: G. FLYNN, DIGNIFIED INTERMENTS, 356 CEDAR STREET, STEAMBOAT SPRINGS. It was moving up the mountain at about twenty-five miles an hour. Jake downshifted the Jaguar into third gear, stepped on the gas and flew past the hearse at seventy-five. Vaguely, he glimpsed the wooden coffin resting behind purple draperies. There were no flowers and no mourners. Mildred Rush was leaving Sky Junction for the last time. Jake Chaffee made the red car go faster and clicked a tape cassette into the stereophonic sound system. He threw his head back and laughed from the joy of being alive, in a car like this, in some of the most spectacular mountains God ever dreamed up.

Liz Drummond, chic in a white cable-knit turtleneck that set off her blond hair and suntan, smiled into her drink from behind a veil of makeup and tinted sunglasses. It was going to be a good day. Duddy-Fuddy was in Denver on some kind of a secret mission. And little Liz was going to play. She sat at a table in a corner of the Sky Bar, one of the few customers in evidence. The day was so lovely, everyone was out skiing or just plain out. Liz tried to control her drinking in public. Right now she was sipping a mug of hot spiced red wine. In her room Liz had tossed down three stiff bourbons while dressing. The hot wine, which she didn't really like, was just a chaser, a reason to be in the bar, to see who might be available for a quiet afternoon in the sack.

The wine was still steaming as she lifted it to her lips. Her glasses steamed a little and through them Liz saw a beautiful shape sauntering through the room as if through a mist on a moor. Buck Washington had come into the Sky Bar. Liz put down her mug, waiting for the smile of recognition. Her glance was an appraisal. She coolly estimated the pleasure she might draw from the black quarterback, and her estimate was high. Liz smiled at no one in particular, and the pink tip of her tongue darted out and traced the contour of her upper lip. Buck Washington would do, and very nicely. He stopped at the bar and ordered a Coke. Then he turned, surveyed the room, and saw Liz. She waved, casually, and with a slow grin Buck picked up his Coke and walked over to her table. He wore tight-fitting blue jeans and a black turtleneck. Liz got a message from every ripple of every muscle in his gladiator's body.

"Looks like we're holding the fort together, Buck."

"Yeah, you and me against the world. Where's Dud?"

"Denver. For two days." Liz always liked to let a man know he wasn't going to be confronted by an outraged husband. But Dud had long passed the point of outrage.

"Poor guy. On a day like this."

"How's your skiing coming along?"

"Guess they'll just have to start the winter Olympics without me. But it's fun, I like it."

"I'm sure," she said, looking at him more meaningfully than the remark required, "that you'll be very good at it." Buck nearly choked on his Coke. God. Another one. He looked through his glass at the woman who sat across the table. Buck had heard a few rumors about Liz Drummond. Liz's downhill course was charted in the sneers of waiters and busboys, several of whom had enjoyed her hospitality in person. It was marked by the careful disdain of certain lady guests and by the thoughtfulness that Cassie Lamont always showed towards Liz, treating her like the breakable object she was. It was a waste. Buck thought. Liz Drummond was still a good-looking woman. But whatever dark odyssey the lady was on, Buck was not about to become part of it. It would be like handing a hypodermic to a junkie.

"You haven't seen Jake?" Buck swirled the ice in his nearly empty glass.

"He drove off somewhere about an hour ago."

"I was looking for him."

"You don't happen to be free for lunch?" Liz got the tone just right: casual, almost an afterthought, take-it-or-leave-it. He left it, just as casually.

"I'd love it, Liz, but I have a lesson in about forty-five minutes." This was a plain lie, and Buck hated lies, and now he'd have to get dressed for skiing, which he hadn't planned on doing. What-the-hell, maybe he even would take a lesson. Then it wouldn't be a lie. He grinned. "Could you give a guy a raincheck?"

"It would be my pleasure," said Liz, sipping her hot wine. "Anytime at all, Buck, anytime at all."

"Wish me luck on de ole debbil mountain." Buck got up and smiled, just from relief.

"See you around." Liz's attention was already wandering, ranging the room like some Distant Early Warning system for the next opportunity. This afternoon must not be wasted just because certain ungrateful darkies thought they had better things to do. She drained her mug of wine and signaled impatiently for another.

Tod Rubin smiled and his face changed character completely. Ordinarily he looked like a scholarly hedgehog, bright-eyed and inquisitive but always alert to scurry quickly back under the hedge in the face of an unexpected sound or sight. Tod's was not a brave face, not a face you'd be likely to remember. It was in fact the perfect disguise for his profession. But now Tod Rubin smiled, a smile that held joy and discovery and a kind of triumph. This was the smile of a man of action, a man whose hands held the course of future events.

What made him smile was the massive brass lock of his own window. For hours Tod had studied the big lock, which was designed to secure the big window and to pivot outwards for fresh air. Now Tod had found a way to open the lock. The answer was in the pivot mechanism. It opened by swinging out from the right. When the latch was fully shut, the window was secure and could only be opened by breaking the glass. But—and here was the answer!—if the latch was not secured, gentle pressure from the outside to the left side of the window would ease the pivot open. Tod was betting that Pepi would leave his bedroom window unlatched. If it was unlatched, the matter would be simple. If not, Tod had a glass cutter and the matter could be made to seem like burglary. Tod knew, for Jean-Pierre had told him, that Pepi was booked solid with lessons. It was a perfect day for skiing. Which made it a perfect afternoon for a bit of breaking-and-entering. Once again, Tod worked the pivot. Once again, he smiled.

René Latour was fifty years old and strong as four peasants. He was also a wizard of sauces, the sauce chef that Raoul Peng had trained at Chez Midas in Paris and persuaded to come to these far, forsaken mountains to work his magic at high prices for the Americans. Not that René had anything against Americans. But he minded the isolation of Sky High, and the fact that there were no women there—at least, not his type. René was a man who loved women. Indeed, he loved life in all its lusty phases. From his burnished copper saucepans flowed sauces of the most exquisite delicacy, sauces that subtly complemented an ocean of fishes and armies of savory calves, lambs, deer, rabbits and fowl. But perhaps more than his sauces and his lamented love life, what René Latour enjoyed most was his indestructible rude health.

He was a big man, René, but solid not fat. His chest like a barrel, belly firm and flat, legs like casks, a little too short for the massive torso, thickset neck topped by a round smiling face ruddy with life and good humor even when its owner was far from the stove glow and copper sheen of his beloved kitchens. And through all his adult life—including eleven months in a particularly sordid German prisoner-of-war camp near Aachen where he had been exposed to every brutality, including the necessity of eating such things as even now it troubled him to remember—René Latour had never been sick an hour, no, not even a minute. Which was why the headaches were so disturbing.

René stood over his own range top with its eight wide-spaced gas burners, watching saucepans like a mother hawk with a nest full of young. In one pan a rich brown *sauce espagnole* was gently simmering its way to perfection. In an immense kettle the bones from yesterday's roast ribs of beef were being reduced to the thick black paste called *glacé de viande* so useful in enhancing other sauces. And in still another pan crushed lobster shells were simmering in a fish *fumet* to extract the last breath of flavor for the next day's surprise: a real Marseilles bouillabaisse. Ordinarily, none of these culinary complications would have given René Latour so much as a moment's pause. But today he had to call up every bit of willpower to concentrate on cooking and ignore this steady, dizzying pain gnawing at the base of his skull. He tried to remember the last time he'd been near a doctor. School? No. Army . . . nearly thirty years ago. Well, why should he see doctors? René shared the deep mistrust of the French working class for doctors, lawyers, and yes, even clergy. Hawks and vultures every one. The doctors would kill you and the priests would bury you and the lawyers would make it all legal, with their hands out, every one. And may they rot in hell, headache or not!

Moving with surprising grace for such a solid man, René sniffed and stirred and tasted his several creations. No little headache was going to get the best of

René Latour. Not when Raoul so depended on him. Not when there had been such a rash of so-called sicknesses among the local help. First, he recalled with a scornful turn of his ruddy lips, there had been the dreadful Mildred Rush with her toad's body and foul tongue and endless complaints. Mildred Rush herself was one big ache, and a good riddance when Raoul sacked her.

But then, just yesterday, Mildred's replacement, a quiet older man named Bill something or other, had also called in sick with headaches, fever, or so he said. Possibly it was the flu. In America they blamed everything on the flu, in France, the liver. Well, who was to say? René was inclined to believe Bill something-or-other, for the man was a reliable worker and not a whiner or complainer like the Rush woman.

René turned away from the heat of the range for a moment and rubbed the back of his head. He felt a little thirsty. He put down the wooden spoon on the damp cloth reserved for his spoons alone, crossed to the nearest sink and poured himself a glass of cold mountain water. There. That was more like it. The pain was still with him but his throat felt better. But, what was this smell? In an instant René was back at his range, and cursing. He had scorched the *glacé de viande*. In disbelief, René turned off the flame: it would have to be thrown away. It had been twenty-eight years since René Latour had scorched a sauce: he remembered it well. God in Heaven, he must be sick.

A finger of morning sunlight inched across the big bed and came to rest on Pepi Prager's sleeping head. Pepi stirred and smiled at the expected warmth: the sun became his alarm clock at seven-thirty every morning. He yawned and stretched luxuriously and threw back the sheet. The girl lying next to him muttered in her sleep and caused Pepi to remember that she was there. Languidly, he reached out and stroked her shoulder and tried to remember her name. There were so many of them, these little girls, and they were really all the same girl. She felt his hand and wiggled a little and turned to him.

"Was I all right?" She had a little mouse face with huge eyes and her body was too skinny for Pepi's taste and she had been less than all right, nervous and too eager and curiously unsexy. Pepi had had to do all the work while the little girl just lay there transfixed with her own private rapture at fucking one of the world's most famous skiers. Pepi could teach her a lot, if he cared to: if only he could remember her name.

"You were lovely . . . lovely." What was her name? "But you ought to learn to relax a little, to enjoy it completely."

"I did enjoy it, Pepi." She said his name slowly, tasting it, drinking in his fame with every letter in the word. He rose on one elbow and leaned over and kissed her lightly.

"Of course you did. But you weren't fucking, my dear. You were being fucked. There is a difference. It takes two."

"You didn't like me?"

"I liked you very much. You are . . . very sweet. I am thinking about your own pleasure." She moved closer to him, sharing the patch of sunlight in the half-dark room. Her arm went around his neck, her cheek against his chest.

"Show me."

"It is a question of . . . response." With one lazy finger Pepi traced the shallow curve of her breast. How old could she be, this little waitress? Eighteen? He surely hoped so. "It is not enough to simply be available. You must participate. With all of your senses. *Here.*" Shifting his body on the bed, Pepi gently brought his hand up behind her head and guided it to his crotch. She wiggled, trying to avoid his grasp.

"Pepi, I don't . . ."

"That can give us both pleasure."

"You can't . . ."

"Suck!" His hand tightened on the back of her neck with frightening pressure. She shuddered slightly and looked at Pepi with a look that was a mixture of scorn and terror and involuntary pleasure. But Pepi wasn't looking at her. He was looking at his wristwatch, a solid gold Rolex, wondering how much time he'd have to put in on this nameless little bitch before he got breakfast. His hand clamped on her neck registered another shudder like a seismograph, and with equal detachment, and then he felt the rough velvet of her tongue on his prick and he smiled. They were like small children. You simply had to show them who was the master.

Half an hour later, the girl left, quickly, saying nothing. Pepi shrugged and got out of the bed and showered. It was going to be a wonderful day. Zipping into his skin-tight blue Sky High jump suit, Pepi laughed out loud. There was something aphrodisiac about that jump suit. They followed it like the Pied Piper, right into his bed. Then Pepi looked at his watch. God in Heaven, five of nine! He took a quick look around the room and smiled scornfully as his eyes passed over the rumpled bed, which would be neatly made and with clean sheets when he saw it next. No wonder he couldn't remember the little girl's name. It wasn't worth remembering.

Before he left his bedroom, Pepi checked himself out in the big mirror. As always, a most satisfactory image smiled back at him. Yes, even if one said it oneself, Pepi Prager was a commendable creation. Once again he checked his watch, liking the heft of the Rolex, the gift of a plump but passionate American widow in Saint Moritz ten years ago. Pepi felt lucky. But then, he'd always been lucky. Part of that luck was the fact that nobody knew he hadn't always been Pepi.

Pepi Prager grinned out of the mirror at his creator, healthy and blond and suntanned, eyes clear and sparkling, teeth, white and perfect, the whole picture charming, a man at least ten years younger than the age that the calendar recorded. Yes. A definite improvement over the original.

There had been a real Pepi Prager.

Carl-Heinz Waldemar had found him quite by chance, a young mechanic at Westerlo, a simple Tyrolean boy who was, alas, not very bright. But the real Pepi Prager had other significant advantages. He was the same age as Untersturmführer Waldemar, and there was a distinct physical resemblance.

Even better, young Prager was an orphan, raised in a

Catholic orphanage outside Innsbruck, an orphanage conveniently devasted in a misplaced Allied bombing raid. Carl-Heinz learned all these things from the young mechanic during a brief friendship initiated by Waldemar during those last days at Westerlo.

Waldemar knew an opportunity when he saw one, and in Pepi Prager he saw a gift from the gods. Young Prager, naturally, was flattered by this attention from his commanding officer. Waldemar pretended to be interested in mechanical things, and the boy was delighted to teach him. Waldemar, in turn, would take the boy for drives into the countryside in the big Mercedes, Prager driving, which thrilled him, and they would stop for beer and sausages in any prosperous looking farmhouse along the way. On these excursions Waldemar learned all there was to know about Pepi Prager. The boy followed him like a puppy.

It was Prager who drove the big Mercedes on the day the SS pulled out of Westerlo. And it was Prager who unquestioningly veered out of the convoy and onto a side road at Waldemar's suggestion shortly after they left Westerlo.

Waldemar, lounging in the back seat of the big convertible, pulled an envelope from his leather briefcase. It was from SS headquarters in Berlin. He showed the envelope to young Prager. "We have a very confidential mission to perform, Corporal Pepi." The boy nodded. The car sped on, moving east through Belgium, into Germany at Aachen, across the Rhine at Bad Godesburg and then south, speeding through farmland, stopping only for fuel and to grab a light snack now and then. All over Germany the great war machine of the Third Reich was crumbling. The usual questions were not asked. Allied bombers came over almost every night in their deadly flocks of hundreds, giving the lie to the Nazi propaganda that assured Germany victory was at hand. One more dust-covered Mercedes with a lone SS officer and his orderly speeding on some urgent mission seemed a natural part of the landscape. They fled south through Würzburg and across the Donau into Bavaria, missing both Augsburg and Dachau for reasons best known to Waldemar, and still further south through Schongau and into the foothills of the Baverian Alps.

It was late June and very hot. Carl-Heinz Waldemar ordered Pepi to head for Garmisch-Partenkirchen. They arrived in the lovely little resort village late in the afternoon. It was quite empty, cool and very quiet. Waldemar requisitioned rooms in the best inn. They showered and changed and had a splendid meal in the deserted dining room of the inn. Both men slept well that night, their first real sleep in two days.

Next morning, early, they moved on again, filling up the car and taking a big picnic basket from the innkeeper's fat wife. The SS, of course, paid for nothing. Waldemar dutifully signed vouchers and the townspeople dutifully took them, and thanked the kind Untersturmführer, and Waldemar accepted their thanks even though he knew and they knew the voucher was worthless. The Mercedes drove deeper into the mountains, past the peak of Kreuzeck which loomed straight up behind Garmisch, and out around the still taller Zügspitze, tallest mountain in Germany, sitting right on the border between Bavaria and Austria. In winter, Waldemar knew, for he had done it, you could ski from one country into the other on the Zügspitze. They talked of many things, Waldemar riding in front now, questioning the young corporal about his background, registering fact after fact in a mental file for future reference. There was no traffic at all on these mountain roads but for an occasional farm wagon or a herd of goats.

They passed an abandoned guardhouse and knew they were in Austria now, home to both of them. Around noon they came on a small mountain lake and Waldemar suggested they stop for lunch and a swim. The corporal agreed enthusiastically: it had been hot work, driving. They pulled off the road and got out the picnic basket. Waldemar had lifted a few towels from the inn, and he produced these from his luggage. Soon they were splashing happily in the chilly water. Waldemar climbed out first and disappeared behind an evergreen with his towel. Prager climbed out soon after, wheezing and grinning cheerfully. The grin was still on his face when the other man's Luger barked once from behind the evergreen and blew half of Pepi Prager's head off, the grin with it. It was not pleasant work, switching uniforms, but Waldemar steeled himself to it. This was, after all, a matter of life or death. The corporal's uniform fitted almost too well. And the picture on the corporal's *Ausweiss* was close enough, considering the times and the usual quality of such pictures. Waldemar had a waterproof oilskin in the boot of the car. He wrapped the corporal's head in a towel and then in the oilskin, laid him on the floor in the back of the car. Then he raised the canvas roof of the Mercedes and threw a rug over Prager's body, which was now dressed in the immaculately tailored uniform and bore the papers of Untersturmführer Carl-Heinz Waldemar.

Then he sat down on the grass and ate a satisfying picnic lunch.

All that afternoon he drove the big car farther and farther into Austria. And all afternoon he kept saying over and over to himself the magic words: "Pepi Prager . . . Pepi Prager . . . Pepi Prager." The new-model Pepi Prager ditched the Mercedes late that night on a secondary road fifty-some miles east of Innsbruck, with the bloodied corpse of "Waldemar" crumpled in a heap beside it, wallet empty, watch gone, all evidence making it look like a casual robbery. And the Lord knew there was plenty of that going on these days. He'd secreted nearly a thousand Reichmarks in gold in his luggage. He had his Luger, a Mauser rifle and plenty of ammunition.

Carl-Heinz Waldemar was a mountain-bred boy, trained to survive, a hunter, a fisherman, a crack shot and crack skier, completely unburdened by any human scruples at all. The body of "Waldemar," he assumed, would be found and reported and recorded officially as dead, thus exonerating any so-called sins of Waldemar. And as for Pepi Prager, well, the world had bigger fish to fry. He wandered for three days until, quite by accident, he came upon a lonely goat farm high up on a nameless alp. Pepi stayed at the farm a year and a half, spending not a penny of his gold, working for bed and board. In 1946 he put on his now tattered uniform and made his way to Innsburck to surrender, pretending shell shock. He was held in a detention camp six weeks, then de-Nazified and let go. Life was hard but there was plenty of work. His gold made it all easier, but he spent very little still.

One thing he bought was skis, and all his spare time was spent in polishing the skiing technique he'd learned as a boy. When there came a time for Austria to have a ski team once again, Pepi was on it, and winning. Soon it all came to him: the success, the women, the money. One summer in the early 1950s he checked into a clinic in Switzerland and had his nose altered just a bit. Gradually, subtly, he began lightening his hair. He won his Olympic gold medal, and then he began teaching. First in Saint Anton, then Saint Moritz for more money, then in America. Yes, he'd been lucky. And he was going to go on being lucky.

Pepi left the bedroom and walked out of the little chalet into the morning sunlight. He didn't notice that the bedroom window was a quarter-inch ajar.

DR. WILLIAM SHEPHERD, M.D. Bill grinned as he strode by the new sign at the end of the path to his rented house. All the eight long years, all the classes he had attended and the parties he hadn't, the uncountable hours of studying for the scholarships he couldn't do without, the thrill of learning the skills of life over death, the awesome responsibility of using those skills and the plain fool's luck of finding this town and this girl and this life: everything was written in the little white sign. He wondered what ever happened to the hand-lettered sheet that read: SKY JUNCTION NEEDS A DOCTOR. It would be good to have that sheet hanging someplace. It had changed his life.

The house was small but tidy. It sat well back from the road behind the old sawmill. It had been built a hundred years ago for the foreman of the mill. The shingles had weathered to a soft gray and the woodwork was crisply white. Bill used the old parlor for a waiting room and the old dining room for his office. The kitchen was big enough to eat in and two of the three bedrooms upstairs had been turned into a living room and a small library. Setting up the office had taken a month: he'd had to shop mostly in Denver. Bill had located a good used X-ray machine, vital in light of the injuries to be expected from Sky High. In fact, he furnished the office with second-hand furniture and equipment, mostly because his budget was small but also for the sense of solidity he got from things like the big old mahogany partner's desk. Zem, who quickly became Bill's decorator, furniture finder, curtain maker, and color consultant, had found the desk and its chair at an auction in Steamboat Springs. She had natural good taste and a horse trader's eye for a bargain. It was fun for Zembra Gibbs to decorate a house: everything at Sky Ranch was kept exactly the way it always had been and neither Zem nor her grandfather would have dreamed of changing it.

Someday, Bill thought, he'd go back to the old farm in Vermont and collect a few family things, but that could wait. Until the time when Zem would go with him, as his wife.

"Now that you've made me a home, how about making me a wife?" They were drinking coffee in Bill's kitchen after supper like old married folks.

"I'll say this for you, Doctor Shepherd, you're a persistent son of a bitch. But frankly, Scarlett, I'm not the marrying kind."

"How do you know if you've never tried?"

"You're right. I don't know. Seriously, you don't think I'm being coy or anything, do you?"

"No. No, I don't think that, Zem. Crazy, maybe. But coy, never."

"I like you a lot, Bill. I thought you knew."

"At what point, exactly, does like turn to love?" Bill looked at her and saw his whole future. The air in these mountains was sweeter to Bill because this girl breathed it. He wondered if he could stand Sky Junction without her.

"It is a well-known fact that love was invented in the sixteenth century, in France, by the troubadours."

"It is a well-known fact that I love you."

"You really want to get married." It wasn't even a question. She knew he did.

"Hell no. I've just been making small talk."

"Gramps would love it."

"That's swell, Zem. But I'm not proposing to Gramps."

"Look, I'm sorry if I seem dumb. You know what you want. You've been to Harvard, you have two terrific degrees, you have all these very high standards . . ."

"And what my high standards make me want is you."

"Bill, I like—maybe even love—everything I know about you." She took his hand. "It's *me* I don't know!"

"Let me introduce you. You're Miss Zembra Gibbs, young, talented, beautiful and beloved. Specially by me."

"What a tragedy. Brilliant young doctor smitten by village idiot."

"Damn right! I want you totally, completely, full-time and legally."

"With all my goods and chattels." She walked around behind Bill's chair and put her arms around his neck. Then she leaned down and kissed him.

"I'd love you naked and penniless."

"Suppose we go upstairs and you can prove it."

"Some people will do anything to change the subject."

"I thought that was the subject."

"What can I do," Bill asked, getting up and taking her hand and leading her to the stairs, "to convince you?"

"If I knew," said Zem, suddenly serious, "I'd tell you." They went upstairs, turning out lights behind them. Soon the whole house was dark.

Unlike most beautiful women, Cornelia de Vos was not a mirror watcher. Her confidence in the impact of her looks didn't need reaffirmation in images thrown back by cold silvered glass. She found affirmation warmly reflected in the eyes of men. Now, dressing for the afternoon's skiing with Pepi and Niris, Cornelia swept her honey-blond hair in place with a knitted headband, and glanced in the mirror as she walked out of her room in Sky Lodge. She wore the white jump suit with the single red circle in the middle of the chest. On this afternoon Cornelia intended to do some of the most serious skiing of her career. Niris had invited her to lunch, but she had declined. After today, she knew, she'd be asked again. The second invitation would be accepted. Cornelia walked down the hallway and out into the bright afternoon sunshine. She slipped on her sunglasses and lifted her skis out of the wooden locker built into the wall by the door. Smiling, she clamped on the skis and pushed off down the slope to the loading platform of the tramway. It was going to be a beautiful afternoon, sure as there was oil under the lands of Bidijar.

Dorothy Dutton was not pleased. Momo had been in a sulk for days. It was one thing, she thought, for his overtures toward the ski instructor to be ignored. But it was quite something else for him to be such a poor sport about it. And his reaction to her biography was far from enthusiastic.

"Artificial pearls," he had sneered, "cast before real swine."

"I rather thought you'd be pleased, Momo. After all, you'll figure quite prominently in the book."

"That is exactly what I feared."

"Why do you care?"

"Why indeed? Can there be some tiny shred of pride left in the long debauched genes of the Ruvo di Putignano-Squillace? Some shard of discretion chafing against the silken prostitution to which our line has reduced itself? I'm not really sure, my love. I guess the simplest explanation, is, it all seems rather vulgar."

"We all want monuments, Momo."

"Monuments are for the dead."

"Don't say that! I mean the book as a lesson for the living."

"A lesson? And who will you instruct with such a lesson?"

"I want my life to mean something."

"It does, Dorothy. It does indeed."

"Why do you choose to make fun of it, Momo? That's hardly in good taste."

"Derision, my love, is the last refuge of the defenseless. What you see before you are the final, feeble death throes of the dying dinosaur."

"The hypochondriac flea would be more like the truth."

"Kindness was never your strong suit, my pet."

"Nor discretion yours. This girlish modesty in you amuses me, Momo. Are you afraid I'll publish some of your little follies?"

"It is the big ones that worry me."

"Well, they'll all be there. The book will be true and true and true. No blackmailer will threaten me again. It shall be a clean fresh wind blowing through the dusty closets of my life."

"The draining of a swamp might be a more appropriate image."

"You cannot provoke me, Momo. I know why you're so miserable."

"Then you know a great deal."

"He doesn't even know you exist."

"The French boy?"

"Belfort. Jean-Pierre. The de Vos woman has him in her pocket."

"Or someplace." Momo looked at his wristwatch. It was late morning. They were still in bed. Then he poured himself some more coffee from the tray at the foot of the bed. "I'm not sure whether you underestimate me, Dorothy, or overestimate me. In any case, you're quite wrong. True, the boy is charming. But my unhappiness—and indeed I have been unhappy here—is not from that quarter." He looked at her and, as always, was amazed at how perfectly the embalmers of the world's greatest beauty salon had worked their grisly art on this woman older than his mother. Even here, in the morning and in bed, she looked hardly a day over fifty.

"What is it, then? Surely not my book."

"Of course not your wretched book. It's no worse than any other toy. Something about this place, Dorothy, has made me realize a rather disconcerting fact."

"And . . . ?"

"The fact is, I'm dead."

"Crazy, more likely, Momo, why don't you spend some time with Doctor Haspenberger when we're in

New York? I think the strain is telling on you . . . this sudden preoccupation with death."

"Not preoccupation, my dove. Death itself."

"I won't continue this conversation, Momo. It is very distasteful to me."

"Death usually is." He kissed her lifted, siliconed, creamed and lacquered cheek, and Dorothy shuddered.

Dudley Drummond was more at home doing espionage in Denver than trying to fit in to the glittering set at Sky High. Dud checked into the Brown Palace Hotel before noon. Soon he had a large phone bill and an even larger bar bill and a serious case of battle fatigue. But he also had a good idea of how Zeke Gibbs was attempting to influence the Colorado legislature to vote against the upcoming bill to widen Highway 317.

Dud was a stranger to Denver but no one with Jake Chaffee's connections would be a stranger anywhere. He had two excellent local "stringers" for his own New York public relations firm, moonlighting journalists who handled Colorado PR assignments on retainer. It was through one of his stringers that Dud heard about the unlikely combination of men who had lunch at the Settlers Club: Zeke and his lawyer, Will Jefferson, Jed Regis and Dave Davis and old Henry Macintyre. Three legislators of such widely differing political coloration they hardly nodded in passing under normal circumstances. The records of Jed Regis' tame conservationist group, Friends of the Rocky Mountains, were open for inspection. Zeke's ten-thousand-dollar contribution was duly and legally recorded.

Soon afterwards, Jed Regis had made two well-publicized speeches using the proposed widening of 317 as an example of the destruction of the natural glories of the West by a few greedy capitalists typified by Jake Chaffee. Dud read the speech and smiled. How righteous would Jed Regis seem, he wondered, when the words of his indignant speeches were contrasted with the timing of Zeke Gibbs' ten-thousand-dollar contribution? Once again Dud Drummond reached for the phone.

Zeke Gibbs slammed his clenched fist hard on the kitchen table. The coffee cup jumped and some of the coffee spilled over and began to stain the newspaper dark brown. Zeke didn't make a move to wipe up the mess. He just sat there in disbelief at the article that took up a good quarter of the front page of the *Denver Post.* STRANGE BEDFELLOWS was the lead headline, followed by: "Influence-peddling hinted in upcoming legislative battle on Route 317 bill." Dud Drummond had done his work well. The article had all the facts, including Zeke Gibbs's ten-thousand-dollar donation to the Friends of the Rocky Mountains.

Zeke read the article and reread it. Then he got up and began pacing the kitchen floor. Jake Chaffee was behind this nasty piece of work, he had to be. Zeke could well imagine what would come next, the insinuations, the legislators who might be on the fence staying away from the vote altogether, fearing any breath of scandal. And Will Jefferson had been so confident! It was all arranged, he'd said. Zeke looked out the window into the clear Sunday morning. He stood very still, trying and failing to control the shudders of rage that swept through his sinewy frame. A mile away at the bottom of the snow-covered meadowland that had all once been his, Sky High lay sparkling in the morning light. Zeke Gibbs felt sick.

13

Jake Chaffee's laughter roared against the walls of Cassie's bedroom like California surf.

"What's so funny?"

"Look at this." He handed her the *Denver Post.*

"Oh. Oh, ho. Looks like you've got the goods on 'em. But Jake, this really isn't funny. He could go to jail."

"Regis? They'll never pin it on him. But just raising the question is enough. I never thought Zeke Gibbs would be that obvious. To just march into Denver thinking he could buy a few votes as though they were that many more sheep for his ranch."

"It's sad, really. He's always had a pretty straight reputation."

"Until he went crazy."

"Was *driven* crazy."

"You think it's my fault?"

"Jake, look: I approve of Sky High. And you. I'm here, aren't I? But it just seems sad. He's really rather splendid, you know, Zeke Gibbs."

"He's a dinosaur that didn't have the good sense to phase himself out with the rest of his kind."

"You're like him, you know, in some ways."

"I'd never ask a girl like you to marry a dinosaur."

"And I'd never accept a dinosaur. But the grit, the determination: that's the same. The absolute conviction that you're right."

"He's a fanatic. The Savonarola of Sky Valley."

"He's America."

"He is the hard rigid shell of what was America, Cassie; there's a difference. The juice is gone and all that's left is bile and bitterness."

"You don't feel sorry for him?"

"I might, someday. Right now I'm too mad. He's piled stupidity on stupidity and achieved nothing. Except slowing me down a little and making it more expensive for me. I'd respect the man more if he up and shot me dead."

"Don't say that, Jake. If he's crazy as you say he just might try."

"No. He'd think it. Wish it. But he wouldn't do it. To his credit."

"It must be terrible, though. To be that old and see your world dissolving right before your eyes."

"The world dissolves a little every day. You've just got to be ready for it."

"Not Zeke Gibbs's world. It stayed just about exactly the same for a whole hundred years. Then you came and broke it like an egg."

"If it hadn't been me, it would've been somebody else. Maybe somebody with less taste and fewer scruples."

"What happens now? About the legislation?"

"Mostly, we sit up here and pray. Dud is cranking out a kind of follow-up program, to make sure the right people get asked the right questions, to keep the thing stirred up. Then, it's just a question of wait and see."

"Dud did it pretty well, didn't he?"

"You bet. The guy is an absolute pro."

"It amazes me that a man with so many smarts stays with a wreck like Liz."

"I have a feeling she wasn't always a wreck. In fact Dud told me that himself, once."

"The world is filled with dumb people trying to change people. They'd love a leopard if only he didn't have all those spots."

"I won't try to change your spots, Cassie." She looked up at him. It always came down to this, sooner or later. The ring she hadn't accepted hung over them and they both tried pretending it wasn't there. But it was. Jake kept it in the vault in Cassie's office, a vault she opened several times each day to get jewels and valuable papers for the guests. And every time she opened the vault she saw that simple blue leather box sitting there like some time bomb that one day would surely go off and break something. Or someone.

"That wasn't what I meant," she objected.

"I've made quite a few mistakes in my life, Cassie."

"Name one."

"Betsy."

"I don't think I want to be your next mistake. Jake, what's wrong with things the way they are?"

"The way things are may be better than nothing. It's simple and easy." He put both of his strong hands on her shoulders. "And just a little cheap. Well, I don't want it simple and easy. I need you, can't you see that, Cassie? I need you the way Charlie needs you. As part of me." Her eyes never left his eyes, even though she could feel a trembling in his fingertips. Without meaning to, he gripped her tighter, so tight it almost hurt. And Jake's eyes, which always made reporters think of hard bright things, steel and crystal, quite suddenly filled with tears. She had never seen him cry. Cassie shifted under the weight of his grip. She put one slim arm around Jake's waist and led him to the door of her bedroom. The strength had washed out of him with the tears. It was like leading a wounded player off the field.

Cassie's little office was just across the hall. She opened the door and led him into it. The vault, concealed behind the redwood paneling, whirred and clicked as she fiddled with its combination lock. Then it swung open. Her fingers found the small blue box and brought it out. She opened the box, took out the ring, and slipped it on the third finger of her left hand. Burke Lamont's narrow gold band fitted snugly next to Jake's ring. Somehow the two rings looked right together, as though it had been intended that way. Maybe, thought Cassie, it had been. She had to stand on tiptoe to kiss him.

"Cassie."

"I love you, Jake. I just haven't had the guts to admit it, even to myself."

"Thank you. Thank you very much." They walked back to her bedroom, in silence. Jake kissed her once again and stepped back a little and started opening the top buttons of her simple, schoolgirl's cotton flannel nightgown. It fell to the floor. He bent to kiss her and her arms went softly around his neck. Then he picked her up and gently lowered her onto the bed and quickly slipped out of his own clothes and joined her. Jake reached for her left hand and kissed it. "You fill in all the empty spaces."

"Jake." Her hand touched his neck now, pulling him closer. And suddenly in the blue night he was a little boy seeking comfort, finding it. Their lovemaking started softly in the night, building stronger and hotter like any well-made fire until it consumed everything, all their thoughts and fears and dreams, love leaping and glowing with a magical life of its own in a mingling so complete it was impossible to say where Jake began and Cassie ended because really there was no beginning and no end.

Tod Rubin was never sure if anyone at Sky High noticed his afternoon strolls, but it seemed unlikely. There were, after all, vastly more amusing people to watch than the slender Viennese. And the casual nature of the resort lent itself to spontaneous comings and goings at any hour, day or night. Armed with this knowledge, Tod pulled on a pair of thin kidskin gloves and made his way out of Sky Lodge, down the driveway and around behind the kitchens.

René Latour stood in the back door of the kitchen taking a final puff on his Gauloise in the vain hope that the harsh French cigarette might drive the headache away. He squinted into the afternoon sunlight, frowned, and set the cigarette butt flying into a snowdrift. René scowled, but not at the slowly approaching figure of Tod Rubin, whom he had never seen before and would probably never see again. He scowled because now for the third day in a row his head was throbbing. Surely he had never known such a thing in France, and just as surely, the pain in his head was being joined by a soreness of the throat. And him with a sauce Duglère to create for this evening's sole filet Duglère. *Merde!* He must go supervise peeling the tomatoes or it would never be done right. Abruptly René turned on his heel and retreated into the kitchen, slamming the door on the bright afternoon and causing a wave of relief to engulf the ever-cautious Tod Rubin.

"Failure in America," said Jake to Pete Woodbury, "is thought to be a contagious disease. Let 'em get one whiff of weakness and they're on you like sharks after a shipwrecked sailor. That's what really worries me." They were going over projections of the sale of condominiums on the time-sharing plan. It looked promising, more promising than anything else they'd thought of. Paolo's sketches were, predictably, brilliant.

"Hang on, pal," said Pete, "we may be leaking a little, but we aren't shipwrecked yet."

"That's what the captain of the *Titanic* used to say. If I, personally, have to bail much harder, my arm's going to fall off." They went back to Pete's endless financial projections. There just might be a way out after all.

From twenty yards away Tod Rubin could tell that Pepi's bedroom window was open. Something about the way sunlight glinted off one side of the double pane let him know it was ajar. He wondered how long it had taken Pepi to grow this careless. Or was it carelessness? Maybe the man really had nothing to hide. Slowly, idly, kicking a small chunk of ice as he went, the Viennese made his way up the drive to the pumping station. Then after a slow survey of the landscape which showed it to be perfectly empty, Tod turned and walked briskly back toward the chalet. Nimbly, looking and feeling as though he knew exactly what he was doing, Tod worked the pivot action of the window latch and stepped over a snowdrift and into Pepi's bedroom.

Once inside Tod paused and listened, and heard nothing. Then he drew the curtains against the chance of being seen by some passerby and began searching.

The layout was simple and handsome in keeping with the rest of Sky High: high ceilings, redwood walls and furniture, stone fireplace in the living room, a compact kitchen and bath, and the one bedroom. The search would be simple then. There were few places to hide anything. Pepi Prager had made no personal additions to the decor of his chalet: the furnishings and accessories and even the Navaho rugs could have been interchanged with those in the Sky Bar.

Tod began his search in the bedroom. He had already decided he was looking for paper, for some sentimental memento that could be produced, reflected on and hidden again without too much fuss. Karl-Heinz Waldemar would have sheaves of medals and press-clippings from the glory days of the SS and from the international manhunts, that followed the trials at Nurnberg, but Tod's guess was that Waldemar would be too shrewd to keep them about. Somewhere in a Swiss vault, perhaps, but never where they might be found by the Tod Rubins of the world. No. What a Waldemar might keep by him would be some photograph or love letter or family memento that would not be identifiable except to one who knew the background very well. And in this Tod was confident. He had studied his prey. He had visited the tiny Austrian village of Obersdorf where Karl-Heinz had grown up to be the pride of the town, handsome and such a skier, so like a recruiting poster in his Kadett's uniform. Tod knew that Karl-Heinz had married, while still in the officer school, a thin blonde girl named Heidi von Meerschaft, heiress to a good Munich brewer, herself a picture poster for the youth of Hitler's thousand-year Reich. Tod knew that Karl-Heinz's mother had died of some unspecified illness while the boy was still in training, that she had never lived to see him married or to see him become an internationally wanted war criminal of the most monstrous sort. Lucky woman, thought Tod.

Tod Rubin moved about the little house with the swift assurance of a surgeon. His touch was firm but gentle, his eyes flicking about like a lizard's, missing nothing, waiting for the almost invisible signal that prey was at hand. Tod had learned the fundamentals of searching and lock picking and electronic surveillance during a six-week crash course given by Interpol, the international police cooperative. He had learned well.

Starting methodically at the front door, Tod made his way through a closet, under rugs, in the creases of upholstered furniture, feeling, sensing, tapping, knocking on the very stones of the fireplace to see if one might have been worked loose. His touch was subtle and where he passed only a camera could have detected a change in the position of some object Tod had lifted. Ten minutes did for the front hall and its closet, the living room, bathroom and kitchen.

What Tod learned about his quarry didn't surprise him. Pepi Prager wasn't a cook or a reader or much of a drinker. The refrigerator was stocked with refreshments that looked like they were kept for guests. Pepi, Tod knew, took his meals at the lodge or had intimate lunches or suppers brought to the chalet on trays. His wardrobe was of excellent quality and came from international sources: shoes from London, boots from Denver, a dinner jacket and two formal suits from Paris, shirts and sweaters and ski clothes from everywhere.

If there was anything distinctive about Pepi Prager's home it was the sterility: the lack of any personal touch. There was not a photograph, not a trophy, no reproductions of press reports, nothing. It was odd, in a man of such apparent vanity, a man whose athletic abilities had won him Olympic gold medals and a multitude of other prestigious awards. A shrewder man, thought Tod, would have invented a few homey touches if only to throw someone off the scent.

For the second time that afternoon Tod stepped into Pepi's bedroom. He tried to put himself in Pepi's shoes. "I have," said Tod Rubin to himself, "suppressed everything about the Nazi past. But there is one thing—a love letter, a photo, something small and rather anonymous-looking on the face of it—that sometimes consoles me in the dark hours. I can't bear to destroy this one thing. It must be where I can get it easily and conceal it again easily. Now: where do I hide it?" The quiet radar of Tod's eyes roamed the room, searching, questioning, rejecting. There was a redwood-famed mirror hanging over the dresser. He lifted it from the wall but there was nothing behind it. Nor was there anything in the drawers or taped to their sides or backs or bottoms. He wondered where Pepi kept records.

Tod sat down in the chair next to the night table. The

less he found, the more certain he became that something was there to be found. He looked at his watch: nearly three. In fifteen minutes he'd have to be out of there. From no motive other than restlessness, Tod opened the bedroom closet door once again and looked inside: the shelf above the coat-hanger bar was empty but for a slightly incongruous felt Stetson cowboy hat. There was nothing hidden in the hat nor on the shelf. On an impulse, Tod began frisking all the garments that hung in the closet. There were ski jackets and stretch ski pants, several pairs of informal slacks and three sports coats including a slightly outmoded but well-cut navy blue flannel blazer. It was in the inside breast pocket of this blazer that Tod felt the crisp rustle of paper.

It was a plain white drugstore envelop, quite new. Tod simply held it in his gloved hand for an instant, not really believing it could amount to anything. He opened the envelop, which wasn't even sealed. Inside was a small wallet-sized black-and-white photograph. It was a studio portrait, posed, a little stiff, the lighting slanted dramatically in the glamorous style of the late 1930s. From the picture the innocent seventeen-year-old face of Heidi von Meerschaft smiled out across nearly forty years. The upper left-hand corner of the picture had been neatly trimmed away, cutting out, Tod was sure, the name of the boy it had been given to. No matter. The girl was surely Heidi. The signature, black ink faded to a rusty brown, was in the handwriting Tod had studied in the Waldemar file, a rounded curiously indecisive hand for one of the young heroines of the Third Reich. It said: *"Ich liebe dich. Heidchen."*

The newest small Nikon appeared from Tod's parka pocket, a miniaturized 35mm SLR with its own tiny flash attachment. He laid the photo down on the dresser in indirect light from the window and took eleven exposures by flash in rapid succession, bracketing his speed and lens openings to be sure of getting several accurate shots. Then he replaced the sad little picture in its envelope and put it back into the pocket of Pepi's blazer. He closed the closet door and checked the room to be sure it was as he found it. From behind the drawn bedroom window curtains he surveyed the little access road. Then he opened the curtains and the window and stepped out onto the road, pulling the pivoting window shut behind him but for the smallest gap.

Tod looked at his watch. Three-fifteen. He'd been at Sky High nine days. But it had taken only half an hour to trap the Wolf of Westerlo.

The next day Tod would fly to Denver and have the photographs developed immediately in a police laboratory. Then, with the evidence secure and enroute to STYX headquarters, Tod would return to Sky High and await the springing of the trap. He smiled, fleetingly, and then frowned. Maybe it was the tension passing, but an unwelcome throbbing had started up at the base of Tod Rubin's well-trimmed head.

Raoul Peng surveyed his immaculate domain with a feeling of helplessness so unfamiliar that at first he didn't recognize it. By God, they were dropping like flies. First the terrible Rush woman, then her replacement, and now his own man, René Latour. René, needless to say, would never complain but Raoul, sensitive to every breath and nuance of his kingdom, knew René was feeling poorly. It might be America, it might be the altitude in these wretched mountains. One thing Raoul knew: it wasn't the food. Still and all, it would pass. He thought of his future at Styron Food Corporation, the contract, the fame, the luxury. It always made Raoul Peng feel better to think about the future. He sighed, and opened an oven to peek at a braising breast of veal stuffed with pistachio nuts.

Maggie della Robbia lay on her bed and tried to blow smoke rings at the ceiling. She was wearing only the rosy glow of a recent hot bath, a light suntan from the neck up, and the weight of the world on her mind. Only by gathering all her willpower had she resisted fleeing Sky High the morning after that sad, aborted love scene with Pete Woodbury. Poor Pete, He didn't deserve such a holier-than-thou puppet to fall in love with, if it was love. Poor Maggie. Poor world. A girl could paint herself into a corner in a mood like this, in a place like Sky High, with a guy like Pete Woodbury.

Maggie put out the cigarette, reminding herself that Pete had been a bad influence in one way: she'd doubled her smoking since they'd met. Maggie closed her eyes and lay back and tried to remember everything her ski instructor had told her about weight shifting. Her mind was somewhere over the fall line concentrating on unweighting her uphill ski when the knock came at her door.

"Who is it?"

"Room service." Pete's voice sounded far away.

"Go away."

"Can't. It's an emergency."

"Just a minute, you lunkhead." Maggie got up and disappeared into the bathroom for a robe. She made a quick towel-turban for her damp hair, frowned into the mirror and opened the door. There stood Pete Woodbury, hair mussed, looking about eighteen in old blue jeans and a turtleneck. He was carrying six perfect paper-white narcissus.

"Stolen, too." He grinned. "For you, Maggie, I have taken up a life of crime." They hadn't spoken for two days. Maggie had come into the bar once when Pete was there, but just as quickly turned and left.

"Pete! They're lovely. Let me put them in water." She went into the bathroom and filled one of the drinking glasses: too short, but better than nothing. "And thank you, sir. They're beautiful."

"Cassie will murder me when she sees they're gone. But I shall have died in a good cause. Think well of me when I'm gone."

"I think well of you when you're here."

"I had an interesting phone conversation today."

"Oh?"

"With Franny. That's my wife. I asked for a divorce."

"Oh. I'm sorry."

"Radical surgery," he said, suddenly looking away from Maggie and out the window, "was called for. The patient is still in shock, but chances for recovery are excellent. Naturally," he continued, turning back to

Maggie and taking her hand in his, "he's going to need help."

"Naturally. Pete, what about her?"

"That's a good question. She's a very insecure lady, is Franny. That's why she needs all the props. I hope this may make her think a little, do some re-evaluating."

"I feel like I did it to her."

"The hell you did! Maggie, I was drowning. Going under for the third time. And not even really noticing it. All you did was make me notice. In other words, save my life."

"She must feel rotten."

"Can I have a drink?"

"I don't have anything here. I'll call for something."

"Never mind." He sat down on the bed. "It's a little weird, you know. I've never been a plunger."

"I've done a lot of making do, myself." She was standing next to him and she put her hand on his head. "I hope you'll be happy."

"I was hoping *we'd* be happy. Us. You and me." Pete reached out and put his arm around her waist and pulled her to him and held her tight. Then, slowly, still holding her close, he stood up and kissed her and untied the robe with his other hand. He brushed the robe from her shoulder and it slid to the floor and still he kissed her. Later, after they made love for the third time in the fading twilight, Maggie looked at him from across the enormous distance of three or four inches and reached up with one finger to trace the outline of his lips.

"It really was an emergency, wasn't it?"

"The best kind. The kind with a happy ending."

"I won't tell you how long it's been," she whispered, "since I've enjoyed . . . this."

"Fucking?"

"Fucking."

"It's important to say what you mean."

"It's more important to be able to mean it."

"I love you, Maggie della Robbia."

"Please: don't say that."

"Why not?"

"I might turn back into a frog again."

Dorothy Dutton smiled. She had a new toy. The tape recorder had been flown up from Denver just this morning, a gleaming new Sony. Momo had gone off in a sulk, but Dorothy was too preoccupied to notice. She had more important things to do. Momo was but one small jagged piece in the great jigsaw puzzle that was her life story.

It had been years—decades—since Dorothy had felt obliged to explain herself to anybody. But now, quite suddenly, the tick of every clock and every sun that set held a warning for her. If she didn't tell the story, once and for all, who could say what might happen after the . . . unthinkable. For even in the most secret corner of her heart Dorothy Dutton could not bring herself to face the fact of death. Setting her life story down was one way to keep death at bay, to deny the undeniable. As she began to speak into the little steel microphone the magic of explaining her wild career took hold. What started as a whim soon became dedication, and dedication turned to obsession as the words formed in her throat. "My story begins," said the richest woman in the world, "in the soft brown dirt of the tobacco fields of Carolina."

Sky Mountain lightly wore the enormous weight of blue above it. The time was one o'clock in the afternoon. Pepi, Niris and Cornelia stood side by side on their skis before starting their first run. They should have been an ill-assorted lot, the Arabian prince, the fugitive Nazi, the butcher's daughter from Delft. But to see them gliding down Sky Mountain was to see three bodies and three spirits fused in one rhythm, perfectly in tune, united as one.

They skied down the China Bowl side by side, separated by no more than twenty feet apiece. It made quite a spectacle. They danced and flashed over the moguls rather than taking the more conventional routes around them. Sometimes all three would be in midair at the same time and sometimes they'd be darting and bobbing and flying at unlikely intervals dictated by the thousand bumps and dimples of the mountain. Their run down China Bowl would last forever in the memories of people who saw them. But in fact it took less than ten minutes.

"Bravo!" said Niris when they stopped at the bottom to catch their breath.

"If only all my pupils were so talented, this job would be a lot more fun." Pepi was feeling benevolent. He even looked on the de Vos woman with more tolerance.

"It really is perfect," said Cornelia. "I think we ought to get in another run on the bowl before it melts or something."

"Agreed!" There was a new measure of enthusiasm in Niris's voice. They skied to the chairlift that serviced the bowl and got on after only the briefest of waits. Cornelia rode with Niris, with Pepi alone, behind.

"The mountains of America," said Niris pensively, "need take a back seat to no others."

"When I was a little girl, in the Netherlands, I would dream of such mountains. It was so terribly flat there."

"I, too, have always dreamed of high places." He turned to her, searching with his dark brown eyes. "What the flatness of the Netherlands did to you, the endless desert did to me. We have always worshiped the snow, in my part of the world. It holds a special magic for us. Did you know that we invented ice cream, anyway sherbert?"

"No! When?"

"Thousands and thousands of years ago, in the enormous kingdom called Persia, in the days before Xerxes, the days before Alexander reduced us to provinces of sheep herders, some great king—it is not known just who—would have special horsemen in relays bringing ice and snow down from the Taurus mountains, like the American Pony Express, you see. And then, in the kitchens of the palace the ice would be mixed with fruit juices and honey and voilà! The first sherbet."

"What a lovely story."

"It's true."

"I always thought it was the Romans."

"Ha!" His laugh was deep and merry. "Nouveaux riches. We taught it to the Greeks, and the Greeks taught it to the Romans. Yet still some of the most interesting ices come from North Africa. There is one made from a dark puree of apricots that is amazing."

"I must try it sometime."

"You will, Madame de Vos. You will." The chair reached the exit platform just as he was about to add something more. They skied down the ramp and waited for Pepi. As Pepi skied towards them he was greeted by Cornelia's most dazzling smile, a smile that could melt rocks. Cornelia was happy. Her afternoon was a success.

Seven years in the bone-crushing competition of big-time pro football hadn't turned Buck Washington into a violent man. Not even the hurt of being black in a white-on-white world made more than an occasional dent in Buck's fundamental good nature. Buck was well aware of the enormous force concentrated in his body and he used that force the way an intelligent hunter uses his guns: rarely, but with deadly effect.

That was why Buck didn't slug the little Italian faggot sitting next to him at the bar in the lounge at Sky Lodge.

Momo was sulking. Dorothy had her money and her memoirs, Jake Chaffee had his mountain, Cassie had Jake, Liz Drummond her bottle, the beautiful French boy had de Vos or she him, but he, Momo, Count Massimilliano Ruvo di Putignano-Squillace, what had he? Nothing and no one! It wasn't fair. He, Momo, who tried so hard, who dressed so perfectly and kept his body so slender and inviting, who smiled at all the right times, who knew jokes and fresh gossip, Momo who had been everywhere and knew everyone, for Momo to be all alone in this glittering mob was simply intolerable.

Leaving Dorothy with her tape recorder and her memories, Momo had gone down to the Sky Bar in search of adventure. What he had found was Buck Washington.

Buck was an occasional beer-or-wine man, not what you'd call a drinker and certainly not a solitary drinker. But this noontime found him sitting on a bar stool in the Sky Bar nursing a cold Coors and waiting for Jake. The college dropout behind the bar knew football and he was in the midst of an unlikely speculation about the Superbowl when Momo appeared on little Gucci feet and insinuated himself onto the bar stool and next to Buck.

"Good afternoon, Mr. . . . ah . . . Washington." They had met. The party at Sky High had been running long enough by now for everybody to have met everybody else at least once.

"Buck! How are you?"

"Well, thanks. Interesting name, that: Buck. It is the male of the deer, is it not?" Absently, Momo picked up the Strega mist that the boy behind the bar automatically prepared for him. Momo spent a lot of time in that bar and his tastes were well known.

"Yes. That's exactly what it means."

"Cheers." Momo took a long appreciative sip of the pale yellow-green liqueur.

"Tallyho." Buck lifted his half-empty beer mug and winked at the bartender. The bartender snorted, pretended the guffaw was a sneeze, and quickly found something to do at the opposite end of the bar. Momo ignored this: the boy was, after all, merely a servant. And everyone knew what the servant problem was in America.

"You're here alone?" Momo asked.

"All by my lonesome, as we say."

"You must make friends. Why don't you join Dorothy and me for supper tonight? I'm sure she'd be thrilled."

"She a football fan, too?"

"I'm not sure." He paused, thinking there must be a thread of logic somewhere in this odd conversation. "But she's American, more or less, and all Americans love football, don't you agree?"

"Some do. Some don't." Buck looked at the dapper little count. It was people like him who gave perversion a bad name. Momo had AC/DC stamped on him in more places than a light bulb ever thought of. Buck didn't care which way people swung as long as they didn't try to swing him along with them, but something about Momo gave him the creeps.

"I think American football is magnificent," said Momo in his most thrilling voice; "the spectacle! the speed! the brutality!" In his excitement, Momo put down his nearly empty glass. He gestured in the air with his beautifully manicured hands. One of the hands came to rest on Buck Johnson's heavily muscled thigh. No sooner did that small fluttering object alight than Buck reflexively covered it with his own hand, twice as big and crushing. Momo, thrilled beyond all expectations stopped in midsentence. Buck's hand closed around Momo's hands with a pressure that was gentle and steady and then not gentle at all. Smiling peasantly, Buck lifted the hand off his leg like some dead object that had found its way there by accident. Momo sat transfixed, first by surprise, then joy, then hope—nothing wrong with a little sadomasochism under the right circumstances—then pain, then pure naked fear. The man was going to break his hand! Momo smiled weakly and the smile froze as the pain increased and sweat broke out on his impeccably shaved face and his eyes widened in terror like some small rodent trapped in the headlights of a speeding car. The scream was just welling up in Momo's constructed throat when Buck Washington abruptly let go of his hand.

"Fuck off, little man." Buck smiled as he said it. Momo, speechless with fright, slid off the bar stool, backed away, then he turned and ran from the room. Buck, grinning, asked for another beer.

Cassie looked at the ring and made a wish. It was a simple wish, simpler than the wishes she usually made. Cassie wished that her headache would go away. It seemed unfair with everything, at last, going right for her, that she should be plagued by a throbbing, splitting headache that proved resistant to aspirin and cold towels and wishes made on diamonds. She must be coming down with something. Sky High was far, far too busy for its manager to miss even ten minutes of her day, let alone get the flu. Well she'd grin and bear it as she'd grinned-and-borne many worse things in her time. Everything was going to be all right. For the first time in years, Cassie felt her future coming into focus, and it was going to be a very good future. Charlie, she decided, would not be an only child. Jake would love having another son, other children. Charlie would like brothers and sisters. And Sky High was the perfect place to bring them up. They'd need a house, of course, but that wouldn't be a problem. Almost for the first time Cassie let herself think how much good Jake's money could do for Charlie, for the unborn kids she and Jake would have together. They'd have a house up the valley a little, not too far, within walking distance from the lodge. Cassie smiled over the pain of her headache. Everything was going to be all right. Very all right.

It was twilight in Liz Drummond's brain. She wasn't drunk and she wasn't sober, and that was just how she liked it. The room was in twilight too, but that was because she kept the draperies drawn shut. It might be dawn or high noon outside. Liz stretched lazily in the big bed and her hand touched the head of the boy sleeping next to her.

Then Liz sensed something unusual. My God! There were two of them! One on either side. That was a first, even for lascivious Liz. She blinked her eyes open and looked at the boy on her left. Not bad, near as she could make out. Then she turned a little and looked at the one on her right. He was older, probably twenty-five or so to the other one's eighteen. How about that? Slowly, almost idly, she sent both hands out exploring under the sheets. What she found there gave three people several more hours of very strenuous fun and games.

Tod's plane landed in Denver at ten minutes after eleven in the morning. The police lab developed his pictures within an hour, an hour Tod spent rather nervously making small talk with a slightly bored lieutenant over bad coffee and worse pastry. The Nikon had done its job well. Of the eleven exposures, six were acceptable and three were near perfect. Tod asked for a dozen copies of the best shot, and when these were processed bade the lieutenant a polite farewell and made his way to the nearest post office. There, he dispatched eight of the twelve prints to STYX by airmail special delivery. Then he checked into a nearby Holiday Inn and made a phone call to an unlisted number in Vienna. After ten minutes of buzzing and ringing Tod got through to STYX. He could hear the phone ringing in the dingy offices in the Neutor Grasse, and quite suddenly Tod Rubin, usually the soul of calm and reason, got choked up and emotional. He was, after all, a long way from home. "Mozart Appreciation Society, good morning!" came the stern and forbidding tones of Fraulein Frantzi. It was Tuesday in Vienna. The Mozart Appreciation Society was their code for Tuesdays. Tod felt homesick, even for the dour and charmless Frantzi. Oh, well. Herr Professor Doktor Knabel finally picked up the phone after Tod had spent three expensive minutes convincing Frantzi that he was himself and with an urgent message.

"Yes, Tod?" The professor's voice rang true and clear over the five thousand and more miles between them.

"Did you get my package, Professor?"

"Yes, Tod, and the results are positive. We sent you a cablegram yesterday. Sorry for the delay, my boy, but your evidence only arrived on Friday, and you know how things are on weekends."

"Well, that's good news. I have even more evidence, a photograph of his wife before their marriage, hidden in his room. It is in the mail to you. Shall I contact the FBI, Professor?"

"We have already done that, Tod. There will be a slight delay. The proper channels must be used, and it will take, perhaps, several days. What I want you to do, dear boy, is stay right where you are at that place . . ."

"Sky High."

"Yes, exactly. An agent will contact you very soon. As long as the . . . individual in question suspects nothing, all is well. Just watch him, be sure he makes no unexpected moves, and enjoy yourself a little. You have done a fine job, Tod. This will be a feather in our cap, to get this one. Your hunch was a good one. We congratulate you."

"Thank you, Professor." This was high praise indeed: the old man was very sparing with his plaudits.

Something unexpected stirred in Tod at that moment. He had been praised before, and justly, but his business of Pepi Prager was not like his other cases. It was more than just an intellectual game, a massing of detail until the evidence spoke for itself. This was something Tod had made happen, by the force of his will, the agility of his instinct, and Tod suddenly realized it was a hunter's instinct, and that the thought of moving in for the kill pleased him more than he liked to admit. A shiver went through him, and he was glad the professor wasn't there to see him blush.

"Just watch, young Rubinsky, and wait. You will be contacted within a few days. And the actual arrest . . ."

"Will be made by the Americans?"

"Precisely. Good-bye, now, Tod."

"Good-bye, Professor." Tod hung up the phone slowly. He hoped to see Pepi Prager's face when they finally closed in. And he wished a certain old lady in Belgium could be there to see it with him.

Zeke Gibbs resisted the temptation to slam the telephone onto its cradle. No point in wrecking the phone company's equipment just because he was mad at his lawyer.

"Will Jefferson *says* we're not licked yet." Zem looked up from the book she was reading. It was after supper in the old ranch house. Bill Shepherd was out making house calls.

"You sound like you don't believe him."

"I don't, Zem. Damned lawyers. They're always so sure about everything. Ten thousand it's cost me and what'd we get? A lot of libelous publicity that's sure going to lose us votes, may just also lose us the fight."

"Would it be so bad, Gramps? If you lost?"

"Zembra, I know you think I'm just a crazy old man. Maybe caring about this valley—what's left of it—makes me crazy. There's such a thing as caring too much."

"I care, too, Gramps. I understand how you feel. I just don't want you to make yourself sick over it, that's all."

"It took Jake Chaffee to make me see how much it

means to me, Zem. Never really thought much about it before he came nosing around."

"I think Aunt Eugenia's more to blame than Jake Chaffee."

"No, Zem. 'Genia was weak, but you can't blame someone for giving in to temptation. It's the tempters and seducers you've got to look out for. That carnival barker down the road flew over there and sweet-talked your aunt right into signing before she knew what got into her. Hell, why should she care?"

"Because it's in her blood. *I* care."

"Well, little Zem, you just haven't had your aunt's advantages. You've been locked up here with an old crazy man all these years, just hearing one side of the story. Hell, there is another side. Maybe it would be a better thing if this whole damned country got itself paved with Macdonald hamburger stands and drive-in movies."

"Gramps!" Zem Gibbs laughed and her grandfather laughed with her. It was the first time in months she'd seen him looking cheerful.

"I don't have to tell you that road really does need fixing." Zeke looked at his granddaughter with a small shy smile. He'd never admitted the truth of the matter before.

"If it hadn't been so narrow . . ."

". . . your mom and dad might be in this room tonight. It's suprising the papers haven't picked that up. But when you're old and alone, Zem, you fight with whatever comes to hand. He's done that to me, Jake Chaffee."

"I just can't help thinking it could be worse. It'd be best if he hadn't come at all. But when he did come, he tried to make the place attractive."

"That raises an interesting question, Zem. Would you rather have your head chopped off by a gold ax or a plain old steel one?"

"If you knew the man . . ."

"Oh, Zem, I *know* the man. He was here in this room. Once. And once was enough. I'm a crazy old timber rattler and I never went to a fancy university back East and my daddy wasn't a famous senator, but I do know that man." Zeke walked over to the window and looked down the valley. The moon rode big in the sky, a fine three-quarter moon spreading soft cool light. The head of Sky Mountain rose proud out of its sheath of dark trees and at its base only a cluster of lights revealed the enemy camp that was Sky Lodge. Zeke paused for a moment and continued: "I know the kind of greed a man like that has in him, Zem. It isn't just your everyday greed for money, it's something worse and much deeper. It's a thirst to play God, the worst kind of arrogance. It's the urge to build empires, a lust for control, to invent new games and win them and let the world wonder why. Some men do it with guns and armies, men like Alexander and Napoleon and Hitler. Jake Chaffee plays the game with real estate and he doesn't much care whose, but make no mistake, it's the same game, Zem, and an evil one. He thinks he can own a mountain. No man owns a mountain. Or the sea or the sky. It's wrong to want to."

"Jake Chaffee doesn't know that." Zem got up and joined her grandfather at the window.

"The mountain," said Zeke Gibbs softly, talking more to himself than to Zembra, "will teach him."

14

Eliza looked at the small blond head riding next to her in the MG. A week ago she hadn't even known Charlie Lamont existed. Now, they were thick as thieves. Eliza's memories of her own dead brother were blurred. If anyone had asked her why she was so attracted to Charlie, she might not have had a ready answer. Maybe it was simple affection. Maybe it was to make up for her doubts about Cassie. Maybe it was one more way to get closer to Jake. But whatever the reason, she saw a lot of the boy and enjoyed every minute. Right now she was driving him to town for ice cream and to have his cast changed for a lighter walking cast. Whizzer, of course, shared the bucket seat with his master. Eliza reached out and rumpled the boy's hair. "You know what you're going to be, C. B. Lamont?"

"No, what?" It sounded like another new game.

"You are going to be my stepbrother. How about that?"

"Will you be my stepsister?"

"That's included at no extra cost."

"What's a stepbrother?"

"It's when my father marries your mother."

"Mommy told me that."

"I'm going to like having a brother, old chum."

"Me, too." Charlie had one arm around Whizzer. "And my chum here," he said gravely, "can be your stepdog."

"It's a deal. I don't have a brother and I don't have a dog, and I can't imagine nicer ones."

"And I don't have a father. I did, but he died."

"I heard about that. I'm sorry."

"My father was a very good skier."

"My secret agents tell me you're pretty good yourself. When you're better we'll ski together."

"I fall a lot."

"So does everybody. I bet even Pepi falls sometimes. Anyway, I think old C. B. Lamont is going to be an Olympic racer."

The red MG pulled into Sky Junction's main street and Eliza found a parking space in front of the old soda fountain. "Decision time!" She turned to her passenger. "What flavor, old chum?"

"Maple walnut, please." Eliza brought two cones back to the car and they sat in silent comradeship for a while, eating the ice cream in the bright mountain sunshine.

"Eliza?"

"What's up, C.B.?"

"Will you stay with me when he takes the cast off?"

"Of course I will, Charlie. I bet we can even talk him into letting Whizzer be with us. Anyway, it doesn't hurt."

"It itches."

"He'll do something about that. And we'll show him what a brave old chum I've got, right?"

"Stepchum. Right."

Maggie della Robbia wondered if the pain was a punishment from God. She'd had the headache two days now and it wasn't getting any better. Aspirin dulled it a little, but the pain was always with her, drumming at the base of her skull with steady urgent messages. No doubt about it, she was coming down with something. Still, she wasn't going to let some dumb headache get the best of her.

Maggie was amazed how quickly her first rush of guilt had turned into pleasure. It wasn't just the sex, although the sex was fine. And it wasn't the fact that Pete Woodbury, lovable, honorable Pete, was really going through with his divorce. Maggie felt good because she was happy in her own skin for the first time in years. It had been—how long?—since she'd had this wonderful, relaxed feeling of contentment.

She'd never go back to Nick. The thing with Pete might or might not be permanent. In her heart she hoped it would go on forever, but that was the wish of the schoolgirl who still lurked beneath the surface in grownup, glamorous looking Maggie della Robbia. Maggie's first impulse had been to call her four children together for a family conference. She had always brought them up to take a share in major decisions, to make them feel they were truly a part of the family decision-making process. But then Maggie hesitated. If sides were going to be taken, she didn't doubt whose side her kids would be on. But Maggie would never, if she could help it, turn her family into an armed camp.

Nick, she knew, would probably sigh with relief when she asked for the divorce. It would let him play full-time instead of having to give lip service to the farce of being a family man.

She looked into her dressing-table mirror and smiled over the persistent pain of her headache. A very sexy looking redhead smiled back, a girl Maggie might not have recognized two weeks before. Her thick red hair was worn loose the way Pete liked it, not in its former prim twist. The well cut burgundy velvet slacks were last year's, but the simple silk shirt above them was daringly unbuttoned nearly to the point of no return. "You," she said sternly to the girl in the mirror, "are a hussy." And loving it.

Jean-Pierre Belfort turned the shower on as hot as he could stand it and stood under the needle spray for some minutes without moving. It was a fine place to think, the shower. He felt the hot needles dashing off his broad shoulders, felt muscles unwind that were tight from a long days' skiing, as he tried to sort out the conflicting emotions that sat like a hard little rock in his gut.

Cornelia de Vos was not, to Jean-Pierre, just another easy fuck.

Jean-Pierre had been halfway down the face of the China Bowl that afternoon trying in vain to drum some coordination into a gangly teenaged girl. Her fundamental lack of any athletic ability was complicated by the fact that she was about cross-eyed with lust for Jean-Pierre. Then he saw Pepi and Niris and Cornelia come flying down the hill looking like avenging angels. He laughed out loud, such was the contrast between his hapless pupil and those soaring apparitions. "That," he said, pointing with a ski pole, "is what it's all about."

Later, as he nursed his pupil down the easiest route, a traverse that led them under the path of the chair-lift, Jean-Pierre saw Cornelia and Niris riding up together, laughing and nodding, their heads nearly touching. Of course Niris would go for a woman like Cornelia, and she for him. And what could a penniless farm boy from Val d'Isère offer a woman like that? One thing, surely: he had offered it and the offer had been warmly appreciated. But Jean-Pierre was not a French peasant's son for nothing, and not for nothing had he spent all his winters since high school teaching skiing to pleasure seekers in the Alps and in America. Jean-Pierre knew the way the world worked, and he was shrewd enough to see when it started to work against him. A month ago his reaction would have been a simple Gallic shrug, another glass of wine and another easy conquest. But a month ago Jean-Pierre hadn't known Cornelia de Vos.

He felt for Cornelia something he'd never felt before. This was not simply one more jet-set body consumed with lust, using a parade of ripe young men to keep middle age at bay. Jean-Pierre knew those women well, and he had used them as they used him, fair trade, nobody hurt, thanks for the tip.

The hot water beat down on him and at last he reached for the soap. Minutes later he was getting dressed and minutes after that he was standing in the Sky Bar scrubbed and shining with health, smiling despite the tight little knot in his gut that was growing bigger and tighter. Cornelia wasn't there, and neither was Niris.

Cassie lay in the shaded room with her head toward the foot of the bed and her feet elevated on two pillows. A damp hand towel masked her eyes and forehead. She had just taken three aspirin tablets. Still the pain continued. She couldn't remember the last time she'd taken a nap. Thank God for Eliza, pitching in with Charlie like that. Cassie hated any kind of pills. Burke and a couple of his racing chums sometimes took little red "uppers" and that had terrified her. She wouldn't be surprised if he'd been on pills on top of the whiskey the night he killed himself, although there was no way to be sure. Well, anyhow, if she wasn't feeling a lot better the next day she'd call Bill Shepherd. In the meantime she had about fifteen more minutes before the alarm clock would remind her it was time to make an appearance in the Sky Bar. She frowned under the cooling towel. Usually Cassie liked the goldfish-bowl aspects of her life at Sky High: being by nature a very private person she realized it was good for her to deal with people in a public way. She liked people, liked helping them with small problems, liked organizing things to run smoothly. Cassie knew she liked the job for another reason too: because she was very good at it.

There was a thumping-thumping-thumping sound from down the hall and Cassie smiled. Charlie was practicing with his new walking stick. Jake had cut him a length of Aspen sapling and rounded off both ends with sandpaper to preserve the floors from scratches and Charlie's hand from splinters. Jake Chaffee would be a good father for Charlie. This thought made Cassie smile. But the small effort that took brought the pain rushing back, and the smile dissolved into a frown.

Noel Northcliff was the most fastidious of men. Like many a poor boy growing up in England in the 1930s, NN had formed his ideas of elegance from the cabaret of Noel Coward and the films of Cary Grant and Fred Astaire. Such was the wit and ease that young Northcliff had set himself as a goal. To a remarkable degree, he had achieved that goal. Noel Northcliff at fifty was a smooth and seamless creation, moving easily through the fabled drawing rooms of Mayfair and Park Avenue and the right bank of Paris. Noel enjoyed every minute of it. His razor-sharp brain was well aware it was all rather silly now, that with every passing year fewer and fewer people cared about the cut of a suit or the timing of a bon mot. But this was his world, he took a certain indulgent pride in it, as though he had created that world like some sly dapper little god. If there was a certain air of impending doom about it all, of dancing under the volcano, so much the better: it merely added to the drama of the last act of Western civilization.

Elegance, to Noel Northcliff, was an end in itself. If he had been alone on a desert island, he would have dressed for dinner, just like the people in cartoons. But NN took it all lightly. The Northcliff wit was a real wit founded in a sense of the underlying madness of life on earth. This is why, when NN found himself virtually trapped in his room at Sky High by a galloping case of diarrhea, he chuckled philosophically and reached for the Kaopectate.

The Kaopectate had long been NN's constant traveling companion, for his work often took him to exotic places that spawned equally exotic germs. He'd had Montezuma's Revenge in Puerto Vallarta, Rasputin's Revenge in Kiev, Vishnu's Vengeance in the Vale of Kashmir and Madame Butterfly's Backlash at plum-blossom time in Kyoto. And always, the Kaopectate had seen him through this most undignified of human afflictions. Idly, as he poured a triple dose of the chalky, horrible-tasting fluid into his tooth glass, Noel wondered who was getting back at him this time. Certainly not Raoul Peng. One of the best things about Sky High was the crisp cleanliness of it all. Here were no festering swamps under a lurid tropic sunset, nor unwashed coolies secretly contaminating the salad. No houseflies flitted from sewer to soufflé at Sky High. Maybe, reflected the world's best-known society reporter as he choked down his medicine, maybe he was simply coming down with *la grippe*. Then Noel frowned. He'd have to do better than that. *La grippe* wasn't funny and it wasn't fashionable. Then a wicked thought occurred to him and he laughed outright. Maybe it was a plague! How lovely, how absolutely delicious, to imagine this court-of-Marie-Antoinette crew awash with the shits. Noel felt better at once.

At the moment Jean-Pierre Belfort was looking for her in the Sky Bar, Cornelia de Vos was soaking in a scented tub of very hot water in her suite upstairs. Her hair was piled on top of her head. She leaned back and sank a little deeper into the tub, replaying the afternoon in her head, word by word, gesture by gesture like an actress in a long-running play considering how to improve the performance. Timing, Cornelia well knew, was everything. In fact that was why she lingered in her tub.

Niris had invited her to supper. Cornelia had begged a previous engagement. Niris had asked her to ski with him the next day. Cornelia would be delighted. And supper? They would see. Cornelia had no previous engagement for this evening, and Niris would almost surely be in the bar waiting to catch another glimpse of her. As would Jean-Pierre. So Cornelia would make no appearance in the bar this night, or in the restaurant either. A simple tray would be sent up to her room. As for Jean-Pierre, charming boy that he was, she must find a way to let him down gently. The stage would have to be cleared of supporting players. The significant part of the drama was about to begin.

Cornelia smiled in the mist that rose from the bathtub. Niris was really a delightful little man. Not little. She mustn't think of him as little. He was, let us say, compact, in the way of many Near Eastern men. Not a Jean-Pierre, of course, but one mustn't think of that. The Jean-Pierres of the world were physical specimens, and the woods were filled with them. Still, she remembered the first night with Jean-Pierre, and the night after that. Cornelia shivered a little in the hot tub. To tell the truth she wouldn't mind it if that boy came knocking on her door right this minute, but she knew he wouldn't. Too polite. And, when all was said and done, a servant. Suddenly Cornelia stood up in the tub and opened the drain. Let them think what they would, Niris and Jean-Pierre too. A bit of mystery never hurt a love affair. Madame de Vos had a previous engagement this evening. With Madame de Vos.

Dudley Lanier Drummond III looked at his wife with something like hope. Dud was an optimist by nature. The fact that for five messy years he had hoped in vain made little impression on Dud. It might be his fault. Maybe he was doing something wrong. Maybe they should have had kids after all. They'd talked about it, the first year they were married. But Liz didn't want kids. "I don't want the responsibility of bringing them into this rotten little world, Dud. And that's that." She had then sipped her martini. That was back before he'd started counting her drinks.

"Why's it so rotten?"

"Why does shit stink? Don't ask me. I didn't make it." Then he had realized she was drunk.

They both drank a lot in those days, but it never seemed out of control. Then the day came when Liz showed up for a lunch date downtown, thoroughly plastered at twleve-fifteen. Then came the binges, the days and weeks she'd vanish altogether, the checks scrawled out to "Cash" cashed in odd places, the collect phone call from Paris asking him to please wire money. The time he found out she was sleeping with the eighteen-year-old son of his next-door neighbors. Most men would have thrown in the towel at almost any one of those signposts, but most men were not Dud Drummond. Dud had stuck with her, through the shrinks and the drinking and the drying-out farms and the open parade of lovers. Dud stuck to Liz with the devotion that makes certain dogs lie growling, fiercely guarding the graves of long-dead masters. Hers was a slow suicide. It was Dud's fate to keep hoping that somehow he'd find a way to pull her back from the abyss.

It wasn't all misery. No one could have withstood that. Some days were much better than others and this looked like one of the good days. Dud had come back from Denver to find Jake thrilled with what he'd accomplished there. Jake showed him a carbon of a complimentary letter sent that morning to Dud's boss in New York. And Liz seemed quieter and more sober than last week. He accepted this happy turn of events as a gift and set his mind to making it last. She laughed, not her bitter cynical laugh but the nice warm laugh he loved. She looked better. The Sky High sun was tanning her and if you didn't look too closely, she was the picture of health. Maybe this was the turning point. Maybe something about Sky High made Liz realize there was hope after all. In any event, this was definitely a new Liz. The only thing she complained about was a headache.

Tod Rubin shuddered all down the length of his thin body, and clenched the sheets as if they could somehow keep him afloat above the pain. Then, slowly, he climbed out of the bed, first planting one foot gingerly on the floor, then following that with the other foot as if getting out of bed was a new adventure for him. He stood up, staggered like a drunken man, and fumbled his way to the bathroom. Even before he found the light switch Tod felt himself getting sick, very sick. Just in time, for the nausea was welling up in him like an erupting volcano, he located the toilet bowl.

Later, feeling a little better and faintly ashamed of himself, Tod stood at the sink washing his face and hands and taking two aspirin tablets with a long drink of good mountain water. He saw a gaunt man with damp, matted hair staring back at him from the mirror. He must get a grip on himself. He'd been working too hard. After all, breaking and entering did not come naturally to Tod Rubin. Or could it simply be disgust at being under the same roof, so to speak, as the notorious Karl-Heinz Waldemar? Tod didn't want to look anymore at that face in the mirror. Quickly, he flicked off the light. He would feel better tomorrow. Sitting down on the edge of his bed, Tod shuddered once again. And once again he felt the sweat breaking out on his forehead. God in heaven. He'd been working too long catching monsters. Some of it must be rubbing off on him. When he got back to Vienna he really must speak to the professor about taking a holiday. Not in a ski resort, either.

Clio, long-suffering Muse of History, was now Dorothy Dutton's constant companion. Not for Dorothy were the innumerable soft temptations of Sky High. No longer was she seen in full sail at high noon sipping beer in the Sky Bar. All day long in simple clothes and minimal makeup, Dorothy Dutton sat hard at work in her room. Reel after reel of tape recorded her long gaudy lifetime. This was a new experience for Dorothy, who hadn't known there were any new experiences left. Never had she worked at a self-imposed task. The machine made it easy, like one long glorious cocktail conversation with a man who never interrupts, grows bored, or fails to be amused.

A second tape recorder was flown up from Denver with blank tapes by the gross, and Momo was set to work duplicating the originals. Dorothy wanted two copies of every tape. The originals would go into a vault in Zurich. This great work must be made safe from fire, theft or loss. Momo, much subdued since his rebuff by Buck Washington, was happy to perform this menial chore. Right now keeping a low profile appealed to Momo's instincts for survival, and survival was the one gift God had allowed the Count Ruvo di Putignano-Squillace.

"Spring came early to Asheville that year," said Dorothy confidentially to the microphone. "My father's château, Duttonfields, had a formal garden of hybrid azaleas and rhododendrons patterned after the spring garden Le Notre created for Vaux-le-Vicomte. It stretched from the side terrace of the château all the way down to an immense oval reflecting pool a quarter-mile away, a fantastic maze of pathways shaped into faceted squares and circles within circles and scrolls and fleurs-de-lis. I would walk through this garden quite alone with my little Yorkshire terrier, Brillo. For I was the only member of the family in all those thousands of acres, in all the cold, uncounted rooms of the château. I was sixteen and very lonely. It was this summer that I discovered sex." Dorothy sighed and pushed the STOP button on the recorder. Momo was in the other room dutifully rerecording yesterday's tapes. She remembered that garden, that spring, and the soft breeze that seemed to wrap itself around you and cling there like crepe de chine. Dorothy smiled gently, but then she frowned. The headache was coming back again. She must be working too hard. Dorothy got up from her chair and went into the bathroom to take more aspirin. For all her hypochondria she was strong as a horse. It was most unusual for Dorothy Dutton to have a headache.

It was windy on top of Sky Mountain. Dud Drummond, awkward on borrowed skis, zipped the parka tighter around his neck. It was the race, he thought, cursing it, that was the agent of his discomfort this afternoon. Dud and Pepi Prager and Jake were mapping out the race courses.

The Sky High Challenge Cup was going to make news nationwide if Dud Drummond had anything to do with it. The winner would ski away with fifty thousand dollars in cash, and there were generous prizes for the runners-up. Dud was counting on Killy. He was pretty sure of Spider Sabitch. Young Hank Kashiwa would be there, as would Henri Duvillard and a crew of unfledged hotshots like Jean-Pierre Belfort, who just might turn the tables on the pros. And there'd be Pepi Prager himself in that well-publicized "comeback" exhibition race.

Sports Illustrated and *Skiing Magazine* were sending crews, and so were the three major television networks. Dud wasn't counting on a big crowd of spectators. Sky High just wasn't all that well-known yet, or that accessible to the big cities. But with coverage like this, the crowds would be there for the next Sky High Challenge Cup.

The three men stood together looking up at the trail called Pepi's Promise. Like Wardance, this was one of the toughest expert trails on the mountain, designed by Pepi to equal the most challenging Alpine downhill courses in the world. Pepi had succeeded. The trail cut down the steepest part of Sky Mountain, plunging and twisting through stands of fir trees, down one steep face that in summer revealed itself for the rock-ledged cliff it was. It would make a hell of a race, and it would be hell to photograph. Already, they had skied the trail three times, Dud sideslipping gingerly down the steepest parts, searching out camera locations that would give a sense of the steepness and danger of the run. At last, they had agreed where the three camera platforms would be built. Then they skied off towards China Bowl, where the main events of the race would be held.

China Bowl was a perfect natural ampitheater: it presented no problem for a television crew. The main events of the Sky High Challenge Cup would be the new kind of race developed especially for the TV cameras on the pro circuit, the double slalom. The classic Olympic courses had individual skiers competing against a stopwatch, which was all very well for the skiers but vastly less interesting for spectators. The new double slalom consisted of two identical slalom courses running side by side down some wide trail. The drama was provided by two skiers actually skiing against each other down these parallel courses, in full view of the spectators and—more importantly—the television cameras. In one brilliant stroke ski racing had acquired all the drama of a horse race.

The three men skied slowly down China Bowl and stopped at the bottom, almost exactly in the middle. This would be the finish line. Above the smooth rim of the bowl a few stands of sentinel spruce trees hid the north face of Sky Mountain. To the left, behind the rim, an immense cornice of snow and black rock raced up another thousand feet to meet the sky, curling up and over on itself the way big surf curls just before breaking. The cornice hung frozen but still threatening over the serene perfection of China Bowl. The great Alpine cornice was called Widow's Peak. It was strictly off limits, the one part of Sky Mountain that scared everybody.

"Now," said Dud, "if we really wanted some action, all we'd have to do is get somebody to come cruising down that."

"You're picking up the insurance premiums, I take it," Jake laughed without humor. What they were doing was routine, donkeywork, but Jake knew how vital every line of publicity could be for Sky High, and the fact that so much was riding on the success of the pro race, of this whole extended opening party, had taken its toll on the well-known Chaffee charm. He looked up at Widow's Peak. He and Pepi had started to climb it one day last July. There were rocks that hid rattlers, and three deep crevasses concealed now by forty feet of smooth-looking snow. The weight of a jackrabbit could break through that snow in seconds.

"There is not that much money in the world," said Pepi quietly, "to get a sane man up that cornice."

"I think we're all set here, Pepi," Jake said absently, his eyes still on Widow's Peak, held there by the subtle fascination of the impossible. "The snow-cats can bring up the materials for the camera platforms."

"We will give them," said Pepi as they turned to ski down, "something to remember."

Maggie reached across the table in the Sky Bar where they were having cocktails and touched Pete's hand. It was still here, warm and real. She wasn't dreaming. She looked at the face of this man who had changed her life. It wasn't a face to launch ships or lead armies. It would never end up on a coin. But Maggie loved that face. She was being brave and trying not to show it. Because Pete was leaving Sky High.

"The papers initiating the divorce," Pete Woodbury had just said quietly, "will be ready for me to sign late next week. Jake's lending me the company apartment until I can find one of my own. Naturally, Fran will get the house and an income and support for the girls."

"How are they taking it?" Maggie was sipping her second daiquiri, but the headache was still there.

"Typical Franny: gotta keep that facade polished. She hasn't told them yet. Wants to wait till we can tell them together. Maybe she's right, at that. And maybe it's a big number to grab me by the heartstrings."

"Don't say that, Pete. You sound hard when you talk that way."

"You're right. As always." He grinned and some of the tension went away. "It's just that I'm used to a lot of game playing, Maggie: the veiled threat, the sly dig, the whole Machiavellian number. You've heard 'em, I'm sure: all dressed up and smiling and tearing each other to shreds."

"I know what you mean. That's why I'm such a flop

as a rich man's wife. Half of it I don't understand, and when I do, it makes me mad."

"Here's to that!" He lifted his glass and touched her glass.

"Here's to getting out of ruts."

"To you and me, Maggie. I haven't felt so good since they let me out of the Army. And that was eighteen years ago."

"I keep telling myself it'll be easy, that he just doesn't care at all. And that may not be true. He cared enough to bounce me off a brick wall last summer."

"If you're in any kind of danger, Maggie . . ."

"No, Nick's a coward. He was drunk and I was making fun of him, which I should have known was a mistake. Very humorless, the Italians. The rich, fat, Cadillac-driving, Las Vegas-going, hooker fucking ones, anyway. Pillars of the church. My Nick not only gave the church a new roof, his company actually put it on. Do you suppose that cancels out a spot of wife beating in Saint Peter's record book?"

"Not in my book."

"Mine, either."

"Maggie, would it make sense for you to get away someplace until it's over? I mean, you don't know how he'll react, do you?"

"I have a fairly good idea." She sipped the drink. "First he'll be shocked: how could I do such a thing? Especially to a sweet guy like Nick. Then he'll get moralistic: the church and all that. Then he'll begin feeling sorry for himself and send me expensive presents in bad taste, which I will return, and then he'll realize how much fun he can have as a free agent, with none of those nagging little guilt feelings. At which point, instead of his formerly loving wife and ex-chairwoman of the Sacred Heart of Mary Association, I will become 'that redheaded broad who took him for a ride.' Nick only knows about two kinds of women: broads and ladies. I used to be a lady. Tell me, Mr. Woodbury: would you mind being seen with a redheaded broad?"

"It would be a privilege. So you're really going to do it?"

"I'm really going to do it. And"—she looked away

from Pete's serious dark eyes and out into the black-and-violet twilight—"not completely because of you, Pete. Although you probably got me going a bit faster than I might have done otherwise. But it was coming. Had to come."

"Marry me, Maggie."

"I can't answer that now. It's all too fast for me. I probably won't file for a while. It may take a year."

"We can still be together. Philadelphia isn't so far away."

"The lawyers might have some things to say about that."

"Mine won't."

"I wouldn't put it past Nick to have me followed. To catch me misbehaving would soothe his bruised vanity. Of course, there are two sides to that one, if he ever wanted to toss the accusations around."

"Marry me anyway."

"I'll say this for you financial guys: you're persistent."

"At least say you'll consider it."

"I'll consider it, Pete. I'll consider it a lot." They sat there for a few moments just looking at each other. Maggie was happier than she'd been for years. But her headache was getting worse.

Liz Drummond counted the little green capsules slowly, lovingly, a quiet smile on her face. There were seven phenobarbitals carefully hoarded from the last prescription. Dud, ever thoughtful, had brought back a month's supply from Denver, thirty lovely new ones. The new ones were red. One before bedtime, the doctor said, for guaranteed sweet dreams. But never, never more than two.

So thirty-seven ought to do it. How Christmassy they looked, the bright red mingling with the darker green. The doctor, a new doctor, young and sleek and very Park Avenue, had asked Liz about drinking. "Well, yes, Doctor, I do take a drink now and then, socially. Or a little wine." How clever she felt. She'd had a very large vodka-and-tomato-juice that morning for breakfast. The glow was still on her. When he cautioned her never,

never to take the sleeping pills after she'd been drinking, Liz nodded solemnly, for all the world a responsible young matron who just had a little trouble sleeping sometimes.

Liz cupped the thirty-seven pills in one hand and walked back to the bedroom. Duddy-Fuddy was off someplace with Jake. She sat at the dressing table and poured a glass full of bourbon. Very good bourbon it was, too, courtesy of Sky Lodge. Then she began taking the pills, four by four, at first mixing the green ones with the red ones and then just the red ones alone.

Nine times her cupped hand came up to her lips, followed by the glass of bourbon. There was one pill left, red and shiny, a perfect little tube with rounded ends, very cheery, a tribute to modern science and technology. Liz swallowed this last pill and washed it down with more bourbon. Then she filled her glass again, and sipped it, looking thoughtfully out the window at the sun setting behind Sky Mountain. "Tension headache got you down? Try Zappo! The ultimate remedy. Look! Headache gone!" Her voice trailed off. Liz blinked. There were two suns setting behind two Sky Mountains. Lovely effect. She must tell Duddy-Fuddy. He could make a fucking PR poster out of it: *See Sky High and Die*. She stood up, slowly, still holding her glass. Step by uneven step Liz Drummond crossed to the bed. She sat down heavily, spilling a little whiskey on the expensive coverlet. "Tsk, tsk. Neatness counts." Liz set the glass down on the night table and swung her legs up on the bed. Her legs were heavy, heavy. She looked at the window. There was only one Sky Mountain now. The room was quiet. Sky Mountain, framed by the redwood window frame, looked like a Christmas card. "Merry, merry Christmas, Duddy-Fuddy," whispered Liz as death rose to meet her.

Dud was in Jake's suite with Jake and Pete Woodbury going over the latest press clippings. Probably the best was a six-page four-color spread in *Sports Illustrated;* it had been shot in late November by a crew from New York, but you'd never know it to see the article. The pictures showed Sky High in full swing, the bars, the kitchen, the tramway and the slopes. The fact that the place had been empty and still under construction at the time of the shooting was never apparent. The article was more than enthusiastic. "Sky High is nothing less than the new standard that all ski resorts will have to measure up to in the future." The article went on to rave about the food, the snow, the luxury of it all, with personal interviews featuring Jake and Raoul Peng and Pepi. The same picture of Jake holding his skis and looking out over Sky Mountain had found its way into the sports section of *Time*. The caption was, simply: "King of the Mountain." The *Newsweek* piece also featured a picture of Jake. They called him the "Snow King." There would be features in *Skiing* and *Ski* magazines, and in the sports sections of Sunday newspapers in eleven major metropolitan areas. That was the coverage Dud knew about for sure. More, undoubtedly, would be coming, especially after the widely televised broadcast of the Sky High Challenge Cup next weekend.

"I'm not too sure about all that Snow King bullshit, Dud," Jake laughed, "but it looks pretty good to me. Why don't you make Pete a few Xeroxes of everything so he can show 'em to our pals in Wall Street?"

"Do that, Dud. It's a very impressive package."

"Thanks. More coming. These things always follow a snowballing kind of pattern. The next thing we want is for people to begin using Sky High as a location, for fashion spreads in the magazines, for ads and commercials. The trick is, make 'em welcome, help 'em in every way, do it for free—but demand a credit. And, if we can get someone to film a feature movie here, and it just happens to have a bit of Sky High identification here and there, that's literally priceless."

"Like all those Ford cars in all those James Bond movies?"

"Exactly."

"Dudley, you make it sound like anything's possible," Pete said.

Pete's mind raced: There might be more in the publicity than he'd dared to hope.

"With enough time—and money—you'd be

amazed," Dud said. "I mean, they once got Eleanor Roosevelt, for chrissakes, to do a margarine commercial."

"You're kidding."

"Scout's honor. Hell, the British royal family endorses all kinds of stuff—by implication, mind you, and discreetly. But it's done."

"It's all for sale, then?" Pete was genuinely surprised. It was a world he'd never been exposed to.

"Let's say it's for rent."

"Under the right circumstances." Jake put down the proof pages from *Sports Illustrated*. "Can I buy you guys a drink?"

Dud Drummond looked out the window, then at his watch. "A quickie, Jake. I've got to check on . . ." He caught himself: "Got to see Liz about something." Jake went to the bar and poured Scotch for Dud and Pete Woodbury. Then he poured himself some of the house Zinfandel. "To Sky High."

"Amen." Pete smiled.

Dud finished his drink quickly and set down the glass. "Thanks, men. See you later." He went out of the room and down the hall and Jake began talking finances with Pete Woodbury.

They were still talking ten minutes later when the door swung open. Dud Drummond stood there, but if he hadn't been wearing the same clothes they might not have known it was the same man who'd left them a few minutes earlier. His face had gone pale and more than pale: it had a gray, drained, translucent quality like something made from wax. His eyes seemed not to focus.

"Dud?" Jake stood up.

"She's . . . she is . . ." Dud stood in the doorway waiting for someone to rewind his key. Then with slow robot steps he made it to the bar and poured himself a glass of Scotch. He raised the glass but missed his mouth and put the glass down as though he didn't know how it got there. "You never heard her laugh," said Dud to no one in particular. "She had this funny little laugh, that you'd have to be very close even to know she was laughing. And when you got that close, you'd want to get closer. A very good sport. That's what people would say. Lizzie's such a good sport. A good sport and beautiful. I never thought I'd be so lucky, to get a girl like that. Liz. She's dead. She's dead, Jake."

Jake had an arm around Dud in a second. "Easy, Dud. Are you sure?"

"Not breathing."

"Where is she? In your room?"

"Sleeping. Dead." Jake led him down the hall and around the corner and down another hallway. Pete followed, saying nothing. Liz Drummond lay peacefully on the bed. There was no expression on her face. She looked younger, at peace with herself and the world. Only the overturned whiskey glass on the floor and the empty pill bottles in the bathroom told the story. Jake reached out for her pulse and found none.

Dud Drummond wouldn't leave the room until the doctor came. It was as though he felt she might wake up again, and he wanted to be there when she did. Bill Shepherd got there in fifteen minutes, flushed and out of breath, wearing blue jeans and a lumberman's wool shirt. He felt her pulse and put a stethoscope to her heart, and sighed. "How many pills were there?"

"I just brought a new month's supply back from Denver. Thirty. I don't know if she had any others."

"Has she ever tried this before?"

"No. That is, not to my knowledge."

"We'll have to bring in the coroner." Bill paused. "I'm not sure where there is one."

"Steamboat Springs." Jake spoke quietly. "Bill, we'll want to keep this just as quiet as we can."

"Of course. Is there someplace an ambulance could pull up inconspicuously?"

"Sure. Behind the kitchen wing. Just tell them to bear right at the fork in the driveway."

"Right." Bill Shepherd picked up the phone. The arrangements were made quickly. An ambulance would be at Sky High by ten that night. There would have to be an autopsy—the state law required it—and an inquest, but it could be a private inquest. Jake stayed with Dud Drummond after Shepherd and Woodbury left.

They went back to Jake's room and had that drink. Bit by bit the life flowed back into Dud Drummond.

"Jake," he said, "thank you for being . . . tolerant . . . while she was here. I used to try to fake it that I didn't know the things she was up to, but of course I did. And in case I'd forget, she'd remind me."

"God! She was lucky to have you."

"Yeah. Maybe." He looked up at Jake from some private dungeon. "Jake, if it's OK with you, I'll just stay on here and finish up everything we've started."

"Sure. Of course. If you feel up to it."

"You always feel there must have been something, some angle you didn't figure, some trick you didn't try. I would have done anything, Jake. Anything."

"I believe that."

"It was an act of love."

"You took very good care of her, Dud."

"You don't understand. Her suicide was because she loved me too much to drag me down with her."

"Don't blame yourself, Dud. You did everything you could."

"That's one way of looking at it." Dud finished his drink and grinned aimlessly at the glass.

"Funny, isn't it? Me drinking, after what it did . . ." Dud held his glass out straight and dropped it. It didn't break, but bounced without a sound on the carpet, rolled and stopped. Dudley touched it with the toe of his shoe. Then he stood up abruptly and brought his heel down hard on the expensive glass, with its bright blue Sky High monogram.

Jake shuddered at the crunch.

"She was so beautiful," said Dud, "you wouldn't believe, how beautiful she was."

"Dudley . . ."

"I think I want to take a walk, by myself, for a while, Jake."

"We'll be here when you need us."

"I know that. Thank you."

"Dud . . ." But Dudley had already turned and was walking out the door. When he had gone, Jake covered his own face with his hands and stood for a long while without moving.

15

Zeke Gibbs sat on his bed, staring at the boots he was about to put on. The day hadn't begun yet and Zeke wasn't sure he wanted it to.

The banjo clock on the bedroom wall said five-to-six. The clock had come to him with Jenny Kimball, a wedding gift in 1923. He sighed and looked around the big gabled room, Jenny's room. She had chosen the wallpaper, dusty pink with sprigs of white roses darkened now to ivory. The furniture was hers or her choosing, and the many-colored oval rug had been hooked by Jenny's hands over one long winter. It was a woman's room with an old man's chill on it now. Zeke had moved nothing, changed nothing, but somehow the life had gone out of that room in the years since Jenny died. Even Zem, who had brought him happiness in other ways, couldn't chase away the gloom that lived here. It had been a room filled with love once. Now it was just a place to sleep, to hang your clothes, but not to dream. Zeke tried to conjure up Jenny's face and the exact sound of her gentle voice, but failed. He reached for the high hunter's boots and pulled them on over his heavy wool socks and the worn corduroy trousers. The clock struck six with muted silver chimes. Zeke Gibbs had a ranch to run and it hadn't been getting the attention it deserved.

Even the running of Sky Ranch seemed like a lonely last-ditch fight these days. Zem came and went and wasn't really interested. It would all die with him. Zeke carried this certain knowledge with him like a ball and chain. He stood up and moved to the dresser and fished out a bulky outdoor sweater. Even the familiar sweep of his own Sky Ranch meadows outside the window gave Zeke no pleasure, because where his meadowland stopped Sky High began. The early morning sun glittered off unseen windows at Sky Lodge. The eternal winter's silence was suddenly broken by the crack and roar of the Sky High ski patrol shooting down avalanches with field cannon, making a harmless soundtrack for the real battle that raged in Zeke Gibbs's mind.

Will Jefferson had tried as best as he could, but the Chaffee gang outfoxed him. Will was of the old school. He thought in terms of clubs and handshake contracts. You scratch my back and I'll scratch yours. In Will Jefferson's mind, everything could be arranged. But Zeke was fighting Jake Chaffee in the fast-moving world of 1973 and no fish out of water could be less at home in that world than Zeke Gibbs or Will Jefferson. Maybe it wasn't right, but it was happening. The war was being lost. There was no self-delusion about Zeke Gibbs. He had underestimated Jake Chaffee once and that had cost him half of Sky Valley. Zeke felt a growing helplessness and, with it, a growing rage. He had tried every way he knew, fair or foul, to tear even just a little piece out of Jake Chaffee's hide. Sure it was spiteful. Expensive, too. Maybe revenge would be about the last pleasure Zeke Gibbs would know on this earth. and maybe it was hopeless from the start. But sure as God made Sky Mountain, Zeke was going to keep trying. Zeke turned and looked around the faded bedroom one more time, not seeing it. Then he walked out of the room and down the uncarpeted stairs to the kitchen to start up a pot of coffee.

Charlie Lamont had been fascinated by Jake from the first. Until Jake came along, Charlie's world had two people in it: Cassie and Charlie. He didn't remember his real father except in Cassie's stories and in old pictures and news clippings. Jake Chaffee made a big impression on Charlie, first because of his size, remarkable even by grownup standards and towering from Charlie's point of view. Then there was Jake's easy smile, very like the smiles on the pictures of Burke Lamont, a winner's smile with magic in it.

It was Jake who spent long afternoons skiing with the boy, and it was Jake who had finally persuaded Cassie to let Charlie ski alone. Even after the accident, Charlie was grateful for that.

Now Charlie came to Jake with his problems almost as freely as he did to Cassie. Cassie watched this with a mixture of surprise and admiration for Jake. It was what she wanted to happen, but being Cassie, she was too used to discounting her dreams to take it for granted. She thanked some lucky star and loved them both all the more.

Jake's red Jaguar convertible was waiting in front of the school bus when Charlie's class got out. Whizzer sat tall in the bucket seat with a good-natured smile, just as though he'd spent his entire life being chauffered in such luxury. The bell rang and a flock of kids burst from the small clapboard schoolhouse like a covey of quail. Charlie came hobbling on his walking cast with the help of the stick Jake had cut for him.

Charlie waved when he saw Jake and smiled. Jake was a legend among Charlie's schoolmates, and the red Jaguar was famous. The time had passed when Charlie considered Jake a threat. With some basic instinct, the boy could sense this person meant him no harm, or his mother, either. Still, Jake awed the boy. This man radiated power. He sketched out a ski trail on a map and in a few weeks a ski trail appeared for real—with Charlie's own name on it! Charlie strained not to limp as he dragged his walking cast towards the convertible. He would have been astounded to know he held this man's happiness right in his own hand.

"Hop in, old chum. It's surprise time."

"What's the surprise?" Charlie climbed over Whizzer so the dog could keep his favorite outside position.

"If I told you," said Jake gravely. "then it wouldn't be a surprise."

"Can I shift?" This was a new and fascinating game. Jake would depress the clutch and tell Charlie when to move the Jaguar's stick shift into gear.

"Sure. Ready?"

"Ready."

"OK. First."

"First." Charlie's small hand grabbed the big T-shaped handle of the gearshift and neatly set it into first gear. Jake released the clutch and the car glided out onto the narrow road.

"Second."

"Second." The car moved faster.

"Third."

"Third." Jake made a U-turn and headed towards town. "Is it a place, or a thing?" asked the boy.

"It's an event."

"Will mommy be there?"

"No. She's resting. Mommy doesn't feel too good."

"Can I tell her about it?"

"Sure. Ready for fourth?"

"Fourth!" The car picked up more speed and in a minute they were slowing down again for Main Street in Sky Junction. Jake pulled up in front of the town's one church, a small wooden building dating from the turn of the century.

"We're going to *church?"* Church was not a big element in Charlie's life.

"Basement." Jake climbed out of the car and waited for Charlie and the dog. They went in the front door of the little white church and down a short flight of stairs to the meeting hall. This was a long, sparsely furnished room that served Sky Junction as a dance hall, a town-meeting place, and occasionally, as a movie theater. There was a small 16mm projector.

Jake drew folding chairs in front of the projector, turned it on and switched off the light. A title appeared, big white letters on a blue background. It read: CHARLIE LAMONT'S FATHER. That flashed off and another title appeared. U.S. OLYMPIC DOWNHILL GOLD MEDAL WINNER BURKE LAMONT. The boy was silent.

The film opened with a long shot of a downhill race on a narrow trail marked with flags on bamboo poles. A straggling crowd huddled at the side of the trail. A black title flashed over the snow: U.S. NATIONALS, STOWE, 1962. Then a tiny figure appeared at the top of the trail, just a dot, coming down fast. The dot grew into a man and the man was Burke Lamont at age eighteen, placing second in his first big race. The figure came plunging down the race course and flashed through the finish line. The camera moved in on that eighteen-year-old face, even-featured and lean and more surprised than triumphant.

Then came a series of similar racing newsreels, cleverly edited to bring forth the most exciting incidents. After about twelve minutes of newsreels the screen dissolved into a color sequence. Here was a blazing blue sky over a perfect snow field dotted with frosted spruce trees. There were no tracks in the snow. Suddenly three skiers came soaring into the frame from the upper right. They all wore identical red jump suits and they skied on identical red skis. They glided and dipped and swirled in a series of perfectly carved S-turns, weaving in and out of each other's tracks as a triple-stranded braid of ski trails spun out in the virgin snow behind them.

The lead skier was Burke Lamont. After the underlying rhythm of the three skiers had been established, the camera began to join in their game. Suddenly the camera singled out Burke Lamont. The camera skied with him, close on his face which was smiling with mystical elation, an older Burke Lamont, caught forever in the full glory of what he did best, a vibrant soaring myth of skiing, spirit untamed and untamable, an image that—Jake hoped—Charlie would find more meaningful than a bunch of fading press clippings.

The close-ups of Burke skiing dissolved into another long shot of the three skiers, later in the day now, backlit by a sinking sun. The snowfield itself was almost completely in shadow except for the tops of the moguls that were still brushed with glittering white like the crests of waves in a stormy sea. They were schussing now, flying over moguls. Suddenly the camera picked out Burke Lamont, head on, skiing towards a long, long lens that must have been half a mile away. He still wore that oddly exalted smile. The camera held him for a minute or two and the focus grew more and more precise as Burke raced closer to the lens. He soared off a mogul and for one magic instant was spotlit by the yellow horizontal sunlight against the darkening mountain behind him, five feet in the air but higher than that in spirit, a creature not of the earth nor of the sky but caught forever somewhere in between, and soaring, always soaring. The camera froze. THE END.

The basement room was quiet. The projector hummed on and soon the film slipped off its reel and began flapping. Jake got up and switched the projector off, then rethreaded the film and switched the machine back on for rewinding. He turned on the light and looked at Charlie. The boy was crying.

"Hey, chum, that's supposed to be a happy movie."

Jake sat down next to Charlie and put his arm comfortingly around the boy's shoulder. "I wanted you to see what a terrific skier your dad was, Charlie." The boy said nothing. "And there's something else. Remember, always, that just because I'm going to marry your mommy, that doesn't mean I think I can really take your dad's place. I'll try. But you'll have to help me." Charlie turned to Jake. He wasn't crying now.

"Why did he die?"

"Charlie, if I knew that, I'd be a lot smarter than I am. Plenty of things happen that we don't want to happen. Like you breaking your leg. It was just an accident. Sometimes people die in accidents. And, if they do, we're very sad, but we have to go on living ourselves, the best we can, just like your mommy did. Just like you're doing. I think your dad would be proud of you, Charlie. And we want you to be proud of him."

"I'll never ski that good."

"Bet you will. You're pretty good right now, and you're just eight."

Jake got up and took the reel from the projector and put it in a film can. Then he handed it to Charlie. "This is yours, Charlie. We're going to get our own projector at the lodge, only it hasn't come yet. I'll show you how to work it, then you can see this movie any time you want."

"Thanks." They walked out of the room and up the stairs, Whizzer silent at their heels. "Jake?"

"What's up?"

"I really like the movie."

"I'm glad."

"He could really ski, couldn't he."

"He sure could. Did you notice the way he came over those moguls? You can learn a lot about skiing from that movie."

"And his skis were really together, Jake. Mostly it looked like one ski."

Jake smiled to himself as they climbed into the Jaguar. The seed had been planted.

"After the movies," said Jake gravely, "it is very important to have an ice cream cone. What do you say, chum?"

"I say maple walnut." And Charlie laughed. It was going to be all right.

Dorothy Dutton and God had a long-standing arrangement. She didn't interfere with Him, and He didn't interfere with her. So it had been for as long as Dorothy could remember. It did not please her one bit, then, when God decided to visit her with this dreadful headache, this burning sore throat, just as she was finally embarking on her life's masterwork. Surely God must have better things to do. Petulantly, Dorothy picked up the phone and asked the desk to get her a doctor. Half an hour later, Bill Shepherd knocked at her door.

"Countess Ruvo di Putig . . ." Bill was stumbling through the name when she interrupted him in her Early Asheville Belle voice, a voice Dorothy saved especially for handsome young American men.

"Don't you bother, Doctor, there is *nobody* this side of the Rubicon that can pronounce that name. Just call me Dorothy." She extended her hand and he shook it, smiling, absorbing automatically a dozen revealing bits of medical information as he got a good close look at this notorious woman. The tone of her skin had messages for Bill Shepherd: it was slack. From the door of her room she might have been fifty. Close up, in the bright afternoon light, she looked more like seventy. The eyes were a little too bright, the forehead a little too smooth, the hair a little too dyed.

"My name's Bill Shepherd."

"Yes. Well, Doctor Shepherd, I seem to have acquired some sort of a pestilence. Which is most inconvenient, since I am hard at work on a book." She gestured toward the tape recorder and a pile of yellow legal pads that lay next to it on a table.

"You have a headache?"

"But not just a headache, dear boy. *Vesuvius* is in full eruption in my poor head. And this throat. Burning. And, just lately, I've felt quite nauseated. Which never happens. Never."

"Let me take your temperature." Bill produced a thermometer from his bag and took a reading: 99.3°. A shade above normal, but not serious. Her blood pressure and pulse were normal. "It's probably a strain of flue, Countess."

"Dorothy."

"Dorothy." Bill grinned shyly. He wasn't used to the very rich. "Are you allergic to antibiotics?"

"Not that I know of."

"I'll prescribe Tetramycin. Three a day. And something stronger than aspirin for your headache. That should do it. I'll check back tomorrow. If you're not feeling better in a couple of days, we'll take more tests. But it looks like a bug. Nothing too serious."

"Well, Doctor, you are most reassuring. When can I expect the medicine?"

"In about an hour. I'll have someone from the lodge run into town for it. Meanwhile, just rest, and drink plenty of fluids."

"Thank you. I will." She smiled a weary smile as Bill Shepherd let himself out. Then she ran to the bathroom and was sick.

Bill Shepherd knocked on Cassie's door to check on Charlie.

"Come in." Her voice was thin with pain and exhaustion. Cassie lay on her bed, fully dressed, with a damp washcloth over her eyes. She sat up as the door opened. "Oh, Bill! I was just going to call you."

"Charlie?"

"No. Me. It's really stupid, Bill, but for two days I've had a headache that just won't quit and I never get headaches."

"Sore throat?"

"How'd you know?"

"Not by magic. You've got a countess upstairs with the same symptoms. Dorothy . . ."

"Dutton? Oh my God. She's sick enough when she's well. That's all we need."

"It seems to be some kind of flu, Mrs. Lamont. Let me take your temperature." Cassie's temperature was a little higher than Dorothy's just over 100°, but still no cause for alarm. "Have you had any nausea?"

"No. But I feel terrible. Achy all over. And I'm really never sick."

"Can you take antibiotics?"

"Yes."

"Then I'll put you on the same program I gave the countess. Tetramycin and a painkiller. And if you're not feeling better in two days, we'll do tests. Some of these new flu strains can be pretty uncomfortable. I'll get your prescription and the countess's to the drugstore now."

"You've really shaped up that tiny drugstore."

"Well, I persuaded him to stock the basic things: antibiotics and anticholesterol drugs and a few standard blood-pressure depressants. But if I need anything fancier than that, it has to come from Steamboat Springs, or even Denver."

"The serum getting through to the beleagured Eskimo village? That's very romantic, Bill." Cassie was feeling better, now that she knew it was just a spot of flu. No flu germ was going to get her down. Not for long, anyway. "Can I offer you a drink? Or coffee?"

"Thanks, but I've got to be on my way. There's a very expectant mother ten miles down the road who needs her hand held. Remember me to Charlie."

"He'll be sorry he missed you. Thanks for stopping by, Bill."

"Right. I'll check back the day after tomorrow. Meanwhile, rest and fluids."

"Check. Thanks, Bill. I feel better already." Bill smiled what he hoped would pass for a confident smile. But inside, he was anything but confident. There was something wrong about Cassie's illness, and Dorothy's too. Something unsettling. He wondered what.

Tod Rubin was anything but a complainer. Self-effacement was his nature and his profession. And all his experience worked to convince him that any problem could be outwaited in calm and in quiet. And so he knew that in time this terrible headache would go away too, and the night sweats and the nausea that came with it. Tod had a mortal dread of calling attention to himself. To call a doctor would be too conspicuous at this crucial moment in the stalking of Karl-Heinz Waldemar. STYX, in the soft cultured accents of Herr Professor Doktor Knabel, had advised Tod to relax, to stay in the background. So in the background he would stay until events developed at their own sure pace. Now Tod lay naked and sweating on his bed in his shaded room at Sky Lodge. He had just taken more aspirin. Aspirin would lower the fever. Tod shuddered involuntarily and closed his eyes.

Cornelia de Vos knew, better than most women, that there are two quite distinct kinds of sex—sex of the body and sex of the mind. Her career was founded on the latter, as were the careers of all the great courtesans in history. It was the pleasure of the chase, more than the satiety of the capture, that inspired men to extremes of generosity. Large emeralds and chalets in Lausanne never rained on girls whose sexual vocabulary consisted only of the word "Yes." For nearly a week now Cornelia had played a cat-and-mouse game with Niris. Niris was something new to her, a man who had everything, from birth, and for the asking. Most of Cornelia's lovers were self-made, men who had fought their way to wealth and wanted all the ornaments of hard-won privilege. Such men appreciated Cornelia for her brains and spirit as much as her beauty. They admired her for the courage and style with which she cruised the world of wealth and power, and they gave her the ungrudging respect one pro grants another. But with Niris it was different. She must learn as she went along. And she must never, never falter. She had expected him to be imperious. But no, he was gentle, almost shy. She had expected a rush of costly presents once his interest was aroused, but Niris sent nothing other than invitations to ski, to lunch, to supper. Cornelia knew that one day soon there would come an invitation to his bed, and she knew she'd accept that invitation, one way or another and sooner or later. In the meantime, she kept the relationship moving forward.

Pete Woodbury didn't want to leave Sky High. Meaning, he didn't want to leave Maggie. It had been a time of discovery, a time of changes. He'd discovered Maggie, but more than that, he had found out plenty he hadn't known about himself. Maybe it was the example of Jake Chaffee, who always went into a situation running for the ribbon.

Pete was suddenly fed up with hedging his bets, with playing the game so safe it wasn't a game anymore. He was approaching forty and he felt all used up. Franny had used him, played on his conservatism, built on his success, made him a counter in some weird game whose only reward was the fair weather esteem of phonies. Sky High had changed all that, and for good.

Pete hadn't solved Sky High's problems, but he had managed to keep them at bay. He had bought them some more time from the Knickerbocker Trust. And the sheaf of positive publicity he'd carry back to Wall Street would buy more time. He was sure of that. Or almost sure. And with a little more time, Sky High's problems would solve themselves. Jake would be in control. The condominiums would be built, and they'd sell like hotcakes and the cash-flow picture would improve dramatically. But before any of that happened Pete Woodbury had plenty to do. He had a divorce to go through, a house to move out of and a new life to build.

And he had a girl to court. Pete sighed and pulled his worn brown leather suitcase down from the closet shelf. He might have a new life but it would be filled with old memories. Franny had given him that suitcase. How long ago? Maybe ten years. It was the first really good piece of luggage he'd ever owned. Well from now on Pete Woodbury was traveling light. He finished packing and closed the suitcase just as Maggie walked in.

"So soon?" She stood behind him and put her arms around his neck.

"Right after lunch. Could a guy buy a girl lunch around here?"

"He sure could. It doesn't seem like it's just been a week, Pete."

"By actual count, nine days. That, by the way, is the title of something. *Nine Days That Changed the World* or something like that. I was just thinking how much my world's changed."

"Mine too. Promise me something?"

"Moon, stars, planets, or all of the above?"

"Promise me you won't blame yourself. The good ship *Titanic* was heading for those icebergs anyway."

"I feel the same way."

"You have my phone?"

"Tatooed on my heart. How long will you stay here?"

"Three days. A discreet interval, as they say."

"Who does a feller go to to ask for your hand?"

"I . . . don't want to talk about that right now, if you don't mind."

"I know. I'm pushy."

"Too lovable, is more like it. A guy like you could take advantage of a girl like me."

"That is my fondest hope."

"You will call?"

"I love you, Maggie della Robbia."

"Oh, Pete. I know." She walked to the window. It was late morning and the Colorado sky hung over the Colorado snow.

Maggie looked out at all this perfection and thought how easy it must be to be a tree. Or a mountain. The day she knew would come, had come. Maggie promised herself that she wasn't going to let Pete know how empty she felt at his leaving. Sure, they were going to live happily ever after. Their life would be just like the landscape outside the window: MGM-perfection. All her life, Maggie had been a believer. She stood there praying to God to let her believe in her own happiness, now, even for just a few more minutes, just until he left.

"You'll have to fight me off, Maggie."

"I may not fight all that hard."

"I'm Charlie Persistence, the Horatio Alger Kid."

"*Luck and Pluck?* I wish us both luck." Maggie

smiled and it hurt her to smile. The headache was worse today. She thought it was from the tension of her deciding to divorce Nick, or Pete's leaving Sky High. "Did I hear you say something about lunch?"

"You did indeed."

She kissed him and they walked hand in hand down to the bar. It was early for a drink but they had one anyway. And wine with lunch. Later Maggie stood in her room watching the blue Sky High station-wagon drive him to the airport at Steamboat Springs. She was all set to cry. But instead she ran for the bathroom and got very sick.

Eliza Chaffee ran her hand down the offset edge of her racing skis. The edge was still holding, crisp and sharp, the way she liked it. She stood alone in a corner of the tramcar as it wafted her up the mountain. Eliza felt a sense of anticlimax. Maybe it was the headache, which had come on her last night and just would not quit. Maybe it was the fact that she still felt like an outsider even if her father did own the place. Everyone there seemed to fit in smoothly, seamlessly, moving with grace and confidence. Everybody but Eliza.

And now, on this perfect morning, gliding up her father's beautiful mountain, Eliza felt sealed off from time like a fly trapped in amber, safe from harm but never to smell another flower, never to feel the sun. Sky High was just a little too perfect for Eliza Chaffee. It was all one big expensive conspiracy against reality, an international plot to corner the market on dreams.

Sky High, Eliza was coming to feel, was her father's Camelot, a place where only good things happened, where the sun always smiled and the only clouds came after dark bearing gifts of fresh snowflakes. Tell that to the dead Liz Drummond. Tell it to Betsy Bellington, suddenly cut adrift from the fiction of her marriage to Jake. Sky High had no room, no comfort, for people in pain: they were bad for its image. Eliza wondered if her father was aware of these flaws in his Shangri-La. And she worried that he was a part of them.

The car eased into its landing dock with a gentle bump and the attendant opened the doors. Eliza picked up her skis and walked out onto the platform. Maybe a few good runs down China Bowl would make the headache go away.

Bill Shepherd was puzzled. Almost idly, he flipped through the pages of the *Merck Manual,* that physician's standby reference encapsulating the symptoms and remedies of thousands of human ailments. Bill had been called back to Sky High again. Two more guests had the same symptoms he'd found in Cassie and Dorothy Dutton the day before. Some nagging instinct told Bill not to be too sure of his first diagnosis. Sky High was having an epidemic of something. That was sure. But was it really flu? A lot of evils could be glossed over by that one little word. But something felt wrong about writing it off as plain flu. For one thing, the timing was odd. Flu usually spread from one victim to another. Bill felt it was unlikely to have so many cases breaking out all at one time.

If he got more calls from Sky Lodge, he'd take blood samples. Which was a pain simply because the blood would have to be sent to Steamboat Springs and flown to a lab in Denver and a whole day would be lost. Bill closed the thick book. He was finding nothing. He didn't know what to look for.

He sat at his desk looking blankly at the closed book. What he needed was a wizard diagnostician, someone who had seen it all and developed radar for ferreting out obscure diseases that came masquerading as obvious ones. What Bill needed, he suddenly realized, was a talk with old Ferris Hunt. Ferris Hunt, near eighty and still teaching seminars at the Harvard Medical School, a crusty, twinkling, elegant little man who had been world-famous for half a century due to the almost mystical infallibility of his medical judgments. He had consulted on kings and presidents and scrubwomen and bums with equal brilliance. Ferris Hunt, Bill thought, would just be finishing his after-dinner coffee. He picked up the phone.

Doctor Hunt was delighted with the call. He never forgot a good pupil and Bill had been faithfully writing letters all through his internship and since settling in

Sky Junction. After the amenities had been exchanged, Bill got to the point and described the symptoms, the mysterious timing of the sickness and his own reservations about the diagnosis. Hunt listened silently. Finally he spoke. "And you've got 'em on Tetramycin. Well if it is flu, naturally, that would be fine. And it could be flu, William. It's one of the possibles." Ferris Hunt always kept closely in touch with the innumerable alternatives he liked to call "possibles."

"The trouble is," Bill went on, "that neither of the patients who've been on the Tetramycin for two days shows any reduction of the fever. And the headaches keep getting worse."

"Fever's higher at night?"

"By about two degrees."

"And you say there's nausea?"

"In three of the four cases. The other has diarrhea."

"Watery and grayish." Hunt stated this conclusively.

"Exactly. And the patients all seem a little dehydrated. I put that down to the fever."

"Well, well." There was a pause at the other end of the line. Bill Shepherd imagined the old doctor sitting in his favorite green velvet wing chair, the delicate blue-and-white Meissen demitasse on the mahogany table beside him. "William, it's good you called. Without being, ah, an alarmist, my boy, there is another possible we must consider. Quickly."

"And what's that, Sir?" Bill detected an atypical urgency in his old professor's usually gentle voice.

"Typhoid."

"My God!" Bill was shocked, not so much because the disease was serious but because it had never entered his mind to consider it. In Mexico, maybe. But in supersanitary Colorado? At Sky High?

"I see you're surprised, William, and well you should be. Typhoid's hardly known in America these days. But the jet airplane, my boy, is a better friend to certain nasty viruses than all the open sewers of medieval Europe or modern India. If it is typhoid, it might have arrived with one of the guests. Or been there to greet them."

"Wow. I'll have a test made tomorrow."

"It would be most prudent to do that. And stock up on some Chloramphenicol while you're at it. Works wonders. It's odd, typhoid fever and ski resorts seem to be developing some kind of affinity."

"How's that?"

"Surely you know about Zermatt?"

"No. No I don't."

"Zermatt, 1964. Greed, of course, being the national industry of the Swiss, the good burghers of Zermatt actually conspired to keep the thing quiet. So bad for business, you understand. The upshot of it was, that virtually all during the skiing season of 1964 people were jetting in and out of the place; only when they left many of them were carrying more than happy memories of the Matterhorn. They were infected with typhoid. Three, as I recall it, died. One in London, one in Los Angeles. There was quite a to-do when finally it all came out; mea-culpas dangling from every Alp. Reparations. Typhoid, of course, can theoretically happen almost anywhere. But it was the cover-up aspect of the Zermatt epidemic that caused such a scandal. And, I must say, justly."

"Damn right. And you can die from it?" Bill was thinking of Zem.

"In perhaps ten per cent of all cases. Of course, there are different strains, different degrees of severity. Many people have mildish cases and don't know it. That's how you get your carriers, your Typhoid Marys. One Typhoid Mary in a big restaurant kitchen can do for thousands."

"Doctor Hunt: how do they die?"

As the answer came crackling over some twenty-five-hundred miles of telephone line, Bill Shepherd felt truly alone, unarmed, besieged by a deadly and relentless enemy that struck in secret. He knew his fear was unprofessional, that this was an intellectual problem, a matter of accurate diagnosis and proper treatment. After all, he did have one of the best medical brains in the world on the other end of this line. But even that couldn't stop the fear from twisting in Bill's gut.

"Internal bleeding caused by rupture of the lower intestines when the diarrhea gets intense. And sometimes brain damage from the fever itself. And dehydration, if the victim isn't nursed properly. But if it's detected early enough and treated promptly with Chloramphenicol, it's no worse than a bout of flu. And of course, William, it may in fact *be* flu. Don't discount that as a possible. But do have tests made."

"Crack of dawn tomorrow. I appreciate your advice, Doctor."

"It's mother's milk to me, William. More fun than crossword puzzles. Well. This call will cost you a fortune. I've enjoyed talking to you, William. Let me know what develops."

"I will. And thanks again." Bill hung up the phone and looked blankly at his office window. It was starting to snow.

Zeke Gibbs closed the barn door on four hundred and twenty fat bleating sheep. He stood in the frozen dirt road and shivered. The air had changed since this afternoon. All the crispness had gone out of it. The breeze had died down and the blue sky was glazed with gray. There was a ton of snow in that sky, the air was heavy with the gathering storm. Zeke's weather-detecting apparatus, which had never been far wrong in nearly eighty years, was flashing silent blizzard warnings all through his wiry old body. It was going to be a big one. He'd better make sure Zem knew, so she wouldn't be caught in that young doctor's bed when the big stuff piled up.

Zeke remembered the last big one, back in, what was it? '62? The road blocked for six days and Marcy Cavendish nine months gone with twins.

In a way Zeke looked forward to the big ones. Every time somebody got to feeling a little too big for his britches old Mother Nature fixed up a way to cut him down to size. Zeke stood in the twilight looking down the valley. The lights of Sky High were glowing softly in the gray-blue dusk. A wish started growing deep inside Zeke Gibbs's mind. He wished the big snows would come and bury Sky High, and everybody in it. Let the snow come. That would suit Zeke Gibbs just fine.

Bill Shepherd didn't wait until morning. He called Jake and asked for a few minutes of his and Cassie's time. Then he prepared a sterile flask for a blood sample and another for a throat smear and left a note for Zem. Bill knew you couldn't fly out of Steamboat Springs at night, but he wanted to have those samples rushed onto the first plane in the morning. In ten minutes he was at Sky Lodge. Jake and Cassie were in Cassie's room relaxing with a glass of wine. She was feeling a little better. Bill took her temperature, which was still over 100°, and asked if he could take a blood sample and a throat smear.

"Well, of course, Bill. But why?"

"Look, please don't think I'm an alarmist, but there's something funny about so many people getting these same symptoms all at once. I just wanted to get a lab check from Denver as soon as I can, in case, well, in case it's something more than flu."

"And what would that be?" Jake's voice was level, edged with concern.

"What I think it might be—and remember this is only a guess at this point—is typhoid."

"Jesus, man. It couldn't be. Not possible. Have you seen our kitchen?" Jake felt like he'd been slapped.

"Jake, we've got to take every precaution. Typhoid isn't such a big deal anymore if we catch it early and have the right drugs. I mean, the name scares people because it's so unfamiliar, like a medieval plague or something. But we have stuff that can knock it right out, quickly, take it down to nothing worse than a bad cold."

"If word got out that there was even a suspicion of typhoid up here, Bill, you can imagine what it'd do to us. We'd go under."

"Word isn't going to go out, Jake. Not until we're sure. But we have to be sure. That's why I'm here."

"Of course we have to be sure." Cassie instantly decided to treat it all lightly. She sensed the dark visions that were flickering through Jake's head. "Jab away, Doctor Bill. I'll send the wagon to Steamboat right away, before this snow gets any worse, and your samples will be in Denver before noon tomorrow." Bill dabbed Cassie's inner arm with alcohol and drew out a blood sample. Then he took a throat smear, sealed it in sterile plastic, and put both samples in a Ziploc bag. He had a label all written out, RUSH TO THE BLOOD LAB IN DENVER, HAND CARRY. That done, Jake poured Bill a glass of wine while Cassie went off to arrange for the driver and the plane. And Jake said what was on his mind.

"You can die from typhoid." Jake stated it rather than asking it.

"Only if it's untreated. And then usually only if the patient's very young or very old or weak." Bill swirled the wine in its big balloon glass, wine dark as blood. "The mortality rate is about ten per cent."

"There are more than two hundred people at Sky High right now, not counting help. You mean twenty of them could die? Is that what you mean?"

"Nothing like it, Jake. No chance. That would mean—for starters—that every single one of 'em got infected. Which is just about impossible. And it would mean the ones that did get it went untreated, which is also practically impossible because I've already phoned Denver to send up enough Chloramphenicol—that's the best drug for typhoid—to treat the bunch. We should have it in Steamboat by noon tomorrow. So we're as well covered as we can be."

"Typhoid, for chrissakes."

"I could be wrong, Jake. It could be some weird new kind of flu."

"Bill, look: if it is . . . what you think it is, are there laws about revealing it? I mean, could we treat people without letting them know what for?" Jake's mind was spinning out responses to the threat because it was more than a threat to the health of a few prominent people. It was undermining the foundations of Jake's dream.

"It would be smart to avoid panic any way we can. But the state would have to know about it, Jake. There'd have to be an investigation. If it is typhoid, we have to seek out the carrier. That's the law."

For a moment Jake said nothing but merely sat looking at Bill Shepherd. All the Knickerbocker Trust would have to hear was that their investment property was breeding typhoid germs. Sky High would become an instant plague spot, a place to be avoided, a joke among resort keepers. And Jake Chaffee was just the kind of man the world loved to see take a tumble. He'd had it too good for too long and that alone bugged people.

"It's funny, when you think about it."

"What's funny?" To Bill Shepherd, just finishing up his first year of private practice, it didn't seem anything like funny.

"Fate always finds a way to stir the pot a little, doesn't she? Just wants to keep you on your toes."

"We're doing everything we can, Jake."

"Bill, look. Don't mind me, OK? I've got a big commitment to this joint. I've spent the last six months sweating my ass off putting out brush fires and now I hear we may have an active volcano on the property. I do appreciate the warning, obviously, and I'm grateful you're doing such a good job. You just go on doing it, and we'll support you every way we can." Jake stood up, signaling an end to the talk.

"Thanks. I'll get to you as soon as I hear anything."

"Do that. Good night Bill." Jake and Bill left Cassie's room together. Cassie was still on the phone in her little office, chartering a plane for tomorrow morning. Bill walked out to the parking lot of Sky Lodge and drove home through the lightly swirling snow, silently. Driving away from a man who seemed to care more about the success of his resort than the people who might die in it.

Five minutes later Jake Chaffee was in his own suite with Dud Drummond. A top PR man is just as adept at keeping things out of the news as he is at getting them in. And this was the talent Jake hoped to call on now.

"The place to begin the hush-up, always, is right at the source. Just hypothetically, you understand, just to postulate a theory, can we get to that kid doctor?"

"You mean pay him off? Never. Don't even consider it. And we couldn't be party to that even if it were possible. Frankly, Dud, it stinks."

"Easy, Jake. I'm not doing my job if I don't explore every angle. You wouldn't believe some of the stuff we've buried in our time. And it really would be the easiest way."

"Next?"

"The investigation itself, however that's handled. You're thinking this might hurt Sky High, and you're right, it would. But it would also hurt the whole damn state. Tourism is a huge industry out here. Typhoid at Sky High is also typhoid in Colorado. So the state would have an interest in cooling the whole number. When the time comes—if it comes—we might check into that."

"Fair enough. The whole thing scares me, Dud. We can't look like we're covering the thing up, even if we are."

"Oh bravo!" They hadn't heard Cassie come in. "You can always change the name. How about Snowgate?" she sneered. Cassie was tired and sick, and now she was furious on top of it all. "You guys really imagine you can manipulate everybody. The public isn't that dumb, Jake. If the thing is handled decently and honestly, they'll accept that. But the minute you try to pull the wool over their eyes, watch out."

"We're doing everything we can, Cassie. You know that. Ordering drugs we may not need, taking every precaution. But if there's a way to soft-pedal the thing, can you blame us for trying?" Jake managed a full Chaffee grin but to Cassie's eyes it didn't quite fit this time. "Tomorrow," said Jake in a voice filled with manufactured ease, "will tell. Meanwhile, who's for a little supper?"

Cassie smiled. "No thanks. I think I'd better get some rest." Jake started to say something, but Cassie had turned and was gone.

All night long the snow fell on Sky Valley. It fell in tiny flakes, lightly, steadily, and the wind died down so that the snow built up an even mantle of powder.

The next morning, the sun did not rise on Sky Valley. Instead, the light slowly bled through thousands of feet of gray cloud cover that hung over the valley like the finest wash of Chinese watercolor, flattening all perspectives and erasing every shadow. Still there were only about three inches of new snow, and the snowfall, though steady, was so gentle people decided to ski in it anyway. Cars moved in the valley and the great aerial tramway went gliding silently up Sky Mountain until it faded into the constant mist of snow.

Sky High stirred to life unaware of the threat that hung over it darker than snow clouds. The snow itself created a special air of cameraderie among the skiers. There was a spirit of adventure in going up the great mountain to face nature. There was a new intimacy in the little groups of skiers laughing and gliding through the perfect new snow. People skied together, closer than usual, because at fifty yards you could be lost from sight or miss a branching of the trail. And while there was no danger, the sense of pioneering was very real. These people who spent their lives wrapped in silk delighted in the chance, however false, to prove to themselves they could deal with reality when they had to. They went out to play in the fairy-tale snowfall that morning the way Marie-Antoinette went to play at her toy farm in the gardens of Versailles, with its perfumed cows and milk pails from Limoges.

The twin-engined Beechcraft took off from Steamboat Springs at half-past nine against the better judgment of its pilot. But the air was still clear at Denver.

By noon the nature of the snowfall changed. There was still no wind but the flakes came faster now. There was a sting to the snowflakes and the skiing was less fun. By noon people were skiing all the way down the mountain and calling it a day. They had made their point, after all, and braved the elements. Why suffer?

Bill Shepherd decided to give the blood laboratory another half hour. Then he'd call. Bill looked at the telephone as though it was a ticking bomb. He really didn't want to have his doubts confirmed. He didn't want to be the one to tell Jake Chaffee he had an epidemic on his hands.

Niris and Cornelia de Vos skied together all morning, more aware of each other than the increasing density of the snow. By noon they were almost alone on the tramcar heading up for one last run. The Ski Patrol had decided to close the mountain at one. Cornelia pulled off her huge yellow-tinted snow goggles and shook the vagrant snowflakes from her corn-silk hair. He looked at her quietly.

"You," he said in a voice that was almost a whisper, "are the most exciting woman I have met in a very long time."

"Considering the source, that's a great compliment." There was a tension in his voice. It was happening at last. Cornelia could sense the scales tipping in her favor.

"When we ski down, my rooms will be empty."

"Shall I pretend not to understand that?" She giggled like a schoolgirl. But inside Cornelia was not laughing. Her mind flicked like a whip from possibility to possibility. The moment had come. Her choice must be the right one.

"Possibly you do not . . . understand," he said. "I have sent my wives and my servants to Bidijar." He looked at his watch. "Right now they are approaching the Mississippi River. By this time tomorrow they will be in Bidijar, which is perhaps where they should have been all along."

"What do you mean, exactly, Niris?"

"I mean that I want you." He looked away from her eyes for a moment and out onto the mountainside. "We have . . . at least, I have . . . felt something special here, on this mountain. You are not like other women."

"And you, Niris, are not like other men. Your reputation precedes you." He looked at her quickly, not expecting such frankness. For a moment he said nothing. She, too, had a reputation.

"You will not find me ungenerous."

"You expect I am for sale? Then you are not flattering, Niris."

"That was not what I mean. I mean to help you. To care for you. To—hopefully—get you to love me a little."

"But you can have any woman."

"Can I have you?" Cornelia didn't answer in words. Instead, she grinned and reached up with one finger and touched the end of his nose. This was so unexpected he had to laugh too. And they were still laughing at this new, unstated, but wonderfully funny joke as the tramcar pulled into its berth at the top of Sky Mountain.

Route 317 wound thirty-five miles north and west from Sky Junction towards Steamboat Springs. It cut through the valley and around the sides of mountains, a narrow snake of a road that by half past twelve that day was evenly covered with six inches of snow. Soon the plows would be out. On a lonely stretch of road about fifteen miles north of Sky Junction old 317 cut into the side of a nameless mountain about three hundred yards above the valley floor. Here was a falling-rock zone, well marked and dangerous. No cars were out on the unplowed highway. It was in silence then, and unseen by men, that the roar of an avalanche grumbled and grew and built into thunder above the empty highway that was the only road from Sky Junction to Steamboat Springs. An immense snow cornice hung two thousand feet above the valley floor, heavy and wet and weakened by the wind. The six inches of new fall was all it took to set the rotten snow slipping.

As it slipped, first very slowly, then faster, it pushed a falling, rolling crescendo of snow, rock, ice, trees plunging down the steep north face in the full wrath of nature stressed to the breaking point. This gushing river of winter's debris scoured the mountainside clean, pushing all before it. The rampant avalanche roared over 317 and swept it out of being in seconds. A roar and rumble like distant cannon fire was audible for miles, but the sound was quickly blotted-out by the curtain of densely falling snow. The path of the avalanche was only about a hundred yards wide but it sealed off Sky Junction absolutely. Highway 317 was buried under eighty feet of snow and rock and broken trees. No conventional vehicle could hope to pass until the road was cleared and that might take a week. As yet, nobody knew this.

Tod Rubin sat on the edge of his bed in a trance of pain. The fever had been worse last night, and more than just fever, there had been chills and diarrhea, convulsions that felt as though they might tear his insides out. Aspirin was definitely not the answer. Perhaps it might be permissible, after all, to call on a doctor. American medicine, Tod had heard, was very good. Slowly, because the soreness had filtered into every fiber of his body, Tod made himself stand up and walk to the bathroom. He must compose himself, he must not seem in any kind of urgent need. He must avoid anything that would draw attention. He would dress and have breakfast downstairs and then casually ask if there might be a doctor. That was the way to do it. Casually.

The first thing Jake did when he was dressed was visit Cassie. He found her in the bedroom standing in front of her closet looking dubiously at a row of slacks and blouses. On the bedside table was an untouched breakfast tray.

"No, you don't. Don't even think of it. It's right back to bed for you until Bill Shepherd gets here. You look pretty bad, Cassie."

"Thanks, smoothie. I didn't sleep much to tell the truth. But I do feel better. In bed, I'd just worry about things."

"Cassie, you'll only make yourself worse."

"There's a lot to do, Jake. The Sky High Challenge Cup, for instance. How are we ever going to get China Bowl in shape in this?" She gestured vaguely at the window.

"If we don't, we don't. Plenty of races have been snowed out before this. The thing is, not to worry."

"Thanks! But I'll worry double if I'm in bed when there's so much to be done. And, truly, I feel better."

"As you say. But I'm getting Bill Shepherd up here anyway. Dorothy Dutton has it. She fainted this morning. Wants to check out."

"Dandy! Are the roads open?"

"Haven't checked. But they won't be, for long, if this stuff keeps up."

"Jake, could we be trapped up here? I mean, if it really is typhoid?"

"Not really trapped. Sure, sometimes it takes them a day or two to get the roads plowed. But Shepherd ordered some kind of special drug that just knocks typhoid right out of business. He'll have it today, so he says."

"I'm sorry I got mad at you last night."

"Don't think about it. My fault anyway. Here. Have juice. You really look pale." He handed her a glass of orange juice and she managed to get a few sips of it down her throat. Then she sat down on the edge of the bed and looked dully out at the snow.

"I feel like low tide."

"That's why I want you to rest, honey."

"Smooth-talking slicker from 'Frisco." Cassie grinned a little flicker of a grin. Then she put her hands over her red-rimmed eyes. "God."

"Just lie down for a few minute. I'll take care of Charlie. We'll come check in on you in an hour." Jake bent down and kissed her and she didn't move. Finally she lay back on the bed and Jake scooped her up into a more comfortable position and drew one of the blankets up over her. Cassie sighed.

"Thanks, chum. Mrs. Lamont is not pulling her oar today."

"Just rest. I'll get Shepherd up here soon as I can, and everything will be all right." Again, he kissed her, lightly, on the cheek and noticed how hot and dry the cheek was, how drawn tight with pain. "I'll be back soon." Jake left the room and closed the door softly behind him.

Bill Shepherd's phone rang and his hand jumped to pick up the receiver.

"Hello?" He expected the blood lab.

"Doctor William Shepherd?"

"Speaking."

"This is Eagle Airlines. We've got a package for you—off the last flight out of Denver. Chlor-something."

"Right. Can you send it down to me in Sky Junction?"

"I can try. This snow's getting pretty thick. You need it badly?"

"We might. Could you send it on the plow?"

"Yeah. They'd do it. Might not reach you till tonight, though. It's going to be slow action out there."

"Tonight will be fine. And you'll call me if there's any hangup? If we have to, we could send someone up from here."

"I wouldn't try it. This stuff's going to get worse, they say. All flights out of Denver canceled indefinitely. It's going to be a doozer."

"Try the plow, then. And keep in touch."

"Right. I'll get back to you, either way."

"Thanks." Bill hung up the phone with a feeling of relief. One down, one to go. The drug was that much closer and before long it would be closer still. Then he'd be in a position to take care of almost any amount of typhoid. If it was typhoid.

Maggie della Robbia forced herself to call the desk and ask about plane reservations. The headache was worse today, and the sore throat didn't help any either. For the first time since she'd come to Sky High Maggie woke to a gray sky raining snowflakes, and the snow was falling upon a Sky Lodge depressingly empty of Pete Woodbury. All in all, a good place to leave. Maggie lay in bed with no appetite for breakfast. She knew she had a fever. The desk clerk was quick and efficient and in minutes Maggie's connections were all set. Tomorrow, six, six-thirty Philadelphia time, she'd be home facing Nick. Maggie looked at her watch as she hung up the phone. Twelve-fifteen. She got herself out of the bed and tried to think about lunch. Unsuccessfully.

Zem Gibbs was at the top of Sky Mountain putting on her skis when she heard the terrible familiar roaring. She knew the sound in her bones. Only an avalanche sounded like an avalanche. There was a distant rumbling, the echo of the rumble, and then silence. It wasn't on Sky Mountain, she was sure of that. No immediate danger here. But any avalanche was a danger, wherever it fell. Death rode those wild snowslides and Zem shivered to her boots thinking about all that unchecked violence and hoping it hadn't touched anyone she cared about. It would touch them all.

The enormous yellow snowplow moved like some fantastic prehistoric spider through the sifting snow. The twenty-foot blade of tempered steel could scoop and sweep and just plain shove the biggest snowfalls out of the plow's way.

Tommy Foster sat warm and proud in the big glass-walled cab of the plow, easy in his skill at manipulating the complex gears and levers that angled and canted the blade so precisely that a man could damn near peel a grape with it at ten miles an hour in the dead of winter. The snow was deep, plenty deep, and still coming. Tommy Foster figured they had twenty-some inches right this minute, and easily another two feet coming if you could believe the radio, which was calling it the worst blizzard since '62. None of this bothered Tommy. He set out from the highway department garages just south of Steamboat Springs to clear Route 317 to the county line. Just the way he'd cleared it plenty of times before, last winter and the winter before that.

Summers, Tommy Foster worked a giant construction crane out of Denver for nearly twelve bucks an hour. He had the feel of big machinery, respect for what the iron monsters could—and couldn't—do. Tommy could place a six-ton steel girder neat as any hustler shooting pool.

But winters, Tommy took it easy. He liked to ski and drink beer and chase girls and his folks' place back in Steamboat Springs was just right for all that. So up he'd go when the cold weather shut down the big construction jobs, back up to Steamboat to ski and moonlight for the highway department.

Tommy Foster sat high in the snowplow's cab. He knew old 317 by heart, had known it all his twenty-three years, but even so it looked weird in the misty light and the fine steady fall of snow. It could be the moon, maybe, or someplace like that. There were hardly any landmarks at all. Only the long posts of the guardrail on his right told Tommy where the road ended on that side. Lucky he was going south and had those markers. By the time he came back again, he'd have his own path to follow.

The snow was deep, but it was dry powder and easy

to move, not like the wet stuff you sometimes got in springtime, heavy and treacherous because it could freeze into glare-ice in about four seconds if the wind came up just right. It was pleasantly warm in the big cab. Tommy had his big sheepskin coat off and a quart of hot coffee in a thermos jug beside him. There was food, too, sandwiches and two apples and a sack of his mother's well-known ginger cookies. Tommy hummed a little tune he'd known forever, and while he hummed he smiled thinking about a certain girl and the way her body fitted the clothes she wore or, better yet, fitted him when the clothes weren't there. He thought about trails he'd skied and how the next time he'd do it a little different, faster, or he'd remember some crazy Denver night, out with construction guys who really lived like there wasn't any tomorrow. Tommy Foster had a lot to think about, a lot to plan and all of it happy. His plow moved down Route 317, slow and certain, carrying its own little world on its back like the most complacent of snails.

The snowplow was supposed to average ten miles an hour. After about an hour and a half of steady plowing Tommy stopped the plow and backed up a little. He kept the engine running because one thing you really didn't want to do out here was stall. He had some coffee plus a few cookies. Lunch. The big brown-wrapped, sealed, insured package for Doctor William Shepherd sat on the floor of the cab. It was important, the dispatcher had said. Some kind of medicine. Tommy had never met Bill Shepherd but he figured this would be a good way to get acquainted. He did know Zem Gibbs. Hell, every boy for a hundred miles who had eyes in his head and wasn't a card-carrying faggot knew Zem Gibbs, or anyway, what she looked like. Which reminded him, he must ski Sky High one of these days. Fancy as it was. With this in mind, Tommy crunched down his last cookie and recapped the jug. He put the plow in gear and pushed on through the storm. Twenty minutes later, he had to act fast to bring the plow to a quick stop. He sat blinking. He couldn't believe what was in front of his eyes. A wall of snow where 317 should have been.

He looked to the right, just to check, and sure enough there were the brown poles that held up the guardrails. But straight ahead was a snow barrier higher than he could see. It rose almost like a cliff: huge chunks of snow and rock, here and there broken trees sticking out of the pile at improbable angles. *Avalanche!*

Tommy had lived all his life in the high Rockies, but he'd never seen the results of an avalanche close to. He quickly backed the plow and turned it and drove back in his own cleared path, just in case the mountain decided to drop another load next to the first one. Then Tommy put on his sheepskin coat and climbed down from the plow to look at the damage. He walked fifty yards or so, still scared of a repeat performance. It was hard to see through the falling snow but by training his eyes on the line of guardrail poles to where they vanished Tommy could get a sense of the thing. The road just disappeared, eaten up. The mound of debris had to be fifty, maybe even a hundred, feet high. Tommy stood silent in the empty road with the fine light snow falling. The avalanche wasn't a mirage. It stayed right where he first saw it, enormous and unyielding. There was no way of telling how far it went or what they'd find underneath it. And he had no way of knowing what you did to move a mountain. Tunnel through? Climb over? Wait till it melted?

Tommy turned and walked slowly back to his plow. No hurry now. He climbed up into the cab and sat there for a minute in a kind of daze. Then he flicked on the police-band short-wave radio and got highway patrol headquarters. He looked at his watch. It was one-fifteen. Tommy Foster was the first man in Colorado to see the great Sky Junction Avalanche.

16

Cassie Lamont hadn't slept at all. The hot flashes alternated with shivering and chills and Cassie tossed in the big bed, fading in and out of a daze that wasn't sleep or waking but a constant wash of throbbing pain.

Jake offered to stay with her but she sent him away, thinking her condition might be contagious. She thought of typhoid, and almost laughed at the irony of it. Typhoid fever was something that happened in other times, other places, like cholera and bubonic plague. Luck had been with Cassie all her life in the health department, and except for childbirth she'd hardly known a moment's pain. Well, she was making up for it now. Cassie sighed and opened her eyes just to see if there was a difference between eyes open and eyes closed. Slowly, slowly her eyelids opened. There was a pale ghost of light at the window and the room was more quiet than she remembered. Cassie felt the gentle presence of the falling snow outside her window, a billion grains of mist crystalized into perfect six-point ice-lace stars, each one different. That, she thought, must be what God and all his angels do when they get bored, think up new shapes for snowflakes. Typhoid fever! God should stick to designing snowflakes. Of course Cassie didn't know for sure that this was typhoid. And she didn't know for sure that it wasn't. Bill Shepherd would know tomorrow. Today, it must be way past midnight.

Cassie tried to move her head to see the glowing face of her bedside alarm clock but all of a sudden the effort seemed too great. Aspirins. She had taken four of them right after supper. And just before bed she'd been sick again. There went the supper and with it the aspirins. Must take some more. Bring down the fever. Cassie moved her arm to push aside the blanket, to clear the bed so she could get out of it and walk the few steps to her bathroom for the aspirin. But the effort of throwing off the blanket was so great that she lay back for just a moment to rest, to gather energy for actually getting out of bed. This was ridiculous. She'd been almost all right this afternoon, this evening. Cassie turned a little in the bed as if moved by some vagrant current in a river. Her head filled with images of ancient, unforgiving gods, grim and vengeful, carved harshly from black stones. "Why me?" she said out loud and trembled at the sudden noise of her own parched voice in the snowbound silence.

Jake muttered some half-awake promise to the new day and reached out for Cassie. Then he woke up for real because his hands clasped air. He was in his own bed and had been since midnight, since Cassie shooed him out with a little smile that didn't hide the fact that she felt like hell.

Jake had the gift of sleep. He worried, but never in the sack. Beds were for love and for sleeping, and Jake usually found a way to get the most out of both pleasures. He made a noise now that was half yawn and half growl and stretched his long bare body under the crisp blue sheets. Snow. It was still snowing. Jake sat up in bed and rubbed his eyes and looked out the huge picture window at a rectangle of white where his view usually was.

He stood up and walked to the window. Still snowing. The new snow of yesterday had been a six-, maybe eight-inch, decoration, a thing to amuse, the kind of snow you built ski resorts hoping for.

This snow was something else. The tiny crystals filtered down with a consistency that carried its own threatening message, more sinister because there was nothing wild about the snowfall, nothing that bore the promise of wearing itself out. Squinting, Jake could see the shapes of enormous spruce trees, sixty- and seventy-footers, totally blanketed with white and more white coming. White on white. Jake craned his neck to look at the roof line of the next building, trying to guess the depth of it. Hard to tell, but there had to be at least two feet of it. That would mean tough driving, maybe no driving. The Colorado highway department was famous and you could be pretty sure they'd get 317 into passable shape before long.

Jake's mind clicked off the careful preparations they'd made for big blizzards. There'd be no shortages of food or drink except maybe dairy things. There was an auxiliary electric generator. The roofs were so pitched and so solid that they could handle virtually any amounts of snow. More than two thousand candles were in the supply room in case both the power and the generator should fail. If that happened they should still get water from the huge reserve tank in the pumping station. It would mean work, but it could be done.

Jake picked up the phone to see if it worked. It worked. That was a good sign. He thought of Cassie. She'd be first on his agenda. Bill Shepherd was going to have to do something about Cassie, and fast. Then the thought that Jake had been managing to keep out of his head came creeping back with the same soft persistence as the massing snow. Typhoid. He was probably just about snowbound in a hotel filled with some of the most influential people in the world, and the chances were excellent that a typhoid epidemic was rampant among them.

Jake saw his own reflection in the white-backed sheet of glass. That's just what he'd be if the word got out, bare assed in a blizzard. If the word got out. What word? He didn't know for sure it was typhoid. But they'd know today. Odd, if it proved to be Cassie's own blood that carried the message that might wreck all this forever. Jake stepped into the blue-tiled shower stall and turned the hot water on full force. It hit him like bullets and he stood there letting it beat against him. Something was going to have to be done and he didn't know what it was or who'd do it. Time was running out on Jake Chaffee. On them all.

Dorothy Dutton had never felt worse in her life. Her heart had been broken once, but the pain she had felt when Jacques Parmentier died was not physical. The fact was, this legendary advertisement for the plastic surgeon's art was tough as nails inside. But not in this cold white dawn at Sky High.

Dorothy had spent the night alternating between nausea and diarrhea and fever. The young doctor was charming, but he was a young doctor nonetheless, and this was the most godforsaken corner of a godforsaken state. Today, she decided, she and Momo were packing it in. Not for nothing had Dorothy endowed the Dutton Pavilion at the hospital in New York. It was a charming place to rest and if Dorothy Dutton was about to be sick that was where she would be. Whatever that young man had given her was distinctly not working. Her head was a furnace and her body felt like a nuclear test range. Something was wrong on this mountain. It had been silly to come here. Neither she nor Momo cared for skiing. And why, she asked herself, had they come?

Because sport was suddenly chic again, just the way the underprivileged had been a few seasons ago, that dreadful year when everyone went to meetings about causes and invited black people to luncheon.

Well, whatever had brought them to Sky High, nothing in the world was going to keep them there. "Momo!" she cried, in a shout that came out as a croak. There was no answer. Dorothy struggled to her feet and made her way across the room to Momo's door. But before she got there she fainted and sank to the redwood floor in a pathetic-looking pile of damp silk and undernourished flesh.

Bill Shepherd's first caller that morning was not a patient but Zem. She breezed in around ten wearing red and looking like sunshine against the snowstorm outside. "I thought," she said, kissing him lightly, "you might want to trade cars. My Jeep is really what you need in stuff like this." She gestured towards the window as she helped herself to coffee from the big enamel pot.

"I might take you up on that. But I have a feeling

most of my patients are going to be concentrated under one roof."

"Sky High?"

"Sky High." He drained his cup and she filled it.

"Zem, what happens up here in a big snowstorm?"

"It snows. And snows."

"No, really. I mean, how likely are we to be cut off?"

"Not very. Not really cut off, that is. Oh, well, sometimes for a day or two. Most I can remember was five days, but that was a long time ago."

"But the plows get through?"

"Sooner or later. They're pretty good."

Bill looked out at the snow. It seemed he'd been looking at that same snow for about a hundred years: tiny flakes coming down so steadily they almost looked fake—light and dry and ideal for skiing but building into a deadly blanket that could smother you quietly, gently, without even the howl of the wind. The phone rang, startling in the quiet kitchen. It rang again, before Bill got up to answer it.

"Doctor Shepherd?" There were crackles on the line and a distant buzzing noise. The unfamiliar voice sounded far away. "Speaking."

"This is Techlab in Denver. You sent us a couple of samples yesterday. To check out for *Salmonella typhi.*"

"Yes?"

"The tests are positive, doctor. We thought you'd want to know pretty quick."

"You bet I would. Thanks for calling." Bill put the receiver down gently. The room was quieter now, heavy with certainty. His eyes met Zem's eyes and that was when the bottom dropped out. Bill realized how absolutely alone he was, that not even Zem could help, that the only hope for all those people was riding somewhere in a snowplow in a blizzard that was getting worse every minute. His hand clenched on the edge of the old desk. His first real test as a doctor. Bill felt like he always felt before tests—good and scared. He reached for the phone. The highway department number was busy. He started to dial Sky High, then thought better of it. This was the kind of news you break in person. Bill looked at Zem and didn't even try to hide his fear.

"Honey, can you hang in here for a couple of hours? I'd like someone to be here when that plow comes."

"Sure. Bill—it's awful."

"Well, it won't be fun. But we can handle it."

"Gramp's curse is coming true."

"Antibiotics are stronger than curses." He managed a small grin and put his hand on her hair. But Zem wouldn't look at him. Her slim body tensed.

"I wouldn't be betting," she answered in a strangely dull monotone, "anything I couldn't afford to lose."

When sleep finally came to Cornelia de Vos she embraced it almost as eagerly as she had embraced Niris. They had earned their sleep. He had been truthful when he said the rooms would be empty. All afternoon and long into the night Cornelia and Niris filled those rooms with the discovery of love. There was nothing frenzied about their lovemaking. They had all the time in the world and took it. Supper arrived on a cart. They ate naked on the rug before the fire, her head close against the black curling hair of his chest, savoring the moment with the unself-conscious ease of latter-day pagans. Through all the love and the leisurely meal and a night of more loving, they said very little. There would be time enough for talk. Cornelia was happy. Her happiness was reflected in Niris, who made love with the single-minded concentration of a young boy but the variety of long and successful practice. Cornelia enjoyed it completely. There had never been a doubt, for her, that things would go well once Niris invited her to his bed. It was creating the invitation that took the doing. Cornelia turned to Niris, touched the end of his nose, and laughed. He laughed with her and they made love again, well and completely. Soon, she thought, they would leave Sky Mountain. They would go, perhaps to New York, or to Switzerland. An arrangement would be made, papers signed, and the Bidijar reserve would start to pump for Cornelia de Vos. She reached out for Niris. She didn't have to reach far.

Bill was strangely calm. He'd lived in the mountains of New England all his life. The quick dirty punches of a mountain winter didn't shock him. And although he had never been religious, Bill could see an almost Biblical logic to his plight, as though someone had set him an obstacle course that never ended, where new and harder barriers slid automatically into place just as soon as the old ones were crossed. There was something about hitting absolute bottom that was perversely encouraging. Other than earthquake or fire or war, this was about as bad as it was going to get.

"An avalanche!" He repeated, dazed, to himself, the news that Jake had received from the highway department just a few minutes before Bill arrived in the Jeep. "No chance of getting a plow over it?" he asked Jake.

"They say not, those highway plows are really just good for flat surfaces."

"A skimobile? Those things go anywhere."

"Maybe. They're kind of flimsy, though, for avalanche debris."

"But, Jake, we've got to get that medicine!"

"How big's that box?"

"Not very. No bigger than a case of beer."

Jake was at the window now, staring out into the snow as though he could turn it back simply by the concentrated force of his will. As he looked into the blizzard Jake knew he couldn't send anyone out into that mess or up an unplowed highway to meet the treacherous avalanche debris. Who had so much at stake they'd risk a kamikaze mission like that? As he watched the steadily falling snowflakes Jake knew who. There was one man at Sky High who had that much at stake. The thought came to him and he brushed it aside. There had to be another way. After all, how many people were really sick? Even Cassie wasn't really that bad; so she said anyway. "Let's go have a look at Cassie," said Jake; "then I'll have a word with the boys in the kitchen."

Cassie was awake now, and dressed, but still lying on the bed. The effort of dressing had knocked her out again. She managed a smile when Bill and Jake came in. It was an odd, dreamlike smile, unfocused. Bill had seen such smiles on the faces of drunks and drug addicts. And on delirious people. He quickly took her pulse—slow—and her blood pressure—low. The fever was up, 103° now. Anything higher would be truly dangerous. Bill got her to take more aspirin but she could barely swallow the water. He told her to rest, to have Eliza or one of the maids give her an alcohol rub to lower the fever if it rose. Cassie nodded weakly, lay back and closed her eyes. They left the room, closing the door behind them.

"Not good," Bill's voice was level.

"She looks terrible." Jake was just about whispering. "Can't you do anything?"

"I'll try her on penicillin. The local guy has that. Maybe any antibiotic's better than none." They were in Cassie's little office now. There was a picture of Charlie and Whizzer on the desk. Bill reached for the phone. It was dead. He looked at Jake. "I've got a Jeep. I'll run down there myself. You get going on having the water boiled, and try making a body count. You can do that without alarming people, I guess."

"Hurry," Jake said. "Just hurry."

Raoul Peng knew about typhoid. He answered Jake's questions calmly in his small glassed-in office, but in his head many small alarms were going off. That this should happen to the great Raoul Peng! Inconceivable! When there was typhoid, they always blamed the kitchen. But Peng's kitchen was surgically clean. Peng thought of Norbert Styron, of the contract that was even now being written, of the fame and the money and the ease that would be his. "Jake, how sure can we be that this is so?"

"A lab test has confirmed it. Raoul, no one's making any accusations. But somehow those germs are spreading. Could be the kitchen, could be the plumbing. But we've got to do all we can. First thing is to boil all water, get flasks of it to every guest room, and to gently insist they don't drink tap water."

"It shall be done." Peng stated this with regal assurance, as one royalty to another. They left it at that and Jake walked back upstairs, deep in thought.

It was almost lunchtime at Sky High. Jake walked into the bar and made a quick house count. It looked right, but it didn't feel right. The wood was polished, the fire blazed in the hearth, glasses tinkled and laughter rode the air, but somehow it had the air of an ocean liner in a storm.

"The Masque," said a familiar voice behind him, *"of the Red Death."* Noel Northcliff had come into the bar just behind Jake, smiling and elegant in cashmere and silk.

"What in hell do you mean by that?" Only Jake's easy grin took the rudeness out of his comeback.

"Simply, my dear fellow, that we are quite stranded, and some of us not feeling altogether at the top of our form. As it were." Noel was looking rather pale underneath the expensive tan, and the smile on his face had a mummified quality about it.

"I'm sorry, Noel, if you're not feeling well. Can I buy you a drink?"

"Delighted. Chablis, please, Jake. You've heard about the avalanche?"

"Just now. Quite a bad one, from the reports. But we won't be cut off for long. The Colorado highway department's the best. And, don't forget, old 317 goes in two directions."

"Both cut off, old sport. The pass is closed."

"I hadn't heard that." Jake frowned. Liberty Pass often closed in bad storms, and sometimes for days. Jake handed NN a glass of white wine and picked up a glass of red for himself. "To your health." Noel looked him right in the eye and found nothing but charm.

"You do have a sense of humor, Jake."

Jake got Eliza to help him find out who was sick. She did it quietly, thoroughly, and kept the whole operation very low-key. Eliza's message was simply that since a doctor was coming later in the afternoon to call on Cassie, did anyone else want to see him? Twenty-three guests and six of the help were sick. Even without any professional training, Eliza could tell that some of them were very sick. Maggie della Robbia and Dorothy Dutton looked the worst of the lot. The Viennese, Mr. Rubin, was gray and washed-out looking, but then he was fairly pale at the best of times. Cornelia de Vos hadn't answered Eliza's knock. Eliza didn't know where she might be and didn't much care. She was the health squad not the morals squad. If Madame de Vos didn't show up by suppertime, Eliza would make further inquiries.

The door to her father's suite was open when Eliza came to make her report at three o'clock. Jake stood in the middle of the living room holding the dead telephone receiver and looking at it with an expression Liza had never seen on his face before. He looked dazed, puzzled. Now a disconcerting thought crept into Eliza Chaffee's perceptive eighteen-year-old brain. For the first time she could imagine what her father would look like when he was old. Then he saw her, woke from his daze and smiled, casually putting down the phone. "OK, Florence Nightingale, what gives?" This was the old Jake speaking, confident, slightly amused, in control. He slipped into that role like a glove. It had never occurred to Liza before that he could also slip out of it.

"Twenty-three guests and six help are down with something. Plus me." Eliza grinned as she said it because she was a Chaffee and a fighter. But her head ached too, and her throat was sore and she knew it was no ordinary cold.

"Let's move you out of the dorm, honey. If you're going to be sick, you ought to be more comfortable." Jake smiled reassuringly. As he looked at Eliza, pale but beautiful, he saw in his mind's eye a brown-wrapped carton about the size of a case of beer sitting in the back of a yellow snowplow fifteen miles up the road. Jake threw his head back in an odd, involuntary gesture like a dog shaking off water. But the terrifying vision was not so easily shaken off.

"Whatever you say, daddy. I don't want to be any more trouble."

"All my troubles should only be like you, young lady." He laughed, kissed her on the forehead and the bad moment was past. "I'll tell them at the desk. There's a single just down the hall here. That way I can keep an eye on you."

"Maybe I'll go lie down for a minute."

"OK, chum."

Charlie Lamont's brown eyes widened. This was something new. Raoul Peng must be making water soup. Everywhere in the enormous kitchen big pots were filled with boiling water. No herbs, no broth, no wine, but plain water. When a pot had boiled for a few minutes one of the kitchen helpers would ladle the water into a funnel sticking out of a quart-sized carafe. The carafes, when filled, were put on trays with clean glasses and brought to the guests' rooms. Everyone in the kitchen was busy with this strange new task, too busy to pay any attention to Charlie. The boy stood in the door for a minute and then turned, thumping back upstairs on his stick and his walking cast.

The blizzard wasn't fun for Charlie. He couldn't go outside except to the one cleared area behind the kitchen where he took Whizzer for a walk twice a day. Whizzer loved to play in the snow, but with the weather and his cast, Charlie wasn't much good for playing with him.

It wasn't much fun inside, either. With his mother sick, Jake moody and Eliza not feeling too well, Charlie was left pretty much on his own. He didn't know what was happening, but he could sense trouble in the air. When grownups went quiet on you all of a sudden, something mysterious had to be wrong. Charlie wished he knew what it was. But there was nobody to ask except his mother, and she looked so tired that he didn't want to disturb her. Something told him not to bother Jake, either. Only Whizzer was the same as ever. Charlie thumped back to his room and got a red rubber ball to throw for Whizzer. Then he got his parka and mittens on and took the dog outside. The snow, where it had been shoveled off the path, was taller than the boy's head now. And still the flakes came down.

On all the days he couldn't ski, Jean-Pierre Belfort made sure he did his skiing exercises. In the summertime this included running ten miles every day, much of it uphill, plus working out with light weights and performing extensive leg and back and stomach exercises. Today, in the blizzard, there was no place to run, so Jean-Pierre did his daily two hundred deep-knee bends while simultaneously performing arm lifts with his hand weights. Then he did fifty one-legged deep bends on each leg. Then a hundred sit-ups. A hundred push-ups. Then, the most difficult exercise of all, the French Olympic team invention called the invisible chair.

Jean-Pierre stood up straight with his back flat against the redwood wall of his dormitory room. Then he slowly lowered himself into a sitting position, back straight, legs straight from the knees down, thighs exactly parallel to the floor. This simple and quite comical-looking exercise put tremendous pressure on the thigh muscles. The first time he tried it Jean-Pierre collapsed in agony after three minutes, even though his then adolescent legs were very strong to start with. Now, at twenty-five, he could hold the invisible chair for half an hour if he wanted to. But ten minutes was enough to keep the muscle tone up. So Jean-Pierre sat on air with his back to the wall and tried not to think about Cornelia de Vos.

And the more he tried not to think about her, the more she filled his room. Tense, straining, Jean-Pierre saw Cornelia, felt her smooth skin, heard her contagious laughter. Cornelia had become so much a part of his mind in these ten days that Jean-Pierre didn't know how to get her out of his head. And now that she had so obviously caught her Arab, Jean-Pierre knew the hours were numbered before Cornelia would wrap up her prize and depart from Sky High, maybe forever.

He gritted his teeth and for one welcome moment managed to think about the upcoming race, the Sky High Challenge Cup.

He wondered, dared to hope, to let loose a dream. Just suppose he were to win? Suppose all the glory and cash and publicity that can come to a top pro racer came to Jean-Pierre Belfort? It wasn't beyond dreaming. He could ski, and ski well. Would she feel differently then? His thigh muscles were burning. Jean-Pierre didn't know how long he'd held this comical position, sitting on air. His legs hurt. He hurt inside, because he was too shrewd not to know that all the silver cups filled with champagne and all the money and press coverage in the world would never matter an instant to a woman like Cornelia de Vos to whom champagne and fame and money were as much a part of her life as the air she breathed.

Suddenly, like a deflated balloon, Jean-Pierre dropped to the floor with a long pathetic sigh. He sat there for a time feeling the pain in his thighs, feeling lost, alone in a wilderness without a map. Then he got up and went to the window. The snow was going to go on forever. No. Nothing went on forever.

Sky Ranch was buttoned up tight to endure the blizzard. It was very quiet in the old ranch house. Zem was reading fitfully, restless, wanting to be with Bill, or anyway to be doing something, anything. Zeke sat at the kitchen table trimming off the wicks of some old kerosene lamps, just in case. They heard about the closing of Liberty Pass on Zem's short wave radio. News of the avalanche had come that afternoon on the phone, from Bill. Just before the phones went dead. Zem looked up at the old kitchen clock. It was after three. Zem imagined Bill Shepherd making his rounds at Sky High, and wished he would have let her help. She felt useless and somehow guilty to be feeling well when so many were sick. But Bill had warned her to stay away from Sky High. There was nothing, really, that anyone could do, he told her, until they got the medicine.

When the phones went out Jake Chaffee suggested Bill move into Sky Lodge for the duration. Bill felt uneasy about that, but he did it. He left a conspicuous note on his front door telling anyone where he could be reached. Then he packed an overnight bag and a few medical essentials and moved into Sky Lodge.

All the original festivity had gone out of the storm. It wasn't fun anymore. People talked about "it," the storm, in tones of quiet apprehension the way you might whisper about a lurking suspicious stranger. "It" was getting worse. There was no doubt of that. "It" might be getting dangerous.

Word of the avalanche spread through Sky Lodge propelled by fear. Feeding the fear was a sense of helplessness. If there had been one bad avalanche there might be others. Where? Was Sky Lodge in the path of some potential death slide? Jake knew it wasn't, and he made a point of saying so. But still there was tension in the air at Sky Lodge, a bottled-up feeling, a sense of human fuses growing shorter ever hour. How could nature have the gall to interfere with the pleasures of the guests at Sky High?

Bill Shepherd made his rounds, starting with Cassie Lamont and Eliza Chaffee. Eliza didn't seem too bad but Cassie worried him. The fever was alive in her even in the afternoon and Bill knew the fever pattern of typhoid is to build at night. She had no appetite and couldn't keep food down. Bill gave her a penicillin shot and hoped for the best. He knew the Highway Department had extra crews out clearing away the avalanche debris, but no one knew how long it would take.

Bill left Cassie and went to see the two dozen-some other people on his list. Of these, only four were serious. Maggie della Robbia, Dorothy Dutton and René Latour were nearly as sick as Cassie. Tod Rubin was in poor shape but wouldn't admit it. That worried Bill too. The self-deluders were the most dangerous kind of patients. Bill did what he could and reported back to Jake.

"The only one who really worries me is Mrs. Lamont."

"She's a fighter, Bill. She doesn't give up." Jake turned away for a moment and looked out at the storm. Jake knew all about control. He'd been bred to it from boyhood, taught by the master, The Senator, until self-control and a kind of easy manipulation of his public face became so natural to him that the performance and the man behind it blended into one personality. But now Jake was stumped. He had no more control over this situation than a leaf in a tornado. What little he could do was make-work, a bit of smoothing here, patching up there, diplomacy somewhere else, pretending to the guests and the press people that nothing was really wrong at Sky High. That performance disgusted Jake, but it was the best he could do.

He thought of Cassie, lying in her darkened room with a cold towel over her eyes, eyes he loved more than he liked to admit. "How bad is she, really?"

"I've never dealt with typhoid before, Jake. But it's weakened her a lot. We'll just have to watch her, do everything we can to keep the fever down and pray she doesn't rupture her intestines."

"How could we tell if she did?"

"Internal bleeding. Blood in the stools. She'd see it."

"I'll stay with her tonight."

"That's a good idea. Get her to drink as much fruit juice as you can. Let me know if there's any change." Bill got up to leave. He'd been on the go all day. What he wanted right now was a shower and something to eat. He thought of Zem. Maybe after he had a bite he'd run up to the ranch. If he had time.

"Thanks, Bill. I appreciate this."

"Hell, it's my job, right? Heal the sick. I only wish . . ."

". . . you had the stuff on the plow. Me too."

"They'll get through."

"Sooner or later."

The air was heavy with unstated speculation. How late was later? "I'll check back with you tonight." Bill walked out of Jake's room and closed the door behind him.

For a moment Jake sat there looking blankly at the door. Then he got up and went downstairs to see how things were going in the bar. It was time for a show of confidence.

Tod Rubin felt no better for the shot the young American doctor had given him. When the doctor left Tod lay down again and tried to sleep. Sleep did not come to him. The fever was less violent now. It came not in surges, as it had yesterday, but slowly, steadily, a little easier to deal with. Tod closed his eyes and thought about Pepi Prager.

For six months now he had concentrated on the man, studied his background in the most minute detail, crossed the ocean and more than half of these vast United States to track down his quarry here on this lonely mountain. When he closed his eyes, Tod could see Pepi, or Waldemar, call him what you will. He could see the handsome even-featured head with its touched-up blond hair, the flashing ice-blue eyes with the telltale speck of brown. Tod could see the cocky smile, the proud walk, and he could hear the laugh, a laugh edged with scorn.

Tod imagined all that grace and glamor behind bars. Tod could see that handsome face cornered and accused and sweating. He could hear the prosecutor's recital of the evidence.

Tod had another vision. He could see a bare prison courtyard and in it a gallows. Pepi Prager—Carl-Heinz Waldemar—somehow still wearing his fancy blue ski clothes, was led to the gallows. A bag over the arrogant head. A noose around the muscular neck. Silence, then the slam of the trap door opening, a jerk, a muffled groan and silence again. A slow thin smile came over Tod Rubin's face as he lay on his bed in Sky Lodge. His dream was very real to him, more real, perhaps, than anything else in his life right now except the fever and the headache. Tod was not, in his heart, a vengeful man. But it was good to think about Pepi Prager in the dock, on the gallows. It almost made him forget the fever.

Dorothy Dutton looked dubiously at a large pitcher of orange juice and four vitamin pills in a neat row beside it. Young Doctor Shepherd had been practically rude. He'd accused her of being undernourished. The famous beer and peanut-butter diet was completely lopsided, he said. But what did he know? One thing was sure: she certainly felt miserable. Imagine fainting! She'd never fainted in her life. Until just now. Momo had found her all in a heap and got her back to bed. She smiled. Momo was being a dear. He loved taking care of her. She reached for the orange juice and took a little sip. It tasted good. She drank some more. Then she looked at the pills again. No. Definitely and absolutely not. No two-bit doctor was going to tell Dorothy Dutton what to do or when to do it. She put down the half-empty glass of orange juice and lay back against the pillow. She must get out of this place. The sooner the better.

Jake Chaffee walked into the bar smiling his winner's smile. One thing you could say about blizzards, they were good for bar business. The room was nearly filled with people. The spruce logs hissed and snapped in the great hearth. Candles glowed bravely from two dozen polished tables and the air was rich with talk and laughter. But there was a special tension to it. People were trying a little too hard to be festive, and in a dozen small ways it showed. The laughter was a shade too shrill, the drinks were downed a bit too fast. Jake moved from group to group, smiling, joking, playing the perfect host. He could sense the sublimated fear. But still, thank God, everything looked normal enough on the surface. No one had uttered the word "typhoid." Jake hated to think what might happen when that news got out. He had convinced Bill Shepherd that there was no point in upsetting people prematurely. After all, they sure as hell weren't going anyplace for a while. What could be done internally was being done. Water had been boiling in the kitchen all day long. There were carafes in every room, and all the guests had been told this was a measure to prevent the spread of the "flu" that seemed to be going around.

Jake's energy was devoted to getting through the hours before news of the disease came out, as it surely would. He'd get through those hours minute by minute, keeping the performance going even if the theater ended up empty, with all the audience gone home. Jake moved from group to group in the Sky Bar, sipping red wine and smiling, shaking a hand here, kissing a lady there. The room felt better when he was in it, as though there had been a chill and then someone turned the heat up a little.

Jake stayed in the bar for exactly one hour. Then he went to look in on Cassie.

Cassie lay in near darkness. Her big bedroom was lit by one small lamp turned to its lowest candlepower. Jake was shocked when he saw her. Maybe it was the dimness of the room but she hardly looked alive. He walked silently to her bedside. "Cassie?"

"Hi. It's all right, Jake, I'm not asleep." Her voice

was low and it had a faded sound as though it came from a long way away.

"How is it?"

"I feel pretty washed-out." She reached up slowly and pulled the cloth away from her eyes, blinked, then smiled a slender smile. "How's Charlie?"

"Just fine. How about a milk shake? Some ice cream?"

"Well. Yes. A milkshake might be a pretty good idea. I'm not retaining much of anything, though."

'I'll run down and make you a shake if I have to myself. Raoul may scorn the idea of something so simple."

"I'll be here. Thanks, Jake." She reached for the cloth again and put it back over her eyes. Jake had come to her hoping for reassurance, but what he saw scared him thoroughly. The milk shake would give her some energy back. He walked quickly out of Cassie's suite and down the hall to the kitchen stairs.

Peng's kitchen was in the full rush of the hour before suppertime. More rushed than usual, because when Bill Shepherd got one look at the invaluable René Latour he'd ordered the doughty *saucier* to bed at once. So Raoul was left to do the work of two men and he did it with cool efficiency, confident in his skill. When Jake appeared, uninvited, to ask for a milkshake, Raoul Peng was the picture of politeness and concern for Cassie. Privately, he thought Cassie was a little schemer, a woman of no background and no morals who had set her net and somehow landed a big fish. Still and all, she had caught her fish, and this gave her power, which made her worth dealing with. Raoul Peng smiled and pretended to consider various milk shakes, and then took Jake by the arm and led him to the big freezer. "We will make Cassie the ultimate milkshake," he said. "We will give her her strength back."

Peng made all his own ices. His ice cream was more than ice cream. It was a rich custard golden with egg yolks and heavy with the heaviest cream, laced with rare liqueurs and extracts of fresh fruit. He had just invented a new one, a small masterpiece, if he did say so himself. It was a banana puree fragrant with the finest white rum and a touch of fresh lime juice to bring out the flavor. He scooped out a generous portion and put it in a blender with some milk and some more heavy cream. In ten seconds Raoul Peng poured out a creamy essence of bananas with a heady perfuming of rum. This went into a tall crystal mug garnished with a slice of fresh lime and two straws. He presented this to Jake on a small silver tray, smiling benevolently. "With my compliments." Jake thanked him and left. This was a new Raoul. Maybe the fever brought out the best in some people.

Cassie was sitting up when Jake got back with the milk shake. "As good as your word," she said, managing a smile. "Thanks. Looks delicious." He placed the tray in her lap and she sipped the thick ivory-colored milk shake through the straws. "Wow. For a nasty little Buddhist dropout, he makes a mean milk shake."

"I think association with you is mellowing him. He was actually pretty nice about it."

"I will believe that," she said, "when I see it." Cassie was sitting up, energized only by willpower. Finally, before she was half finished with the milk shake, it got to be too much for her. She sat back a little further, sinking into the pillows, and just managed to keep the tray steady on her lap. "I don't think I'd better take any more of this just now, Jake. But thanks. It's great."

"Try to get some rest, Cassie. Want some aspirin?"

"No. I've had enough." Jake took the tray from her and she slid down in the bed. Jake went into the bathroom and rinsed a fresh washcloth in cool water, squeezed it out, folded it, then laid it on Cassie's forehead. "Thanks." Her voice was very far away.

"I'll be back in about an hour."

"Fine." Jake felt a little better as he left her. She'd done something at least, gotten her to drink part of the milk shake. That had to do some good. A little rest and she'd be feeling better. She'd have to.

Tod Rubin woke up from his sleep feeling better. Maybe the shot that young man had given him was working after all. He got up out of bed and stretched. He felt almost himself again. He would go and mingle with the others, not draw attention to himself by being sickly. That, surely, would be what Herr Professor Doktor Knabel would wish. Tod smiled at the idea of pleasing the doktor. Then he took a shower and got dressed.

The bar was thinning out by the time Tod got there, pale but smiling. Jean-Pierre Belfort, who was almost never alone, was alone tonight, standing at the bar drinking beer. A charming young man. Tod would invite him to supper. STYX could afford that small luxury, he was certain. They would have wine, they would be merry, they would talk of skiing. He approached Jean-Pierre and shook hands in the formal Viennese manner.

The French boy smiled, momentarily coming out of his sulk. Yes, he would be pleased to join Mr. Rubin. Hadn't Mr. Rubin taken two hours of skiing lessons from Jean-Pierre every morning for a week? And Mr. Rubin was a pleasant man, in his quiet, slightly odd way.

Anything would be fine with Jean-Pierre that got his mind off Cornelia de Vos. For once again, Cornelia had failed to appear in the bar. Nor Niris either.

He turned to Tod Rubin and smiled. "I'm am as hungry," he said, "as an elephant." Tod had never particularly thought of elephants as being hungry, but of course, they must eat something to grow that big. Maybe this was a chic new kind of joke. If it was, he, Tod, must be chic too. So he laughed and ordered a Scotch although he didn't really like it. In Vienna, Scotch was very chic, very expensive. They finished their drinks and went into the dining room.

"Good-bye, Nick, you fat slobby Wop!" Maggie della Robbia cried. In her fever she saw the lights of Las Vegas, a billion lights, all different colors, a dancing cowgirl in a blue neon hat, an enormous high-heeled shoe made of ten thousand yellow light bulbs. Then Maggie was in a huge gambling room, all green with dark red draperies, and in the middle of it all a huge roulette table, green and long as any football field.

This table held the biggest roulette wheel in the world, and in the center of this huge wheel rose a tower of dark wood. Maggie della Robbia stood on this tower, singing and laughing at the crowd, rouged and wearing purple eye shadow and two-inch fake lashes, mother-naked but for one pink ostrich feather in her hair. She danced a go-go dance and told dirtier jokes than she knew.

The room was crowded with men and all the men were Nick. Nick, fat, sweating, with his sausage fingers dealing out crisp green bills. The room had a thousand Nicks in it, all the same, and Maggie sang for them all, but no one listened or applauded or even saw her, how nice she looked, how her breasts stayed up though she was past forty, how prettily her ostrich feather moved in the breeze.

The wheel slowed and stopped, and suddenly from the far edge of the immense room there came the sound of two hands clapping. Maggie looked up but she couldn't see beyond the circle of light from the chandelier above this one great table. The room was silent now, but for the clapping. The thousand Nicks stood as if frozen, fat fingers on fat rolls of money, open-mouthed but silent.

A pathway opened up. At the end of the pathway, a slim young man was walking towards the table. He got closer. He was carrying flowers, six white narcissus.

Pete Woodbury.

Pete walked quietly up to the table and held out the flowers. Maggie smiled sweetly, a little girl's smile, and gracefully bent to take them. Then she stepped down from the central tower of the great roulette wheel. Pete held out his hand to her and she took it. He reached up and caught her as she stepped off the table into air. Then, still holding her hand, Pete led her up the aisle like a bride, passing through the silent crowd of Nicks. They got to the end of the aisle, where the door was, and Maggie turned, paused, sniffed the delicate white flowers. "Good-bye, Nick! Good-bye, you fat slobby Wop!"

Maggie woke up sweating, not remembering the dream. It was dark in her room. She was meant to be on a plane tomorrow. Fat chance. She remembered the doctor, the shot, sleeping. Suddenly Maggie felt very thirsty. She'd take an aspirin. Four aspirins. And lots of water. She stood up, shakily, and felt her way into the bathroom. Flicked on the light. Jesus, Mary and Joseph, what a sight. Thank God Pete wasn't here to see her like this. Suddenly the diarrhea gripped her.

Maggie sat heavily on the toilet. Disgusting. To be that much a prisoner of your body. To be this much out of control. Suddenly she felt dizzy. She gripped the edge of the sink and the dizziness passed. In a minute or two she felt stronger. Maggie reached for the toilet paper, wiped herself, and stood up. Half in disgust, half in fascination she forced herself to look in the toilet bowl. She knew what to expect—a grayish slime. But what she saw was blood. My God. Internal bleeding. She'd better get to that doctor, fast. Slowly, holding on to things, Maggie made her way inch by inch out of the bathroom. Hold on to the sink. Hold onto the door frame. The edge of the bed. You're almost there, you'll make it. Around the bed, the phone. Just reach out. The last thing Maggie saw was her own hand reaching out for the telephone. She had no way of knowing the phones had been out since noon. She reached for the receiver and took one step and the dizziness came over her again. With a low moan she sank to the floor, still reaching out for the phone.

"First," said Niris as he bit into the apple, "we will go to New York. Then to Paris. Then, perhaps, some skiing?"

"At some point," Cornelia murmured, slicing Brie, "I will have to show up in Geneva. Business."

"Skiing on the way. Do you like Gstaad?"

"Rather stuffy, Gstaad."

"I've had a house there for ages."

"That's what I mean." She laughed, teasing him. "And there's hardly a royalty that doesn't. Gstaad is the only ski resort with more footmen than skiers."

"You," he said, chuckling, "are impossible."

"No, Niris." Suddenly there was a different note in her voice, an edge to it. "I am very possible. But only on my own terms. You must not think of me as, well, as a plaything."

"I think of you," he said, meaning it, "as magnificent. And what you want, shall be yours. If we have to ski in Coney Island."

"It won't quite come to that, I shouldn't think." She offered him a chunk of crusty bread with Brie on it.

"No," he said, smiling, reaching out to touch her hair, "I should think it wouldn't." They were still in his rooms, where they'd been ever since the snow started falling. By now Niris's jet had landed in Bidijar. There it would refuel and head right back to Steamboat Springs to pick them up. Arrangements would have to be made. Niris would prove just how generous he could be. She had asked for nothing. She would get much. For Niris, whose life was crowded with beautiful and available women, had never met the equal of Cornelia de Vos, and might not again. So he determined to make the most of the liaison while it lasted, and to make it last just as long as possible, whatever that might take. Cornelia lay back, resting her head on his chest. They were lying naked on the rug in front of the fire. "It's wonderful," said Cornelia softly, contentedly, "the way things happen."

Tod Rubin's dinner with the young ski instructor was a success. Being a trained investigator, Tod was easily able to draw Jean-Pierre out of himself, and soon the young man was chattering happily away about his childhood in Val d'Isère, how he'd ski to school four miles in the winter, how Killy, who had grown up nearby, was every schoolboy's idol, how young Jean-Pierre got into racing and onto the French Olympic team, and into teaching. Tod heard about Saturday's race, the Sky High Challenge Cup, and Jean-Pierre's hopes for it, how Pepi Prager was to do an exhibition run, the growth of the new pro ski-racing circuit in America. Most of this was news to Tod and he listened attentively, missing nothing. Tod subtly asked questions concerning Pepi Prager but found out nothing he didn't know already. By dessert Jean-Pierre had quite recovered his good humor. They had coffee, and Jean-Pierre, eager to reciprocate for the fine meal, invited Tod for a drink in the Weinstube. Tod already had drunk more wine than he was used to, on top of the unaccustomed

Scotch, but Jean-Pierre's offer was too good-natured to refuse. What harm could be done, after all? Tod signed the check and they got up. He felt a little dizzy, standing after sitting through the leisurely dinner. His forehead was hot. Maybe the wine, maybe the damned flu or whatever. No matter. The young doctor had said to drink fluids, and if wine and Scotch weren't fluids, what was? Of course he'd have a drink with Jean-Pierre. Maybe two. The French youth's enthusiasm and cheer were contagious. What joy, to be this young and this exuberant! Tod thought of himself at the same age, all dark suits and pallor, his idea of a wild time being a glass or two of wine and a game of chess. Well, one could always learn.

The Weinstube was crowded and cheerful. It was the only place in Sky Lodge where you couldn't see the interminable snow. A pretty girl sat on a tall bar stool playing a guitar and singing Spanish folksongs. There was one empty table for two, near the edge of the low-ceilinged room. Tod and Jean-Pierre took it and sat down.

Everyone knew Jean-Pierre. People passed, smiling, joking, nodding to Tod exactly as if he belonged there. It was the first time since he'd come to Sky High that Tod Rubin felt he belonged. The girl finished her songs and was replaced by one of the waiters, a boy of college age with a banjo. Tod had never heard a banjo. The boy was skillful, very jolly, and he sang a fast-paced song about someone named Susannah. People laughed and clapped and the boy began another kind of song, a song about being lonely in a mining camp. The room grew quiet. Tod noticed Pepi Prager at a table for six, the center of his group.

Jean-Pierre and Tod ordered a round of beer, but only after Tod insisted this must be on him. The boy protested, but not too violently. They talked, and Jean-Pierre told amusing stories about some of the other ski instructors and waiters, of scrapes they got into in town, of adventures with girls, of midnight departures through bedroom windows and how awkward it was for two to make love in a sleeping bag designed for one. Tod laughed appreciatively although he had no such stories to give back. His headache, which had gone away in the afternoon, was beginning to return. He'd finish this beer and go to bed.

Tod set his nearly full beer mug on the table in front of him. He turned to look at a girl who had just walked into the room, someone he hadn't noticed before. Suddenly there was a jolt and a splash, wetness and cold all over his legs. Automatically he jumped up. There stood Pepi Prager, all apologies. Apparently Pepi had been striding past on his way to the men's room and jolted the table.

"But, Mr. Robbins . . ." Pepi produced three napkins out of nowhere and mopped up the table. His face was a mask of exaggerated concern.

"Rubin," said Tod, quietly. "It's perfectly all right, really. Don't bother about it." Jean-Pierre had produced more napkins and was also mopping. A waitress came and gave Tod a towel. He wiped the front of his trousers and the seat of the chair, and sat down.

"Your drinks," said Pepi with an alligator grin, "will naturally be on the house. And please accept my apologies. Again." Pepi's eyes sparkled and Tod could see the brown fleck in his left iris more clearly than ever. How he hated that smugness, that arrogance, that unconcealed disdain! The very effusiveness of Pepi's apologies was itself an insult. Tod looked up at Pepi and felt his rage building. The waitress appeared with fresh beers for Tod and Jean-Pierre.

Pepi looked at the Viennese. He had seen this man before, and at Sky High. Of course. Jean-Pierre's pupil. The Jew. Pepi, remembering, became more concerned, more unctuous. The trousers must of course be cleaned, also on the house. More smiles, more tense assurances that everything was just fine. Looking at the Jew, Pepi guessed that everything was not fine. He wondered why not. But then it passed from his mind and he went away. Tod finished his beer. The fun had gone out of his evening. As soon as he gracefully could do it, he signed the check, shook hands with Jean-Pierre and made his way back up to his room.

Tod got out of his clothes and took another shower. His head ached but somehow he didn't want to go to bed. He took two aspirin tablets and got dressed in fresh clothes. That felt better. The touch of Pepi Prager had been on the old ones. How he'd love to wipe that sneering smile from Prager's face!

He sat there in the comfortable armchair by the window looking out into a blizzard that, for all he knew, might go on for a week. The roads were closed in both directions. That was a nice touch, bottling him up with Prager like two bugs in a glass jar. The phones dead. There had been no communication, no FBI, or CIA or whatever they'd be.

Yet Knabel had said the gears were in motion, that it would not be long, for Tod to stay where he was, watching, waiting. Tod suddenly stood up, pacing, remembering Pepi's face, the unctuous smile, the terrible underlying disdain of it.

Tod Rubin had never let himself get personally involved with his work before. His subjects were always at a distance, and if they got too close. Tod found a way to increase the distance. This was the secret of his success. But being so close to Pepi Prager did something to Tod's mind. Tod, who had so prided himself on self-control, felt that control slipping away, felt it replaced by an irresistible desire to lash out, to hurt, to erase that bully's grin forever. For the first time in his life Tod could understand why men killed.

Tod threw himself across the bed. *How they drag us down! Lie with the beasts and you become a beast.* Tod pulled the pillow over his throbbing head, trying to wipe out the image of Pepi's grinning face. But the image persisted all the more clearly for the immense weight of concentrated hatred focused on it.

Tod lay there with the pillow jammed over his face for maybe twenty minutes. He dozed, his head swam in and out of a daze made up of equal parts of fever and alcohol and hatred, a potent combination. In his daze Tod saw the old wooden schoolhouse in Westerlo as la Mère Olivier had described it, the children sealed inside, the gasoline spilled, the lighted cigarette tossed from Prager's lips with the same arrogant disdain he showed tonight, then the flames and the screaming. The man was a beast, not a man but something evil in nature, something aside from humanity. And there he was, all warm and handsome in Sky Lodge, that arrogant grin on his face.

Slowly, half in a dream, Tod Rubin stood up. He ran a hand through his tousled hair and walked to the closet. He pulled down a locked suitcase from the shelf and opened it. Inside was his briefcase, also locked. He opened this. There were five clear copies of the photograph he'd found in Pepi's chalet last week. Tod picked up one of the photos and smiled bitterly. Suppose, just suppose, that Prager would find out someone knew his secret. Imagine that face then!

Moving like a robot Tod selected one of the photographs and put it into a pale blue Sky High envelope. There were such envelopes in every room. On the front of the envelope he wrote: Karl-Heinz Waldemar, Untersturmführer SS. Then, on impulse, he removed the photo and on the back of it in the same careful block letters, he wrote: Remember Westerlo. Tod sealed the envelope and put on his parka. Eleven-thirty. Pepi would stay in the Weinstube for at least another hour. Tod put the blue envelope in the chest pocket of his parka and walked out of his room and down the stairs. No one was about. He walked down the long hall to the side door that led out onto the terrace that connected with the path to Pepi's chalet.

The terrace and the path had been freshly cleared: there was only an inch or two of fresh snow to deal with. No one had been on the path for hours. Tod's footprints were the only ones in sight. He walked up the path through the falling powder into the silence and the darkness. There were lights inside Pepi's chalet and a small outside light on the door frame.

Tod looked at the door. There would be no way to slide the envelope underneath it. But there in the middle of the door hung a simple modern brass knocker, large, bold, shaped like the letter U. There was no wind at all. The weight of the knocker would hold the envelope. Tod unzipped his parka pocket and slipped the pale blue envelope under the knocker. Yes. It would hold.

And even if it fell, he'd find it. He stood for a moment admiring his handiwork.

"How charming," said a mocking voice behind him, "to have an unexpected visitor." Pepi Prager stood close behind him, alone and smiling his damnable smile.

17

Jake would never forget the expression on the chambermaid's face. She was a small, thin girl about Eliza's age. He couldn't remember her name.

Jake stood in the doorway of Cassie's suite, blinking the sleep from his eyes. The knocking had roused him out of an uneasy slumber. For a moment he forgot where he was, slouched in an overstuffed club chair, his long legs propped up on a smaller chair. The knocking had kept up, ever more insistent. He looked at his watch. Nine-fifteen in the morning.

Instinctively he looked at the window and quickly looked away, having seen what he feared to see. More snow. Jake groped his way out of the two chairs, stiff from the makeshift arrangement, and lumbered to the door. The girl's eyes got bigger in her rabbit face. She had expected Cassie. The words stuck coming out. "Mrs. . . . della Robbia!" She threw her small hands up in front of her mouth as if to keep the words in. Or to keep from being sick.

"What's wrong?" Jake kept his voice even, quiet, controlled.

"I . . . think . . . she's . . . dead."

Maggie della Robbia lay where she fell, one pale hand reaching out for the phone. There was no pulse at all. As Jake let go of her wrist he could feel the stiffness of it. He looked at her. The gray light was not kind to Maggie's dead face. Dead. Pete Woodbury's woman. Jake hardly knew her. Even her beautiful red hair looked dead, disarrayed. Slowly Jake stood up and put his hand on the chambermaid's quivering shoulder. She recoiled as if she thought he might somehow punish her. "Why don't you get some rest?" Jake heard himself reassuring the terrified girl, calming her fears as if he had no fear of his own. "Have a little breakfast, lie down, take a hot bath. I'll handle this. And I'll get someone to take over for you today. OK?" Jake even managed a little smile, hating himself for doing it, resenting this necessity for always keeping up the façade. The girl stopped her whimpering and nodded. Jake saw her out of the room, locked the door and went for Bill Shepherd.

In the face of all the warnings, all the evidence, Jake had pushed this threat into some far corner of his mind, hoping it would go away, hoping for a miracle. That was all over now, gone with the last breath of Maggie della Robbia. There would be no pretending now. A plan began forming itself in Jake's brain, one small glimmer of hope flickering against a flood tide of despair.

Bill Shepherd looked down at Maggie but saw his old professor, Ferris Hunt, and remembered Hunt's words, quiet and edged with the unmistakable authority of his years. It had been a lecture, during Bill's first year of medical school. "The day will come," Hunt had said, "when you lose a patient. You'll probably feel like a murderer. You will think of a hundred things you might have tried to save him, or her. When that moment comes you are going to be more alone than you have ever been, or ever will be. And you'll probably think all this"—Hunt's hand made a sweeping gesture that took in all of Harvard Medical School and all medical schools everywhere—"is in vain. Let me tell you it is not in vain. All we can do is to try."

Funny, Bill thought, how those long ago words stuck with him. Funny, too, that their logic did not ease his feeling of total hopelessness. Bill looked around the room. Then he checked the bathroom. The blood in the unflushed toilet told him all he needed to know.

"She ruptured her intestines." The two men stood together, looking helplessly down at Maggie's cold body.

"We'll have to somehow keep an eye on all of them."

Jake's voice was low, colorless. "Bill, if we'd known she was bleeding, could you have done anything?"

"Hell, yes. That's why it's so terrible. There's a whole routine, naturally. Elevate the lower body a little. Give them coagulants. Plasma. Give them a fighting chance, anyway."

"Do you have those things? Plasma? Coagulants?"

"Some. I've got calcium lactate. That's your basic coagulant. And there's four or five quarts of plasma in my refrigerator at the office."

"I think maybe you ought to get them."

"No sweat. The Jeep's outside. I never imagined . . ."

"No. Of course not. Bill, what do we do with her?" Jake gestured at Maggie's body. "We can't leave her like this."

"Is there a way of turning off the heat in this room?"

"Sure. They're all on individual thermostats." Jake remembered how he'd fought for this extra luxury just as all the costs were skyrocketing and the bank had begun its heavy-breathing act. It was a luxury, Jake had argued, that rich people felt entitled to. Even, it seemed, dead rich people.

"Well, that simplifies everything. Give me a hand, would you?" They lifted Maggie onto the rumpled bed and straightened her out as best they could. Jake got an extra blanket out of the closet and pulled it up over her head. A dull ache began deep inside Jake Chaffee's gut. He found the thermostat and turned the heat completely off. Hell, they might be trapped like this for days. The rage came up in him like a wave of sickness, fear mingling with guilt. He hadn't killed Maggie. But Jake felt as miserable as though he had. He turned to Bill. "You'll get the plasma and everything?"

"Right away. Then I'll check everybody on the list. And keep checking them. Jake, if it makes any difference, the odds are probably with us now."

"What do you mean?"

"Very few people ever die from typhoid. About ten per cent. We've got less than thirty on our sick list. So there's about five per cent."

"That's just swell. Just ducky. And when do you suppose the other shoe will drop?" Bill didn't answer this.

The pain on Jake's face told him a reply might be dangerous. They took a final look around the room and at the figure under the blanket. Then they walked out and locked the door behind them. In Jake Chaffee's head, the plan was growing, gaining strength. It just might work. It just might have to.

Tod's mind whirled like the snowflakes that were all around him. He felt the bear-paw grip of Pepi's big square hand firmly on his shoulder, a gesture that might have looked comradely from a distance, had there been anybody to see it, but was in fact a trap. Pepi was in control. Too late, Tod knew, to reach out for the innocent-looking blue envelope that hung against the redwood door of Pepi's chalet. Too late for many things. He was, as always, unarmed.

Pepi reached for the envelope and thrust it into his pocket without reading it.

"And what's this?" The forced heartiness stayed in Pepi's voice, a mockery of humor. "Can it be the bill for your trousers, Mr. Robbins, so soon? Well, at any rate, we must have a friendly drink on it, OK?" He put his key in the lock but still kept his hand on Tod's shoulder. I could break and run for it, thought Tod. I could shout and raise the alarm.

But Tod did none of these things. The whirlpool had caught him, and somehow in his slightly drunken and more than slightly feverish way his dilemma fascinated him. It was like watching a movie on a small television screen. Look! Now the little detective is being ambushed by the master criminal. Now the master criminal is opening the door. Will the wily detective go inside? Will he ever come out?

"Ha, ha, ha-ha!" Tod couldn't suppress the hysterical laughter. "But of course. I would be honored."

Pepi took Tod's parka and removed his own, seeming to forget about the envelope; he hung both parkas in the closet. Pepi moved into the kitchen, poured two generous glasses of a fine old cognac and handed one to Tod Rubin.

"To your health." Pepi grinned and to Tod he looked exactly like the wolf in a children's book Tod once had, handsome but with several teeth too many. Tod lifted his glass and sipped the cognac. Pepi lit a fire in the fireplace, which had been laid and ready. But even with the fire and the cognac, the room was a chilly place. Then came the moment Tod knew must come.

Slowly, casually Pepi went to the closet and came back with the blue envelope. Then he looked at what was written on the front of it. Pepi Prager put his glass carefully down on the stone mantelpiece. He looked at the name on the envelope in silence. His face registered nothing, not surprise, not fear, not bafflement. Slowly, deliberately, he opened the envelope and pulled out the photograph. He looked at this photograph carefully, examined the message on the back, and then put the picture back into its envelope and threw them both into the flames. Now, for the first time in this extraordinary performance, he looked at Tod Rubin. "Who are you?" Pepi's voice was even, low, registering nothing but control.

"That," said Tod with a confident smile, "is far less interesting, Herr Waldemar, than the question of who Pepi Prager is."

The flames grew in the fireplace, reaching for the pale blue envelope. The envelope had landed right-side up and both men watched in silence as the flames charred the bottom of the expensive blue paper. Flame poured along the bottom edge of paper until it reached the corner. Fingers of orange flame reached up toward the name that stood out so clearly against the blue: Untersturmführer SS was the first to be consumed. Then the name Waldemar and then Karl-Heinz.

"I am," said the flat even voice, "and I have always been, Pepi Prager."

"There are those," Tod replied, once against outside himself and thoroughly enjoying the show, "who would disagree with you, *Herr Waldemar*. And I am one of them. But who you are is hardly for me to decide, is it? Those are really official matters, and it is officials who will decide them."

"Who are you?" There was just the slightest edge to Pepi's voice now, a hint of concern. "You come uninvited to my house with meaningless accusations."

"If they are indeed meaningless, Herr Waldemar, how ever did you guess they are accusations? Actually, it is only one accusation."

"There is no proof."

"There is proof and proof to spare. There are people alive who knew the good Untersturmführer Waldemar, who have recognized his photograph, who will testify against him. As do the ghosts of the children of Westerlo testify against him, and the others."

"This is nonsense." Pepi sipped his cognac.

"This is only the beginning of a process, Herr Waldemar." Tod relished the sound of "Herr Waldemar." It tasted good on his tongue. The movie in Tod's head was slowing down a bit. It needed some action, a confrontation on top of the confrontation. He stood up and walked close to Pepi, who remained leaning against the mantelpiece. "For almost thirty years, you've had it good, haven't you? You very nearly brought it off, even as many others have brought it off. You think it your privilege as one of the master race to kill and to mutilate and to walk away from it all smiling and be praised. You curdle my soul in your arrogance." Tod paused, amazed by the force of his own eloquence. Prager-Waldemar stood as he had been, one elbow leaning negligently against the rough gray stone of the fireplace. "You know too well who you are. And what you are." Tod actually smiled at the ski instructor, a confident, sneering smile, a scaled-down version of the expression he had learned to hate on Pepi's handsome face. Well, arrogance could cut two ways, and now it was Tod's turn. Tod looked into the fire: the envelope had disappeared completely now. There was a slight mist on Tod's gold-rimmed eyeglasses. Slowly, almost languidly, he took them off and polished them with a pocket handkerchief.

Then he put the glasses back on and once more faced Pepi-Karl-Heinz. A new sense of power was raging in Tod Rubin now. So this was how it felt to hold the whip! A dangerous, thrilling feeling. No wonder it was contagious. Yes. One could get quite used to this kind of power, to seeing a victim squirm. The fire crackled and hissed. Pepi's expression did not change. He was obviously waiting for Tod to continue. So Tod did continue: "And what you are is sickening. You make me ashamed to be a man, ashamed that we belong to the same species."

"But you are wrong, Herr Robbins." Pepi's voice had silk in it. This was the first time he'd used the German "Herr." Tod thought that was rather careless of him. Then Pepi continued, in the same soft tones: "We do not belong to the same species. *You are a Jew*." Pepi looked at this thin, mouselike man who stood sweating and defiant before him. From under what rock, Pepi mused, had this obscene creature crawled, with his quivering nose and sudden threats? Pepi saw the man for what he was: an enemy of the Reich. The Reich had many enemies, in many places. It was no more than a kind of jealousy, of course, a refusal to accept superiority when confronted by it. The enemies of the Reich, however misguided, must be dealt with. Pepi sighed, and a smile formed on his perfectly sculpted lips. His obligation was to instruct the misguided people who insisted in obstructing the great and inevitable triumph of the Reich. The hostages at Westerlo had been enemies of the Reich, children or not. And the Jews? Scarcely more than insects, but to be dealt with nonetheless. But, wait: the man was going to babble on some more. Pepi decided to listen. It was really quite amusing.

"The game is over, Herr Waldemar, Herr Wolf of Westerlo. The evidence is in the hands of those who know how to use it. What you burned is but a token. And when the snow stops, your masquerade stops with it. There is no place to run, Herr Waldemar, no place to hide." Tod's head hurt. The image before him was starting to blur a little, to come in and out of focus. Still he went on, fascinated by his own bravado, thrilled by what he was saying even before he said it. What would Professor Knabel think of him now? Was this the timid dutiful Tod Rubinsky the good professor kept urging to come out of his shell, to be more involved in the world? Well, he was involved now, and liking it. It would be a new Tod Rubinsky the professor would see next time. Tod gestured rather dramatically towards the window, and the snow outside it. "Yes! When that is finished, *Waldemar*, you are finished."

Tod never felt the blow. Pepi simply shifted his weight a little as anyone might do after standing through such a tirade, then flashed out a rigid fist in one lightning karate blow to the side of Rubin's neck, a perfect, precise stroke loaded with the full force of Pepi's rage and frustration. There was a small clicking noise, almost metallic, the sort of noise a cheap alarm clock makes just before it rings. It was the sound of Tod Rubin's neck breaking. He was dead before he hit the floor.

Pepi looked down at the crumpled figure with scientific detachment. Another enemy of the Reich accounted for. A wave of calm suffused him. So they had found the picture of his beloved Heidi. What did that prove? Heidchen had other admirers before she met Karl-Heinz: they'd often laughed about it. Half a dozen young Austrians might have such a picture. And who was this little worm, anyway, to think he could intimidate Pepi Prager? Probably some sort of blackmailer. Disgusting. Pepi took a sip of cognac. Then he reached out with his toe and nudged Tod Rubin. Dead, and good riddance. No one had seen him come.

Pepi walked casually to the window. Already snow was covering up the footprints. He thought for a minute, then went into the bedroom and looked out that window. He put on some high rubber boots and a white parka that would blend with the snow. Carefully, patiently, he eased Tod Rubin into his parka, zipping it up, pulling gloves on stiffening hands. Then Pepi turned off all the lights and dragged the body into his bedroom. He eased open the window and looked out: all clear. The path led conveniently up to the pumping station. Beyond the pumping station were the woods, and in the woods a deep ravine. Just the sort of ravine a drunk and unsuspecting visitor might stumble into and break his little neck. Pepi looked at his watch. After midnight. Nobody would be out at this time on such a night. Pepi pulled Tod Rubin's body after him out the window. There was nobody on the path, nor would there be until the morning. Seven or eight hours of blizzard would obscure all footprints. Pepi hoisted the man onto his shoulder as easily as if he had been a sack of turnips. Then he marched up the path into the storm. Somehow Pepi Prager felt almost like singing.

All through the long night snow fell on Sky High. Cars in the parking lot sporting bumper stickers that read THINK SNOW were buried beyond the bumpers. The flakes sifted out of the sky with a gentle remorseless silence that was more terrifying than raging wind or stinging sleet. The snow just kept coming and coming. It was building up at the rate of over a foot a day, and Wednesday would be the third day of the blizzard. The flakes wove their way through the aspen branches guarding the ravine of Sky Creek. They made a white shroud for Tod Rubin.

Fifteen miles up Route 317 the snow fell on two big yellow plows working around the clock to clear away the avalanche. Three crews worked eight hours each, gouging out the immense frozen heap that lay across the road. It was very slow work because every time a few feet of highway was exposed more debris would slide down to replace what had been scraped away. In thirty-six hours the highway department had cleared only twenty yards out of a hundred yards of road buried by the avalanche. They had no idea how far they had to go. Still they kept on, day and night, sending one plow back to the garage only when a fresh one had arrived, all fueled up and ready to take its place. The brown-wrapped carton of Chloramphenicol was moved dutifully from plow to plow to make sure it would be on hand when the breakthrough came.

The highway department men worked steadily and heroically but to very small effect. They worked at the risk of their lives because nobody knew when another avalanche might get going. Mountain wisdom told them avalanches very seldom happened during a snowfall, but you never knew. Usually the great plows worked in sequence, one behind the other, but sometimes it became necessary that they work together, side by side, pushing and straining to get some huge sixty- or seventy-foot-tall spruce out of the way. They were making some progress and a sense of urgent mission was in the air. The men worked away through the night, silently cursing the snow as it fell and kept on falling. They had food and coffee and they were in touch with headquarters on sputtering shortwave radios. They knew, as they worked and cursed and worked harder, that sooner or later they would break through and open up the road. Then everything would be all right. Until the next time, and the time after that.

Jake Chaffee had breakfast alone in his room. A shower and a change of clothes helped only a little. His eyes were sore from the restless night and his muscles ached from being cramped into Cassie's chair. Jake ate mechanically, hardly noticing what he was doing. Typhoid was one thing. A typhoid death, and on the premises, was something else. They're really sticking it to you, Jake, he thought, and no wheeling around it, no dealing out from under it, no way. He counted and recounted what he'd actually lose if he lost Sky High. None of what he counted was money although, God knew, if Sky High went so would most of Jake's liquid assets.

In the last analysis it was all about pride. What Jake had to lose was his opinion of himself and the image he carried in the eyes of the world. He'd lose a sense of his own momentum as a man, as a force in creating things, as a winner. Jake had always dealt in the currency of ideas, the force of his energy, his charm, the weight of his dreams, and these things could not be borrowed or begged the way you can borrow or beg money. Jake was looking out the window when the knock came on his door.

"Come in, it's open." Cornelia de Vos stood there all in white, beautiful as ever, smiling. He smiled back. "Good morning."

"I can help, Jake."

"Help what?" He managed a laugh, standing up as he did it, motioning her to a chair.

"With the sick ones. I was trained as a nurse, you see. Not many people know that." Cornelia sat down and accepted the coffee he offered her. "I realize you're short of help, what with all this"—she gestured at the blizzard—"and it seemed to me I might be useful. If you need me."

"I appreciate your offer." Jake didn't know what to make of it. He was used to jet-set whims but Cornelia seemed on the level. He wondered how much she knew, whether she knew it was typhoid, whether she'd panic. What about the Arab boyfriend? Would she really help or was it some kind of crazy Magdalene act, a bit of chic slumming for the beautiful and bored? "We seem to have a little epidemic on our hands, Cornelia."

"Typhoid, to be precise. I know."

"We're trying to avoid a panic. Medicine is on the way, but, well, you know about the avalanche."

"Yes. And you have the young doctor, is that right?"

"Right. And you could help. What we have to do is simply keep an eye on people. The one real danger is internal bleeding. Other than that, it's just a question of keeping the fever down."

"Alcohol baths and all that? I can do that."

"Good. Why don't you go see Bill Shepherd . . . Doctor Shepherd? He's in room 203." Jake wasn't going to tell her about Maggie. And he wasn't going to let his own fears get contagious. Cornelia de Vos was a very cool number. Chances were, she'd be an excellent nurse. "And, thank you very much."

"I always like to keep busy, Jake. Don't even think about it." She smiled and left the room. Jake took a last sip of coffee.

Count Massimilliano Ruvo di Putignano-Squillace looked across the room at his wife and smiled a benevolent smile. She was delirious again and raving. For hours she had drifted in and out of the extremes of fever, now plunging into a glazed sort of trance that was neither sleep nor wakefulness, now starting up with a brittle consuming energy that left her eyes unnaturally bright and her voice as loud and cutting as it ever was in drink.

Momo looked at her and saw money. He saw great piles of it, freshly printed stacks of dollars and Swiss francs and Deutschmarks, and gold, mines full of gold.

He saw it all very clearly, all in one huge vault to which he, Momo—court jester, gigolo, doormat, and stud and pimp and butler all in one—had the only key. There was, of course, her son. The English boy. Lord Westfield. Half would go to him. But the other half would be more than enough for Momo. It would be enough for a dozen-dozen Momos. She sat up in the big bed and waved her arms melodramatically in the air, the Gorgon unchained, one strap of her orchid silk nightgown drooping off her shoulder. "You're a worm, Momo!" She tried to scream but the sound was more of a croak. "You're nothing but wormshit. Lower than a worm. All my life I've been surrounded by worms!"

"But of course, you have, my flower." Momo spread a little of the whipped butter on his breakfast croissant. "And have you ever thought, Dorothy, about what attracts worms? It is decay, my sweet: the stink of rotting flesh." He smiled as he said this, making it almost into a caress. But Dorothy didn't hear him. She subsided into her pillow and closed her eyes, back in her trance again. No matter. The croissant was excellent, as always. Life with Dorothy had its compensations. Life without her was going to be heaven.

Zem was pure Gibbs and Gibbses had never been known for their ability to sit and wait. Now as she sat in the kitchen of Sky Ranch cleaning up after breakfast, Zem made up her mind. Damn-all if she wouldn't go down to Sky High and find out what was going on, no matter what Gramps thought. Two days she'd been cooped up here with nothing to do but fret about Bill Shepherd. It was the longest time she'd gone without seeing Bill, and if two days could do this to her, well then it was high time she got whatever it was out of her system. Zem stood up at the big old stainless-steel sink and left the iron frying pan to soak. She looked at her grandfather. He was sitting quietly at the kitchen table polishing an old flintlock pistol that had been in the family even before the covered-wagon days.

"Gramps, I've got to go down there." She didn't have to specify where "there" was. "He told me not to, but I'm real worried." Her grandfather kept right on with his polishing, moving the oiled rag in small circles on the deep-grained walnut handle of the pistol. If Zem hadn't known better she might have thought the old man was hard of hearing. In fact Zeke Gibbs had ears like an Indian.

She put on her parka and gloves. Still the old man said nothing. She walked to the door, half expecting him to do something to stop her. Finally he looked up and caught her eyes and held them. "If you have to Zembra, you have to." He only called her Zembra when it was some moment of great seriousness. Zeke had never actually forbidden her to go to Sky High, but she knew the depth of his hatred for the resort. "I'll be back as soon as I can, Gramps." She closed the door and walked to Bill's old VW, which he'd loaned her in exchange for her Jeep.

Cassie Lamont started bleeding about the same time Zem Gibbs left Sky Ranch. Cassie was alone and felt the diarrhea coming on again and dragged herself to the bathroom. Later she saw the blood and nearly fainted at the sight of it. But she didn't quite faint. Holding onto the walls for support, she made her way very slowly down the little hallway to Charlie's room. He was there, sitting on the floor with Whizzer, reading.

"Charlie, old chum," she said, trying to sound cheerful, "would you do me a favor and go find Doctor Bill? He's around here someplace? Or Jake, if you can't find Bill. I'm not feeling too good."

"Sure, Mom." He was up and off in an instant, and before she made it back to her bed Bill Shepherd was at her side. She looked at him blankly for a second before she spoke.

"I'm bleeding, Bill."

"We're prepared for that. Try not to worry. The first thing is to lie down and get your feet elevated. Here." He gently took the pillows out from under her head and made a low platform for her feet. Then he got more pillows and built the platform until her feet were eight or ten inches higher than her head as she lay there. "Just rest, Cassie. I've got some stuff in my room that will fix you right up." Bill said this with a confidence he was far from feeling inside.

Bill was never one to make excuses for himself. Nonetheless, he felt that Maggie might have been saved if only he'd been there when the bleeding started. Now he had a second chance. He knew exactly what to do. But the knowledge was no comfort at all.

When Jake came into her room he stopped in the doorway, shocked, saying nothing. Cassie lay sleeping, very pale against the blue sheets. Bill Shepherd sat next to her, monitoring her pulse. A bottle of straw-colored fluid was upended in an aluminum rack next to the bed, and a tube ran from the bottle into a vein in Cassie's arm. The only sound in the room was an occasional small gurgle as a bubble floated to the surface of the plasma bottle. Bill saw Jake and put a finger to his lips. Cassie mustn't be disturbed. It would take two hours for the plasma to feed into her system. With luck, and with the help of the calcium lactate coagulant he'd given her, the bleeding would stop and the plasma would compensate for the shock that comes with blood loss.

Bill got up and motioned Jake into the hallway. They went into Charlie's room, which was empty. Bill had sent Charlie to play with Eliza.

"How bad is it?" Jake's voice was low.

"Bad. All bleeding's bad. But it's been stable for half an hour. I've given her a coagulant. The plasma will keep her from going into shock. She's got a good chance, Jake."

Jake just looked at him, not hearing the words. He'd always wondered what a hanged man feels at the moment the trapdoor falls open under his feet. Now he knew. And now the plan that had been putting itself together in his head since the first word of Maggie's death clicked into action full-blown. Suddenly Jake was in control again. What he was about to do was risky. No, more than risky: it was damn near suicidal. There was just enough logic left in Jake's brain to realize that, but all the logic in the world wasn't going to save Cassie. Jake grinned, an odd, quick flash of a grin that disturbed Bill Shepherd more than the look of shocked disbelief.

Slowly, as through a mist, Bill's image drifted into Jake Chaffee's consciousness. He was droning on with his words of small comfort. He was saying something about how Cassie had a chance. Well, Bill Shepherd didn't know it, but Cassie was about to get more of a chance. Giving her that chance might cost Jake his life, but he knew the instant he had opened her bedroom door that all the life he had was in that room, and ebbing fast.

"Chance!" Jake reached out and touched Bill on the shoulder, a light touch, as if to convince himself the young doctor was real, really there, not part of this deepening nightmare. "OK, Bill. Now listen. Listen hard. I'm going to leave you in charge of her—and the others. Dud Drummond will help. He can do the hotel things. Did Cornelia get to you?"

"Yes."

"She'll help too. And Dud can get you any of the staff you need, anything from the kitchen. They all know him."

"Jake, you aren't thinking of . . ."

"You bet I am. And don't, for chrissakes, say anything. Especially not to Cassie if she wakes up. If! Jesus!" Jake's voice was still low but there was a new tension in it, new urgency.

"Jake, that's suicide."

"And what, exactly, is this?" He pointed in the direction of Cassie's room. "Look, Bill, it's something to try, OK? Don't try to stop me. Just take care of her." Again, he touched Bill's shoulder, but this time it was in reassurance. Jake Chaffee was going into action. Everything was going to be all right. That was what Jake had to believe if he was going to keep his sanity, and he did believe it. He looked at his watch. Ten-fifteen. "With any kind of luck I'll be back by dark. Hell, it's only fifteen miles." He left Bill Shepherd standing there staring at a big battered teddy bear on Charlie's bed. The teddy bear stared glassily back at him. So be it.

Jake talked to Dud Drummond while getting dressed. He dressed deliberately, mechanically, and very warmly. Thermal long underwear. Down-quilted ski pants. Two Shetland sweaters over a silk shirt. And his heaviest down parka on top of all that. He had huge yellow-colored snow goggles that covered half his face. A knitted Peruvian ski mask that Cassie had given him, a one-piece heavy wool helmet of brightest yellow with crazy patterns of red and black. The helmet would be the last thing to go on: it covered his entire head but for the goggles. He selected his warmest quilted mittens and pulled on his high fiberglass Nordica ski boots, science-fiction-looking contraptions of bright yellow with locks and hinges and a warm lining. Jake wasn't planning to ski to the avalanche site, but he was going to be prepared for just about anything. He had no cross-country skis. He'd have to make do with downhill skis. He briefed Dud Drummond and then sent him to the kitchen for a vacuum flask of hot sugar-loaded coffee and some sandwiches. He picked up the knapsack from the back of his closet and put the food inside. Then he zipped into the parka and went out the backway past the kitchen, seeing no one but a couple of kitchen helpers. He picked up his skis and poles and put on his goggles and the crazy-looking Peruvian ski mask.

The huge garage door rose quietly. Jake's red Jaguar crouched ready and shining at the back of the garage. He looked at it affectionately and smiled underneath the mask. It was not a day for Jaguars.

The three Sky High snow-cats sat side by side in the garage. The snow-cats were big and peculiar-looking machines that ran on tracks like military tanks. The tracks were deliberately wide because the purpose of the snow-cats was to groom the ski slopes. They did this by running up and down the trails, beating down the snow if it was too deep, chopping up moguls if they built up too much, breaking up icy crusts. There was a tiny glassed-in cab on top of the snow-cat and from this position the driver could see everything around him. The cats had very powerful headlights and flashing red warning lights, because the most efficient way to use them was at night. The warning lights were superfluous for daytime use, Jake had always thought, since the cats made such a grinding, clanking racket that no skier could be unaware of their approach. Jake had driven the snow-cats often. They were amazing vehicles, capable of clambering up and down almost any grade. And they had a huge capacity for gas. He checked the fuel supply of the nearest cat and found it full.

Methodically, his pilot's training coming to the surface even though Cassie's life might be ebbing with every minute's delay. Jake made a thorough check of all the snow-cat's systems. There was enough gas to get him to Denver if he had to. Jake found a rope and tied his skis behind the cab. He put a snow shovel and the food inside the cab and then, after a moment's thought, dug out some signal flares, the same flares they'd used on the mountain that night when Charlie got lost. That was everything. Then he climbed into the cab and started the engine. He flicked on the headlights and engaged the gear. Slowly, groaning and clanking like some reluctant dragon, the snow-cat lurched out of the warm garage into the continuing storm.

In the lobby of Sky Lodge, white narcissus sat drooping, in a copper bowl. No one had watered them for three days.

Bill Shepherd stood up and kissed Zem Gibbs. She was the first happy sight he'd seen in two days. "The first thing a wife has to learn," he said with a chuckle, "is obedience. Did I or did I not tell you to stay the hell away from here?"

"What wife?" She grinned, her cheeks flushed from the snow outside. "Who'd marry a mean skinny critter like you, William Shepherd, always laying down the law?"

"What I would most like to lay," he whispered in her ear, "is not the law. I'm glad to see you, Miss Gibbs. In fact, I can put you to work, if that's what you had in mind."

"It was." She sat down, and suddenly all the worries came flooding back. "How bad is it. Bill?"

"Bad. We lost one. But don't say anything, yet."

"Who?"

"I didn't know her. Mrs. della Robbia."

"Red hair?"

"Yes."

"God almighty." Zem looked at Bill, but what raced through her mind was her grandfather's curse. One dead already, and they were trapped. "How's Cassie?" she asked.

"She started in bleeding. And that's bad. But she seems to be holding her own. What I'd like you to do, if you will, is sit with her while I take a look at the others."

"Sure. Isn't there anything else?"

"That'll do just fine, Zem. We've got two problems. One is the damn fever. The other is not letting people know too much about it. We've got to avoid panic. And these people just might panic."

"I can believe it. Well, Doctor, turn me loose." He showed her to Cassie's room. Cassie was still dozing. The bottle was about one third empty now. Cornelia de Vos came into the room softly, beckoning Bill into the hallway.

"I've been to them all, Bill. All but one, that Mr. Rubin seems to be hiding. But there's nothing dramatic in the rest of them. The man Latour that you were worried about, he seems better. The Dutton was asleep and I didn't disturb her. But her . . . husband is there, watching. The rest seem all right."

"Thanks. Why don't you get some rest? I'll see Latour. Then we can check them all again after lunch. It seems to be holding. No new cases."

"Please God." She smiled, and the situation immediately improved. Then she went up to her room.

"Well," said Niris, "Florence Nightingale returns." He hadn't been happy about the nursing.

She kissed him.

"There's really no one else to do it. Are you still angry?" It was a game, she knew. He was testing her devotion. And devoted she would be, but never a harem slave.

"If ever there was an excuse for selfishness, it is you. But no, Cornelia, I am not angry. One should help. In fact, as I waited for you, I wondered, could I help myself? Is there anything I can do?"

"Just be patient. It will either get much better—or

much worse soon. And the snow won't go on forever."

"There is no forever," he said, and started nibbling her ear, "there is only now."

Jake wasn't a mile down the road before he began wishing for two things: a road map and a compass. The road he was on presented no problems. It was a town road and recently plowed. Even with the very low visibility he could follow it. But when he came to 317 it would be another story; 317 was a state road and Jake knew where the state snowplows were and what they were doing. And though he'd driven 317 up to Steamboat Springs more times than he could count, it would all look different now, buried under three feet-plus of snow. The snow-cat could go over just about any terrain, road or no road, but how, Jake wondered, was he going to be able to tell what was north, when he couldn't see the sun?

It was after eleven o'clock now, going on to noon, and the light was flat gray all around him. But Jake didn't turn back. For one thing, he wasn't sure there would be a compass at Sky High. He couldn't remember ever having one. He'd have to trust his instinct and his memory. The snow-cat rumbled on alone. Nothing moved, even on this recently plowed town road. Sky Junction knew what to do in a blizzard: stay home. Jake kept his big snow goggles on even inside the cab. Somehow the yellow lenses helped him see further through the snow. There was an insidious glare about this pale gray world. If you looked into it unprotected you could become snowblind.

Jake moved into Sky Junction proper and turned right on 317. It would be cleared for the length of the township. Then he'd be on his own. He checked the odometer of the snow-cat: 324 miles. When that odometer read 339, he ought to be at the avalanche site. If he followed the road. If, and if, and if. Jake thought of Cassie and of Maggie della Robbia dead in the chill of her unheated bedroom. But Cassie would not die. She could not and so she would not. Jake turned his mind back to the job of getting this tin monster to the avalanche site. He was moving along at a good clip, about ten miles an hour. Then he got to the town line. The snow was more than three feet deep.

The snow-cat ran right into this wall of unplowed snow, lurched, groaned, and gouged its way up on top, pressing the snow down in pleats with the wide tank treads as it went. The visibility was about thirty or forty feet. Beyond that, everything dissolved into a white blur, despite the powerful headlights, despite Jake's yellow-tinted goggles. Landmarks? A line of trees on the left, just perceptible. A deserted gas station on the right, then nothing. A funny row of bumps at regular intervals on the right. They must be the tops of the fat creosoted poles that held the safety cables. Jake smiled to find himself issuing orders—to himself. There would be a lot of those poles, the best guides. *Just hang to the left of them and you'll be all right, Jake.* Unless they're covered up which they will be if this crap keeps on falling, which it probably will. A big old barn looming faintly in the distance on the right? Yes. There ought to be a barn there, gray, with a fading sign in yellow. Can't see the sign, just the shape, and just barely but yes, that's right. Nothing again. Now the land is rising a little and that's right too. It'll rise a little and then it will dip a lot. But wait. After the dip, a curve to the . . . left. And what would be the landmarks there? He couldn't remember, and not remembering panicked him. *Cut it out, Chaffee, do it inch by inch. You'll make it happen, like you've always made it happen. Believe that.*

The snow-cat moved on, lumbering up the slope and carrying its own little world along with it. It heaved itself to the top of the rise and started the descent, packing the snow as it moved. Even through three feet of snow there was a feel to the road, an evenness that, Jake hoped, would also make itself felt as unevenness if he left the road. He looked at the odometer. It read 327. Three miles gone. Twelve to go. *Go, Jake Chaffee. Go, Jake.* A remembered cheer. From what? It didn't matter. And who would be cheering Jake Chaffee now, on this gray December morning? Cassie Lamont? She was lying in a daze of fever, balancing precariously on the edge of death with a disease that he, Jake, had somehow given her, given tham all? Zeke Gibbs would cheer, if Zeke could only see him now. It would make old Zeke very happy, wouldn't it? Well, fuck you, Zeke Gibbs. You don't get me down that easy. The snow-cat was descending faster now, with no landmarks visible in any direction. Still and all, that was what Jake remembered: nothing. No landmarks. At least that's what he thought he remembered. *Go, Jake.* The huge snow-packing machine moved on. Jake's mind raced ahead of it, analyzing and rejecting a thousand possibilities, fighting back despair. This was a race he had to win. No matter what it cost.

Pepi woke smiling lazily. He stretched and relaxed and yawned, smiling with the feline satisfaction of a hardworking man who knows he's slept too late. He rolled over onto his stomach and looked at his big gold Rolex. The time was eleven-fifteen. Shocking. On an ordinary day he'd have skied Sky Mountain three or four times by eleven-fifteen.

Pepi reached out beyond the bed and pulled back the curtain. Still snowing. Good. He thought about the Jew, how well it had gone after the initial surprise, how easily he'd pulled it off, slapping him down like a mosquito, getting rid of the body in the ravine. There was, of course, the possibility that the man had been telling the truth, that an investigation was in the works, that there might be other enemies of the Reich. But Pepi had been Pepi too long to credit this. He'd been Pepi for nearly thirty years, longer than he'd been Karl-Heinz Waldemar. So anything that touched on the long-gone Karl-Heinz seemed dim and unreal to Pepi Prager. He sighed and climbed out of the bed. The most important thing on Pepi's mind was what to order for lunch. He suddenly realized how hungry the night's work had made him.

Dorothy Dutton mumbled in her sleep. The words were unclear, but they were French. Tossing, sweating with fever, her hands clutched at the damp bedsheets. Her eyes were shut but Dorothy could clearly see the château of Parmentier-la-Fôret in the moonlight, candles making a soft apricot glow in every window, a light plinking tune being played on a harpsichord. Then there came a low growling noise which got louder. A lipstick-red Bugatti raced up to the great front door of the château, a dark and startlingly handsome young man at the wheel. He got out of the car and walked around it to help the girl climb out. The girl, young, slim, rather pretty in a sad dark way, magnificently gowned in pale yellow, rose from the low red sports car and allowed herself to be led into the château. The huge oak doors of the château swung open on their ancient hinges and for a moment the couple stood framed in the great archway, illuminated by thousands of candles that set the reception hall of Parmentier-la-Fôret ablaze.

One word escaped Dorothy's fever-parched lips: "Jacques!" Four aspirin tablets lay by her bedside. The young doctor had come and gone and instructed Momo to be sure she took them as soon as she woke from her fitful sleep. Momo, earnest, quiet, eager to help, had assured the doctor of his best efforts. Bill Shepherd left to check out the other fever victoms. That had been half an hour ago, and Dorothy seemed to be dragging herself up out of the depths of the fever. Moving silently in his handmade Italian loafers, Momo came up to the beside table and scooped up the aspirins. Then he went into his own bathroom and flushed them down the toilet.

Nothing moved in the gray and white landscape. Jake looked at the odometer: 330. Nine miles to go. And it was twelve-thirty. He'd been moving for more than an hour. Sometimes he couldn't tell whether he was on the road or off it. Then he'd see a landmark tree, a line of marshmallow bumps that indicated the tops of guardrail posts, a remembered farm. And where the hell were the telephone poles? As he looked down at the mileage indicator it clicked into 331. Nearly halfway there. Assuming he really was on the road.

Noel Northcliff was very pleased. It was going to be the story of the year. Typhoid at Sky High. Edgar Allan Poe's *Mosque of the Red Death à la Mode*. Trapped in a blizzard with the world's most glamorous people, helpless against the ravages of nature. It would finish

Sky High, of course, but it would make a sensation for Noel Northcliff. He was very glad he'd come. Noel sat at the desk in his room sipping tea flavored with orange peel and cloves, and writing his elegant longhand with a solid gold fountain pen on the rich Sky High stationery. It would be, he thought, a Daniel Defoe *Journal of the Plague Year, circa 1973*. Just the sort of thing his public really loved, a disaster befalling God's favorites.

Cornelia, in passing, had spilled the beans. But Noel had guessed, long before that. He'd seen typhoid before, but only in places like Tunisia or Mexico. Fascinating to think how it ever got to good old sanitary Colorado. That, he had no doubt, would come out in time. Secretly he rather hoped it could be traced to the more-haut-than-thou kitchens of Raoul Peng. Be that as it may, the story would grow into a gasser. He'd have it written and verified and the instant the phone service—dammit—was restored. Jake might hate him, but ultimately it was all Jake's fault, wasn't it? And by the time Noel got through with Dorothy's biography, it might just be that he'd find himself fixed so that the hate of a hundred Jake Chaffees couldn't touch him. It was going to be a blockbuster, the Dutton book. More of a blockbuster than Dorothy dreamed. Noel put down the teacup, reached for his pen, and smiled.

Cassie was paler now. She lay flat on her bed with her feet raised on pillows. Just looking at her worried Zem Gibbs. The plasma bottle was almost empty. The room was very quiet, insulated by the blizzard.

Cassie hadn't moved at all in the nearly two hours Zem had been sitting with her. For the first time in her life Zem felt really helpless. She knew she wasn't supposed to be able to do anything for Cassie, but that didn't stop her from wanting to. Anything! Maybe when Cassie woke up Zem could give her an alcohol rub, or anyway cold compresses. Or play with Charlie. It was terrible, the waiting and the silence, this sense of being a prisoner. Zem looked at the magazine, not really seeing what was on the page. Why didn't Bill come back? Where was Jake with that damned medicine? She thought of vultures and her grandfather's crazy notion about the curse of the vultures. Or was it so crazy? She looked at Cassie across the beautifully furnished room. Here was a woman with everything to live for. Dying!

The plasma gurgled again. What would she do if it ran out and Bill wasn't there? Would that be bad? She had heard about people dying from air bubbles in their veins. Suppose Cassie got an air bubble while she, Zem, sat there not knowing how to prevent it? God, it was terrible being ignorant. She stood up, frightened in earnest now, determined to go looking for Bill. But just at that moment he appeared, looking at his watch. Naturally he'd timed it. He greeted her silently, then went to Cassie and felt her pulse and frowned.

The plasma had just about emptied out of the bottle. Gently, firmly, Bill pulled off the tape that held the needle in Cassie's vein. She moved a little and emitted a small noise that was half-sigh, half-grunt. He pulled the needle out and wiped the puncture hole with cotton dipped in alcohol. Then he gently replaced her hand on the blanket and motioned Zem to come out of the room. She followed him down the hall and into Cassie's little office, empty now. "I don't like the look of her. We'll let her rest for an hour, then start another bottle of plasma. There's no way of telling how much blood she may have lost."

"She looks awful."

"It almost has to be a ruptured intestine. If we were in a hospital we could just go in and sew it up. But we're not in a hospital, or anything like it."

"God!"

"We're doing everything we can, Zem. If Jake gets back soon enough, the Chloramphenicol ought to subdue the infection almost completely. The question is, can we keep her stable until then?" Zem said nothing. Hand in hand, they walked back to Cassie's room. They sat down in silence to resume the vigil.

Buck Washington had been standing on his head for nearly fifteen minutes when the girl woke up and saw him there, upside down and bare-assed naked, participles dangling, six-foot-two of black quarterback balanced against the red paneling of his Sky High bedroom. She rubbed her eyes and laughed. "You look," she said, giggling, "like the trophy in a fishing tournament."

"Yeaaah, honey," Buck said slowly, drawling it out in his best stage-darky imitation, "Black Marlin! I do this every morning to get the old juices flowing."

"The old juices were flowing pretty good last night, Buck." She wasn't really a pretty girl, not his usual type at all, and Buck had a feeling she'd decided to make him her Token Black Bed Partner, but what the hell, here he was on this goddamned mountain in this goddamned blizzard and she'd practically propositioned him last night in the Weinstube. Not to mention the fact that after about two womanless weeks Buck Washington's juices needed a little flowing. He did a half somersault down from the wall, landed at the foot of the bed and bowed as she applauded. Then he vaulted onto the bed and kissed her. Before long the juices were flowing well and truly. "I love you," she said.

"No, honey. What you love is my friend there." Buck laughed, and as he laughed he wondered why he hadn't seen Jake Chaffee for so long.

"I don't understand you at all." Niris was puzzled. Where he came from nurses were not people one knew socially. "Don't I please you?"

"You please me very much," Cornelia replied with a smile. "But these people need help, Niris. There's no one else in the place with any medical training, but for the doctor. I wouldn't feel right if I didn't help." She had made the rounds twice now, soothing fevered patients, giving alcohol rubs, administering aspirins. Luckily, there was plenty of aspirin; and in the milder cases, it seemed to do some good.

"That is all very well, I'm sure"—he was being sulky now, a spoiled child—"but I need help too. Have you thought of that?"

"And we have all the time in the world, once the crisis is past. Really, it won't be long. Maybe a day, maybe two. We can leave as soon as the snow stops." Cornelia had just showered and changed her clothes. She bent to kiss him as she left the room. He pulled her down onto his lap.

"I will simply have to get sick, to have such a delicious nurse. Then you will find time for me, perhaps?" But he said it smiling, out of his sulk. She freed herself and stood up.

"Perhaps. But promise me you won't get sick."

"You are very persuasive Cornelia. I promise. And the promises of Bir-Saraband are kept."

"I'm sure they are," she said as she left to find Bill Shepherd.

High in the cabin of the snow-cat, Jake Chaffee lost all sense of time. The big cat rumbled through three and a half feet of new snow with its own pounding rhythm, and even though the noise was loud in Jake's ears it was so steady that it, too, became part of this dream landscape, this world with no edges to it, no beginning or end. The odometer had climbed in the last hour. It read 335 now. And his watch told him it was one-fifteen. So he was averaging five miles an hour, a walking pace. That meant three hours up and three hours back before dark. Hell, he'd be lucky to make it back period. *Cut it out Jake,* he told himself. *No time for negative thinking. You can and you will. You have to.* He was more sure of the road now. After the downhill run just outside Sky Junction, 317 ran along its own cut, carved into the mountainsides a few hundred yards above the valley floor. There were guardrails, and Jake kept to where he could see the tops of the poles that held the steel safety cables. He knew there'd be nothing at all between him and the avalanche unless some poor bastard had been trapped out here, which was unlikely. So keeping to the left hand side of the highway wasn't a problem. Going over the edge would be, but it wasn't really a cliff, just a steep rock-strewn bank. The cat could climb up or down just about anything, however steep. Now the odometer read 336. It was driving by braille, feeling your way. There would be one advantage coming back: he'd be able to see his own tracks. The snow-cat packed and pleated the snow in a clear-cut swath. He was building his own highway back to Sky High. Back to Cassie.

It was lunchtime at Sky Lodge. Dudley Lanier Drummond III circulated in the bar radiating a cheer he didn't feel. There was a new mood on the crowd, a kind of silliness, a feverish merriment that seemed to say, "Well, as long as we're trapped here together, we might as well be having fun." One group drank champagne all through lunch and then went out to build snowmen—and snowwomen—on the terrace. They were probably the first erotic snow sculptures Colorado had ever seen. The tone of the conversation in the bar and the restaurant was pitched higher than usual. Three rich Texans got up a very high-stakes poker game in the bar. More than a hundred thousand dollars changed hands that afternoon. If these people were aware of the sickness they didn't show it. When anyone asked for Jake, Dud told a version of the truth. He'd say that Jake was out trying to groom some of the slopes with the snow-cat crew. And at least two fragments of that excuse were true: Jake had ordered the other cats out to pack the slopes as best they could. The blizzard would end, after all, and they had a serious commitment to the Sky High Challenge Cup on Saturday.

Pepi Prager showed up for lunch, resplendent in a sky-blue silk turtleneck, smiling, joking, a walking advertisement for the good effects of skiing and clean living on the body and the spirit. He got together with Jean-Pierre and two other instructors to suggest a skiing-in-the-blizzard lesson for anyone brave enough to volunteer. They'd simply climb up Sky Mountain as far as they could, and then ski down again. Maybe, Pepi added, the snow-cats could be persuaded to pull them up the mountain with ropes. A dozen people responded to this novel plan. Entertaining, and being entertained, was an instinct too deeply ingrained in the guests to be obliterated by a mere snowstorm: if fun wasn't going to be handed to them on a tray then they could make their own fun, and cleverly too.

No one noticed that Tod Rubin was missing. Tod had made himself as inconspicuous as possible. He had succeeded better than he might have wished. Nor did anyone inquire after Maggie della Robbia. The merry-go-round had slowed down a bit in the last few days. Now it was gaining momentum again, and Dud Drummond would do anything to keep that momentum going. He asked Pepi to give him the names of the bold skiers who went out into the storm with the instructors. They'd all get a bottle of wine this evening, compliments of Sky High.

In a life filled with physical risks, Jake Chaffee had never feared death or even thought about it much. He had seen men shot out of the air over Korea, men he knew and liked, but jet pilots in combat are fatalists and Jake Chaffee knew he was bulletproof. He never questioned his luck because there had always been so much of it.

The first death to touch Jake Chaffee where he lived was that of Jon, his ten-year-old son, and even that had produced more outrage than questioning. Jon's death was terrible for all of them, but it came so quickly, so much like lightning, that the boy's dying had a special unreality about it. Jake never saw him dead. Even the death of Maggie della Robbia didn't touch him personally. When you came right down to it, all Maggie's death really meant to Jake was to emphasize the threat to Cassie. And Cassie could not die. Life would not be imaginable without her.

Jake looked out at the road shrouded in snow. In his head was a picture of Cassie pale and gray against the blue sheets, the plasma slowly filtering into her thin arm. He looked at the odometer for the hundredth time: 337. The snow-cat moved forward by inches, but at least it moved, steadily, surely, unstoppably. God, but he hoped it was unstoppable.

Zeke Gibbs stood in the back hall of the old ranch house looking at his Stetson on its peg. He tried to remember just how old that damned hat was and couldn't. Older than Zem, that was for sure. The color had deepened with age and sweat but it was still just as good as it ever was. Zeke slid the wide-brimmed hat onto his head and wondered if he'd outlive it. Probably not. He walked out into the storm, snug in his worn sheepskin coat to check the barns. The snow felt good on Zeke's face. Even the bleating sheeps' voices disappeared, soaked up by the storm until the bleating and baa-ing were only a whisper. Zeke checked his barns, all five of them, and found them in good order. He walked down the newly plowed driveway and gazed out into the storm. At least the drive would be open if Zem did decide to come back this day. Zeke doubted she would. He loved the girl and he even liked her young doctor. But Zem had left him already. Zeke Gibbs looked out into the blizzard and shivered, not from the cold. Then he turned and went back into the ranch house.

The hour had passed. Cassie was still sleeping, if you could call it that. To Bill it seemed more like a coma. Her pulse had come back to normal, a good sign, but her color was off. There were no external signs of bleeding. He decided not to wake her but to give her a second quart of plasma. That would make two from his total supply of five quarts. Knock wood, none of the others seemed to need it yet. Maybe the Dutton woman. But he wasn't going to worry more about her unless she actually started bleeding. Thank God the little husband was there to report if she did. Cornelia was being helpful with the others. So Bill was able to concentrate on Cassie. Cassie needed all the concentrating she could get. Gently, fearing to wake her, Bill Shepherd picked up Cassie's arm. Then he swabbed the vein with cotton dipped in alcohol and deftly slipped in the plasma needle. The slightest frown passed across Cassie's forehead, like a ripple on a quiet lake. It came and went in silence. Only the gentle movement of her chest under the blue blanket showed she was still breathing.

Now Jake was climbing in the snow-cat. The road curved up and to the right, following the contour of a mountain. The odometer read 338 now. One more mile to go. One mile left to go? Face it, Chaffee, it could be two. The fifteenth mile could be short or long and what the indicator said was "about fifteen miles." How wide could an avalanche be? How many angels could dance on the head of a pin? How did he know the stuff would still be there at the slide site even if he did get there?

Doubting the future was a new and painful feeling for Jake. He fought it back the way you fight back nausea. The cat roared and churned up the old highway. The tops of the guardrail poles were harder and harder to see as the snow got deeper. Some places, they vanished altogether. In other places, they appeared only as fat rounded bumps on the smooth surface. But it was good he had started off when he did. Otherwise those guide-posts might have vanished altogether and then where would he have been?

There wasn't much to do besides think, and Jake didn't want to think. The cat practically drove itself except for gearing up or down. Jake decided he wouldn't look at his watch again until he counted out loud to five hundred. He got to sixty-three and looked. Two thirty-six. That was when he began singing. Jake wasn't a singer, not even a singer-in-the-shower, but now he sang, head back, off key, faking the words more often than not, concentrating hard, anything to get his mind off what he was doing and what might happen if he didn't do it. "In olden days," he bellowed above the engine's insistent roar, "a glimpse of stocking/ Was blah-blah as something shocking/ But now, heaven knows/ Anything goes!" Jake had finished all he remembered of Cole Porter and was about halfway through Rodgers & Hart when the cat lurched and his mind lurched back to reality with it.

There in front of him was a wall of snow.

Quickly, because the engine was straining and about to stall, Jake let in the clutch and kicked the snow-cat into reverse. He backed up in his own tracks, carefully, thinking he must have got turned around, that he was facing into the side of the mountain instead of the open road ahead. He backed slowly, then looked behind him and saw the cat-track trailing straight away, back and back until it lost itself in the falling snow. So he was on the road. He hadn't swerved. That *was* the avalanche. The odometer read 338. Good. He was that much closer to Sky High. To Cassie. Jake threw the cat into neutral and climbed down onto the road. He walked up as far as he could, an easy walk on the hard-packed snow. God help anyone trying to hike through this snow without benefit of packing: it had to be three-and-a-half feet deep. Jake strained to hear, hoping the highway department might be working just a few feet away, but with the growl of his own snow-cat ringing in his ears, it was hard to hear anything. What had looked like a wall of snow wasn't really a wall but a very steep incline. Jake could see how the avalanche had swept down the mountainside and across the road. There were big rocks and broken trees and lumps of ice bigger than cars imbedded in the debris. It didn't look like a safe place for the snow-cat. It didn't look like a safe place for anyone.

Suddenly Jake felt hungry. Hell, why not, it was nearly three o'clock. He climbed back into the warm cab and ate two sandwiches and drank a cup of the hot, sweet coffee. Avalanches, he knew, were seldom wide. They tended to concentrate their force in narrow chutes. That very concentration made them deadly. But while the snow-cat could climb almost anything, Jake could imagine breaking a tread on some jutting rock, or getting a broken tree jammed in the machinery. These were things a man could climb around—provided, of course that the avalanche was truly spent.

Jake savored the last of his coffee. Then he threw the cat into gear and slowly turned it around. He wanted everything set for his getaway. Instinct told him to leave the engine running. It was hard to tell how cold it was, but why take the chance? Truckers did it all the time, he knew, in these mountains. That decision made, Jake went into action. He emptied the knapsack and slipped it on his back. Untied his skis and poles from behind the cab. Got out two red rocket flares. Brushed the snow off his skis and stepped into the bindings. The precise little click they made locking onto his boots reassured him: the mechanism was all in order. He bent down to fasten the long leather safety thongs around his legs. They'd prevent the skis from running away from him if he fell and the bindings released. Then Jake slid his hands into the leather loops that sprouted from the handles of his tempered magnesium ski poles and pushed off towards the avalanche.

His plan was simple: he'd go around the debris on a level with the highway instead of trying to climb over the whole thing. Jake stood silent on his skis for a moment before he left the security of the road. His face was completely hidden behind the goggles and Cassie's knitted Peruvian mask. He felt warm and ready for anything. Impulsively, Jake pulled one of the red flares out of his knapsack and lit it. The flare went off with a hiss and rose high above the avalanche. Then it ignited and for a moment the sky turned bright pink. That, at least, would tell the highway people that something was coming. Then, sure in his heart that he'd done all he could do, Jake Chaffee pushed off the road.

On paper it would look simple. The hardest things often do. Jake merely wanted to keep level with the road and skirt the outer perimeter of the avalanche debris. He knew there'd be obstacles. He knew it was the long way around. But on the face of it, the plan seemed simpler than trying to climb up and then down again wearing racing skis.

He eased away from the security of the road, edging his skis, cutting into the rough sloping surface of the snowslide, feeling it solid underneath him. He prayed it would stay solid. After all, Jake reasoned, the damn thing had had three days to settle. The skis flexed, slid, edged. They kept Jake from sinking into the snow. He came on a big black rock. Jake chose to back up a little and climb above it: better to have that rock fall away from under him than down on him. He edged on and on. It was slow work for skis made to fly down perfectly groomed racing trails. Even where the snow was clear it was lumpy and jagged with ice. Here was a huge broken spruce tree stuck into the snowslide. He clambered above that, too.

Just after he made his way around the broken tree Jake heard an ominous crashing sound. In an instant he was flat against the slope, digging into the snow, arms over his head, making himself as small as he could. Jake never saw what it was that came crashing past him. A rock or maybe a big lump of ice—but big it was and solid and ready to kill. For a minute longer Jake crouched where he was, listening, straining, hearing nothing. Then he eased himself up and edged onward.

Dorothy Dutton had long denied there was such a thing as death. She wouldn't admit it to herself, she would not permit death to be mentioned in her presence, and when people she knew died, she forgot it. This could have been traced to the death of Jacques Parmentier, had any psychiatrist been so bold as to try. Dorothy's life was lived for the moment. This drove her lawyers mad. None of them, ever, dared approach her on the subject of a will. To write a will implied that one acknowledged death. Dorothy Dutton no more acknowledged death than she acknowledged invitations from people she'd never heard of. Even now, feeling absolutely rotten, Dorothy tossed the whole thing off. It would pass. Now, as she opened her eyes in the big room at Sky High, the first thing she saw was dear Momo. Momo smiled. Dorothy smiled back. Odd. Momo seemed to be coming in and out of focus. "Have I been sleeping long?" Her voice was dry with fever.

"You had a bad dream, my flower. You cried out something in French, but I couldn't hear what it was."

"I'm thirsty, Momo. Have we some beer?"

"Has the Pope vestments?" He rose from his seat and got a bottle of Moro XX from the tiny bedside refrigerator.

"You're too good to me, Momo." He held the glass to steady it as she sipped. Her hand was shaking. The doctor had said on no account was she to have alcohol.

"Feeling better?" His voice was low, crooning.

"Much. I think . . . yes! Let's go for a walk. The fresh air will do me a world of good." She flung off the blanket and started to sit up. She was halfway out of bed when a wave of sickness hit her. The diarrhea was coming back. Momo helped her to the bathroom. She looked very pale. When she was finished, Momo helped her back to bed again. In her fever she forgot to flush the toilet. Momo did this for her, and saw the blood. Momo flushed the toilet twice. Then he closed the door and tucked the blankets lovingly around Dorothy's shoulders. She was shivering from the chill that followed the fever. "I think, my dear, that we'll have to postpone that walk." Momo kissed her lightly on the forehead. "Sleep well," he whispered, "get a nice, long rest."

Jake Chaffee looked at his watch. Three-forty-five. Already the light was beginning to change, slowly, subtly turning more gray, less white. On a clear day the sun set a little after five. Today he wouldn't even have an hour's worth of light left. Not that it really mattered: the visibility was so poor it couldn't be much worse in darkness. Instinctively Jake tried to go faster. He pushed a little harder with his ski poles, slid the skis a little faster on the short open spaces between rocks and branches. It seemed—though he could hardly be sure—that he'd rounded the outermost edge of the slide. He seemed to be heading back towards the mountain instead of out away from it.

Looking behind him, Jake could see where his skis had made their own thin tracks in the steep lumpy surface of the slide. Going back would be simpler. Right ahead there was a rock a little bigger than a watermelon. Jake edged up over it and felt a sickening lurch as the rock jerked out from under him and rolled twenty or thirty feet down the slide. Only by digging in his poles, edging in his skis and holding absolutely still did Jake keep himself from sliding with it. He waited, spread-eagled on the slope, hardly daring to breathe. Finally he eased himself over, inch by treacherous inch until the weak spot was passed. Then he heard the rumbling.

Jake froze, sure it was a new avalanche gathering. A rumble, a scraping sound, a kind of roar. Then he heard a shrill and unmistakable police whistle. His knees went silly on him. The highway department! Jake edged himself a little farther and pulled out the other flare. He aimed it up and in the direction of the noises. Again the sky flashed pink. The rumbling stopped. Jake moved further. He could see lights now, just faintly, ahead and to the left. They must have backed off when the second flare went up. The slope was gentler now: this was the far side, gentle as the beginning. Somehow he'd climbed higher than the road.

Now Jake could see the lights clearly, and behind them two big yellow plows. He wondered if they could see him. It didn't matter. They had stopped, waiting. He pushed on, edging and sliding and finally actually skiing the last fifty or a hundred feet, gliding over the lumps of ice and compressed snow and right down onto the newly plowed surface of Highway 317. Tommy Foster got to him first. The boy jumped down from his plow, ran up to this weird-looking monster-man clambering up the road in his crazy mask and knapsack.

"I believe," said Jake Chaffee as casually as he could manage, "that you guys have a package for me."

Twenty minutes later Jake was back on his skis again, edging out onto the face of the snowslide, leaving four astonished highway department workers in his wake. The Chloramphenicol was snugly packed in his knapsack and four of Mrs. Foster's well-known ginger cookies were warming his belly. Tommy Foster had promised to radio to headquarters that Jake had gotten through, picked up the medicine and headed back. This could be broadcast shortwave and hopefully someone at Sky Junction would pick it up and get the message to Bill Shepherd.

Going back was easier, even in the fading light. Jake was more confident now. He moved faster on the same little ledge he'd created coming up. He rounded the outermost edge of the slide, where the big tree was, and climbed back over the black boulder with no trouble. It was four-thirty as he rounded the boulder. The gray was darker now. Soon it would be really dark.

Jake moved on, pushing it as fast as he dared. It felt good to move, to push it, to be doing something positive. He was curving back towards the mountain again. It couldn't be long now. He'd promised the highway department guys he'd send up one more flare when he made it back to his snow-cat. Otherwise, they'd come looking for him. He could feel the slide evening-out now and the going was easier and easier. Soon he'd be warm in the cabin of the snow-cat, driving all out for Sky High. Jake smiled underneath the mask. He was getting very close now. There. He could just see the edge of the slide. The beginning of his side of the highway.

Jake paused, safe now, breathing a little hard. He suddenly realized that he heard nothing at all, no sound but his own astonished breath and the whispering of the snow.

The engine of his snow-cat was not running.

18

Momo's first impulse was to order champagne. But, no. Champagne would be a little obvious, not to mention redundant. There would be plenty of time for champagne. So Momo strolled into the Sky Bar and asked for a glass of chablis. He lifted the glass in silent salutation to a dream come true at last; Dorothy Dutton had died quietly in her coma ten minutes before. He, Momo, was suddenly and thoroughly rich. Dear pathetic old Dorothy, who would never acknowledge death. Momo joined Noel Northcliff, who asked for Dorothy. "She's resting, Noel, very peacefully."

Momo knew the New York state law by heart: the husband of a woman who dies intestate with one child splits the estate fifty-fifty with the child, plus two thousand dollars. The two thousand dollars always struck Momo as very funny. He sipped the cool white wine. He'd have an amusing little supper with Noel—he'd say it was at Dorothy's insistence, that she felt simply terrible he'd been cooped up so long—and after supper he'd go back and discover her body. A tragedy, of course. But unavoidable. Momo looked around the elegant bar with an unaccustomed benevolence. Sky High had been very, very good to Momo, Count Ruvo di Putignano-Squillace. He sighed contentedly and resisted the impulse to buy everybody a drink.

"Jake?" Cassie's eyes drifted open. "Jake?" Her voice was thick, drowsy, distant.

"He'll be back soon," Zem said, not believing it. "How are you feeling?"

"Awful." She tried to move her arm and felt the needle and the tube. The plasma bottle, grimly upended in its chromium rack, was half empty now. Cassie's eyes focused on it, and as she watched in quiet dread two air bubbles swam slowly to the top of the pale yellow fluid. "That bad." It wasn't really a question. Cassie stated it as fact.

"It's just a precaution, Cassie." Zem came up and stood next to the bed. "Bill will be here in a minute. He told me to give you two tablespoonfuls of this." She picked up a bottle of calcium lactate and poured a tablespoon full of the creamy white fluid.

"Ick. What's this?" Cassie made a face but dutifully swallowed the chalky medicine.

"Calcium lactate. It's a coagulant. You were bleeding a little. But it's stopped now." Cassie just looked at her.

"How's Charlie?"

"He's fine. With Eliza. Do you feel up to eating anything?"

"No thanks, Zem." She looked at the plasma again. Then Cassie put her head back on the pillow and shut her eyes.

Jake Chaffee stood in the gray twilight silently cursing the dead engine of his snow-cat. He was a competent mechanic and still he couldn't figure out what was wrong: the fuel gauge showed more than half full. It wasn't flooded. The spark plugs looked all right. It might be something in the carburetor, he guessed, but there was no time and no equipment to tear the damned engine apart out here in the midst of a Rocky Mountain blizzard with night falling like a rock.

Maybe, just maybe, if he trekked back around the avalanche, someone on the road crew could help. But that would be another hour gone, and what could they do that he couldn't? He'd wasted twenty minutes as it was. The decision made itself. Jake knew that coming from Sky Junction he'd only averaged about five miles an hour. Hell, he ought to be able to average at least that on skis. He didn't kid himself it would be easy. But he was warm, he was in good shape, and every minute counted. Jake didn't let himself think what might be happening at Sky High, or what might happen if he didn't get this medicine back there fast.

He got another flare out of the cab and lit it. The sky flashed pink again. This was his promised signal to the highway department men that he'd made it back around the avalanche safely. Then he tucked the last two flares in his knapsack and buckled on his skiis. Five o'clock on the nose. With any kind of luck he'd be back in three hours. With any kind of luck.

Jake figured the knapsack weighed about twenty pounds. It was a good knapsack and it rested easily against the soft quilted down-filled parka. After a few minutes of poling and sliding he hardly noticed the extra weight. Jake Chaffee never had the patience it took for cross-country skiing. He wanted the beauties of nature to come at him special delivery. He thought about the differences between cross-country skis and what he was wearing, and cursed himself for not hunting down some cross-country skis before leaving Sky High.

Cross-country skis were longer, for starters, and made of wood. Jake's skis were the latest Olin fiberglass racing model, short and sleek and with offset edges honed like knives. They responded quickly as though on a fast downhill run. But for walking, longer skis would have been easier. The boots and bindings on cross-country skis were different too. Jake's racing boots were rigid fiberglass shells that came halfway up his shins and higher still in back, angled forward to keep his weight where it should be, skiing downhill. The bindings gripped the big boots front and back like a vise, keeping the boots absolutely flat and rigid, doing everything advanced technology could do to make his leg, ankle, boot and ski into one single instrument of speed. And that too was as it should be for downhill racing. But cross-country was another story entirely.

Cross-country skiers moved with long, loping strides, thrusting their elongated skis far forward in a continuous lurching motion that looked ungainly but that was in fact very efficient. And to generate the maximum reach, cross-country ski bindings were loose at the heel to allow a few inches of up-and-down flexibility. The boots, too, were more supple, lower and made of leather.

As Jake forced his skis forward, sliding first one and then the other, never lifting them from the packed-down snow, he realized there was no way to loosen the grip of his bindings on his boots. He could feel the top edges of his boots digging into his leg, hurting. If that kept up he'd get blisters and real pain. He stopped and bent down to adjust the top two clamps of each boot, loosening them as much as the clamps allowed. There. That was a little better. He pushed off again.

The two men who checked into the Holiday Inn just west of Denver that afternoon could have been any kind of businessmen. They registered as employees of the Worthington Corporation, 1010 F Street, Washington D.C. The reference would have checked out. The Worthington Corporation was a dummy organization maintained by the FBI to give cover to agents employed on specially delicate assignments. The two men from Worthington were on a mission of the greatest sensitivity. They were to arrest Pepi Prager, and they'd come all the way from Chicago on a train to do it, since nothing had flown into Denver after Monday noon. They were grimy from the train ride. They showered and unpacked and then met in the coffee shop. Then one of them made a phone call from a pay phone in the lobby.

It was dark now. The light had faded out so subtly that Jake couldn't have said what was daylight and what was night: he was moving in a kind of trance, pushing through the snowfall, thrusting one leg as far forward as the pain would let him, then following with the other leg, trying for a little glide to make the motion easier, reaching out with his ski poles to pull himself forward. Probably, a small voice of logic told him through his daze, he'd have a bit more downhill than uphill between the avalanche and Sky High. The stretch of road he was on now sloped downhill, but only a little, maddeningly, not enough to ski.

There would be at least two steep hills to climb, he remembered. Two at the minimum. A ironic grin came and went under the grotesque Peruvian ski mask as Jake thought how many times he'd swept down this same road at more than a hundred miles an hour in the red Jaguar.

Push, reach, pull, thrust, push out again. The rhythm of his movement had its own hypnotic fascination. After a while even the pain developed a personality of its own, unpleasant, maybe dangerous, but still a companion, something to remind Jake Chaffee that he was alive and moving, that this wasn't just a bad dream. The pain burned into Jake's legs with every thrust of his skis. He knew how tired he was, and welcomed the pain as a way to keep awake. It was his silent companion now and he fought it inch by inch: it was more his enemy than the distance or the darkness or the snow.

The dark was never black. The snow gave off a glow of its own, and although Jake could see no more than maybe ten feet in any direction, ten feet was enough. The tracks he'd made coming with the snow-cat saved his life. Without the packed snow underneath him to make the going easier, without the foot-high wall at the edge of the packed snow, Jake would have been exhausted and lost before he'd gone a mile. He kept close to the edge, feeling the barrier when he couldn't see it, making sure his skis were cutting right angles across the even horizontal tracks of the big snow-cat. He was going uphill now. Odd, how you never realize the steepness of a hill until you walk it. Still, he kept up the rhythm, push, thrust, pole, pull, push again. Slow work. Hard work. Life-or-death work.

Bill Shepherd was bone-weary but it was more in his head than his body. All day he'd been fighting this feeling of helplessness, of working against impossible odds, of having both hands tied behind his back. He stepped into Cassie's room and managed a smile for Zem. It wasn't a very convincing smile. Bill went to Cassie and felt her pulse, then threw himself down in an overstuffed chair and sighed. Zem said nothing. There wasn't much to say. The second bottle of plasma was half gone now.

Jake came to a crest in the road. He could feel the beginning of a slope more than he could see it and stopped for a minute to catch his breath. Six-thirty. He'd been at it an hour and a half now. It took real effort to imagine anything in the world but falling snow and this endless pushing, stretching out, pulling on, pushing all over again, living all your life on one frozen treadmill. Who was it, he tried to recall, in mythology, the guy doomed to keep pushing the big rock up the hill, only the rock kept rolling back down on him just as he got it near the top?

God, but it felt good to stop. Jake stood tall, and suddenly he was aware of the weight of the knapsack. *Welcome that weight, Chaffee,* he told himself, *Cassie's life might be riding on it.* His breath steamed out in white clouds against the white of the falling snow. No wind. You could be thankful for that, if you were looking for things to be thankful for. No earthquakes, no erupting volcanoes, no lightning bolts. There was quite a list, if you put your mind to it. Suddenly Jake wanted to sit down. Just for a minute. He could actually time himself on the stopwatch. No. What he really wanted to do was lie down.

He couldn't lie down. Jake looked down at his skis, just visible against the snow, and felt the slope again. Maybe he could ski down. He tried to remember if there was any part of the road steep enough to be dangerous for a skier who couldn't see. No. Slowly now, deliberately, aware of the need to conserve himself, Jake pushed off. There was just enough of a slope to let him glide. Small favors, maybe, but it felt wonderful. Nearly as good as lying down. *But you aren't going to lie down, Jake, or sit down or even stop for more than a few seconds.* He moved down the gently sloping road giving himself pep talks, wondering if he could be moving faster than the damned snow-cat. It was possible. Anything was possible.

In room 403 of a Holiday Inn just outside Denver a meeting was going on that would have gladdened the heart of la Mère Olivier, had she been aware of it.

In a room at Sky High two pairs of eyes watched Cassie Lamont fighting for her life. The plasma seeped into Cassie's veins slowly, slowly, and Cassie herself lay motionless in a sleep that was indistinguishable from coma. Bill Shepherd and Zembra Gibbs stayed with her and ate a light supper from trays. Neither of them asked the unanswerable question: *Where was Jake Chaffee?*

Cornelia and Niris ate supper from trays also, alone and together for the first time that day. Cornelia had checked in with Bill, and Bill gratefully told her to take a few hours off, get some rest, eat. They'd do a bed check later on. So far the fever patients seemed to be holding their own. Neither of them knew about Dorothy Dutton.

In the Sky Bar, Momo was bringing forth his very best and most amusing anecdotes. He had kept a small group in stitches for nearly an hour. Suddenly a look of concern crept onto his face. He glanced at the thin golden wafer of a wristwatch that Dorothy had given him last Christmas. Six-thirty. Would they excuse him, he pleaded, he must just run up and see if there was anything Dorothy required. He'd be back by the time his next drink arrived. Smiling but ever the attentive husband, Momo walked upstairs and opened the door of his suite, blew a kiss at the stiffening corpse of Dorothy Dutton, and returned to the bar.

There was a point of light in the distance. Jake began inventing fantasies about the light—that it was a house, that the house had a skimobile, that the skimobile sped him to Cassie's bedside in five minutes. All of which could happen except that nothing was going to get Jake Chaffee off the packed trail of his own snow-cat. The light could be nothing. He checked the time: seven-thirty. Funny. It seemed like five minutes since he'd fought against his desire to lie down, and it was more than an hour. Two and a half hours. If he was averaging five miles an hour, he ought to be nearly there. If.

Jake tried to reconstruct Main Street in Sky Junction in his head, tried to imagine where the first house would be that had access to the plowed part of 317, where someone might give him a lift. He drew a complete blank. He could see the road in his head, he could see Bill Shepherd's house at the edge of town, and logic told him there had to be other houses with people in them, but damned if he could remember where.

Push on, dammit. He looked for the light and it was gone, or maybe it had never been there at all. Maybe he'd finally gone bonkers. Uphill now. The road going uphill. Push, slide, stretch, pole-out, pull in. Left, right, left, right. Jake tried to remember marching cadences. Fuck marching. The snow kept falling and falling. It was massing on the snow-cat's track now, and probably two or even three inches had built up in the time it had taken Jake to travel this far from the avalanche. The track was still clearly defined. It was just that the moving was harder. Push. If the hill got much steeper he'd have to herringbone, or sidestep. That would squeeze the few remaining drops of energy right out of him. It was getting, dammit, steeper. Steeper and curving. Curving more. Which meant one good thing. This had to be the big downgrade just outside town.

The pushing was much harder now. His skis had some kind of magical stuff on the bottom, like Teflon, that kept them permanently slippery, absolutely wonderful for downhill, only this hill went up. Now the rhythm became push, slide back, brace yourself with the poles, push. He'd have to herringbone. Shit. He stopped but wouldn't let himself rest. If he started to rest he just might not stop. Herringbone. Jake lifted his right ski to make one side of the herringbone V. Lift, toe out, edge in, pole, pull, lift the other ski—Jesus, they both weigh a ton—other ski, toe out, edge, pole in, pull—and congratulations, you just made your first V. A thousand of them might get you up this hill which, by the way, just happens to be Everest and the north face of the Eiger all rolled into one handy package just for you, Jake, nothing but the best. Toe out, like a fucking duck. Now the other one. That's it, pole, pull, two V's are better than one. Only when the pain came back did Jake notice it had gone away for a while. How long? He thought of Charlie, stuck up on the mountain with his leg smashed, alone with the dog. Wouldn't mind having old Whizzer here now. Do the old Saint Bernard number, tie some of Bill's medicine around his neck and send him scampering back to the lodge. More V's. Now he could see the top of the rise. Pole. Pull. Pray. The top of the rise! He could glide a little now. The pain was going away again.

Even the gliding, sliding of his skis was heavy going now. He had to be nearly at the edge of town, nearly at the end of his cat track. The plowed town road had to be somewhere just ahead. It was, and the change in surfaces took him by surprise. The cat track ended in a rough little ledge. Two feet below, the town road lay smooth, untracked under a few inches of new snow. It had been plowed for the third time that afternoon.

Jake lost his balance on the ledge. He fell heavily, forward and to the left, not a skier's fall but a drunken lurch downward. For a moment he lay there, numb, the breath knocked out of him. Up. He must get up. It was strangely comfortable, lying there. The weight of the knapsack pressed him down. There wasn't much pain anymore. Jake opened his eyes and saw his gloved hand stretched out on the road, pointing towards town. Towards Cassie. The last thing Jake thought of was Cassie.

Pepi Prager turned on his smile and saw the girl beginning to melt. She was one of the better-looking rich Texans, honey-haired and big-titted and quick to laugh. She'd be warming his bed before long if history was any kind of teacher. He reached out for her hand. She'd have tales to tell, this one, when she got back to her oil wells. Not every girl at Sky High was so favored, to share the bed of Pepi Prager. He smiled, teeth gleaming against the tanned, perfect face. It was going to be a good night.

Bill eased the needle out of Cassie's arm. That would have to be it for the plasma. At least for a few hours. He wished she'd wake up so they could get some nourishment into her. If she didn't eat before long, he'd have to consider glucose injections. And where in hell was Jake? Cassie moved a little. A slow shudder rippled through her thin body. She opened her eyes, looked up and saw Bill. "Where's Jake?" Her voice was like a bad connection on a long-distance line.

"He'll be back soon. Could you take an egg-nog?" Bill smiled. Her talking was a good sign.

"I could try. I feel—kind of hollow." Bill told Cassie to rest, to save her strength. He sat down heavily in Jake's big chair. The room was filled with the frightening fact of Jake's absence. Bill made up his mind that if Chaffee hadn't shown up in half an hour, he'd send out a search party.

It might be a damn-fool errand, but Zeke Gibbs was glad to have something real to do. A man could go crazy just sitting around the ranch house waiting for the snow to stop. So when one of the ranch-hands asked for a lift across town to look in on his ailing sister, Zeke was pleased to oblige. There was no danger to it. The town kept the roads clear, even in a storm like this, even though anybody but a crazy old reprobate like himself would be stuck to the fireside until it stopped. Zeke and the young hand piled into the Jeep pickup and roared off through the dusk in four-wheel drive. The normally ten-minute drive took nearly half an hour but they weren't in any hurry. Zeke dropped the boy off and told him to stay with his sister until the blizzard snowed itself out. Then he got back in the pickup and headed home. The boy's sister lived clear across the valley. As Zeke came to the intersection of 317, he could see the town had plowed it. This made him wonder if the boys from the state highway department had broken through the avalanche yet. Hell, he was out anyway. He'd just take a little run up the plowed-out stretch of the road and see if anything was happening.

Eliza Chaffee lay on top of her bed with all the lights out. Bill had told her to rest, even though she really didn't feel that bad. It had been fun helping the glamorous Cornelia de Vos, but then the headache came back and Bill packed her off with aspirins and advice. It was pleasant, lying here, listening to the barely audible whisper of the snow. She closed her eyes, and began to doze off. Where, she wondered, was her father?

It was dark now. Zeke kept the pickup in four-wheel drive and drove it close to the wall of snow thrown up by the plow on the right of the road. He felt kind of like a plow himself, creeping up the silent highway. It was no night to be out, no night to be fighting avalanches. Still, in these parts a man learned early to take the weather as he found it. He was near the town line now. There. The plowed stretch of highway ended in a low wall of snow. They hadn't broken through. He'd have to back and turn. He threw the gearshift into reverse, eased it back, then forward, turning. What was this? His high beams picked out a pile of rags, nearly covered by snow. Something glittered. A ski! Some lunatic had come out on skis in this storm! And got what he deserved, too, by the look of it. Zeke threw on the emergency brake and climbed down from the truck.

It could have been any fool. Zeke stood there for a minute, looking down. He was alive, at least. Zeke saw the faint mist of the man's breath on the big yellow goggles. That crazy looking knitted helmet might have kept him from freezing his ears off. Zeke squatted next to the unconscious figure and pulled off the goggles, and lifted the knitted mask.

Something went out of Zeke Gibbs as he squatted in the road looking down at his mortal enemy. If Zeke had a dollar for every time he'd wished Jake Chaffee dead, it would be money enough and more to buy back Sky Valley. Now Jake lay at his feet, unconscious, half-frozen, near dead. What a simple thing it would be just to leave him there. Zeke looked over his shoulder with a quick furtive motion, as though he expected witnesses. Only the falling snow was there to see. The Jeep's tracks were being covered already. By dawn there wouldn't be a trace. Later on, when he had time to think about it, Zeke could never quite remember all the things that crowded his mind as he bent over Jake Chaffee, alone in the fine deadly snow: the curse, maybe, or the fact that Highway 317 was well on the way to claiming one more victim. Whatever he thought, Zeke didn't think for long. Automatically, and with the unexpected gentleness that is part of real strength, his old fingers began working at the release mechanism of the bindings of Jake's skis.

Cassie was sitting up now. She held the big glass of eggnog in both hands, and dutifully sipped at it through a straw. It was delicious, but for all she noticed, it might have been liquid chalk. The very act of sitting up took a lot of her strength. Drinking the eggnog took more. And fighting back her fears about Jake was worst of all.

Zem was in the room, and Bill too. Neither of them was good at faking confidence he didn't feel. Bill sneaked a glance at his watch. Ten minutes more: then he was going to get someone to go look for Jake. A loud knock echoed off Cassie's door. Bill looked at her. "Come in," she said in a low voice. Something about her voice kept Bill's eyes on her instead of the door. Then the door swung open. Cassie's eyes got very wide.

"Gramps!" Zem was on her feet and halfway across the room.

Zeke Gibbs stood in the doorway, a little dazed to find himself at Sky High, and in a lady's bedroom. He carried Jake Chaffee in both arms like a broken toy. "I have something, Ma'am," he said quietly to Cassie, "That belongs to you." Then he laid Jake gently across the foot of the big bed, turned and left the room. Zem followed, chattering, asking a dozen questions all at once. Zeke said nothing. It was only later, when Bill Shepherd was helping to get the ski boots off him, that they noticed the blood flowing from Jake's legs where the unyielding tops of the boots had rubbed the flesh raw.

Thursday morning came to Sky High in a burst of sunshine.

Jake had been taken up to his own room, cleaned up and bandaged and put to bed. He slept twelve hours. Now he was up and showered and ready to face the world, his world, or whatever might be left of it. He didn't remember falling, or being picked up by Zeke Gibbs, or any of it. Jake was walking stiffly and both shins were bandaged, but he felt fine. Bill Shepherd had made his rounds with the Chloramphenicol the night before and already there was good news. Fevers were down, heads were clearer. The epidemic would soon be under control.

Jake's first stop was Cassie's room. She sat up in bed, pale but restless, smiling. The internal bleeding had stopped. Jake bent to kiss her and held her hand, and kept on holding it. He needed the touch of her to convince himself she was really there, and he with her.

"For a fast-talking slicker from 'Frisco," she said softly, "you do some pretty fair cross-country skiing." Her hand tightened in his. "You saved my life, Jake. And other people's lives too. I don't know how any of us can thank you."

"It's all part of the service, darling. You can thank me by resting a lot and eating a lot and turning into my Cassie again. Promise?"

"Promise." She just looked at him. They didn't need more words than that.

Dorothy Dutton was dead. Jake heard it from Bill after breakfast. That made two, two dead, and maybe a third because nobody had seen Tod Rubin for two days. Jake said nothing while the news sank in. It probably meant he'd lose Sky High. For the first time, as he sat there, Jake realized he was able to imagine a life without Sky High. But it was hard to imagine going through all the rest of his life feeling like a murderer, and that was exactly the way he felt: guilty. Except for him, those people would be alive now. Bill's protests didn't register. Still, he had to go through the motions of running Sky High.

There was the pro race to set up. There was the bank to deal with, if that wasn't a lost cause already. There were a thousand pieces of his dream to be picked up and patched together somehow, and Jake set out to do that as best he could, for as long as they left him.

By noon the Sky Lift was running again and the slopes were dotted with skiers. The snow had never been better, or the sky more blue. To look out any window from the lodge, you'd never know there'd been a blizzard, or fever, or death. The radio said Liberty Pass would be opened by nightfall. Jake sent the second of his snowcats up 317 with a mechanic to bring back the cat he'd abandoned. That was done by noon, and soon all the snow-cats were put to work grooming and packing Sky Mountain. The Sky High Challenge Cup would be the world's first look at Sky High on TV, and Jake was determined it would look its best.

The telephone service came back around noon. It was a few minutes after four o'clock in the afternoon when Jake's phone rang. "Mr. Chaffee?"

"Speaking."

"This is Peter Hartmann, Mr. Chaffee." The voice was terse, low key, competent. "I'm with the Federal Bureau of Investigation, and I think you might be able to help us in a matter we're looking into."

"Naturally, I'll be glad to do anything I can." Jake had no idea what the man might be leading up to.

"It's a very sensitive thing, Mr. Chaffee, and we would rather not go into it on the phone. Could you reserve me two rooms for tomorrow night?"

"Sure. You may have some trouble getting up here, though."

"We'll get there. And thank you for your cooperation." Hartmann clicked the phone once and it died. Jake hung up slowly, puzzled. Terrific! Plague, blizzard, avalanche and now crime. He wondered what would be next. Then it dawned on him that the phone was working and he dialed Pete Woodbury in Connecticut.

Pete Woodbury was packing. He moved about the bedroom in the white clapboard-and-fieldstone house he'd shared with Franny and the kids, methodically choosing and sorting and discarding. All he really needed to pack right now was clothes, so he could move into the Chaffee Development apartment as soon as possible. The dividing of books, records, paintings and other items could be left for later. That would be a moment not to look forward to, if Franny kept going in her present bitter state of mind. She had passed the scene-making stage. Now Franny had lapsed into dull, overly polite, sullen servitude filled with one-word answers and veiled menace.

Pete had slept in the guest room since his return. The girls had taken it well, quietly, no tears. Hell, half of their friends had split parents, sometimes multiple splits. And soon they'd be going away to school anyway. The phone rang and Pete picked it up absently, lost in indecision about a slightly threadbare but comfortable pair of blue jeans. He decided to keep them, remembering how disreputable Franny thought they looked on him.

He picked up the phone and heard what Jake had to tell him. Pete sat on the edge of the fourposter bed he'd shared with Franny. He tried to focus on an old Currier & Ives lithograph that hung on the wall but his eyes blurred with tears. Jake finished and said how sorry he was. Pete said nothing. Maggie, dead. Images of Maggie flickered through Pete's mind with relentless burning clarity. Maggie on the jet to Denver, with her blushing and her needlework. She never did finish that little pillow. Maggie, laughing, letting her glorious red hair down for the first time. Maggie on skis, a careful, graceful skier. Maggie in bed, glowing. Pete could imagine Maggie every way but dead. She'd never be dead as far as Pete Woodbury was concerned, no matter what the truth was. But she'd be gone, and now the life Pete had been planning for the two of them was gone too, evaporated without a trace, blown away, a thing without substance or form.

Pete knew that for all the rest of his days he'd carry the aching memory of something that had never happened. His life with Maggie was reduced from all it might have been to a few stolen hours on Sky Mountain.

He looked numbly at the lithograph, seeing it clearly for the first time: THE OLD HOMESTEAD read the title, and there it was, Victorian and idyllic, decked with gardens, a hoopskirted lady forever calling to a little sailor-suited boy who ran down the faded lawn. Pete wished a futile wish: he wished that he and Maggie were part of some old picture on some happy wall, frozen in time, together, inseparable.

"Pete?" Jake's voice was quiet, concerned. Pete didn't know how long he'd been staring at that dumb picture.

"Yeah. I'm here."

"If there's anything I can do . . ."

"No. Thanks. I'm just a little numb, Jake. God. She had four kids. You don't think of people dying."

"I know, what you must be going through, Pete. I nearly lost Cassie."

"I know, Jake. I'm glad for Cassie." Pete closed his eyes. He was thinking how differently things might have turned out if he had been at Sky High with Maggie, when she needed him. "I'm going to send all our clippings to Knickerbocker by messenger, tomorrow."

"Pete, if you feel like you need to rest . . ."

"Thanks, but work is probably the best thing for me right now. Keep my mind off things."

"Cassie and I will look forward to seeing you back here. You know that."

"It'll be nice to be back." In the one place he knew Maggie. Pete hung up the phone and sat for a minute in silence. Then he dragged himself to his feet and finished packing.

The longest drive Jake Chaffee ever took was the mile and a half from the garage at Sky Lodge to Zeke Gibbs's ranch. Jake did it in the afternoon, right after the FBI man's call. The sun was still bright, and the top was down on the red Jaguar, as usual, and none of it made Jake feel the least bit cheerful. He didn't know what he was going to say to the old man, or what kind of reception to expect. Jake just knew he had to say something to the man who saved his life. He knocked on the neatly painted door. Zeke opened it himself.

"I came," said Jake evenly, "to thank you." Zeke looked older today than Jake remembered him. He stood in the doorway, tall and sinewy, only the bright eyes seemed alive in a face like old leather. Those eyes looked Jake up and down, and at the sleek convertible in the drive behind him. "I would have done the same," said Zeke, "for a dog." The door closed.

There had been an exodus from Sky High Friday afternoon. The charter was flying out of Steamboat Springs again, and the highway department had finally broken through the avalanche after four days of round-the-clock labor. Most of the sick people who could be moved left. But, to Jake's surprise, many others stayed on. The worst was over, they figured, and there was the promise of one more weekend of fun. More reporters arrived, and a television crew came up from Denver by bus. Jake took the head of the camera crew up the mountain to show him the camera sites. His legs were still painful but he put up with the pain: the television coverage could do a lot for Sky High.

There was an air of anticipation in the dining room that night. Several pro racers had checked in, a new infusion of celebrities added to the well-known faces already there. Cassie felt better. Jake had supper with her and went to mingle with his guests. Pepi appeared, smiling, joking with some of the newly arrived racers he knew from other resorts, other races. Tomorrow was going to be a big day.

Jake was having a nightcap in his room when a knock sounded on his door. He opened it to see Noel Northcliff, smiling.

"I hope I'm not intruding, Jake."

"Not at all. Have a drink."

"I came," said Noel as Jake handed him a cognac, "to tell you about a Noel Northcliff First. I had written a rather bitchy piece about the recent unpleasantness." Noel sipped his cognac and smiled inscrutably.

"You mean the typhoid?" Jake hadn't figured NN for a blackmailer, but you could never tell.

"Exactly. *The Masque of the Red Death,* as it were."

"And that was a first?" Jake forced a smile. What in hell was the man leading up to?

"No. The first was that I tore it up. And wrote another piece, which I phoned in that afternoon." Again, the inscrutable smile.

"And?"

"And you're going to be a hero, Jake Chaffee. If I do say so myself, it's an effective bit of melodrama: the blizzard, the fever raging, the avalanche, even death itself. And the playboy innkeeper risking all to bring back the vital medicine. They'll be on the edge of their seats. All twenty-six million of 'em."

"I guess I should say thanks."

"It is we who should thank you, Jake. I had a touch of it too. You may have saved my life."

"That wasn't really why I did it."

"I know. But, so what? When that paper hits the stands, you'll be the biggest hero since Rin Tin Tin."

"That won't bring Dorothy back, or Mrs. della Robbia."

"Dorothy had a long, full life. And few regrets. As for the other lady, very sad." Noel smiled, thinking of the book he would write from what tapes Dorothy had made before her sudden death and from the file he had at home, on microfilm. Her life would not go unrecorded. He, Noel, would write her epitaph three hundred pages long. It would be a triumph of journalism. It would be a gold mine. "Well, Jake, I'm leaving tomorrow. I just wanted to thank you in person. You've earned what you have here."

"Thanks, Noel." Jake finished his drink and went to bed. He'd need more than a complimentary gossip column to save Sky High.

Saturday dawned cloudless and bright as though there had never been a blizzard in the Colorado Rockies. Jake was having breakfast with Cassie when the phone rang. He picked up the receiver. "Yes? Who? Sure. My room, in ten minutes." He hung up slowly.

"Who was that?"

"Would you believe the FBI?"

"I'd believe anything." Cassie managed a smile.

"That's who it is. Now what in hell can they want?" He got up, kissed her, and walked out of the room.

Hartmann and his associate Blake were waiting for him. Peter Hartmann was the senior officer. They were two militantly average-looking men in off-the-rack suits and town shoes, not even pretending to be part of the Sky High group. Quietly, dispassionately, Hartmann told Jake the whole story of STYX and Tod Rubin and the chance discovery by la Mère Olivier of Pepi's photograph in the skiing magazine, of the investigation, of the evidence.

Finally Jake stood up. On any other day he would have been shocked and unbelieving. But as it was, Jake was reduced to simple wonderment: what new spitball was God getting ready for him now? First typhoid, then Nazis. Peng, no doubt, was secretly Tojo. It was almost funny. Almost. His reaction was instinctive: Sky High came first. You do not arrest the ski pro on the day of the big race.

"He's gone, you know." Jake said it quietly. He had to make a deal with these men. He needed time.

"Prager?"

"No, Rubin. Nobody's seen him for three days. He didn't—couldn't have—checked out. Clothes still in his room. He had a touch of the fever. We were afraid he might have gone delirious and wandered off into the storm."

"You've searched?"

"Of course. But there's four feet of new snow. We might not find him until it melts."

"I suggest," said Hartmann, "that we have a word with Mr. Prager." Jake took a deep breath and looked at his watch. "You know we're having our first big pro race today. Pepi may be on the mountain already. I'd consider it a favor, gentlemen, if you could make your move after he does his exhibition run."

"He's been on the loose for thirty years," said Hartmann standing up. "I can't see how an extra hour or two will make much difference. He can't get away: there are state police checking every exit."

"You'll have our fullest cooperation." They shook hands.

Outside Jake's door, Pepi Prager stood frozen. Then he darted around the corner and down the hall. He'd heard it all. He stood in an alcove, getting his breath, thinking how to buy time. So the Jew had been in earnest. And the stupid Americans thought they had him cornered. How little they knew of heroes! What a surprise Pepi Prager had in store for them! He walked down the stairs into the crowded lobby, smiling, at ease. They would learn what manner of man was Karl-Heinz Waldemar.

China Bowl had been turned into a carnival on skis. Already, at noon, the bowl was filling up. Spectators on skis with all manner of picnic equipment and cameras were settling into advantageous locations. Bright groups of ski racers made practice runs down the sides of the bowl, dressed in harlequin colors and wearing racing bibs with huge numbers and SKY HIGH printed on them. There was no sign of Pepi.

Jake moved from group to group, checking that the camera crews had all they needed in the way of food and coffee and help from the Ski Patrol. Peter Hartmann and his partner came up around noon, conspicuous in their city clothes and borrowed overshoes. Even Charlie Lamont was there, by special permission, hobbling gamely through the snow on his walking cast. Still, no Pepi. If he didn't show up soon, they'd start without him, and a full-scale search would begin.

The Skytop restaurant was serving sandwiches and quiche lorraine, coffee, beer and wine. Jake had a quick sandwich with Charlie, but his mind was not on eating. Where the hell was his star, Pepi? Surely Pepi didn't know that he was in any danger. The double-slalom racecourse stood empty, waiting, marked with blue flags on tall bamboo poles. The TV cameras were in place. China Bowl, Jake thought, never looked better. There it was, a perfect half globe scooped out of Sky Mountain, white under its new powder, the cobalt sky above, and all of it framed by the looming Alpine cornice of Widow's Peak.

Then Jake saw Pepi.

It could only be Pepi Prager. Jake sensed this with a terrible foreboding because the tiny figure was too small at that great distance to distinguish features. Jake stared silently at the little dot of blue, then went to the camera crew and borrowed a pair of binoculars.

High beyond the rim of China Bowl Pepi Prager was side-stepping his way up the smooth deadly face of Widow's Peak. Jake could see the man clearly. Pepi's sky blue jump-suit fitted him like another skin. He was already a third of the way up the cornice, frowning with concentration, obsessed, beyond all limits of reason or reality. Pepi lifted one foot up, then followed with the lower foot, up and up. He must have been climbing for an hour, Jake figured. Jake kept his binoculars focused on Pepi, trying to remember where the crevasses were on Widow's Peak.

The great white curling lip of snow hung over the top of the cornice like a frozen ocean wave about to break. And Jake knew it would break if the slightest vibration disturbed it. Still Pepi climbed and climbed, leaving a mile's worth of hash marks in the white velvet snowfield behind him. Jake felt a hand at his elbow. "I suppose," said an ironic voice, "that there's no way to get him back down here." He might have been discussing next year's tulip crop in the netherlands.

"Not without a helicopter."

"Some exhibition run." Hartmann's laugh had no humor in it.

The sun felt good on Pepi's face. He liked being close to the sun. It made him feel clean. A fine thing, to be his age and in such shape. How many men so old could climb so high and scarcely breathe hard? The rhythm was easy now. The first strain had gone. Pepi edged up and up, hardly looking back, always concentrating on the next step, the right placement of the skis. He had promised them an exhibition run. They would get a run they'd never forget. He smiled. The virgin snow felt good under his skis. He was halfway up the cornice now. How much higher did he dare go? Dare? He, Pepi Prager, would dare anything, anyone, anywhere. Daring was the story of his life. Let others crawl. He would soar high above them. Look at them down below, far below, tiny specks, insects.

Pepi looked up and ahead. He was traversing the cornice as he climbed it. Two hundred yards above him the blue shadow of the cornice crept down the slope to meet him. That would be the place. There, where the knife-edge of blue met the dazzling white. He must not begin his run in shadow. Up and up he moved, first the upper ski and then the lower ski. He looked out across the valley. From here you could see everything. Sky Lodge lay miles below, white against the evergreens. Then the little toy town, the road, other mountains. Pepi climbed, never pausing.

Other people had spotted him now. A ripple of excitement passed through the crowd. So this was the exhibition run! Few of them knew the danger. They figured it for another dramatic stunt, and the world of ski racing is filled with such stunts. "Jake, is that Pepi?" Charlie's voice was shrill.

"I'm afraid so, Charlie. He's doing something very dangerous."

"Why, Jake?"

"Frankly, old chum, I think he's crazy."

"Really crazy or fooling-around crazy?"

"Really, truly crazy."

The television cameras were zeroing in on Pepi now. He was edging up closer and closer to the shadow of the rim. They got the focus and more than seven million Americans sat in disbelief of what happened next.

There was the shadow, so deep and blue and smooth it almost had a substance of its own. The shadow beckoned Pepi Prager, invited him into the folds of its blue veil, out of the spotlight. But Pepi liked the spotlight, liked the heat of it, the glitter beating down on him.

So he stopped climbing.

Pepi stopped and stood tall. His skis clicked together with a military precision. He stretched up, checking the tightness of his bindings, the security of his leather safety thongs. All was in perfect order. Then, slowly, keeping his skis at absolute right angles to the sharp drop-off of the slope, Pepi twisted his torso so that from the waist up, at least, he faced straight down the immense cornice. There they were, far below, his audience. The fools. Slowly, his body rigid at attention, Pepi slipped his right hand out of the strap on his ski pole. He raised his right arm in a gesture that some people took as a benediction and others as a Nazi salute.

Then he dropped his arm and reached through the leather loop of his ski pole and pushed off down Widow's Peak.

A noise rose up from the crowd that sounded like a violent wind ripping through a pine forest. Only there was no wind on Sky Mountain that day. Pepi started his run in the direction his skis had been pointing in the climb. The snow, of course, was very deep. He began to run slowly, even poling at first, the snow up to his knees. He swept out to the right, following the line of the shadow. Then he turned, a great sweeping turn to the left that scattered powder.

Pepi was going faster now, gliding in the deep powder more like a surfer than a skier. From the bottom of China Bowl the man himself was hardly visible: they judged his progress by the trail he spun out behind him the way invisible jets drag white contrails across the sky. But Jake Chaffee saw him plain. Jake had the binoculars on him, and the TV cameras were broadcasting him. Jake followed every movement. It was on Pepi's second turn that the cornice began breaking off.

There was no noise at first, no warning. Suddenly a huge chunk of overhanging snow simply wasn't there and the smooth lip of the cornice had a big jagged gap in it. The cornice fell for nearly a minute before they heard the roar. Tons of snow and ice fell straight down and hit the snowfield and that started the avalanche for real.

The whole slope behind Pepi Prager shuddered with the impact of the falling cornice. Then it came tumbling down. Widow's Peak was very wide, and it might have been possible for Pepi to ski out of the avalanche's path on either side. But whether he didn't hear it or feel it or simply did not care, Pepi continued making his perfect graceful S-curves in the unmarked snow as the avalanche built force behind him.

The avalanche was plummeting straight down the slope with the full weight of uncountable tons of snow and ice. Pepi turned and glided. The great wave gained on him, roaring, building a crest of snow and giant blocks of ice that kept tumbling over and over on itself. Pepi skied on, heedless, a strange smile on his face, a look of triumph.

The avalanche would have caught Pepi Prager in minutes but the mountain itself got him first. He made another turn, perfect, a model of its kind, turning left again, still smiling, up to his knees in it, when suddenly he simply wasn't there. It looked like a movie-maker's trick. First Pepi was there, and then he and his ski tracks vanished completely into the smooth snowfield. Then Jake saw the crack and remembered the crevasse, one of three deep gashes in the slope, thin brutal gorges hundreds of feet deep, that had been glazed over with the heavy snowfall, waiting for the slightest pressure to open them again. The avalanche roared on, undeterred by the narrow crevasse, until it spent itself harmlessly a mile down the slope. Jake stood silent, staring up at Widow's Peak, unable to grasp what he'd seen. A quiet voice, Hartmann's voice, drifted into Jake's unfocused consciousness: *"Earth, conceal not the blood shed on thee!"* Jake started.

"What's that?"

"It's from the memorial plaque the Allies put up at the Bergen-Belsen Nazi death camp." Hartmann's voice stayed low, a contrast to the excited babble around him. "I guess," he went on, "that we can call off the hounds now."

"I guess you can."

The Knickerbocker Trust building dominated a corner on Wall Street in lower Manhattan, a huge pile of limestone and bronze designed to impress—an impregnable mausoleum of money. The building tried to be Greek but succeeded in being Roman: there was no lightness to it, no grace. It squatted on its corner like some immense stone toad, faintly menacing, fat but still greedy, waiting for its next victim. Pete Woodbury was used to banks and bankers but walking into the chilly recesses of the Knick always gave him a little shudder. Which, he thought ruefully, was probably just what the architects had hoped for.

The elevator whispered to a stop and the bronze door slid open. Pete stepped out onto the deep green carpeting and walked down the wide, empty hall to the reception lobby. Green was the prevailing color inside the Knick: deep, money green. The reception lobby featured real antique chairs upholstered in green leather, whaling prints and a real defrocked dowager with beady eyes and an aura of lavender sachet about her. "Peter Woodbury for Mr. Harkness." The beady eyes didn't move.

"Mister Jason Harkness or Mr. William Harkness?"

"Mr. William Harkness." My God, thought Pete.

The dowager called Bill Harkness's secretary and soon the girl appeared. Pete gave her the best smile he had on him, and she smiled back. Pete reached for his handkerchief and wiped his forehead as he followed the girl down the carpeted hall. He hoped the fear didn't show.

Bill Harkness had a second-from-the-top-level office, which at the Knick meant splendid: a silk Tabriz on the floor, chestnut paneling that had obviously come from some old English country house, a working fireplace, lots of books and brass. Harkness got up from behind a desk that was a little too elegant for him. Bill Harkness was a prime specimen of the golfing-shooting-yachting school of banker, tall and ruddy with always a trace of a tan and a body that even at sixty could probably fit into his Yale Varsity football uniform, Class of '35. He smiled a lot, but there was a working brain in there someplace too. Pete hated the type but liked this particular example of it. At least, he'd liked the man until right now. Pete had no idea what Harkness was going to do. This was the day of decision. Pete had done his homework, sent complete projections on the condominium scheme, complete with time-sharing revenues.

Harkness waved Pete into a seat and the secretary served them coffee. Then he lifted the thick folder of Sky High's press clippings. "Some press you guys bought yourselves, Pete."

"If we'd bought it, it would have been even better." Pete made himself smile. *Play it like your life does not depend on the outcome, Woodbury.* "You really can't buy that kind of write-up. It's like the Broadway reviews."

"I'm about to hit you with another kind of review, Pete."

"Shoot." Pete felt his stomach land with a thud at his feet. Here it came.

Harkness sipped his coffee and put the cup down. "There are people here who aren't very happy with Jake Chaffee. Oh, he's had his successes, but, frankly, it's more a question of . . . style. He's a little, well, flashy for us. Naturally we don't blame you guys for inflation. But serious questions have been raised about the man's stability." The Knick's idea of stability, Pete thought ruefully, was to be stiff in your tomb. "Friday," Bill Harkness went on, "we had a finance committee meeting. We went over several ongoing projects. You guys aren't the only ones with problems. In any case, I presented your proposal. It got a very mixed reception. Well, to make a long story short, in true Knickerbocker tradition . . ." Harkness paused and helped himself to some more coffee. To Pete, it was the longest sip in the world. Harkness put his cup down and went on: ". . . they copped out. Left the matter in my hands entirely."

"And . . ."

"I was just about stumped, Pete."

"It's a tough decision, either way you go."

"I'm glad you understand that. I turned the thing over and over in my mind all weekend. We'd just heard about the typhoid, and that sure didn't look good. Until this morning"—Harkness was grinning—"this morning my wife gave me this." He held up a much-thumbed newspaper page. Pete hadn't seen it before. Harkness passed it to him. "Believe it or not, something our maid reads." It was Noel Northcliff's society column and it read: "The Playboy as Hero: Chaffee's Bravery Saves Lives at Posh Resort." Pete skimmed it, smiled, gave it back.

"It's typical of Jake," Pete said, "that he never mentioned this." Harkness cleared his throat theatrically. "Well, Pete: any man who'd do a thing like that is a man I'm proud to be associated with. You can tell Chaffee that for me. The papers are being drawn up this week, just as you proposed them." Harkness grinned conspiratorially, a small boy's grin. "Oh, we're not out of the woods yet. We'll run into the usual old fuddy-duddies, you can bet on that. And I'm not going to make it too easy on you. But you'll get your extensions. The Knick will not pull the rug out from under you." Pete Woodbury felt the relief rush through him as though someone had thrown on an electric switch. For an instant he was silent: it was that much of a surprise. He couldn't think of anything spectacular to say to this man who had just given Jake Chaffee a reprieve on the dream that held his life together. So all Pete said was: "Thank you, Bill. You won't regret this."

"No. I'm sure I won't." Harkness smiled and Pete gave thanks to the Yale football team or Horatio Alger or whoever it was who'd given this man of the 1970s such an untypical belief in human courage. Harkness showed him to the door, with much smiling, handshaking, patting of backs. Yes, they'd have lunch later in the week, sort out the details. Pete restrained himself from kissing the dowager who manned the reception desk. He didn't even wait to get back to his office but called Jake collect from a pay phone on the corner of Wall Street and Broad.

Zem Gibbs stood in her grandfather's big bedroom at Sky Ranch holding up the delicate flow of ivory satin and Chantilly lace that had been her great-grandmother's wedding gown. "Gramps, it's lovely!" Zem, as usual, wore blue jeans and cowboy boots and a man's shirt but the reflection that floated back at her from the slightly rippled surface of the old mahogany mirror showed a girl's beautiful face poised above the Victorian confection of a wedding dress. "We'll have to do some fixing, but it'll work." She bent her head to smell the fabric, stored all these years in home-made sachet. Her grandfather sat in the big old rocking chair watching her. He smiled, knowing the answer to his question even as he asked it. "You're happy, Zembra?"

"Very. Very, very." She hesitated, not wanting to endanger this moment. Her grandfather had been having reverses, she knew, in his war with Jake Chaffee. The Legislature had just voted to widen Highway 317. That avalanche, which had changed so many lives, had turned the tide on that question, too. The highway had to be made safer. Only Zem's announcement that she'd decided to marry Bill Shepherd had lightened her grandfather's gloom.

As Zem had explained, after the long typhoid siege, she had never completely realized how much she needed Bill until she took a good, hard look at the possibility of losing him. "And we can always take a trip around the world together, can't we?" she laughed.

"Don't see why not," Zeke said. "Surprised a smart gal like you didn't think of that before."

The old man liked Bill. And even more than that he liked the idea that Zem would be staying in the valley now, that she'd undoubtedly have kids, that there'd still be Gibbs blood on Gibbs land. But now Zem was going to ask her grandfather for a favor that might set him off again, just when he seemed to be recovering from his latest bitter disappointments. She took a deep breath, refolded the gown, and gave it a try. "Gramps, if I asked you for a really important favor, would you do it?"

"You know I would, honey, if I could."

"It would make me very happy," she said, softly, looking Zeke Gibbs in the eye, "if you'd invite Jake Chaffee to my wedding." There. It was out. Zeke said nothing. Whatever he'd been expecting, it wasn't this. Money? Some special present? A fancier wedding than just the parlor of Sky Ranch? But this: Jake Chaffee! He stood up and turned to the window. He could see all the way down the valley to Sky High and it seemed as though he was looking the length of a battlefield. Zeke put his big leathery hands in his pockets and stood there for a moment looking out. Then he turned to Zem. His gaunt, handsome old face was solemn. Then it broke into a little mischievous smile. "Honey," he said, "if you wanted Adolf Hitler and the Emperor Nero at your wedding, I would do my best to get them for you." She ran across the room and kissed him.

The dying light clung to the top of Sky Mountain with the tenacity of a rejected lover, flattering, turning white ice to gold, dragging out the inevitable moment of departure. Jake sat with Cassie at a window table in the Sky Bar, shamelessly holding hands, sipping white wine and watching the last of the sunset. They'd just got back from Zem's wedding. "I was sure the old bastard would shoot me."

"He's quite a nice old bastard, really."

"Careful, lady, you are spoken for." Jake's divorce was moving slowly through the California courts. Before the year was out it would be final. She pressed his hand lightly. The two gold rings gleamed on her left hand, the one simple band and the other dramatically criss-crossed with diamonds.

"I guess I am, at that." She looked across the table

into his eyes and found them changing as they did a dozen times each day, from one shade of blue to another. A girl, thought Cassie Lamont, could do worse. Much worse. "What next?"

"Us next."

"That's all?"

"That's everything."

And it was.

Epilogue

It was Zembra Gibbs Shepherd who accidentally unraveled the mystery of the Sky High typhoid epidemic.

The Colorado state health department made a thorough investigation and found no conclusive source: they merely assumed that Mildred Rush had been a carrier. Then, one day in June when the last of the snows had melted off the lower slopes of Sky Mountain and the wild flowers were making their first glorious showing, Zem took her new husband on a picnic up the mountain. She wanted to show him the Indian cave she'd discovered as a girl, with its mysterious drawings scratched on the stone. The cave was part of a granite outcropping right next to Sky Creek. Laughing and chattering, Zem led Bill through the aspen grove to the cave site. They'd brought a flashlight, the better to see the drawings. Zem stood in the cave's entrance, flicked on the light, and stepped in. Suddenly her voice shot back to Bill, low, urgent, all the fun gone out of it. "Oh, no! Bill, come quick." He thought she'd come on a nest of rattlers. But it was worse than that. In a second he was at her side, looking down the strong yellow beam of light.

"Jesus." There lay a skeleton in the remnants of blue jeans and a few other moldering items of clothing, a sleeping bag, a knapsack. The bones had been picked clean and a few dark brown feathers scattered on the cave floor showed how. "Those vultures, Bill: remember?"

"The curse wasn't a curse, then," he answered. "This is what they were after." It took the health department to piece the story together: the youthful dead man had been carrying a passport bearing the name Wallace Hill. From police reports it was determined that he had three drug convictions and had last been known to be on Crete, living in a cave with a colony of hippies. This report came over the phone to Bill Shepherd. It all sounded very remote. No one knew how the boy had come to the cave on Sky Mountain, but the autopsy showed skeletal traces typical of one who had been carrying typhoid in his system. It was undoubtedly the typhoid that killed him. But not before he'd somehow infected the water supply at Sky Lodge. They'd never know for sure, but the assumption was the boy had been alive but sick with diarrhea, using Sky Creek as his plumbing, just when the pipes to the Sky High reservoir were being laid in the creek bed. That, said the inspector, would be all you'd need.

The FBI saw no reason to publicize the Prager case, even after Tod Rubin's body was found. The coroner's verdict on the Rubin death was "misadventure." Both Jake and the FBI men were sure Pepi had killed the man, but there was no way to prove it: the ravine was steep, Rubin had been sick, it just might have been accidental after all. In Vienna, Professor Doktor Knabel closed out the Waldemar file and sighed, less because Tod Rubinsky had died than because he'd never really lived.

The Count Ruvo di Putignano-Squillace moved quietly back into the refurbished family palazzo south of Rome, where he proceeded systematically to destroy his liver and what scraps were left of his reputation.

Eliza Chaffee returned to college with a new goal in mind: she wanted to become a doctor.

Cornelia de Vos always remembered Sky High with fondness. Her bankers in Liechtenstein were more than pleased at her success there, for Niris was, and continued to be, very generous. And if Cornelia sometimes thought of Jean-Pierre Belfort, it was with affection more than regret.

As for Jean-Pierre, he got lucky the day Pepi Prager's luck ran out. The race went on as scheduled, everyone's nerves on edge. Jean-Pierre took a first in the double-downhill and second in the giant slalom, winning five thousand dollars for the afternoon's work. This was enough to gain him a foothold on the pro skiing circuit. He had about five years as a racer, did quite well, saved money, had fun. At thirty he retired to Val d'Isère, opened a small restaurant, married a local girl and had four sons. He skied less, worked hard, put on a little weight, prospered. And sometimes, late in the afternoon, Jean-Pierre would stand in the window of his restaurant watching the shadows creep across the valley, and his plump cheerful wife would have to call his name twice to wake him from a dream of having been young, on Sky Mountain, and in love with Cornelia de Vos.

Noel Northcliff got rich off the book he wrote about Dorothy Dutton. *Rich Girl* he called it, and it sold like hotcakes. Everything in it was true except for the account of her death. NN printed Momo's version, not believing a word of it.

Dud Drummond stayed on at Sky High. Jake offered him a job as permanent PR man and sales manager for the condominium development. He learned to ski, gradually got over Liz's suicide, and did very well promoting Sky High.

Pete Woodbury went through with his divorce, spent two miserable years as a New York bachelor, and finally realized he was never going to find another Maggie. That was when he found someone who suited him nearly as well, a widowed lady lawyer with no kids but a deep streak of honesty and a well-developed sense of humor. They married and were happy.

Raoul Peng left Sky High in June. His contract with Styron Food Corporation came through after all. Raoul's cuisine would be missed more than the man himself. Jake and Cassie persuaded René Latour to stay on in Raoul's place—at Raoul's salary. This made Raoul furious and Latour happy. The food at Sky High continued to be superb.

Zeke Gibbs lived six more years, long enough to see his first three grandchildren, two boys and a girl. And while Zeke would never be at ease with Jake Chaffee, some sort of truce developed between them. Jake and Cassie went to his funeral, as did half the state of Colorado. They mourned the passing of an era, and the death of a man.

Only Sky Mountain was unchanged, proud in its perpetual cloak of white, the Colorado sky bright above it, the one permanent thing in a churning current of love and hate and dreams.

ABOUT THE AUTHOR

TOM MURPHY, JR., a one-time advertising copy writer, is the author of a previous novel, *Ballet*.